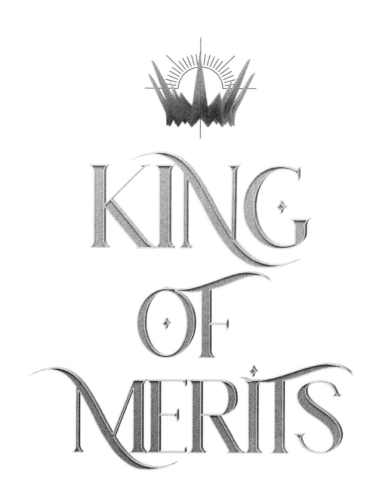

KING OF MERITS

JUNO HEART

King of Merits: A Fae Romance - Black Blood Fae Book 3

Cover and chapter header design by: saintjupit3rgr4phic

Map Design: Isle Brookes Design

Editor: Bookends Editing

ISBN: Ebook: 978-0-6487442-3-8

ISBN: Paperback: 978-0-6487442-8-3

ISBN: Hardback: 978-0-6487442-9-0

v221028

Winds will whip, sparks will fly, waves will churn, earth will rumble

Aer, the Sorceress of the Seven Winds

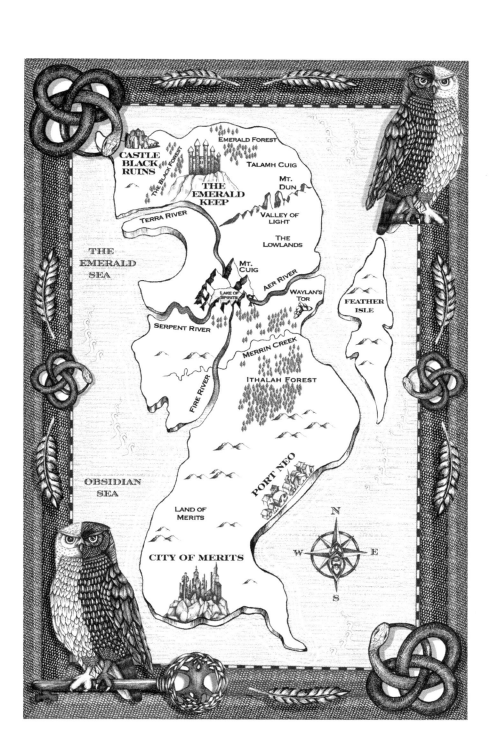

Prologue

Riven

Heavy as a mountain, my crown bows my head low as I peer into the druid's well—long spikes of black crystal reflecting in the water like arrows piercing my skull.

Arrows of sorrow.

The well's mirrored surface ripples, revealing two more crowns. Golden crowns: a matched pair of twisted fire and rubies.

The dark water before my eyes displays the grandeur of a coronation, the Fire King and his Queen of Flames, their smiles as bright as sunshine and blazing only for each other. All around them bustles the luminous Court of Five. Magic and revelry, music and mayhem, love and light and joy.

A bright court, the opposite of mine, lit by all I can never have and will never deserve.

It taunts me. Terrifies me.

My gaze seeks the red-haired child with quicksilver eyes, eyes that show no mercy. Ever's daughter. The one, who when she comes of age, I must ensure I never meet. Never gaze at in person, even though I long to do so with all my being.

But I must never allow it.

Never.

Yet night after night I descend ancient stairs to the druid's well...again and again to view images of her as a young woman grown. To see her smile and dance.

And while I watch, I vow over and over...

Never her, I whisper.

Never her.

She is my kingdom's enemy, and if given into my hands, the cure to their cursed blood.

The girl is *their* cure. The girl is *my* curse.

The curse I long for but won't ever allow myself to surrender to. I won't.

A wave across the silver water, another ripple, then the Bright Court is gone.

Then *she* appears. Merri grown, ribbons of long red locks catching on branches as she wanders through a forest, lost and alone. She stops at a pond to drink, and as she does so, the very fabric of the spring day rends, breaking as a dark force moves closer.

Danger lurks behind the leaves, hidden deftly by the forest. A crack, a rustle, and then a tall traveler appears behind her. His cloak is dark, silver hair twisting around his shoulders despite the stillness of the air and trees. No breeze. Not a whisper. But magic moves inside him.

He bends, placing a jeweled hand upon the blue velvet covering her shoulder.

She turns.

Silver eyes skewer. Silver eyes tantalize and enslave the stranger, trapping him in the bonds of a long-ago cast fate.

The man smiles, the left side of his mouth curling with long-bridled intent.

Is this being good or evil? Does he come to help or harm?

Dark humor shivers through me. Why do I ask when I already know the answer?

For the man in the woods is *me*, Riven Èadra na Duinn.

I am the Silver King.

And Merrin Airgetlám Fionbharr is my destiny.

The destiny I must forever shun.

Red floods the surface of the water, concealing the image of the couple, shrouding them in crimson blood.

In the vision, just as it always does.

In life, as it must never do.

1

Land of Five

Merri

With a flick of my wrist, my bedroom chamber's teal drapes fly open, and I scowl down at the Faery city of Talamh Cúig. Most mornings, the sparkling emerald and black surfaces of the buildings fill my heart with joy.

But not today.

The dream that woke me still clings to my skin like a cloying velvet gown worn on a hot summer's day. But here in the Land of Five, it's springtime. My favorite season. I should be happy. And I would be...if not for the dream.

The dream of snow and winter.

The dream that is light and bright before it turns a deep suffocating purple, the color of bitter longing.

This nightmare of the silver fae with haunted eyes has plagued me since childhood. It doesn't occur every night. And, sometimes, not every moon turn. But when it does, it lingers until the next time, following me through the brightest days and tormenting me during the darkest hours until morning light creeps across my green and gold walls, saving me.

Every day, I ask myself, why do I see this fae? What's so special about him?

He performs no remarkable deed nor utters a single word, only stares with his mournful gaze. His silence entices me into a void of white where red flows from deep gashes and wounds—whose injuries these are, I never know.

Sighing, I move away from the windows, snatch my favorite bow and quiver from the floor, and throw them on my bed. With my fingers, I rake knots from my hair, tugging hard on the long red strands.

I dress quickly in hunting leathers and a light emerald cape, hoping a ride before breakfast will erase the vision of the fae with the sorrowful, glowing blue gaze.

Halfway to the door, I skid to a stop. Cara! I'd forgotten all about her. Backtracking, I close in on the happily snoring lump and then give the bed furs a good poke.

"Wake up, lazybones," I say, "or you'll miss a ride through the mountains."

A muffled squeak resounds from under the covers. A long brown nose wriggles out, followed by shiny black eyes blinking in confusion.

"No? Not interested? Goodbye then. I hope you enjoy your day with Arellena." My elven chambermaid is famously stern and not very fond of my roommate. "I believe she plans to spend the entire day here, sorting and mending clothes. I'm sure you'll be a great helper."

A mass of brown and purple fur explodes from the bed, landing on the shiny wooden floor at my feet. I laugh and scoop up my adorable mire squirrel and tuck her warm body into the crook of my neck. Her striped tail wraps gently around my throat as she scolds me with angry chirps.

"Worry not," I say, patting her with one hand as I collect the bow and quiver with the other, and then sling them over my shoulder. "I wouldn't have left you behind. I know how Arellena terrifies you."

As I stride through beams of sunshine in the Emerald Castle's hallways, I mock salute the striking images of my father, Prince Ever, and King Raff, fighting ferociously side-by-side in their gleaming armor from the tapestries that line the walls. Thankfully, at breakfast time, they behave a little more civilized. Mostly.

When I enter the Great Hall via a back staircase, a chaotic scene greets me. I bite my cheek, trying not to laugh. It's impossible.

Father and King Raff are arm wrestling, their wild movements sending goblets and platters sliding along the rectangular table. My mother sits in Father's lap, heckling him to decrease his chances of winning.

Raff's mire fox, Spark, screeches and bounces atop Isla's shoulders, her furry little hands buried in the queen's golden hair and distracting adorable baby Aodhan from his breakfast.

Magret, Alorus, Orlinda, and Lord Gavrin play quiet games of hnefatafl, and next to them, my younger brother, Wynter, clomps the heels of his boots onto the six-pointed star in the middle of the table. Chunks of jet-black hair hide the devious twinkle in his brilliant eyes that are so similar to our mother's. My eyes are silver, like Father's, the color as changeable as the weather our magic controls.

Tumbled cups, messy food platters, and all manner of entertainments, such as wooden puzzles, instruments, paper scrolls, and arrow fletchings cover the table's surface. Yes, my family breaks their fast like an encampment of warmongering giants rather than refined, graceful fae royalty.

A small band of winged musicians, drunk and already falling over each other at this early hour, play haphazardly from the dais, and Balor chases my brother's black wolf around the table in time to the lively beat, snapping at his tail as they go.

When the king married my mom's cousin, a human like Mother, fun-loving Raff and Isla became rulers of the Elemental fae, and the strict courtly standards that my grandmother, Varenus, upheld are only adhered to on important, formal occasions. Of which breakfast isn't one.

With a deep breath, I straighten my spine and sally forth into the fray.

"Good morning, brat," says Wyn as I pad across the floor toward him.

With my sharpest nail, I flick the tip of his straight nose. *Hard.* "You'd do well to remain silent if you can't respect your elders. Heed your wolf's manners. Ivor could easily best Balor with those formidable fangs but regularly quashes his beastly nature to maintain goodwill."

Wyn rolls his eyes in reply.

"Good morning, sweetheart," says Mom. She tickles my father's side, helping Raff gain the advantage and send Dad's fist crashing into Lord Gavrin's bowl of curd porridge. The king winks at me, straightening his sunstone-encrusted crown. Next to Raff, Alorus and Orlinda smother giggles.

I greet the loud chorus of "Morning, Merri" with a grin, then blow kisses to my parents. Humans who met them would never believe that Prince Ever and Princess Lara could possibly have two grown children. They barely look a day older than me and Wyn.

Wyn throws a grape, and I catch it before it hits my nose. "I'll speak as pleases me, Sister. And if you continue to be annoying, I'll toss Cara into the mix, and we'll see how your rodent fares against my wolf."

"Don't call her a rodent." Cara's whiskers tremble against my neck. I soothe her with a gentle chin scratch, then blast Wyn with an icy wind that tears his hair toward the ceiling. Unsurprisingly, a frenzied mess is quite a good look on him.

"Stop that, you terror." He laughs, smoothing his hair in a battle against my air magic.

"Make me."

"If you insist." With a click of his fingers, the walls begin to shake, emerald-colored dust powdering my hair and face. Spluttering, I create a breeze and blow it back at him. Curse his filthy earth magic!

"Show off," I say, releasing his mop from the wind spell.

Like me, Wyn is a halfling, but in an unfair trick of fate, his powers are almost as strong as a full-blooded fae's and more powerful than mine. My air magic is unreliable, and my visions are often hard to decipher. Or completely useless if they're about a certain silver-haired fae.

"Dear Son. Sweet Daughter," says Father. "Must you act like bog trolls every mealtime?"

I aim a pointed smirk at Lord Gavrin who is busy mopping porridge from his face.

"Yes, Father, you're right," says Wyn. "I humbly beg your pardon and will attempt to follow *your* fine example at all times in the future."

"Which means he can do as he likes." King Raff laughs. "He has you there, Brother. In human years, your son is a mere youth of sixteen and already smarter than you."

"Or just more insufferable," I suggest.

"Come and join us, Merri," Isla says, bouncing Aodhan on her lap.

The little prince is a beautiful golden-haired child with eyes of brightest amber, like his father's, the king. It saddens me to think that when he comes of age, the family's vile curse will course through his veins.

"I've made chocolate croissants," continues the queen. "Your favorite."

Smiling, I pour pear juice into a goblet and swipe a delicious pastry from a plate. I take a drink, then a bite, and say around a big mouthful, "I'd love to sit awhile, but I don't have time. I'm going riding."

"Before breakfast?" Mom asks, her hair tumbling around her shoulders as she speaks, dozens of threaded emeralds glinting among the strawberry waves.

My hair is even brighter, making it hard to hide unless I don a cloak with a hood, which I always do when I venture into the forest. A Princess of Air doesn't see many interesting occurrences, but a stealthy stranger does.

"No, Mother." I take another large bite, bitter-sweet chocolate melting on my tongue. "As you can see, I'm eating it now."

"It's difficult to believe you could willingly choose to forgo my company," Wyn says in his annoying, deep voice.

One year my junior, he has the voice of a king—as arrogant and charming as our father's. He throws a purple grape at me. "Here, your rat looks hungry. No, don't thank me."

Refusing to argue, I smile serenely and offer Cara some of my croissant.

I gaze at my pouting family and shrug. "Sorry, but I need to get outside and let the wind chase a bad dream away. A hard ride toward the Dún Mountains should do the trick."

Frowning, Isla studies me. She does that a lot, examines me as though I'm a puzzle she needs to solve, and asks questions about my dreams as if they contain the answers she seeks. I don't know why she does this. She thinks she's subtle, but trust me, she's not.

Mother smiles, her fingers stroking Father's neck as she hugs him closer. According to her, my dreams are typical for a young girl and they'll go away when I meet the right fae, the one whose actions, not just their handsome face, will speak to my heart.

Be patient, she says, and I just shrug. I'm not interested in love, anyway.

"You have your bow?" Father asks. "The draygonets are on the move again. Kian saw a weyr of them not far from Serpent River only two days past."

Bending at the waist, I flourish a curtsy, making my quiver full of arrows pop over my shoulder. He gives Mom a dimpled smile, confident in the knowledge he's raised a child who's not entirely reckless. Like he was. And still is.

Their happiness warms my heart, and I think again how disturbed humans would be to see their parents glowing blissfully before their eyes, as strong and beautiful as they've ever been, but it doesn't bother me. An ageless appearance is the way of the fae and the mortals who form mate bonds with them, as my mother and Isla did with Father and Raff. In one hundred years, I'll likely remain unchanged, too. In appearance, at least.

Wyn issues a sharp whistle, and his wolf pricks his ears, his alert orange eyes fixing on my brother. "Ivor and I will come with you," he says, swinging his long legs off the table, boots thudding onto the marble.

"No, you won't." I push him deeper into his high-backed chair, my fingers snagging on the chain of white daisies lying against his chest.

I fasten a button on his forest-green shirt that hangs raggedly open as if he doesn't give two hoots about his appearance, which is a ruse.

Wynter only behaves like a lazy troll so the ladies of the court can take care of his every need. But he's capable of doing anything he sets his devious mind to, including dressing himself properly.

"You broke my necklace," he shouts, feigning great offense.

"Oh, boohoo. I'm sure there are a bevy of sweet sprites hovering around the corner, ready to make you a new daisy chain. Fret not, dear one."

Secure in the knowledge he is precious to me, he flashes the dimpled smile that makes all of Faery weep, his smattering of freckles glittering in the soft morning light. And he's not wrong about his value. I'd stick a blade in anyone's eye to protect him.

Not that he needs defending—he's skilled with his sword, and his magic is strong. Wynter inherited all the advantages of a Prince of Five, while I bear the shortcomings of my halfling constitution.

Unfair, in my opinion.

Isla's words circle through my mind: *Power may follow the Elemental male line, but you, darling Merri, are destined for something far greater than to sit upon the Throne of Five and look pretty for the rest of your days.*

Whenever I ask her what this amazing destiny is, she finds an urgent matter to rush off to, looking oddly guilty. Even stranger, she never repeats these words in front of my parents. Or Wyn, for that matter.

I give a mock bow to my family. "Okay, later, guys," I say as I spin to face the exit, my eyes on the bronze star decorating the arched doors that lead to fresh air and freedom.

"Some of us here happen to be female," says Magret, who, despite living with humans and halflings for many years, still insists on taking everything we say literally. "Have fun on your ride, Merri, but please remember that if your grandmother's spies hear you speaking like that, there'll be seven hells to pay when you return."

Tell me about it. Grandma Varenus greatly disapproves when I speak in *the mortal gibberish*, as she calls it. I've picked the slang up from visits to Mom's birthplace over the years and admit I'm very fond of it.

Earth. What an extraordinary world. My favorite mortal hangout is, of course, Max's Vinyl City diner, where Mother and Isla worked when they were young. I hope we visit the human realm soon, though Father says we're needed here, and it's therefore unlikely.

Truthfully, I'm glad Varenus only dines with us during the grander feasts. She disapproves of the way we tease each other and set the dining table on the floor in front of the dais instead of on it.

When Grandmother lectures, my parents only grin secretly at each other. But her callous words hurt me, make me feel inferior, and I'm glad I don't have to suffer her disdain very often. *And certainly not today*, I think, as I hop down the last steps onto a city pathway.

Outside, it's a perfect day, a clear blue sky and a sweet-scented breeze blowing my dream a little further away. Thank the Elements.

Fae are opening up market stalls that line the silver-paved streets behind the castle, calling out greetings as I hurry past. I shout back to them and breathe deep the delicious smells of cinnamon and baking bread as I leap over a low wall and take a shortcut to the stables.

When I round the bend into the cobblestone courtyard, five moss elves appear, the sleeves of their bark-colored tunics sweeping the ground as they bow low. They don't look happy, their dark hair framing deep frowns.

It is a family I know well and love dearly, for the older members have been my playmates since I first arrived in Faery as a child. The tallest of them scratches one of his curling horns, and then tugs impatiently on the hem of my cloak.

"Good morning, Tanisha, Marelius, Jasper, Fern, baby Velvet. What disturbs you on this fine morning?" I say, keen to pass by and be on my way.

Pointing at the stalls, they speak in the fast Elvish of their tribe, a language I'm not fully fluent in. The only word I understand from their excited babble is Kian because it's repeated so often.

Oh, not again. The moss elves despise Kian and spout regular dire warnings about him for the slightest of reasons. Cara chirps loudly in my ear, and I know she agrees with them. I'm not fond of Kian either. But he's infuriating, not dangerous.

"Is Kian in there?" I ask, pointing at the stables.

"Yes," says Tanisha, the matriarch of the clan. The others nod furiously. "No good. No good."

"I'll be fine." I squat down and meet the elves' worried gazes. "Relax, everyone. I'm well aware that Kian is a pain in the neck, but I won't be with him for long. Nahla and I are going riding."

Marelius, Tanisha's mate, hugs my leg and tries to drag me toward the market district. Although tall for a moss elf, the top of his head only comes up to my knees.

"No, Merri, stay," he pleads, his eyes bright beams of gold against his mossy-green skin. "We elves have some very bad feelings today."

Don't they always? A distraction is needed.

"Hey, I have good news. Queen Isla is looking for someone to entertain Aodhan after breakfast. You should hurry along to the Great Hall, because Salamander is probably heading over right now, trying to beat you to it. You know how obsessed the fire mage is with her little fire prince."

Hugging each other, the elves squeal and move away as one bouncing mass.

They take great pride in being the favorite playmates of the royal children and maintain a fierce rivalry with any member of the court who challenges their positions as chief babysitters.

Dusting my hands off as I watch them dash toward the castle's teal spires, I try not to feel too guilty about using my halfling skill and twisting the truth into an almost-lie, something a full-blooded fae can't do without experiencing extreme pain. Wyn is skilled in the art, too, but rarely chooses to employ it. Mainly because he refuses to do anything that might make him appear less fae and more human.

Warm sun on my back, I stride into the stables and find Kian with his head practically grafted onto Seven's, the imp's rainbow-colored horns tangling with his red locks as they whisper next to Jinn's stall.

"Morning," I boom, startling them into bumping foreheads as they look up.

"Hello, sweet Merrin," says Kian, his voice sending chills over my skin as he struts forward, peacock-blue cape rippling behind him. In his richly embroidered outfit, he's dressed far too finely to be mucking out horse dung. Not that he'd ever lower himself to such a task. I wonder what mischief he's up to.

"I guessed you would be riding out early on such a fine day," he says, stopping in front of me. "I've already saddled your mount for you."

"That seems kind of you." I'm fully aware that he's never nice without an ulterior motive. He probably thinks I'll invite him to come along, but I'd rather take an amorous mountain troll on an outing than Kian Leondearg.

Jinn and his daughter, Nahla, nicker from their stalls in greeting. "Hello there," I say, drawing out a small bunch of carrots from my pocket. "Care for a treat?"

Jinn gobbles two with astonishing speed, but Nahla turns her head away, which is most unusual. Normally, she'll eat anything she's given, including my cooking, which is brave of her. Perhaps she's feeling poorly.

Stroking her warm neck, I ask, "Are you all right, dear one? We can go to the meadow and lie about in the sun if you're not up to a gallop."

My horse neighs loudly, nudging me with her nose. If it weren't for the white star on her face, she'd look exactly like her coal-black father. "Fine, then. A ride it is."

Giving Kian my back, I hook my bow onto Nahla's saddle and then climb up into it.

A barely dressed Seven scampers up beside Kian and links arms with him. She gives me a cheerful wave.

"I'm certain I heard you swear off dallying with Kian three Beltane festivals ago," I tell the imp.

Her one black eye blinks innocently at me from the middle of her brow. "Although full of himself, Kian is rather pretty, and I do like to check now and then to see if his bed skills have improved."

"Or stable skills," I suggest.

Kian's bright-blue eyes glitter darkly. Foolishly, he reaches out to pat Cara who has crawled down to my forearm, and she sinks her teeth into his fingers.

"Blasted mire trolls!" He snarls, raising a hand to slap her snout.

My anger wakes the sky, thunder shaking the walls, and Kian holds his palms open, a gesture of surrender. "Calm yourself, Princess. I won't retaliate against your creature, although she deserves it many times over."

Patting Nahla's coat, I click my tongue, and she moves out of the stall, knocking Kian sideways.

"Would you like company?" he asks, already opening Jinn's stall as though sure of my answer.

Jinn screams, kicking the walls, clearly wishing they were Kian's breeding organs or his pocket potatoes, as Isla is fond of calling them.

"I prefer the company of my animals, and even if I agreed to bear yours, you couldn't keep up with us anyway." I stab two fingers at my chest, the black and gold feather ruff around my neck stirring with the movement. "Air magic, remember? Nahla and I ride like the wind."

I bend and kiss Nahla's neck. "Let's go, girl."

And we're off, flying through the courtyard.

2

The Silver Pond

Merri

W e clip-clop between the city's vine-covered walls, then wind down the green-tourmaline pathway that leads to the massive jade gates at the entrance to town.

Terra River's waterfalls roar below us as we trot along the golden bridge, then Nahla breaks into a gallop, her hooves thudding over the grassy plains of the Lowlands, the Dún Mountains a dark line in the distance. I let loose a long shout. Freedom at last.

Smiling, I scan the azure sky. The seven órga falcons circle above, calling to each other as they angle their wings for home and swoop over me, their bellies as white as fair-weather clouds.

With the castle's green towers disappearing behind me, I fix my gaze on the mountain and lean low over Nahla's neck, her hooves barely touching the ground as we fly along.

Bearded firecrest swallows follow in our tracks, flitting through the long grass in rainbow-colored flocks. Greencoats, the small trooping fairies of the Lowlands, colorful rabbits, mice, and all manner of tiny creatures scatter, taking shelter as we thunder past.

This is blissful, Nahla and I racing with the wind under an expanse of blue sky, Cara curled around my neck, and the last wisps of this morning's dream finally dissolving. Energy courses through me, power, joy. Life is better than good—it's perfect.

Without warning, everything changes.

Nahla's pace falters, and she slows to a clumsy trot, then a walk that zigzags aimlessly across the green plains. Something is very wrong. I give a light tug on the reins, and she stops, hanging her head listlessly.

As I dismount, Cara crawls around my shoulders, her striped tail wrapping too tightly around my neck. "Calm down. Everything's all right," I tell her. "Nahla isn't feeling well, that's all."

I cradle my horse's head and stroke the white star on her face. Her brown eyes are glazed, her ears barely flickering. She looks exhausted. Sick. Or worse—bewitched.

A bubble of fear expands in my throat, and I lift my eyes and scrutinize the plains, shocked that I barely recognize them. I squint eastward in the direction of Waylon's Tor. The usual cuts and curves of the landscape that indicate the way to the

Crystalline Oak have disappeared, and in their place, a purple mist hovers, stretching as far as the eye can see.

I spin on my heels, circling around and around and can see no pathway out, no familiar landmarks. This has to be magic. Powerful magic.

But whose?

"Hello?" I call out, as if whoever trapped me in this fog will happily pop out and introduce themselves. Of course, no one answers.

I'm completely lost, which makes no sense at all. My brother and I have spent our lives ranging over this territory, and I know it as well as the Emerald Castle's every nook and cranny.

Closing my eyes, I inhale deeply, examining the insidious purple vapor. The taste of strong power vibrates over my tongue. I let my senses drift along the air currents but don't get very far. Something blocks me, a spell too dense to penetrate. It feels like high magic. Could the insane air mage finally have escaped her prison deep in the Emerald Forest?

A veil of gray clouds covers the sky, and no matter how hard I try, I can't sweep them away. I may be a halfling, but I'm an Elemental Princess of Air. A little cloud manipulation should be a cinch.

Okay. So this is bad. I need to get home, and fast. Talamh Cúig is north-west, but with this darned fog, I can't see the sun or sense the currents on the breeze.

I'm lost.

Hopelessly lost.

Nahla makes a distressed sound, and I kiss her nose. "I think we should keep moving. The fog might clear if we do, and we'll go slowly. Do you think you can walk?"

My horse whinnies in agreement, and Cara crawls farther underneath my hair. Bravery isn't my mire squirrel's greatest strength.

"All right. Let's do this." With jerky movements, I string my bow, then gripping it tightly, I take the reins with my other hand and lead Nahla forward.

The strange silence that surrounds us is eerie and complete, as if the seven realms have imploded and left only the three of us alive. Knowing it will be futile, I call my father in my mind. I get the answer I expected—more oppressive silence.

Think rationally. How do I escape this?

So far, no creature has jumped out of the gloomy vapor and attacked us. And if they do, I have my bow. I'm not a sitting ballybog, stuck in the mud, flailing my limbs while I wait to have my head kicked off my shoulders. I'm a fighter. I'll survive. I just have to keep moving until this mist clears, until I can see where I am again.

Maybe Nahla knows. "Nahla, can you take us home?"

She nickers and changes course, speeding up. Hope flares in my chest as I walk beside her, periodically attempting to surf the air currents, not entirely convinced I should trust my spell-drugged horse's sense of direction.

My thoughts meander to my parents. I think of Mom, how she coined the term surf-the-currents to describe Dad's and my ability to send our magic along the air and seek disturbances in its patterns and learn from them.

Dad always teases her when she admonishes him for not paying attention during important court events by replying that he's busy *surfing* for the benefit of others. This answer always wins him a clip over the head, which he loves.

At this moment, I'd give anything to see them.

Nahla and I struggle along blindly for some time. The skin on the back of my neck crawls as if unseen eyes are watching close by. My muscles ache, my mind growing sleepy and dull, and I have to remind myself to keep a firm grip on the cherry wood of my bow to stop it from slipping to the ground.

With every step I take, the grass looks more comfortable and softer than a bed. I consider lying down to gather my strength while I come up with a plan.

Yes.

A little rest sounds wonderful.

My steps halt. I close my eyes, lowering myself to the ground. I'll just stop a moment...

Cara screeches and buries her claws in my hair, digging her nails in hard.

"Ouch! Why in the Elements are you attacking me?" Stupid question—because when I open my eyes, the answer is obvious. While I was busy falling asleep on my feet, a winding pathway has appeared in the fog. I intend to follow it, no matter where or *what* it leads to, because even a battle to the death would be preferable than wandering in this purple haze for all eternity.

We walk slowly, the mist guiding us along a shifting, writhing tunnel. Barren trees appear at the edges of the fog, their skeletal branches sprouting leaves as we go until, finally, the mist lowers to knee-height, and we come out in the middle of a thick, dark forest.

Silver light shines through arrow-straight fir trunks, the trees opening onto a dark glade, a pool of sparkling water at its center. No birds chirp or call. No animals scratch or yip or growl. This place is weird. Unnatural even for Faery, because there have never been any forests on this side of the Dún Mountains.

So where am I?

My pulse pounds. I draw an arrow from my quiver that's strapped to the saddle and hold it alongside my bow. I whisper soothing words to Nahla and walk steadily forward because whatever this is, I intend to face it head-on. Even if my arms are too shaky to aim straight.

The temperature drops. A cold wind rises, howling like a mad creature as its icy tongue licks over my skin. I try to manipulate it, to change it, but I can't.

Dropping Nahla's reins, I fasten my cloak tighter and move as if in a dream toward the water. My thoughts turn sluggish, my heartbeat, too.

I stop at the pond's edge, my gaze scanning the boughs of a gigantic ash tree, and I admire the way its gnarled branches reach over the water, embracing it. It's such a pretty sight. So comforting.

Nahla wanders into the trees to nibble on some grass. I'm not worried. She'll be fine. Nothing can harm her in this lovely, special place.

As I crouch down beside the pond, preparing to scoop clear water into my dry mouth, a pair of dragonflies lands on my arm. Their electric blue bodies distract me, reminding me of my mother's tattoo. I swallow past a dull ache in my throat, yearning for one of Mom's warm hugs.

But, no, I don't need my mother in this wonderful place—so dark and cold and beautiful.

Yes, it really is enchanting.

To think that only a few moments ago, I was desperate to go home, but now I feel quite happy to stay here forever. Lie down. Fall asleep. *Rest*.

What was I doing? Oh, yes, having a drink. Then I'll sleep.

I dip my hand in the water, the icy temperature making me draw it back briefly. It's winter-cold, freezing. Then I take a sip and close my eyes.

A twig cracks nearby, then a deep male voice echoes behind me, paralyzing my muscles. Cara shivers against me, but for some reason, I can't lift a finger to comfort her.

"What are you doing here?" he asks, his angry tone alarming me.

Okay. What happens now?

I should turn around and face my foe, leap up with my bow drawn, but I can't move. And, also, my bow seems to have vanished.

"You shouldn't drink that," he says.

My hands shake, my insides, too. I'm very familiar with the dark timbre of that voice. I know it well, because I last heard it this morning in my dream.

Forcing my muscles to relax, very slowly I peer over my shoulder.

A tall figure, wreathed in shadows, stands on the edge of the trees. Silver hair. Pale skin. A cruel expression. His lips part and his shockingly blue eyes widen.

"*You*," he breathes out.

My gaze focuses, and I stare, taking in every inch of him.

The fae standing before me is a young warrior with a face as beautiful as the brightest star in the midnight sky. His expression severe and cold, he glitters like a god of old.

A wavy curtain of snow-white hair frames his cheekbones and the bluest eyes I've ever seen. His clothes are black, his spiked crown, too. He wears a dark tunic over leather and silver armor with pointed shoulder pauldrons in the typical style of fae royalty.

The jeweled sword belt hanging from his lean hips holds no weapon. One arm is folded behind his back in a genteel pose, but in contrast, his lips form a feral curve.

Without a doubt, this is the fae who haunts my dreams. I know his face as well as I do my own. He doesn't look friendly or pleased to see me here, but that doesn't change the fact that I'm drawn to him like no other before.

He's a dream come to life. An attraction spell made of flesh and bone come to lure me to Dana knows what or where. Perhaps to my ruin. Or my death.

This is madness. Or deep magic. No, I must be hallucinating. Why else would he stay silent, unmoving, like a ghost?

All fae know the best way to dispel an illusion is to talk to it. That usually sends them packing in a puff of indignant smoke.

I point at the pond. "I've already drank some water. It tasted fine. What do you predict will happen to me?" I try smiling, and blue-tourmaline eyes stare back. "Well, has it been poisoned or enchanted?"

The charged silence grows heavier. He doesn't move. Nor do I.

As we stare at each other, my heart hammers against my chest.

"You wear a beautiful crown," I say. "Are you a prince of this lonely place?"

"No. I am not that." He takes a step toward me. Then another. His intense gaze traps me, keeping me in place.

"Where are you from?" I ask.

Silence.

"Shall I guess? Have you come from one of the dark realms, Tech Duinn, perhaps?"

He cants his head again, studying me. An elegant hand lifts and reaches toward me as though he wants to check if I'm real, then it falls against his thigh.

I fumble onto my feet, brushing twigs and dirt off my clothes. "You don't say much. Or, indeed, answer any questions."

Wind rustles the leaves as the temperature drops to glacial. Soft flakes of snow begin to fall, swirling lazily from the ashen sky above. Snow? It's springtime. Or at least it was in my world this morning.

As my dream fae steps closer, snowflakes melt on our hair and shoulders, but they don't touch the trees nor the surface of the water. Or the grass. Only the two of us.

Cara is a warm lump beneath my hair, snoring softly and not affected by unfolding events. In this mysterious threshold place, perhaps the silver fae and I are the only two creatures who matter.

He moves forward, stopping only a finger's length away. Too close.

The air between us vibrates and pulses. And I, the Princess of Air, can barely draw breath as his gaze traces my face, lingering on my freckles, my hair, then repeating the pattern. His attention is suffocating, dangerous, but I want more of it.

So much more.

"So, are you going to tell me where you're from?" I ask.

Slowly, he shakes his head, and then slays me with a soft smile.

Frustration builds in my stomach. "At least give me your name."

His smile grows, then twists into a grimace. He lifts his cold fingers and skims them down my cheek, his feather-light touch scalding like frostbite. I gasp.

Why is he touching me? And why in the realms am I letting him?

This is wrong. I should back away. Or run. But I don't. I just stand there shivering.

"Why would I give you the gift of my name?" he asks. "You could easily use it against me. Would you do that, Merrin? Plot my downfall?"

My pulse races. "How do you know *my* name?"

"I have always known it."

"So, was it your magic that brought me here?"

He ignores my question, his thumb dragging over my lower lip.

My limbs grow heavy, and I sway toward him. "You're right," I say. "I can't plot against you if I don't know who you are." Or *what* he is, for that matter. "So the reason you won't tell me must be because you're afraid of me. Am I right?"

He laughs darkly. "You ask too many questions."

"And you answer none of them."

"It is safer if I don't." He gives me a sad smile. "I always imagined that if I found myself in this moment with you, I'd be strong, but I'm weak. Your freckles make me want impossible things."

"Tell me... tell me about these impossible things. And name the worst of them first."

His gaze drops to my lips, and he leans closer, his mouth parting.

My heart pounds as I tilt my chin up. "Is it a kiss you want?" I ask, my voice thin and breathy. "If so, that's neither horrible nor impossible."

Against my lips, he says, "You cannot know how much I wish to—"

"Wait," I cry out, stepping back. Something bright flickers near the sharp point of his ear. "Look! The snow falling around you has turned red, red as blood."

Just like in my dreams.

"What?" His hand swipes the air, capturing tiny flakes of crimson. He frowns as they melt on his palm. "This is a warning. I should not have touched you."

Around me the snow swirls pure and white, but on the mysterious fae, it falls flecked with blood. His expression darkens, now full of pain and terrifying to behold. The arm he keeps behind his back tenses as though he's tightening his grip on something he's hiding there.

A noise like glass shattering startles me, and the whole pond ices over.

What is happening?

I shuffle backward as a branch snaps in the trees behind me. The sound makes the fae flick his head up, and I look over my shoulder, my jaw dropping at what I see.

On one side of the glade is a golden stag, a jeweled black crescent moon strung between its enormous antlers. On the other side stands Kian. His red hair is dry, untouched by snow, his cornflower eyes wide with what appears to be glee.

"Merri," Kian shouts, taking a step forward. "Quickly, move away! He has a blade drawn behind his back. He'll kill you."

The ground shudders and the nameless fae spreads his arms, a black-bladed dagger held loosely in his left hand. "Untrue. I was not about to slit your throat," he tells me, his eyes burning with fury.

I focus my energies and attempt to raise a barrier of wind between us. Nothing happens. In this strange place, my magic is impotent. Kian's must be, too, or he would've already struck out at the stranger whose anger, it seems, can still affect the elements.

Kian takes another careful step toward us. As always, his chief concern is his own neck. "Well, maybe he can say he wasn't going to murder you at that moment, Merrin, but perhaps he planned to or was about to abduct you away to the Merit kingdom, just as his brother did to Queen Isla."

"His brother? What?" My gaze shoots to the silver fae.

A breeze parts his cloak, revealing a flashing pendant in an ornate frame. "You're a Merit!"

"Yes," says Kian. "And no ordinary one at that. Before you stands the Merit king himself, his court our long-sworn enemy."

All these years I've been dreaming about a Merit? My legs buckle, and it takes all my strength to stay upright. "You're Riven? The King of Merits?"

It makes no sense. He can't be the king. With his soft, translucent skin and lambent eyes, he's far too young and exquisite to be the ruler of that dark and terrible land.

"It is true." The fae points his sword tip at the ground. "That's why I couldn't tell you my name. I didn't want to frighten you, Merrin."

"Frighten her?" Kian snarls. "You're her natural born enemy. I'm sure you would sooner crush her skull than calm her fears."

"I've heard stories about you," I tell the Silver King. "According to our queen, out of El Fannon's two sons, you're meant to be the good brother. But if that's the case, then why would you bring me here?"

"Queen Isla knew him when he was but a prince. Power must have changed him," says Kian. "I swear he was going for his sword, Princess Merrin. I saw it. He no doubt wished to take your lovely head from your shoulders and carry it back to his court as a trophy."

Kian draws his sword and struts around the clearing, maintaining a measured distance from Riven. The king, with his weapon now sheathed, looks far more dangerous.

If I don't tread carefully here, this incident could ignite a war between our courts—a truly horrible outcome. What would the diplomatic Queen Isla say if she were here?

With my mind racing, I turn to Kian. "No. I don't believe he was planning to harm me. It didn't feel that way at all. Times have changed. Temnen and King El Fannon are dead. Their reign of terror has passed, and it's time we forged a more amicable relationship with the Court of Merits."

The king stares at me, his body frozen like an ice sculpture, dark-red snow staining his hair and cloak. I don't understand why a king would stand in silence and let Kian speak ill of him.

Kian scoffs. "If he meant you no harm, then why would he pretend to be someone other than who he is? The worst of the Merits may be dead but, lately, I hear whisperings about their court that disturb even me."

Yes, the rumors must be dire indeed if they trouble Kian, a lover of mayhem and debauchery.

"He must have a reason for not introducing himself. Perhaps he'll explain it to us now." My gaze locks with the Merit's. "Speak plainly, King Riven. Were you planning to murder or abduct me?"

"No," he says. "This meeting was an accident. I have no knowledge of how you came to be in this liminal space."

"This is my kingdom! We're somewhere in the Lowlands, north-east of Talamh Cúig."

He laughs, a rumbling sound that vibrates deep in my stomach. "If you cannot guess what has happened here today, then you're very naive for a Land of Five princess."

"What?" Heat flushes through me. "King or not, your manners need a polish."

"This is high magic," he says. "Although not mine. And obviously not yours. It's a border land, a space between worlds. Neutral territory, if you like."

"Listen to how he distracts you from the issue at hand." Kian takes a tiny step toward Riven. "Let me frame a different question. King of Merits, have you ever imagined causing harm to Merrin Fionbharr, be it by your hand or another's?"

I sigh. What is Kian up to?

The king's fists ball at his thighs, his knuckles white as bone. His mouth opens but no words come out of it.

"See?" Kian points a finger at the Merit. "He cannot answer truthfully without admitting his schemes! He is a fiend, wishing only for the downfall of your family through any means possible."

Time stills as I stare at the Merit king, the snow suspended in the air around his tall form. Part of me never wants to forget this moment—his face, the harsh bone structure, the too-lovely features, the angry pout of his lips. The rest of me wishes I'd never seen such a perfect being.

He likely wants to destroy my life in some way, and I want to do unspeakable things with him.

Why?

I do not know.

All fae are beautiful. He shouldn't have this effect on me. A tear runs down my cheek, my heart freezing over.

Riven's palm lifts toward me. "Merri, please—"

A black and white owl alights on the ash tree branch nearest the king. "Riven. Riven!" it calls. "Come. Come now!"

With its fierce green eyes fixed on me, it ruffles its bi-colored feathers, soft and white on one side of its body and rows of tiny black metal scales on the other. If I remember Queen Isla's stories correctly, it's a techno-beast, most likely the king's bonded creature.

The king inspects the owl, his black crown glittering darkly against the moonlight shade of his hair. "Meerade," he says, in a broken rasp.

The owl shrieks, and the air warps and buckles, a jagged tear forming in the space between me and the king. Snow continues to fall on him, but spring blossoms appear on my side of the glade. The Merit king is right; this is a place between worlds, a portal that's caused our separate kingdoms to somehow merge. An accidental meeting that should never have happened.

Riven's body shudders and blurs. He bends and retrieves something from the ground, quickly stuffing it under his cloak, then he fades, vanishing in front of my eyes.

A sound like the keening of a thousand banshees rises, growing louder and louder until I think my ears might explode. Then it disappears, and all is silent.

The Merit's world has gone, leaving Kian and me surrounded by the Lowland's bright-green plains.

"Well, that was quite a morning," I say. "Do you think he's dead now? The king, I mean."

"I wish it were so. But some Merits possess the ability to disappear in such a way. They call it transferring. They can reassemble their bodies in the exact spot they concentrate their minds upon."

"Quite a useful talent. I remember Raff speaking of it. Where are our horses? I presume you brought one and didn't slither all the way here on your belly," I say as dizziness overcomes me.

I've never fainted in my life, and I don't recall feeling like this before, horribly lightheaded and nauseous. I blame Riven—the King of Merits—for turning my world upside down.

Cara wakes and crawls into my arms, the movement making my stomach lurch. I hug my shivering mire squirrel tighter, wondering why I've been dreaming about the Unseelie king my whole life.

I whistle, and Nahla and Kian's chestnut stallion appear in the distance, their manes streaming as they gallop toward us. The urge to laugh shudders through me, just as it always does whenever I think of the name Kian gave his horse—Khan—so ridiculously similar to his own. It's endlessly entertaining—even when one's head is spinning madly.

"Merri." Kian's palm presses into my back as he nudges me toward his horse. "You are unwell and should ride with me. We'll return home slowly."

The thought of being that close to him makes my stomach roil again. I want to protest but can't find the energy to make a fuss. "I'm fine. But Nahla is feeling a little wobbly today, so you're right. It's probably for the best."

Wearing a sly smile, he nods, and ties Nahla's reins to Khan's saddle.

"Kian, wait. My bow," I say as he helps me into the saddle. "I dropped it somewhere."

Kian sneers. "No. The Merit took it."

Riven took my bow? I suppose I should be glad he didn't shoot me with it.

As Kian prepares to mount, I shuffle backward in the saddle. "You ride in front." At least that way I can attempt to keep as much distance as possible between our bodies.

He scowls but obeys. As he should. After all, I'm his princess, and he's been my fawning follower since as long as I can remember, always appearing when he's not invited and slobbering in my wake. It's repulsive. And unnerving. So I try to never be alone with him if I can help it.

As Kian drives the horses forward, I release a deep sigh.

Disoriented and weak, I'm in shock and not just from the aftereffects of high magic. At the in-between place, I felt a deep connection to the Unseelie king—the fae who has long haunted my dreams. When our eyes first met, something locked into place, link by link, breath by breath. But I have no idea why.

Because he is yours, whispers the wind in my ears. *Always yours.*

Pleasure shivers down my spine, a sign I'm not opposed to the idea, even though a match between the Merit king and a Land of Five princess is a ridiculous idea. My parents would never allow it. And besides, according to Kian, he just tried to kill me, which isn't an ideal start to a courtship.

But then again, my father did try to kill my mother within minutes of meeting her. Perhaps my rendezvous with the Merit king was auspicious after all.

I glance over my shoulder at the Dún Mountains, their indigo curves growing smaller as we ride away from them in the direction of the Emerald Castle. Home.

As I turn back around, my head spins, and I press my forehead against Kian's cloak. "Actually, I do feel quite sick."

Then the plains dissolve into blackness.

3

The Silver King

Merri

I wake to an alarming sound: Kian's shrill voice bleating in my ear.

"The Merit king has infiltrated our lands," he announces as if speaking from a high lectern, his words vibrating against my cheek.

What? Where am I?

My eyes fly open to find my nose squashed against Kian's indigo-blue cape. Ugh. Revolting! Now I feel even worse than I did before I passed out on the plains, whenever that was. Earlier today? Another lifetime ago?

I groan and clutch my head.

"The Merit king? No. That's not possible." Across the room and moving closer, my father's voice sends cool strands of air magic to enfold me, soothing my aching lungs. "Put her on the couch, Kian. Quickly. She's waking up, and when she does, it won't do her any good to find herself in *your* clutching embrace."

Father. He knows me so well.

Sinking back against soft cushions, I gaze at a flock of falcons painted on the walls, their wings outstretched as they spiral toward the ceiling until they become tiny specks of gold. *Falcons.* I must be in my parents' chambers, then.

Clothes swish and people whisper as they bustle around me. Cara snuggles into my shoulder. Balor's nose wets my cheek, and Spark is crouched over a platter atop a sideboard, munching on slices of apple and tossing discarded pieces over her shoulder onto the floor, ever the disorderly creature.

"Drink this," Isla says as she sits next to me.

Before I can hoist myself onto an elbow, she spoons a tonic into my mouth. I splutter, coughing up the sweet liquid. "How long were we gone?" I ask.

My mother stands before me in the dull light, a sweet-smelling shadow of silk and warmth, and bends to press her hand on my forehead. "Not long." She wraps a green and gold robe around her chest, and under it, her skin is bare. Frowning, she drops onto the divan beside me. "It's just past lunchtime, sweetheart."

"Lunchtime?" I lurch upright, nearly toppling Mom and Isla from the couch. "That's not right! We were gone for ages—hours and hours. I'm sure of it."

On the other side of the room, the rumpled bedclothes on my parents' gigantic four-poster bed come into focus. "If that's true, then why are you guys getting out of bed in the middle of the day? I saw you at breakfast and..." Then I notice Father's cobweb-gray shirt, the buttons misaligned, his barbed silver circlet sitting askew, not on *his* head but on Mother's, her red hair twisted and tangled around it. "Oh, right," I mumble. "Please don't answer my question."

My parents don't even try to hide their grins. Father squeezes Mom's shoulder then joins King Raff on the couch opposite me.

Silvery veils flutter in the tall lancet windows flung open to reveal the distant Dún Mountains, the light turning Dad and Raff into glittering silhouettes.

Leaning forward, his gold eyes grave, Raff says, "Tell us everything that happened, Merri. Begin at the start."

Hands clasped behind his back and lips forming the shape of a dried prune, Kian struts to my side then points at me. "I can tell you what happened. The Merit king attacked her!"

"What?" choruses my family, all glaring at me with either worry or fury, or varying degrees of both.

Thunder rumbles nearby, the room darkening then flashing white as lightning streaks overhead. I flinch. Spark screeches, leaping off the table then scampering into Raff's arms. Given the little lightning display, I'd say Father is the *most* furious of them all.

"Dad, please. Just let me explain," I say. "Kian is exaggerating. Be calm and let me tell you the whole story. It's not that bad. I promise."

A muscle twitches in his jaw. "How does one exaggerate an attack, Merri? It either happened or it didn't."

"Ever, let her speak," says Mom, and the thunder quiets, rumbling far off in the distance. Only Mother calms his storms with ease, one look, a soft word. A loving touch.

Silver eyes skewer me. "Then you had better hurry up and tell it," he growls out. "Because I am inclined to leave this room at a run, saddle Jinn, and head south toward the Merit kingdom. My sword has much to say to Riven na Duinn. And me? I have only three words. *Die, you—*"

"Brother!" Raff's palm shoots out. "Please. Stay and listen to Merri's tale. An all-out war with the Merits is not the answer. It never has been. You know this."

Burrowing into the cushions, I take a sip from the goblet of water Isla passes me. I clear my throat. "So, after breakfast, I rode out toward the mountains, thinking only of riding fast, feeling the wind in my hair. But before long, Nahla didn't seem herself, and by the time I realized she was unwell, she was unsteady on her feet, and it was too late—we were lost. If I had to guess the cause? To me, she seemed spellbound."

"How did you become lost so close to home?" asks Raff. "Did you make it past the mountains?"

Passing the goblet back to Isla, I shake my head. "No, we were on the plains and mist came out of nowhere and surrounded us, transporting us to a forest glade. There was a beautiful clear pond, and I was overtaken by thirst. When I dismounted to take a drink, a stranger appeared from the trees. The Merit king, although, at the time, I didn't know who he was."

"And he attacked you for no reason?" asks Isla.

"No! He seemed as shocked by my appearance as I was by his. We spoke. I tried to find out who he was, but he wasn't very keen to tell me. It started snowing. Some of the flakes were bloody. What can I say? The whole experience was strange, out of place, out of time. But never at any point did I feel that he wanted to *hurt* me."

Isla's hand rests on my knee, her gold gown shimmering as she leans close. "What did he look like, Merri?"

I take a breath, then pause for a moment, wondering how to describe such a singular, ethereal creature. "A star," I whisper. "A celestial being."

Isla smiles, an impish light twinkling in her blue eyes.

"And when it began snowing, he drew his sword?" asks Raff.

"No. Kian sneaked up and startled us. That was when Riven went for his sword. I think Kian's arrival caused the problem."

Kian's back stiffens, his proud expression souring. "You were fortunate I was there to save your life, Merrin!"

I snort. "Save me? Right now, I'm wondering if it was your fault I found myself in that enchanted forest in the first place. In the stables, before I rode out, Nahla wasn't herself. As I mentioned before, I suspect she was spellbound. Did you enchant her, Kian?"

Everyone stares at the vain, red-haired troublemaker. The air thrums so hard from Father's fury that glasses tremble on all surfaces.

A deep scarlet blooms over Kian's face. "I...I would never hurt you, Merrin. Surely, you must know that." He turns to my father. "Ever, my dear friend. You know I'd never wish harm to befall your child, don't you?"

Slowly, Father stands. A chair smashes against the marble floor as he removes it from his path with an explosion of air magic. He stalks forward, cracking his knuckles one at a time in the way he usually does when he's about to shift into his griffin or wreak havoc upon some poor soul or unlucky town.

I swallow the lump in my throat.

"Ever, please!" Kian inches backward. "You *must* know that Merrin is precious to me."

Father's nose wrinkles. "The scent of misdeeds sullies the air. It reeks of your brand of mischief, Kian. So. Answer the question and answer it without evasion. Now! Did you or did you not enchant my daughter's horse?"

"No," Kian says, white swallowing the pretty cornflower blue of his eyes as the odor of fear permeates the air.

"No, *what*?" Father growls, slamming his fist on the sideboard.

Kian pivots on his heels and scurries toward the door like a terrified mouse.

Isla moves to stand beside my father. Purple flames shoot from her palm, aimed at Kian. "Stop walking, Kian Leondearg. Answer Ever's question or I'll begin asking my own. But be warned, a queen's interrogation is not easily lived through."

Kian takes another step and his red mane bursts into flames. He pats his head, leaping and squealing like an angry changeling.

Queen Isla smiles.

Spinning like a top, Kian screams and screams until he finally gives in. "All right. All right," he says in a weak voice. "I beg you to put the flames out. I shall answer the stupid question."

The fire disappears, and he strokes his undamaged hair, which is as bright and lustrous as ever.

"Did you use a spell on Nahla today?" Raff asks. "Think carefully before you attempt to evade the question again."

Kian's shoulders curl forward as his palms open in surrender at his sides. "Yes. Yes, I did it."

A wild wind circles the room as Father takes several steps forward, crashing goblets, books, and platters to the floor.

"Wait! Please," begs Kian. "Please, Prince Everend. I have more to say."

Power vibrates against my skin, the sizzle before Dad's storm breaks. The intense energy presses against my limbs, holding me in place and preventing me from leaping on Kian and scratching his deceitful eyes out.

My parents' chamber disappears; in its place, an image flashes across my mind of Kian lying among ruins, those cornflower eyes fixed on the sky in an unseeing gaze. A sun emblem glitters on his forehead, a tattoo or magical glyph, I can't tell which. Heart pounding, I focus on his vacant death stare, a flicker of hope igniting in my chest.

Could this be a promise of things to come?

As terrible as it is to wish for his demise, I can't help it. My family has waited a long time for a reason to give Kian what he deserves. To deal out retribution for his forever meddling in our lives, causing grief and heartache for his own amusement. Well, now that the moment has finally arrived, we're all frozen, silenced by the shock of his treachery.

King Raff is the first to move. "So be it. What you did, Kian, was a deliberate act of harm that could have resulted in, at best, Merri's kidnap, or at worst, her death. Some would go as far as to call it treason. Therefore, the punishment shall fit the crime." He lifts his hand, readying to signal the guards.

"Wait!" says Mom. "First let him explain why he did it. It's only fair." Mother. Her heart is soft, perhaps because of the human sentiment still residing deep within it.

Kian's steel-capped shoulders drop, his gaze skimming the floor—probably searching for a crack that might open and swallow him whole.

Raff nods. "Fine. Explain, then. Why did you do this terrible thing?"

Kian lifts his chin. "I only wished to draw Merri away from court to speak with her alone. It's no secret that I have long admired her, but no matter what I do, I cannot seem to hold her attention. I used a disorientation spell on Nahla and then tracked their progress so that when they faltered, I could be the one to come to Merri's aid and grow in her esteem."

Ugh. My stomach lurches, a cold sensation slicing up my insides. Even when Wyn and I were children, Kian creeped me out. He was always lurking around the periphery of our games, preening and gloating like a demented peacock.

"How did you obtain the power to create such a spell?" asks Isla. "Your earth magic couldn't create a forest glade out of the Lowland plains without assistance."

His chest puffs as he prepares to boast. "As you correctly assume, Your Majesty, I didn't summon the glade. I was as surprised to see it as Nahla and Merri were. I lost my bearings in the mist, and it took an age for me to locate them. The glade was no creation of mine. Would that I had the skills to manifest such glorious spaces instead of manipulating soil and producing gemstones at will."

Earth magic is actually very cool, and Kian has always been an ungrateful fool, coveting what others have instead of appreciating his own gifts and talents.

Kian's gaze catches mine. "Princess, I saw the Merit in the act of drawing his blade even before he heard me arrive. I swear it was so."

And fae cannot lie. So it must be true. My heart sinking, I look away.

"That is troubling news indeed," Raff says. "But, Kian, hankering after what you cannot have was always going to bring about your downfall. Vow now to let go of your fixation on Merri, be the friend and loyal servant that she deserves and your punishment will be mild. This time. But if you bother her again, banishment will be your best fate—the worst, I promise you, does not bear thinking about. Ever, what do you recommend he suffer for his crime?"

"To begin with, a night in the dungeons, just as he tried to inflict upon Isla when she first arrived in our lands, and I'll bestow a fitting penance in the morning." Dad cracks his knuckles. "I'd like to consider *all* the options."

"As you wish, Brother," says Raff, the golden wands of citrine in his crown gleaming as bright as his grin.

The guards, Orlinda and her mate, Marlin, lead Kian from the room, and Isla sits down beside me, sighing loudly. "I can't believe

Riven meant to harm you," she says. "What about you, Raff? Do you think he could've changed so much since the time we were the Merits' prisoners? He was our ally then."

"No." The king frowns. "Back when he was only a prince, his greatest ambition was to create peace between our lands. Yes, he is a Merit and therefore not entirely trustworthy, but what would he gain by hurting our Merrin?"

"Nothing," Isla replies. "And I would trust his sister, Lidwinia, with my life. She loved Riven then, believed in him, and hell, probably even killed her own father to ensure her brother ascended to the throne as quickly as possible. This whole situation is fishy. There's bad magic here. I feel it in my gut."

"Then we need to consult the mages this evening," says Mom. "They probably felt the magical interference or have intelligence from the wild fae."

Their voices drift over me as the memory of the Merit king's fingers, smooth as glass on my cheek, chills my blood. The look in his eyes, wild, intense. And definitely unhinged.

The Merits have long been obsessed with humans, and I'm a half-blood. Perhaps he *did* plan to abduct me.

"Kian was right about one thing," I say as I draw the attention of all in the room. I swallow hard. "The Merit king was definitely hiding a blade behind his back. At the time, it didn't feel like he was going to hurt me, but now I wonder... For what other reason did he have his sword unsheathed?"

"Maybe he wished to take a lock of your hair as a memento of your meeting," suggests Isla, an uncertain smile on her lips.

Father laughs, a dark sound. "Then I shall make a memento of his shining silver head. And perhaps Kian's scarlet one, too."

"Don't punish Kian too harshly," I say. "Yes, there's no doubt he's an obnoxious mischief-maker, but he did come to my rescue. If he's correct about the Merit king, then who knows what might have happened to me if he hadn't intervened?"

"Merri's right, Ever," says my mother. "As misguided as Kian's scheme was, he didn't plan to hurt her. But we can't be so sure of what the Merit intended." She turns to Raff. "Riven must have created the glade. His magic would be strong enough to form the rift and hold it for a period of time. And if that's true, such an act could be seen as an invasion of our territory. After Raff and Isla's imprisonment, our Council declared that if any Merit entered our land without invitation, it would be considered a declaration of war. Riven knows this, and yet he broke the agreement."

Raff says, "Then there must be a price to pay. A severe one to deter similar incidents."

"What? No, that's a bad idea!" I wring my hands in appeal to the king and queen. "Riven and his sister helped you escape from the Merit kingdom. They saved you from Temnen. They were your friends, weren't they? You can't go and declare war on them. Any reprimand should be mild. Riven didn't hurt me."

Isla links her arm through Raff's. "I agree with Merri. We wouldn't be alive today if it weren't for Riven and Lidwinia's help. I put my trust in Riven back then, and I'm willing to give him the benefit of the doubt now. Personally, I don't think he planned to hurt her."

Raff picks up a hnefatafl piece from a low table and turns it between his fingers. "I'm not so sure. Remember, Isla, there are many in Riven's court who think him insane or at the very least unbalanced."

"You're speaking of the past, my love," says Isla. "Lidwinia writes to me about how their courtiers are learning to live without the cruelties El Fannon encouraged. She refers to her brother with only love and respect. I trust them."

Father's eyes darken to chips of pyrite. "And yet the Merit drew his sword against a princess of our land. He may have planned to kill her. Or perhaps he did not. Either way, I want to raise an army against their city. Riven must learn that we're not to be trifled with, then he won't dare to come near my family again."

Mom looks appalled. "Ever, I wasn't suggesting you start a war. I was thinking more along the lines of a stern letter or a meeting to renew the terms of our agreement, and certainly not of you slicing his head off with your sword!"

While they argue, I get up and drift over to the window and stare toward the mountains in the approximate direction of where the glade appeared. Why was I so certain it was Kian's arrival that caused the Merit to draw his blade? Now I'm doubting my memory, my instincts. My heart. Because of Kian.

"Merri?" Mom's voice breaks through my turbulent thoughts.

"What?" I turn, rubbing my arms and yawning. "I'm sorry. I lost focus."

She comes over and folds me in a warm embrace. "Go and rest. You look exhausted. Have dinner in your rooms if you wish, and we'll update you with anything we learn from the mages in the morning."

Flashes of color—silver, bronze-gold, deep reds, and shimmering blues—whirl through my mind. The mages four, the fifth still imprisoned in the Emerald Forest, her power tethered to the moss elves. "Is Father going to start a war?"

Mom laughs. "No, darling. Don't worry. We'll make him see sense."

"Thank you. See you tomorrow." I blow kisses at my family and race for the door, longing for my soft bed. "Let's get some sleep," I tell Cara, and she answers with a gentle snore from my shoulders, already a step ahead of me.

I make it as far as the hallway when the queen's voice halts my escape, calling my name. With quick steps, we walk toward each other.

She clasps my hands tightly. "Merri, at this time, there's so much I wish I could say to you." A strange, wistful smile flashes over her face. "Unfortunately, I have no choice but to keep this simple. Please remember that things aren't always what they seem. You must strive to keep an open heart. Holding on to hate only grows more of it in a never-ending cycle. Understanding and forgiveness are always the correct choices. Hold strong to these ideas no matter what. Promise me?"

Isla's heart is pure. What she asks can only be good and right. I can see no problem in giving her my word. "Of course," I tell her. "I promise to try to always think and act with an open heart and mind."

With those words, her gold-painted lips stretch into a luminous smile. "Good. Thank you." She strokes my cheek. "One more thing, Merri. Stay away from Kian, won't you?"

"No problem there. I learned long ago to keep my distance from him. He's a major pain in the butt."

She laughs at my use of Earth slang and glides back toward my parents' rooms.

In my chambers, I peel off my dirty cloak and leathers and fall into bed, tugging Clara into my arms. The moment I close my eyes, a vision overtakes me, engulfing me in darkness.

First, I hear the sound of water lapping, then my body is swayed by a gentle rocking motion. Wooden splinters dig into my feet, my bare legs curled under me. My eyes flare open and, other than the white of my robe glowing in soft folds over my lap, I see only black.

Horror pounds through my veins as cool water sprays my face. I'm in a boat! My hands are in a strange position, crossed over my chest, and I'm gripping what feels like two sword hilts. I test that theory, slashing them through the air in front of me. Yes. I'm holding heavy blades. I place one over my knees, retaining the other in case I need it, and tug a silken blindfold away from my eyes.

A starless night sky surrounds my tiny boat as it bobs on a jet-black ocean. Above my shoulder hangs a golden crescent moon. I look left then right, trying to locate the deadly rocks I know will be lurking out there in the inky sea. I can *feel* them.

As soon as I pick up an oar, another blindfold wraps tightly around my face. I tear it off and another appears. Then another. And another. With a frustrated scream, I place the second sword over my knees, bow my head, chest laboring with gasped breaths while I think.

This is a dream. This is a dream. Just a dream.

But I can't sit here and do nothing, can I? I should paddle, but in which direction?

I don't know. I don't know.

I grip the swords again, crossing them over my chest as I lift my chin and straighten my back.

I'll wait here in the darkness, thinking, before I do anything rash.

I'll wait here in my dream.

I'll just wait.

The water's song goes *lap, lap, lap.*

My body dances to the rhythm of the moon.

Sway. Sway. Sway.

A voice calls in the distance, low and rough.

"Merrin? Come here to me. Quickly, come now."

It is the Silver King.

The Silver King is calling me.

Presenting a problem.

A dilemma.

Do I answer?

4

The Hunter

Riven - Two Years Later

"The princess comes," says Meerade, the points of her talons biting into my right shoulder.

Torchlight flickers over the limestone walls of the druid's cavern, and I lean closer to the scrying well. I say nothing as I bow my head and wait for the vision in the water to solidify.

Yes...

Yes, my owl is correct—Merri has come at last. Since our meeting in the in-between-land two years ago, she hasn't once appeared in these sacred waters. I would know if she had because I come here every night to check, to be sure she's truly gone. Because that is what I want—Merrin Fionbharr eradicated from my mind forever. Isn't it?

So, why has she returned after all this time?

My knuckles bleaching white as I grip the well's edge, I study the image with growing dread. Today, instead of a forest, she runs across a frozen lake, her wild red hair flying behind her. Her arms and feet are bare, and her wet, silver gown clings to her legs. She looks cold. Terrified. As though she's fleeing for her life.

I'm not familiar with this dark, ominous place, where even the tree branches look sinister, bowing over the banks and creating webbed shadows on the surface of the lake. No. Correction. They're fissures in the ice, not shadows.

"Don't fall," Meerade screeches. "Take care!"

"It's all right," I tell her. "These visions aren't real, remember?"

The fissures crack open, spreading along the ice, and Merri stumbles...

"Riven?" says Lidwinia, who has used her nefarious sibling skills to creep up on me while I was distracted. She presses her cheek against my back, her fingers digging into my upper arms.

Not now. Don't interrupt now.

I need to see what happens to the girl. I glance away from the scrying well. "What do you want, Lidwinia?"

"I apologize for disturbing you here. I know you dislike it, but you've left me no choice. You've been down here too long, and I have news. Also, your courtiers wish to see you."

Before turning to face her, I check that the image in the water has dispersed, and praise the Oak it has. The last thing I need is for Lidwinia to see me mooning over Merrin Fionbharr.

"Sister." I kiss her brow. "What news do you bring?"

"I've received a message from the Elemental king. He wishes to meet with you to discuss the prospect of our courts coming together for Samhain rituals this year, as was sometimes tradition even under Father's rule."

My jaw drops. Surely, Lidwinia is joking.

After the peculiar meeting at the pond with Princess Merrin and the red-haired Elemental courtier, a Land of Five envoy arrived at our court with a decree that was clear and uncompromising. If I dared show my face in their land again, I would be captured, murdered, have my kingdom invaded, and my people destroyed.

Unconcerned by the threat, I shrugged my shoulders at the time. With our court's powers, a blend of technology and magic, we're not so easy to defeat. And I possess no desire to spend my days bent over battle maps planning strategies that would lead to the death of thousands of fae—both Elementals and Merits. No desire at all.

"That's absurd. You *do* realize Rafael thinks I tried to kill their pretentious Princess of Air?"

"Merrin? Isla tells me she's as sweet as honey and one thousand times nicer. No doubt she would forgive you for any transgression." She arches a dark brow at me. "I suppose they must have come to their senses and realized what happened that day was an accident."

"Elementals acting sensibly? Now, that would be news worth celebrating."

"Now, now. Retract your claws, Brother." Grinning, she pats my cheek. "Once, you were quite fond of Queen Isla, so—"

"Yes, but she's only *married* to an Elemental."

"Well, regardless, it appears they wish to reconcile. In three days' time, King Rafael wants you to meet his small hunting party in the forest at the northern base of Mount Cúig, near Terra River. The horned annlagh has risen for the first time in over a century and is in pursuit of a mate."

"I thought that beast was fabled."

"Unfortunately not. You will hunt the creature. If you manage to slay it before he or a member of his court does, then you'll be forgiven your earlier trespass upon their land and—"

"But I did not trespass—"

"Shh, I know." She smiles, her snake-like tongue flickering as her fingers stroke Meerade's metal wing. "I remember well how it went. One moment you were fortifying boundaries along the city's eastern walls, the next you were in a foreign forest by a pond. And there was Merrin."

"Yes. There she was. Suddenly and for no good reason." Merrin Airgetlám Fionbharr. Bane of my life. My one and only obsession. Perhaps that is reason enough.

"Anyway, if you kill the annlagh, we'll be invited to celebrate Samhain at the Elemental Court again. Peace, Riven! It's what you've always wanted. Plus, there is the fact that your aging spell has lifted. Have you ever considered the idea that the fae who caused this to happen might be an Elemental?"

"Never. I prefer not to think of it at all." Or that I started aging again the very next day after I visited the in-between world—with Merrin Fionbharr.

I leave the podium and walk over the surface of the water, my trick making my sister grin. "This could be a trap."

"Nonsense!" she says. "The message contained the authentic royal seals, magical and impossible to forge. I trust the Elemental king, and I trust his queen even more. But he's requested that you go alone, which I admit does put you and our land in a vulnerable position. But it must be as he asks. How will you protect yourself?"

I flick my right hand, and a ball of light spins in the air. "My magic is at least equal, if not stronger than the fire king's."

The ball rotates between me and Lidwinia, growing in size until its brightness is blinding. I cast it against the limestone wall. It explodes, forming a diaphanous barrier around our bodies. I click my fingers, and arrows of violet stalactites shower down from the roof then bounce off my magic's protective shell.

"I'm not worried about *my* safety, Lidwinia. Rafael's brother, Prince Everend, is of more concern, constantly threatening war. He can't let go of his grudge and refuses to believe I didn't plan to hurt his daughter that day. I want peace between our kingdoms. Long term, *stable* peace. And I aim to achieve it. So, if Rafael's message is real, it's very good news indeed. In fact, I must chance that it is and make ready to leave tomorrow."

"Good. And I'm pleased to tell you that Ever won't be joining the hunting party."

Because if he did, no doubt he'd try to rip my head off with a lightning bolt the moment he laid eyes on me and destroy any hope of accord between our kingdoms. "Either way, I will attend the meeting."

"Excellent, Your Majesty." Wearing a mischievous smile, she dips her hand in the well and splashes me. "I'll send a message to the king of Talamh Cúig on your behalf. And if the Elementals hurt you in any way, I'll grind every single one of them to dust."

Ah, my slightly insane sister is truly a marvel to me—mostly level-headed and benevolent in nature—but if those she loves are under threat in any way, she transforms into a bloodthirsty creature.

I smile. "Tell Rafael to bring his biggest bow. He'll need it if he wants to best me in the hunt for the annlagh."

Three days hence, I'm on the northern side of Mount Cúig tracking a set of large hoof prints through the forest and wondering why the Land of Five king truly wishes to meet with me.

Certainly, it would be convenient for Rafael if I kill the horned annlagh without him needing to lift his bow, but does he truly wish to discuss resuming *Samhain* festivities of all things? I read his message. It was simple and to the point—exactly like the king of Talamh Cúig.

The designated meeting place near Terra River is too far from the Merit City for direct transfer, so Raghnall and I materialized in Ithalah Forest, and I traveled the rest of the way on horseback.

So, here I am, hunting the annlagh who in turn hunts for a mate, with Meerade scouting the skies ahead for trouble. Given there are no female annlaghs, when it surfaces from hibernation every hundred years or so, it must take by force any creature who has the misfortune to cross its path—dryads, pixies, even kelpies—but hopefully not fae kings. I give a brief snort at my once-in-a-decade joke.

Understandably, the beast is a great nuisance in the Land of Five, and the Seelie fae are eager to be rid of it, but so far today, I haven't encountered a trace of them on this hillside, which is odd. But the Elementals are strange creatures, ruled by whim and whimsy. Perhaps they decided to attend a banquet instead. I wouldn't put it past them.

Regardless, I stalk onward through the forest, my bow drawn, as I attempt to quash images of shiny red waves spread against a background of snow. Merri, the Princess of Talamh Cúig has somehow invaded my thoughts once again. Must I always be plagued by her?

In truth, whenever I close my eyes, I see her face. That day at the pond, I should have killed her then and there and put an end to this torture. I was gifted with the perfect chance, but I couldn't do it.

I could not do it.

In the flesh, the Elemental brat was everything I prayed to Mab she wouldn't be—and so much more. Why did the sight of those moonlight eyes turn me to stone? Immobilize me so I could barely speak, let alone draw my sword and turn that pond red as I'd always dreamed I would?

I must never succumb to the insidious spell the Elemental princess has woven through my bone and marrow. If I did, I would forever be at her mercy, just as the Black Blood curse foretells. My kingdom would be lost. My people defenseless. And the Elementals would have what my father always swore they wanted—full control and to reign supreme over both our lands.

Damn the curse and its secret words that repeat through my mind with every crunch of my boot over bracken and stone.

A halfling defies the Silver King,

From dark to light, her good heart brings.

Enemies unite. Two courts now one,

Should merry win, the curse is done.

This will never come to pass. I won't let it. It's one thing for my courtiers to rhapsodize over human pets, but a Merit queen with human blood ruling over them? No thank you. The idea is laughable. And terrifying. Mostly because the weakest, sickest part of me wants this. Longs for it.

Crunch.

My body bounces off a tree trunk, and I stumble backward over rocky mounds. "Where in the Blood Sun did that come from?" I mutter, rubbing my nose.

"Daydreaming fool!" says Meerade. "Heed where you walk."

"I *was* paying heed, you insolent rodent eater."

"Shh," she hisses. "Too quiet! Forest is too quiet!"

"Not inside my head. If you were privy to my thoughts, you would find the conversation both loud and chaotic."

She bites the point of my ear. "Be quiet now and listen, King of Merits."

Slowing my breathing, I do as my wise owl bids and listen.

I stop in the brush and plant my feet wide, muscles taut, ears pricked, and I hear...*nothing.*

Insects dance along shafts of sunlight between the spruce trees, but I hear no chirping of birds. No scratching of creatures. No laughs or whispers from the Elemental hunting party who are meant to be scouring the forest nearby. I am alone, and where the hell are they?

Bow drawn beside my cheek, I spin slowly in the eerie silence. Then I notice the lack of weight on my left shoulder. My owl has vanished. "Meerade?" I call.

Branches snap behind me. I swing my head around, expecting to see either a hideous horned monster or my owl. But it's Olwydd, my dead brother's bird—a foul omen indeed.

"What are *you* doing here?" I snarl out.

Black-pebble eyes spin in its evil little bronze head. Whirring with a click-click-click, it alights into the air, disappearing above the trees. I look up, marveling at how clear the sky is, unmarred by the violet clouds that often blanket the Merit City.

"Good riddance to stool pigeons," I say. No doubt he's gone to find the Fire king to alert him of my presence and fabricate some transgression on my behalf. Olwydd has always been a traitor.

On a heavy sigh, my eyes move from the treetops to the forest ahead. Perhaps, for fun, I should hunt the Elemental party instead of the beast? I unhook my water pouch from my belt and take a long drink. As I reattach the pouch, a stand of trees sways and parts, and I spy enormous silver antlers glinting between moss-covered branches and moving toward me with speed.

I pull my bowstring tight and draw a slow breath, releasing magical energy that should throw a wall of protection in front of me...except...nothing happens. "What in the realms?"

The creature breaches the trees, its roars shaking the ground beneath my boots.

The thing moves at the speed of light magic, so fast its grisly limbs and maw blur as they drive forward. I loose my arrow, and the annlagh knocks me to the ground, all breath leaving my lungs in a hard whoosh.

"Stupid, stupid king," it says, its knee on my chest and clawed fingers clamping my neck.

How could my magic fail me so thoroughly? I don't understand.

I wheeze and stare into translucent eyes that burn with power as old as time. "How did you...?"

"*How*, you ask, oh, dense one?"

The beast's fetid breath makes me gag as its drool drips on my cheek and slides under my collar. Dewdrops glitter like jewels on its antlers, but the grass and leaves are dry.

"Stand," the annlagh says, leaping off me and moving a few strides away.

I swipe my bow from the ground as I lurch upward, withdrawing an arrow from the quiver on my back, then nocking it while the beast stares, unmoving.

Aim true.

I draw the bow tight. The string cuts into my soft-leather glove, but my fingers won't release it. The creature's eyes track the blood that drips from my fingers, my arms shake, and still, I cannot loose the arrow.

"Riven Èadra na Duinn," it says. "I have long wished to meet you."

I blink once, and in that instant, the beast disappears, leaving in its place a willowy woman dressed in silver, a cloud of white hair billowing around her head and shoulders. Her features are indistinct, shrouded in a glamor, but her voice is as clear as a crystal bell.

This is no annlagh, no Elemental courtier, but whoever in the seven realms she is, she's more powerful than an Unseelie king. I should be quaking with fear, but I'm not. I am resigned and ready to face my fate. Whatever it may be.

She smiles, or at least her mouth twists in the rough shape of one. "Your fingers are bleeding. Lower your bow, for you cannot possibly use it."

I let it fall to the ground. "Who *are* you?"

"Your question could be better formed, King of Merits."

Sighing, I look to the sky. "I have long despised nitpickers of language. It reveals a shallow nature."

"You are amusing, Silver One."

Well, *she* can talk about shining things—she's the one who glows like a winter moon.

"You would do better to ask *what* I am, not who."

"Fine. What are you, then?"

"Oh, Silver King, you are foolish," she says, ignoring the question she forced me to ask. "You come into the territory of your family's long-time enemy and do not even think to wear your crown of jet. A crown that offers you much protection."

"A king's crown is not made for hunting." Against my will, my fingers go to the obsidian circlet on my brow. I raise my chin at the white lady. "I ask again—what in the realms are you?"

"A friend."

I breathe a laugh through my nose. "I sincerely doubt that."

Milk-white hands reach for me. They shoot golden light into the center of my chest, the pain arching my back and rumbling a groan from my lips.

"Answer one question, Riven na Duinn. Who is it you seek?"

"Always Merrin Fionbharr." The words burst out of me, beyond my control. I grind my teeth against the pain of this fiend's terrible magic.

"Yes," she says. "You do. And for what purpose?"

"To…" I swallow a moan. "End. Her."

"Wrong answer, Silver King."

The spear of light falls away from my body, and a golden bow appears in the lady's hands, a long arrow already nocked. Aiming at my heart, she draws the bow tight, then releases the arrow. It hits my chest with a loud thunk.

"I'm wearing armor," I say daftly as my hand goes to my chest panel, finding it split, blood seeping from the seam.

No.

That's not possible.

In a trance, I gaze down at the fletching bouncing at the end of the arrow that protrudes from my chest. Gripping the shaft, I draw a breath to speak. "But how—"

Laughter tinkles, the sound charming, like water dancing over stones in a brook. "Be careful, Riven. Don't pull too hard on that. I need you alive. Now would you be so good as to hurry up and pass out? You're as strong as a fomórach. I'm sure you don't wish to behave like those impulsive giants and make everything worse, do you?"

"Did…did Rafael send you to kill me?"

This time, her smile is clearer, and I can almost make out her facial features. She slinks forward and places two cool fingers on my lips. My teeth chatter against them.

"Shush now. Time for all good kings to go to sleep."

Then she pushes me backward, and I slide down the hill and fall into a turbulent sea. No. That can't be right. I'm in a forest. It must be a bed of writhing sweet grass. A cushion of gnashing wild flowers. A pillow made of storms and smoke and cool breath.

I fight my heavy lids, my eyes searching for the white woman, but she's gone. Disappeared like a phantom. Thank the Blood Sun, for I did not like her much.

Slowly, slowly my blood travels through my veins, my heart growing weaker with every panted breath. Where is Meerade? My vision clouds, then dims. My energy fades fast, but I lift my heavy hand and press it against my wound, feeling the blood seep hot between my fingers.

I never imagined my end would be so pitiful. So wretched and lonely. I wish Lidwinia were here, and Elas, too.

Releasing a painful sigh, I watch the translucent leaves move against the sky. So blue. So peaceful. A soft whinny sounds nearby. Raghnall! "Go home," I tell her in my mind. "Go now."

In the distance, an angel speaks of death, then an unpleasant weight crushes my chest. Waves of red block my view, narrowed silver eyes frowning down at me.

Ah, of course, a vision of the Elemental princess has come to ruin my final moments and force me from this realm into the next. I suppose that is fair. I had planned to be present at her last breath, too.

A chuckle escapes my lips, more of a cough than a laugh. A strange time for humor, but it's amusing to find myself staring at this girl, a ghost come to haunt me into my grave.

I want to raise my fingers and touch her freckles, glittering like tiny stars on her lovely face.

I try to lift my head and bid this phantom Merri farewell. I part my lips, and all that comes out is one word, "You."

The phantom frowns but doesn't dissolve or utter a single word.

"You," I say again.

Then the darkness takes me.

5

To Capture a King

Merri

Today, the Lake of Spirits on top of Mount Cúig shimmers, the surface of the water resembling rainbow moonstone—flashing silver, blue, pink, and peach.

I can't peel my eyes from the beauty of the lake, the source of our Elemental powers, as I dry off after my monthly swim. Feeling revitalized, I tug my clothes on quickly, competing with Magret to be the first dressed.

"Merri, we should hurry back," says Magret, pulling her mauve tunic on and squirming to drag her large antlers through the neckline. "Your mother wants you back in time to meet the Shade Court royals who are arriving in advance of tomorrow's feast."

That's right. Beltane. I'm trying to forget about it. I turn my frown away from Magret as I tighten my sword belt, then tie on my soft gold cloak.

"She wants me home in time to be trussed up to meet Prince Landolin."

"Merri! Lara only wishes you to meet one of your own kind who'll make you as happy as Prince Ever has made her. She hopes you'll find love. What mother does not wish this for their beloved child?"

I can think of quite a few, but I won't name names. Fae females can be ruthless in their matchmaking schemes, caring only for social connections and advancements. *Love* usually has nothing to do with it.

I wish I could confess the truth to Magret. Tonight is an orchestrated ruse, and I only have to pretend to be amenable to a match with Landolin, because our High Mage has already foreseen our bond will fail the Beltane rites. Thank the Elements.

"Well, then," I say, smoothing my bitter expression. "Where are all the halfling princes hiding who want to leap over the Beltane fires with me? Besides Wyn, I'm yet to meet one, and if Mother wishes me to wed my *own* kind, then a halfling is what she'll need to present. Or do you think she and Father will let me take a trip to Blackbrook to find a human husband?" I already know the answer to that stupid question. A big fat *no*.

Magret's pale skin darkens and wildflowers sprout around her bare feet, a sure sign I've angered her. "You know your happiness is her main concern. Tell her your dreams, and she'll help them become your reality."

True. Mom doesn't want me to marry someone I despise, but if she knew whose snow-cold kisses I dream about each night, if I told her I have a dreadful crush on the Merit king, who may or may not have tried to take my head off with his sword when I met him two years ago, she'd lock me in a tower and ask the sea witches to hide the key in the deepest part of the ocean.

"All right, Magret," I say as I mount Nahla. "Let's leave at once, so we can be home before nightfall, and I can meet the Shade prince wearing clean clothes and my best fake smile."

Our horses pick their way down the wooded hillside to Terra River at the base of the mountain, where they stop to drink their fill, and I stretch my legs in the stirrups.

The forest glows with golden afternoon light, insects swooping along gentle currents of air. Closing my eyes, I send a gust of wind swirling upward, collecting fallen berries and leaves to twirl through the tree trunks.

Magret laughs, flicks her hand and creates a path of brilliant red poppies that trails haphazardly over the riverbank.

An iridescent gyendad, the freckled wasp my father first thought Mother resembled, escapes my mini-tornado and lands on my forearm.

"Hello, friend," I say, moving my arm in a slow circle and filling my lungs with the day's warmth. The creature shoots into the air then buzzes along the path of poppies that rambles through the woods.

My gaze follows the wasp, snagging on a peculiar sight. Underneath a copse of rowan trees, lies a body, the flowers surrounding it an icy white instead of red.

"Magret, look." I point at the sleeping figure—possibly a demi-giant by the size of it. Or maybe a very large fae.

She reaches for her bow and nocks an arrow while I dismount quietly. I draw my bow and quiver from the saddle and do the same, stalking forward.

"Merri, let me go instead," her voice hisses.

I shake my head, lifting my palm to stop her, and then draw my bow tighter. Crushing red poppies underfoot, I creep toward the body. Closer. And closer still.

A black cloak and long silver hair swirl through the glowing flowers, and my heart leaps into my throat.

It's the Silver King.

My mortal enemy.

The fae I dream about who wishes me dead.

The weight of my bow shakes my arms. I should ease my burden and loose the arrow. Kill him, if he's not dead already. But I can't make myself release the bowstring.

"He's fae," I call over my shoulder as I prowl onward, neglecting to inform my companion *which* particular fae.

Dropping to my knees beside the king, I rest the bow near my calf. His pallor is gray, his lush lips pale and bloodless. He looks vulnerable. So beautiful. So...almost dead.

Oh, snap out of it, Merri. Stop ogling him and do something.

I feel his forehead, then his cheek. Both are marble-cold.

I ease his cloak aside, then the top of his leather chest plate. A necklace lies against his throat above his Merit pendant. It's an arrowhead strung on a chain of twisted gold feathers—air symbols that sing to my soul—the initials M.F. engraved upon it. My initials.

This is the arrow I lost along with its bow when I met the king at the in-between world.

Why does he wear this?

And speaking of arrows, there's a rather large one jutting from his chest armor, dark blood still trickling from the wound.

A branch snaps as Magret moves closer. "Merri, who is it? An Elemental?"

"No." I frown over my shoulder at my friend—wildflowers woven through her white hair and antlers, her corded gardener's muscles tensed, and the bronze-tipped arrow she's drawn aimed at Riven na Duinn's heart. "Stay there, Magret. I don't want to scare him to death." Not yet, anyway.

Her pale eyes narrow, but she gives a sharp nod. I breathe a sigh of relief. Magret wouldn't hesitate to kill him if she knew who he was. Thankfully, Riven hasn't visited the Elemental Court since he was a child. She's likely never seen him fully grown.

I rest my weight on my hand beside his chest and lean close, then use my thumb to part his lips and blow a slow stream of gold-tinged healing air into his lungs. With a gasp, he sucks down the magic, his lids slitting open, and I'm pierced by a bolt of startling blue. His eyes are a wonder to behold.

Riven's pupils dilate, and he tries to lift his head, promptly thudding it back onto the carpet of flowers beneath him.

"You..." he croaks, an elegant but shaky finger pointing at my nose.

"Merri!" says Magret. "Come away from him."

"It's fine. I know this fae. Now shush and let me speak with him."

"But—"

"Please, Magret." Heart pounding, I inspect the injured Merit.

When I first met Riven, he was tall and ethereal—a boy still developing into a man. Now he looks older, perhaps a few years past my age, and he's larger, more muscular, and harder all over.

But in Faery, appearances can be deceiving. With glamors and spells, tricks and curses, only a fool would believe their eyes over the words they hear spoken. In words lies the truth hidden behind every selfish motive, foul deceit, and ridiculous ruse.

According to tales, in actual fae years, this Merit has been alive far longer than me, cursed to be ageless until he meets his mate, when henceforth, it's rumored he'll begin to age at the normal rate of our species.

This is a full-grown king lying before me, not the exquisite youth of two years past, so he must have already met this paragon of Merit beauty. My foolish heart pangs at the thought.

"You…" he says again, then loses consciousness once more.

"Who is he, Merri?"

"Be patient. I'll tell you soon." I push Riven's shoulder to rouse him. "Yes? I'm certain you were about to say something fascinating."

This time, his eyes flare open, pupils almost swallowing the blue irises. "You're her," he slurs. "The Elemental brat."

Charming. I remind myself he's a Merit, and I shouldn't expect courtly manners from *his* kind, although, surely a *king* could do a lot better.

"Obviously, I am she. And you're the wretched Merit king. A would-be murderer of innocent girls."

"Merri!" shouts Magret, lifting her bow again. "Come away."

Gritting my teeth, I throw a gust of wind at Magret. Her hair unravels from its loose braids and wraps around her face, effectively gagging her. She gives a nod of resignation, easing the strain on her bow, but keeping it aimed at the Merit's chest.

"You're wrong about that day. I didn't try to—" Riven breaks off and laughs, an unexpected action for someone with an arrow sticking out of them. "Merrin, look, you have moons around you."

"What?" My head lashes in all directions, but I see no moons. This fae is delirious.

He laughs again. "You have the full moon at your brow, and the dark one rests over your stomach. Two crescents and the half moons lie at your sides. You have the silver lady's entire circuit on your body, full to waning, then waxing once more. It is astonishing."

"What?" I glance at my chest, my thighs, then turn my forearms over, but there are no magical moons to be seen. "Oh, quit your rambling. You're unwell and not making one tiny bit of sense."

"Tell me," he says, barely stifling a groan. "Do you know the final verse?"

"Of what? A ribald song of the Dark Court? An Elemental lovers' lament." I shrug. "Perhaps I do. Perhaps I don't. If you care to explain what in the realms you're talking about, I'll attempt to answer."

"I'm sure you know it." His eyes roll back. "Um. Something about... Someone defies the king. Merry melts the silver one—no, that's not right. The Silver King goes forth... I believe I've forgotten it."

"You're concussed. It's a wonder you know your own name. Actually, *do* you know it?"

"Yes. I'm a king of Faery, and we don't suffer trifling annoyances such as having arrows pointing out of our bodies or halflings hovering over us. Unseelie royal blood is…" He grips the arrow shaft, his knuckles white. "Curse the Blood Sun, this hurts."

"Yes, you're a king! And here you lie, proof that royalty can be felled by an arrow just as easily as lesser fae or *halflings* can." I stab my finger at the enormous long bow on the ground beside him. "What are you doing hunting in our lands again? You know the penalty."

"But your uncle…"

I raise my brow, and he shakes his head, wincing as he collects his thoughts. "I mean your step uncle, the king. Or whatever he is to you. Some kind of relation, yes? Well, it's by his invitation that I'm here, hunting the annlagh."

"The annlagh isn't due to surface for another fifty years. And did you say, Rafael invited you? No way. After your last visit, my father wants your head on a platter. Raff wouldn't dare cozy up to you while Dad has you marked."

"Cozy up to…what does that mean? And marked for what?"

"Forget about it. Before you pass out, you need some water." As I stand and retrieve my pouch from Nahla's saddlebags, I hear a loud grunt behind me, and I turn just in time to watch him pull the arrow from his chest.

"Now you've done it!" I tell him. "That arrow will be bewitched at best, poisoned at worst. By tugging it out, you've probably sealed your fate—a painful death in a foreign land with no loved ones by your side."

He has nothing to say to that, except a moan, then he gives me a crooked grin. The fool!

I drop to his side and stem the steady trickle of blood with my palm. Again he loses consciousness. Wonderful. What am I supposed to do with him now?

"Get on Nahla, Merri," calls Magret, attaching her bow to her saddle. "Hurry."

"I can't just leave him here to die a slow death!"

Magret raises a pale eyebrow.

"I can't. *Can I?*"

"Yes, you certainly can. And you must." She springs onto Juniper's back. "Mount your horse. I beg you, do it now. Nothing good will come of helping this fae. For Dana's sake, he's the Merit *king*."

Everything she says is true, but I can't abandon him. Although, even if I wanted to help him, which I think I do, I can't simply waltz through the castle gates and dump him in the Great Hall, a souvenir of our outing.

Look who we found, folks, the King of Merits out dying in a field of poppies!

We may as well feed him to the frost wolves. Or my father's cold mercy. No. Sorry, Dad. That won't be happening today. Not on my watch.

The hidden antechamber behind the wall of my bed springs to mind. Secluded and soundproof, everyone except me seems to have forgotten the room exists. Who would know if I tucked the Merit king away in it? But, then again, if he happened to die there,

I'd have a rather large problem to dispose of. That thought gives me pause. He doesn't look very light. But still...

"Magret, what choice do we have? If we leave him here, he dies. Take him home—my father will crush his lungs and then gut him as he struggles for his last breath. We'll have to sneak him into the castle and hide him."

"*Where?*" she asks, baring her teeth. "Under a log in the Onyx Courtyard?"

"No, in my antechamber. We'll nurse him back to health and help him escape when he's well enough. He's an Unseelie king. He's strong. He'll get better quickly, or if the magic he's been infected with is as potent as it seems, he'll die fast enough. Either way, he won't be our problem for long."

"*Your* problem. You've lost your mind, Merri. This man has stolen your reason."

She stares at me.

I glare back, waiting for her to break.

"Oh, fine! How will we transport him to the castle?"

"Good question." I tear a long piece of fabric from my tunic and gently roll Riven onto his side. "Couldn't you have arranged to be shot a little closer to my home, Riven?" I glance over my shoulder and find my horse happily eating rowan berries nearby. "Nahla, come quickly."

She whinnies and trots over, then sniffs the Silver King from his boots to his neck. Snorting, she nudges my shoulder, distracting me while I do my best to bandage Riven's chest.

"Yes. I know he's pretty, but try to think of him as more of a murderous viper lurking in the grass than a juicy berry to nibble on. Don't be fooled by his looks." That's what I'm telling *myself* over and over, anyway. "If you kneel low, Nahla, we can drag him across your back."

Slowly, my horse lowers herself to the ground.

Magret crosses her arms. "It's almost a day's ride to reach Talamh Cúig," she grumbles.

"I'm aware of that."

"And we'll need to move fast if we're to arrive before your precious burden perishes. Have you considered the journey itself may kill him?"

"Of course. At times like this, I wish I could shift into a flying creature as our full-blooded royal males can. Or transmute from one place to another like the Merits."

"But you cannot, so—"

"Magret, please stop pointing out the obvious and come and help me."

We spend an unreasonable amount of time wrestling the listless lump of Merit onto my mare's back. My air magic barely works on him, which is strange. He's in my land, so even my diluted halfling power should be strong enough to affect him.

Finally, we tie him securely behind my saddle and set off at a canter, following Terra River toward the Dún Mountains and home.

An indigo dusk is settling over the castle when we pass through the jade gates, a large, oiled cloth I borrowed from a farm draped over the Merit's body, so he looks like the spoils of a draygonet hunt. Given his bulk, he's quite the catch.

I wait in the stables for Magret to return with her brother, whose help we sorely need, peeking under the cover now and then to be sure Riven is still alive.

"What's this?" Alorus asks, nearly taking my eye out with the point of his left horn as he reaches for the cloth. "It's about the size of a full-grown okapri."

Okapris are like huge peaceful cows from the human world, but in Faery, their bodies are striped.

I slap Alorus's hand away. "Fear not," I tell him. "We haven't suddenly turned into savage hunters who bring down the gentlest oafs of the land for our pleasure." I hold my breath, then release it in a whoosh. "It's a Merit. We found him unconscious near Terra River."

Alorus's yellow eyes widen as he lifts the covering and peers beneath it. "Son of a draygonet, he's the size of a bear, and dressed rather finely, too. Who in the realms is he?"

"He's *my* captive, and you're not to tell a soul or ask Magret a thing about him. After you help him to my chambers, you're to pretend you've never seen him."

"Your chambers! What madness—"

Squeezing his shoulder, I give him a smile of fake concern. "If you don't think you're up to the task, or don't wish to help your princess, please tell me now, and we'll arrange to have your memory wiped. Then you can go about your business in peace."

"Alorus," his sister scolds. "We have no choice but to hide him as quickly as possible, and we can't do it without you. *Please.*"

He turns to me. "Princess, whatever you're planning it will likely be dangerous, not only for you, but possibly for the entire kingdom. We should alert our king."

"No! Trust me. Please. I know what I'm doing," I say, staring at his left eyebrow while I think of a task I'm proficient at—something simple, like removing Nahla's bridle. "The less questions you ask, the less you'll have to worry about." Or be unable to lie about if anyone at court decides to stick their noses into my business.

Sighing, he bows low. "Of course, Princess Merri. I'm always at your service."

"Wonderful! Now, please, carry him to my rooms via the secret stairs. And hurry, Alorus. We don't want my father to catch us in the act of hiding a Merit, do we?"

"No, we certainly don't." Alorus releases the catches in the trapdoor hidden in the roof of Jinn's stable. I kiss my father's steed's black nose as he wickers a greeting, then hoist myself into the dark passage above.

"Quickly," I say, helping Magret through.

With a groan, Alorus hefts the Merit king over his shoulder. "Seven hells, if you two get me killed, I'll never speak to you again."

"Indeed, you won't be able to," says Magret. "Now hurry!"

We wind along the cobwebbed passages without incident, then exit by a narrow door concealed in the hallway that leads to my apartments. Just as I release a huge sigh of relief, we round a bend and crash straight into the queen, tumbling her tray of pastries to the floor.

"Oh! Sorry about that!" she says. Scraping damp tendrils of blonde hair from her face, she squats down and collects her croissants. She's been on a cooking spree again and still has the apron tied around her golden gown as proof.

Magret bends to assist. "Let me help you, Isla."

"Your Majesty," says Alorus as he attempts a stiff bow. I elbow him, indicating he should keep moving past the queen.

Without looking up, Isla says, "I'm glad you made it back in time to greet the Shade courtiers, Merri. Well done. I know you're not thrilled about taking part in the Beltane rites with Landolin, but it will all work out as it should." Lifting her tray of restored sweets, she stands and gives me a secret wink. "I've just made Raff and I some snacks. Fancy one? It'll be ages until dinner."

As I open my mouth to reply, she looks over her shoulder at the fast-retreating faun, and my stomach sinks to my feet.

"Alorus?" she calls, laughing. "What the heck have you got there?"

Alorus's broad shoulders stiffen, but he doesn't turn around.

In the silence, my heartbeat drums in my ears, thundering when the queen's skirts swish as she strides toward the king.

"Whatever it is, Alorus, it's bleeding on the floor runner. You'd better tell me what you've got. Now, please."

"Something the ladies brought back from their hunt."

"Yes, and what is it?" The point of her boot taps the floor as tendrils of smoke wind from her fingertips. A second later, those fingers reach for the cloth.

"Stop," I shout. "It's a fae from another court. We found him unconscious near Terra River."

"*What?*" She lifts the cloth from Riven's head, gasps, and lets it drop, turning narrowed blue eyes on me. "Merri! This is no ordinary fae. You've captured none other than Riven na Duinn, the Silver King of the Court of Merits."

"I know who he is. And for that reason, we must hide him quickly. Come, Alorus." I march past Isla and open the door to my chambers. "Will you assist us?" I ask. "Or will you dash off to tell Raff?"

Queen Isla places her tray on the floor against the wall. "Merri," she says, smiling brightly as she strides closer. "I prefer not to lie to Raff, but I'm still human, albeit a magically altered one, and unlike full-blooded fae, I *can* lie and *will* lie to protect those I love. Of course I'll help you."

Alorus lays the king on the divan under the window in my sitting room, then I send him and Magret off to gather bedding and nursing supplies.

Standing regally in the center of the room, Isla regards me. "What were you thinking by bringing him to your chambers? Many of us, including Ever, could possibly sense his power, subdued as it is. Your father's air magic is strong enough. Imagine the hell to pay if he discovered Riven. You've risked much to keep this Merit safe."

Safe? I don't care if he's safe necessarily, not after he tried to kill me. *Allegedly.* I don't want to be personally responsible for his demise or the ensuing war it would start. Pacing across the floor, I rake my trembling hands through my hair, uncomfortable reality sinking in.

By the Elements, what have I done?

"Chin up, Merri. Since I'm queen, only the High Mage and Raff can rival my magic. I'll ward the room, cloak its boundaries from snoops. We'll work this out. Don't worry."

Chanting under her breath, she collects ash from the cold fireplace and sprinkles it in each corner of the room. In the air, flame sigils leap to life in each quadrant, then with a loud whoosh, a line of fire runs between them, joining them together.

Isla's hand sweeps the floor, the roof, the walls, and orange and blue flames follow its path, blanketing all. "By salamander, dragon, and flickering tongues, by citrine and gold, this fire cloak will hold. Thus I have willed it, and now it is done."

Grinning, Isla brushes her hands off. "Mm. That made me hungry. Got any food up here?"

I laugh. "No. You'll have to eat the Merit king's provisions when they arrive. Or perhaps your pastries in the hallway."

While we await Magret and Alorus's return, the queen perches on the edge of the divan at Riven's side, dropping pastry crumbs all over him. Finally, Isla puts the croissant aside and sends fire magic into his wound, healing him as best she can.

She lifts his eyelids then pinches the sharp blade of his cheek before caressing it. "Such beauty," she murmurs. "He's so unlike his horrible slug-headed brother, both inside and out. You remember the stories about Temnen?"

I nod. Boy, do I remember. I grew up on them, hanging off every word of the tales about two human girls falling in love with cursed fae princes and becoming Land of Five royalty—a princess and a queen.

Deep in thought, the golden queen purses her lips. "Temnen was such a creep."

"But while Riven is pleasing to gaze upon, by blood and upbringing, he's still a Merit," I say, unwisely reminding her that he could be dangerous. Stupid me. I don't want the queen to have second thoughts and send for an executioner. Or worse, my *father*.

Having the Merit king here is an opportunity to study him, work out why I dream about him and why he wanted, or perhaps *still wants*, to kill me. I hope I haven't ruined my chance.

A diversion is needed.

I give Isla a sly smile. "So, Temnen had the forehead antennae, his sister Lidwinia, the snake-like tongue. I wonder what slimy appendage Riven na Duinn might be hiding beneath his clothes."

"Merri!" She cuts me a look, amusement flashing in her sky-blue eyes. "I wouldn't think too hard about that if I were you."

It's strange how pleased she looks right now, her palm resting comfortably on the unconscious king's chest armor. As if it's been there before, or she's harboring a secret passion for him. I need to understand what this is between them. And if they *do* share a secret, I must know it.

"When I found him, Isla, he was rambling, barely conscious. He said he was in our land on Raff's invitation, which can't be true."

Her eyes widen. "You're correct. It isn't true."

I pull my dagger from the strap around my thigh and point it at Riven's throat. "Should we...?"

Isla draws my arm back. "No need for that. I'll send a salamander through the flames with a message to his sister. Tangled threads are at work here. I feel them crackling through my veins. It isn't dark work, but it's complicated. Have patience while I unravel them for you. The Silver King is yours to tend. Take good care of him."

I draw a quick breath and speak, my words a shaky whisper. "Aren't you worried he'll try and hurt me?"

She throws back her head and laughs. "Riven? No, I'm not. As far as he's concerned, trust your instincts as you've already done by bringing him home. He's not your enemy. I promise."

And who is she to promise such a thing? How could she know for certain?

My gaze flicks between her fond smile and the king she's directing it at. Something is amiss here, and I have no inkling what it might be. Stretching my fingers subtly, I sift through the air between us, searching for a clue, but finding none. I sigh loudly.

The queen turns her smile on me. "Relax, Merri. All is well. Riven is at your mercy."

"And still I plan to chain him to his sick bed."

She stands and smooths the front of her gown. "I'd better leave before he wakes. Make sure he believes that only you, Magret, and Alorus know he's here. Don't mention me. As much as possible, I'd like to avoid lying to Raff and your parents. But if you need assistance with anything, let me know, and I'll be here in a flash."

"Thank you," I say, so glad to have Isla on my side.

"When he's well enough, we'll need to get him out of here without Ever finding out. Or Grandma Varenus." She shivers. "Ugh. That would be a disaster."

"My lips are sealed."

She sashays to the door. "Once you have him set up in the antechamber, come straight to the Great Hall. Don't be late for the Shade Court's reception."

"I won't be." As much as I'd like to skip it, I'm obliged to show up and chat pleasantly with Prince Landolin. I just hope he's grown into a much nicer fae than he was the last time we met, which was an age ago.

"Good," says Isla, flouncing out of the room with purple and gold flames in the shape of wings flickering behind her, a fire goddess hurrying back to her king. Which leaves me with nothing to do except to gaze down at *him*.

The Merit king in all his resplendent glory. Pale as death, beautiful as a glittering star.

A dream come true.

What is Isla thinking, leaving me alone with him? Has she lost her mind? I'm not certain yet.

But I have without a doubt lost mine.

6

The Princess of Air

Riven

Like a meteor from the skies, I crash back into my body, waking with a jolt to find silver eyes peering down at me and an expanse of frowning brow above them.

No.

Please, no. Not Merri.

I release a low moan.

If I'm dead, this is a horrible punishment—doomed to spend my afterlife seeing my face reflected in the Seelie Princess's eyes.

Merri.

Why?

Why her?

"Finally, the *king* awakes," she says, her scarlet tresses tickling my throat as she hovers over me, palms planted on either side of my body. She utters the word king as if it's the greatest of insults.

"Where am I?" I croak, struggling to lean on my elbows as I gaze at my surroundings.

The room is small, containing only the bed I lie in, an empty hearth, a carved rosewood cabinet, a curved bench opposite, frosty-green walls, and a ceiling so high it's invisible. Candlelight flickers from crystal sconces and there's not a window in sight, the room's atmosphere strangely warm and intimate.

Merri sweeps her upturned palm around the space. "In case you're wondering, this room is a secret chamber, and I'm holding you in it until you recover."

"In the castle's dungeons?" I shake the chain that tethers my ankle to the foot of the bed, and it chinks musically. "And is this cold iron?"

"No, and not quite. I don't want to hinder your healing, only diminish your magic so you can't try to kill me again."

"My magic is already diminished on account of my being in your land. Right now, I'm easy prey. Easy to end. Given our last meeting and your family's reaction to it, I'm surprised to find you helping me. Or are you?"

"I'm in two minds. The idea of twisting another arrow deep between your ribs is not without appeal, and if you don't behave, I just might do it. But, at the moment, I want you well enough so you can return to the Merit lands as quickly as possible. Hopefully, before someone discovers you."

"No one knows?"

"Only my most trusted friends."

This is bad news. Why would Merrin want to keep me a secret? It would be better if she handed me over to the Fire king straight away. At least then I could go out fighting, and the end would be quicker. So long as Prince Ever had nothing to do with it, that is.

"What are the terms of my captivity?"

She taps her chin, the soft point of her heart-shaped face. "I haven't decided yet."

"My court knows I've journeyed to your kingdom. If they don't hear from me, before long, they'll send an army. Is that what you want?"

"They won't. It's been taken care of. Don't worry. You only need to lie back and heal."

I slow my breathing, attempting to gather some of her life force and pull it inside me, so I can sift through her feelings and motivations. But it doesn't work. She's either blocking me or my power is useless because I'm unwell.

"Lie back, Riven." With a gentle push, she forces me down into the mattress. "The arrow's poison was strong. You're lucky to be alive."

She rises and goes over to the bench, fills a goblet from what looks like a water jug, and then places it on the small table beside me. "Drink this as soon as you're able. Don't forget."

"More poison?"

"Only one way to find out." Narrowed silver eyes rake my body, and her lips curl in a sneer of distaste.

Anger burns deep in my chest, and I shake my foot again, testing the strength of the chain. She looks at me with pity.

"You should let me go, Princess. What's the point of holding me here?"

"To keep you alive."

"And why save me today? Why not leave me in the forest to die?"

"That was yesterday, Riven. You've been unconscious for some time. I saved you because, unlike you, I'm not a coldblooded killer."

So, like her father, she believes I intended to harm her that day by the pond. She's not entirely wrong.

"You saved me because you're tenderhearted. Aren't you afraid I'll try to hurt you again?"

"You can't harm me in my own land."

"Oh, Merrin. Merrin." I give her my most irritating smile, the one that never fails to make my sister thump me over the head. "You're young. So innocent. You have no idea what I could do to you in the space of a breath."

"Air is *my* element. As a Merit, you don't even have an affinity. Honestly, I don't understand your techno-magic, and whenever someone begins to speak of it, my eyes glaze over. Remind me how it works again?" She stifles a yawn.

"My magic is not the same as other Merits'. I've worked hard to retain my connection to nature, so you and I are not so different."

Dark-red brows rise as she gestures with her hand for me to elaborate.

I drop my head back on the pillow. "If you promise to feed me well, I might describe it in stimulating detail another time."

A long brown snout peeks through her thick red locks, sniffing the air. The nose must belong to her bonded creature. I struggle onto my elbows again and squint at the unattractive hairy lump. "You have something in your hair. What is it? A rat?"

She retrieves an animal the size of a squirrel, its brown fur banded with purple. It has small round ears, inquisitive black eyes, and the bushiest striped tail I've seen on any creature Seelie or Unseelie.

The princess smiles. "She's a mire squirrel."

"Does she have a name?"

"Cara."

My throat tightens. "My mother's name is Ciara. It's similar."

"Oh? And is she as sweet as my little Cara?"

The animal races down Merri's gown, leaps on my bed and into my lap. She chirps as I stroke her thick fur.

"Yes, she was very kind for an Unseelie mother, remarkably so for a Merit queen."

"Was?" Merri's bow-shaped mouth twists, the tips of her ears turning pink. "I'm sorry. Of course, I remember the stories now. She died when you were a child. It must've been terrible to lose your mother so young."

"Yes," I say, my voice dropping low. "Magnified a thousand times over because she was murdered by my father, whose every thought and action was only to increase his power and influence, no matter the cost to others." I groan. "Why am I telling you these things? The poison on the arrow must've contained a loose-tongue spell."

"I doubt it. You speak as if you reject your father's customs and yet," she points at my chest, "you still wear that wretched object."

I fist the twisted metal chain that Merri's arrow hangs from, my pulse quickening. Has she seen it? The blanket slips down to my waist, revealing my bare chest and the fact that I'm naked beneath it. Of course she's seen the arrow lying against my chest. But does she recognize it?

With relief, I realize she's staring at my Merit pendant inactive against my skin, her arrow lying under it. Still, a distraction is required before she looks too closely. That arrow is mine, and I'm not giving it back.

"Couldn't you find me any clothes to wear?" I ask.

"Unfortunately not. You're too big to wear anything of mine. Suitable items from our laundry will be delivered at some point later today."

I grin at her, then glance down at my body. "And you had the pleasure of divesting me of my clothing?"

She laughs. "No, that was Magret's duty. As was the full report she gave me afterward."

That comment wipes the smile from my face. "I trust it was favorable."

"Don't worry, Riven na Duinn." She scoops up the mire squirrel and saunters toward a green door set into an ornate gold archway. "I'm sure on the whole you're quite fashionable in the Merit Court."

What does she mean by that? She can't possibly have found me lacking.

"You're leaving now?"

"Yes. I have a festival to dress for." She raises an eyebrow while I stare blankly, then shrugs and whirls around, her hand reaching for the doorknob. Her shoulders drop and she faces me again.

"Your mind has much healing to do. It's Beltane tonight. Can you not feel it in your blood?"

That explains the warmth sliding through my veins. I'd wondered if it was her presence that caused the effect, but apparently not.

"Then why do you look so unhappy?" I ask. "This is the Bright Court after all. Isn't Beltane a joyous festival for your kind?"

"Not if you have to jump the fires with someone you have no interest in..."

I lurch upright, pain blazing through my ribs and head. "You mean your family has selected a potential husband?"

She nods.

"Who?"

"The oldest son of the Shade Court."

"*Prince Landolin?*"

"The one and only."

"That fae is a scoundrel. A demon dressed in silks and diamonds. Merrin, he would only bring you sorrow."

"Tell that to our court's advisers. They're convinced Landolin Ravenseeker is the most desirable fae in all the seven realms for their princess to align herself with."

Then by some foul trick or glamor, he has managed to fool them completely. He's not evil through and through like my deceased brother, Temnen, was. Nor is he rumored to live for cruelty alone as my father did. But Landolin is weak and vain, and he could *never* make someone like Merri happy. Not even if his life depended on it. As it will, of course, with Prince Everend as his father-in-law. One misstep and the Prince of Air will exterminate him painfully.

"Anyway, Riven, your reputation is worse than Landolin's. You're the Silver King. The mad king. What High Fae family would consider you a worthy suitor? Not one is my best guess." Smiling, she pats her creature. "Come, Cara, let's leave the Merit in peace."

The supposed mire squirrel scurries from her mistress's arms and hides under her unruly mane of hair, popping out to chirp at me.

"At least Cara seems to like you," Merri says.

"Wonderful news." I wince as pain spikes my temples. Sarcasm is a sly form of lie, and it cannot be uttered without consequence.

"Good night, Riven." Merri slams the door and locks it. The grind of the bolts sliding into place sets my teeth on edge.

Like an obedient Unseelie king, I follow Merri's directions and gulp the goblet of water before lying back to consider my options. As I'm injured, poisoned, and chained to the bed, I quickly conclude they can be counted on one finger.

My only choice is to remain under her care while I heal and hope my powers return soon.

Then I'll escape, but perhaps not before I bring a swift and merciful end to Merrin Fionbharr, the girl I've watched forever.

My secret desire and the greatest threat to my kingdom.

7

Beltane Fires

Merri

"**Y**our dancing has improved since we last met," says the Shade prince, removing his hand from my waist to run it through his royal-blue tresses.

As we dance, he regularly breaks rhythm to pet his hair, perhaps making sure the comely locks are still attached to his narrow head. I admit he wears it in a lovely style far prettier than mine. The sides are braided at his temples, and the rest is worn loose, rippling over his shoulders and glinting with threaded moon flowers.

Coal-black eyes skim my emerald gown, fixing on the golden dragonfly embroidered over my chest. "The years have transformed you, little butterfly, and since you've emerged from your chrysalis, your appearance is more to my taste. At present, I feel somewhat favorable to the deal our parents plot together in mannerly whispers."

Somewhat favorable—what an insult!

I give him a bland smile and say nothing.

Dressed in shadows and diamonds, the prince is handsome and lovely to look at, but he's obsessed with his own beauty, never missing an opportunity to peer into a mirror-like surface. And when he gazes into my eyes, it's his own reflection he's admiring, never me.

Wearing my frozen smile, I pretend to be charmed as we twirl over the grass oval between the nine sacred hazel trees, zigzagging through the crush of bodies dancing wildly around the old city's tournament space.

Tonight is Beltane—my favorite festival of all—and I refuse to let Prince Landolin ruin it.

Wyn waltzes past with a beautiful southern witch in his arms. He winks and sprays the Shade prince and me with a puff of glittering dirt, then spins away.

Landolin frowns at my brother's disrespectful use of earth magic but stays silent. No doubt his family has instructed him to avoid a brawl tonight at all costs.

Wyn isn't happy about my potential union with the Shade Court. He says they're an evil lot who torture stray humans for fun, which makes me doubt the judgment of our court's advisers and political schemers. To them, my happiness is apparently of no consequence.

I wish I could tell Wyn the truth about tonight. And I pray to Dana that Ether is correct about the outcome. Because if she's wrong, well...that doesn't bear thinking about.

It's a beautiful, clear night for a festival. Moonlight falls on the king and queen's table, which is set beneath the ruins of Castle Black. Opposite, steep cliffs fall into a wild, thrashing sea, and fae from both the Shade and Elemental Courts fill the rows of stone benches that climb around the edges of the arena like a sparkling staircase to the stars.

Three small bonfires burn a line down the middle of the arena, the heat almost singeing my eyebrows off as we weave our way past them. Later this evening, couples will interlink hands and leap over the fires—a test of their bonds, both old and new. Landolin and I will join them, and if we make it over all three without being burned, the courting contract will be sealed and plans for our marriage will begin in earnest. But that's not going to happen—our High Mage swore it wouldn't.

Sorrowful blue eyes flash across my mind, and I miss a step, stumbling against Landolin who doesn't smile or laugh, just scowls in displeasure at my clumsiness. "Sorry," I say, biting my inner cheek to stop myself laughing.

It seems only one of us has a sense of humor.

One dance is all it takes to remind me why I could never be happy as his wife. He won't find happiness with me either. Thank Dana, it could never happen, anyway.

Landolin releases me near a sea witch, one of the guards of the seven sacred hazel trees, her white robes and black cape billowing in the jasmine-scented breeze. She watches with a sly smile as the surly prince bows stiffly before striding away without a word.

I blow a kiss of thanks to the witch, grateful for her service to our court. Beltane isn't the sea witches' favorite festival, but they take their role as guards of the hazel grove very seriously and would never miss a celebration.

All around us, music swells. High fae and wild creatures alike shriek and laugh as they spin and fly about to the rhythm of the flutes, bells, harps, and bodhrán drums. I sway along at the edge of the crowd, chatting with a group of woodland sprites.

"How do you like the Shade prince?" whispers a close by voice.

I jerk as the Queen of Fire draws her arm through mine and pulls me toward a table overflowing with sumptuous delights.

I admire the flowers and vines tumbling over crystal bowls of wine, platters of juicy fruits, steaming pies, and plates of sweet bannocks.

Later tonight, we'll offer the leftovers to the spirits of the old ones, and they in turn will care for our land and gardens over the coming year.

I tuck my hair behind my ears, stalling for time. "Well...his midnight-silk attire is very fetching, and the diamonds dripping from it are even more delightful."

Sparks swirl in Isla's eyes. "And other words that suit him are ostentatious, distasteful, and let's not forget boorish."

I laugh. "I agree."

"So you don't like him?"

"No." I wince. "Nor is he very fond of me, I'm afraid. I'll be sorry to disappoint Lord Stavros and Lord Gavrin when we fail the jump tonight. I know how important they believe an alliance with Landolin's court is, especially at the moment, but—"

"As your parents have already explained to you, we'll be fine without the Shade Court. Both Raff and Ever are home, their magic fortifying our boundaries, and the curse will lie dormant until Aodhan comes of age. At present, our kingdom is strong enough. We don't need Landolin, so we're free to bake and eat and dance without worry."

She pops a bright red cherry in her mouth and smiles. "Besides, we have an even stronger ally than the entire Court of Shades who is currently resting in your chambers. Rather fortunate circumstance, don't you think?"

Isla laughs at my gaping mouth, and her expelled breath sends a mass of sparks floating onto a nearby faun's leg, setting his fur alight. He squeals, and the queen's fingers flutter through the air, the large sunstone ring flashing with power as she douses the flames. "I'm so sorry, Nyeel. That wasn't intentional."

Nodding and smiling at the folk, we make our way to the high table and settle into our seats, giggling at Landolin, who's dancing with Seven.

The one-eyed imp's sinuous moves display her many charms, and the enthusiastic tongue the prince licks her with signals he's forgotten all about me. I can't say I mind very much.

After conversing with Raff and my parents, Isla turns back to me and speaks in a low, heavily warded voice, rendering our words indecipherable to those around us. "Tell me how that king of yours is going, Merri. Is his health improving?"

"My king? I'd be a fool if I thought I could own Riven na Duinn. He's the kind of fae who will only ever belong to himself."

"Perhaps. But even when I knew him as the outcast prince, his people owned him, and he will always put their interests first. I haven't decided if that's a good thing yet."

"Exactly. Therefore, he could never be a trustworthy ally," I say, my voice rising much higher than I intended.

"That remains to be seen. If nothing else, the Merit king's time at our court is an opportunity. Maybe for us. Maybe for him. As they say, time will tell."

"I'm confused by the way you speak of him, Isla. One moment he sounds innocent and alluring and the next, quite devious. Shouldn't you make up your mind about Riven before I spend too much time alone with him?"

"Where you're concerned, he's definitely the latter. Dangerous and armed with an insidious charm." She tugs my wrist, drawing my attention away from the dancers. "Listen, Merri. Something strange is afoot with this whole Merit king business."

"An understatement if ever I've heard one."

The queen grips my hand under the table. "Last night, I sent a message through the hearth flames to Riven's sister to advise her of his injury, to let her know I'll keep her brother safe while he heals. A whole day has passed, but I haven't had a reply."

"Your message could have gone astray."

"Unlikely, the salamander is a magical creature. There's no physical journey for it to make."

"Could it have been intercepted somehow?" I ask.

"Virtually impossible. And it would be a brave fae who dared to interfere with a missive from a queen of Faery. My best guess is that on hearing her brother was attacked in our land, Lidwinia was too furious to reply, and is calculating her next step, which I suppose is a fair reaction."

"Concerning."

"Yes, very. And regarding us finding the creature responsible, I concocted a story about a pixie, poison-shot by a stag beast who turned into a woman. Our mages seek it as we speak. As a queen of Faery, I must say the ability to lie is very useful. The High Mage is conducting extensive investigations but, so far, hasn't turned up a clue. It's beyond odd. Usually, nothing of this gravity would get by Ether."

This news turns my blood to ice. The idea of an entity running loose in our land who has the power to lure the Merit king into forbidden territory and the gall to make an attempt on his life without first seeking our permission terrifies me.

Who could be so brazen? So powerful? Only a creature from the Dark World, a barren realm of monstrous entities long segregated from ours, could achieve this. My skin crawls as I wonder if the border magic that separates us is weakening, or if a being has somehow gained the ability to breach the wards at will. Both options are dire for my kingdom.

"Isla, are you tempted to tell Raff I have the king in my chambers?"

"No, Merri. Absolutely not. It would sign Riven's death warrant." Fireflies dance around the queen's hair as she drums her fingers on the table. "And I won't, unless you tell me there's no other option.

Help him heal. Befriend him if you can, and mend the rift between our courts. And, please, always, *always* remember to be guided by your heart and never by your fears."

I take a deep breath, my gaze lifting to the stars before it drifts over my family seated along the high table. Blissfully ignorant of the recent troubling events, they look happy, and I plan to do everything in my power to ensure they remain so.

Grandma Varenus sits beside my father, her face solemn and white hair sparkling like sheets of moonlit snow. She arches a brow at me and clicks her fingers. Ice crystals form in the tree branches above my father's head. She claps her hands, and they instantly melt, pouring onto Dad's head.

I laugh as he scowls, wringing his wet hair out on her plate. Fortunately, he's wearing his golden armor, so if she retaliates, at least he should survive.

Rearranging the crown on his tawny mane, Raff points at Balor, Spark, and Cara chasing each other through the dancers' legs. Rising, he makes a joke that I don't quite hear, offers Isla his hand then sweeps her down the stone steps onto the grassy dance floor.

Sparks from the bonfires gather and eddy around them as he takes his queen in his arms. With a flick of his hand, he steps back and twirls her off, alone, into the crush of dancers. The drums pound faster, fiddles and flutes growing frantic. He springs after her, pulling her body close as they dance together, their feet hardly touching the ground.

Before long, horns blow, heralding the beginning of the fire ceremony. Tiny chill bumps spread over my skin as I leave the high table and follow the king and queen onto the tournament ground. I suppose it's time to find Landolin.

Happiness and a twinge of jealousy claw at my insides as I study my family. I want what the king and queen and my parents have. A soul mate. True and everlasting love. Difficult to find and impossible to have with a fae like Landolin Ravenseeker.

Despite what the Land of Five advisers think, vain and shallow, the prince is not for me, and besides, his realm exists on a plane beneath ours, bleak, dark, full of mysteries and secrets. I'm a lover of the bright forests, an admirer of the chaotic human cities, and I could never be happy living in the shadows.

Beneath my feet, tiny rocks stir—a warning that Kian, brandishing his earth magic, is about to appear. Before I have time to hide in the crowd, he slips out from behind a hazel tree dressed in princely crushed velvet, an emerald circlet on his brow, and green tourmaline decorating his hair and clothes.

Head bowed, his hands smooth over his tunic, too busy admiring himself to watch where he's walking, which is straight into a group of goblins. "Kian Leondearg!" the tallest one calls, no doubt hoping to draw the vain lord into their circle of rowdy troublemakers.

Alas for me, Kian grants them a dismissive nod and steers out of their way. His gaze snags mine, nostrils flaring wide as he changes course, heading directly for me.

I straighten my spine and calm my breathing. By the Elements, I am not in the mood for Kian's nonsense tonight.

"Dearest Princess," he says, bowing low before rising in a dramatic cloud of gold dust. "Good evening."

"I see Father has granted you use of your magic again," I say, giving him a small smile.

Leering at me, he presents a garland strung with translucent halite, twisted dried tubers, and petrified wood—a beautiful offering of his element's bounty. "You look especially enchanting tonight, Merrin."

I glance down at my gown. In the usual fae style, the silver and blue panels of glossy fabric display a lot of skin, but fleetingly, still retaining secrets. Spun with precious metals, dyed with bright forget-me-nots, and imbued with air magic, the fabric floats around my limbs like falling feathers.

The dress is beautiful, but its purpose—to snare a prince—is suffocating, and I long to be back in my hunting leathers, rambling through the forest with Nahla and Cara. And perhaps even Wyn.

A vision of silver hair snaking through snow-white poppies flashes in my mind. Then eyes of the deepest blue, flaring wide with confusion and pain. Damned Riven again.

Kian's fingers curl around my arm, his nails digging sharply. I shake him off and nod at his gift lying in my open palm. "Thank you, Kian. It's gorgeous. But you shouldn't have."

It's bordering on an insult to give such a lovely gift to a fae he isn't courting, to me, who has never once encouraged him.

His smile morphs into another leer. "How beautiful the bonfires are this evening. Will you do me the great honor of leaping with me this Beltane night?"

He has to be joking. If not, his boldness and stupidity are astonishing. Father has warned him what will happen if he continues to bother me and, still, he can't seem to control himself.

As I take a breath to tell him that what he asks is impossible, the garland is wrenched from my grasp by long fingers flashing with diamond rings. Prince Landolin has arrived. With a scowl, he tosses Kian's gift into the air, and it turns into a bat and flies off into the trees, screeching.

"There goes your precious present, jester-haired courtier. Who are you to ask Princess Merrin to cross the fires? A prince I've not yet been introduced to?"

Kian splutters.

"No? It is as I thought, then. You're no one." Landolin extends his arm. "Come, Merrin, the ceremony begins."

Courtiers form a chanting circle around a line of small ceremonial fires on the ocean side of the tournament area, their jaws gnashing against the night sky as smoke wreaths their bodies. They strike vicious poses, their blood wild and pumping lustily in anticipation of the Beltane rites.

I long to escape Landolin's tight grip and romp through the spectators with friends, laughing and singing as I did when I was a child. Back then, I naively believed when I married my prince, it would be for love and love alone. But peace, our politicians advise, is more important than tender touches, the thrill of those only growing weaker over time. Love is meaningless in the greater scheme of things. Apparently.

"Ready?" asks Landolin.

I nod, and we join the couples who will take part in the ceremony, gliding to the front of the line. As royalty, the prince and I will open the rites by leaping first. In truth, I'll be glad to get it over with.

Conflicting emotions roil inside me as the drums pound faster, the crowd's chants rising in a frenzied crescendo. My leap must look authentic, but I'm terrified that I'll miscalculate, and we'll make it over the flames unscathed, and I'll be bound by ancient rites in a loveless marriage with the Shade prince.

The four mages stand straight as taper candles beside the king and queen, their expressions radiant and their diaphanous gowns trimmed with ivy leaves and large blossoms that glow like fire opals.

From the high table, silver eyes flash in the dark, and my father's air magic gently lifts locks of my hair in a reassuring caress. He smiles, and my mother waves and gives me a human-style thumbs up.

King Rafael opens the Beltane ceremony with a lively speech that has the court in stitches. It sounds entertaining, but my mind is whirling so fast I barely understand a word of it.

While I wait for the fires to reduce so the rites can begin, I stand in a daze, hypnotized by the flames.

Who will take care of the Merit king if everything goes wrong, and the Shade Court spirit me away to their shadowy underworld?

I picture Riven lying alone, in pain in my antechamber. Magret and Alorus have promised to check that he fares well tonight, but I'm anxious to see him for myself.

Over the last couple of days, I've discovered there's nothing that feeds an obsession quite as well as having a nightmare turn into flesh and bone and take up residence near one's bedchamber.

Mother moves to the front of the dais, a stunning vision in silver and gold. She sings a springtime song about growth and warmth and young love in bloom. It has the desired effect on the crowd, and bodies move slowly in the flickering firelight, eager for the ceremony to be over so they can disappear into the forest and become one, their couplings enhancing the prosperity of our land.

The ashes from the bonfires will be collected for use in spells and sprinkled over the gardens to enrich and enliven the soil. New unions. New marriages. And if we're well blessed, in several moon turns, many sweet fae babes will be born.

Part of me longs to retreat to a dark forest bower, illuminated only by fireflies and starlight, and celebrate Beltane in the ancient way. But not with Landolin. Once again, it is the King of Merits whose face blazes before me.

Riven.

My nightmare.

My enemy.

My addiction.

"Merrin, it is time." With his finger, as is customary, the Shade prince paints a stripe of ash from my forehead to my chin.

I bend, gathering ash in my palm, and return the action, carefully pocketing a handful to anoint Riven with later. He must be protected too.

The Merit may be my enemy, but I want to give him the best chance to survive his poisoned wound. Why? Well, the answer is complicated.

King Raff smiles at Landolin and me, beckoning us toward the first fire, the flames of all three now burning low. "Use of magic will disqualify you. The powers of Beltane will determine the suitability of your match. If it's deemed prosperous, Dana and the Old Ones will bless your union." He kisses my cheeks, then the prince's.

We slip our shoes off.

With my fingers tight around Landolin's, I face the flames. "By the Elements Five, may destiny unfold as it should. Steadfast and true, my feet will fall as best serves the Court of Five and our honorable and faithful allies of the Shade Court."

Landolin's black eyes meet mine, his gaze cold. His lips curve in a smug smile. "As it is spoken, so may it be. As the gods old and new bear witness, what I make mine in the shadows is mine forevermore."

That sounds ominous...and rather permanent.

We nod at each other, then we leap.

We soar above the first fire, the heat scorching the bare soles of my feet. Over the roar of the crowd, I hear Landolin hiss. Is he burned? If so, our bond is broken.

A dark thrill courses through me.

The dewy grass soothes my feet as we run forward then leap over the second fire, flying so high above it we laugh with joy. Grass again, then more running, and then the third and final fire.

My lungs ache as I fill them with air. Our arms swing back hard, then up we go, sailing above the heat and noise of the fire. I land a moment after Landolin, jerking him backward on purpose. Pain sears from my feet to my heart, and we both stumble forward.

The fire. We landed on the edge of the fire. Relief floods through me. Our bond is broken, and I only hope the prince doesn't realize that little yank I gave wasn't accidental.

Courtiers gasp as one as flames lick up our clothes, my mother's scream the loudest. We stand immobile, like burning statues. Eyes wide and our fingers still tangled tight, we wait for King Raff to end our torture.

In two breaths, Raff arrives, his sunflower scepter pointed at us and his amber eyes wild. "Come! Tine bheannaithe," he commands, and the flames spin away from our bodies, spiraling into the head of his scepter.

"I'm sorry," I say to Landolin as I grip my knees and bend over them, panting. "Are you hurt?" Other than a little blackening of our clothes, we seem unscathed.

He inspects his feet and legs. "I'm fine. Although, I was rather fond of these breeches." He waves his hands and black shadows whirl around his legs, remaking his satiny pants. "Don't worry, Princess Merrin. The shades have decided—you're not supposed to belong to me."

Thank Dana, the flames, and every single star in the sky.

My dress hangs in tatters around my thighs, but I won't waste my energy reforming it from cobwebs and air in a show of magic just for the Shade prince's sake. Before bed, I plan to visit Riven, and I need my strength so I won't appear weak in his presence.

The Beltane couples leap the fires in pairs, some fail and others, whose bonds are strong, triumphantly receive Raff and Isla's blessings before quickly escaping into the Emerald Forest.

My parents bring us goblets of wine, and I gulp mine down inelegantly. Landolin thrusts his empty cup at me, then steps away to whisper in Seven's ear—better hers than mine.

Mom squeezes me in her arms. "Well done, darling. I admit I was terrified that Ether's vision of you and Landolin not making it over the fires was incorrect and you'd be taken away from us."

Father says, "I'm sorry you had to go through that, Merri. I would never allow such an unworthy fae to have you, no matter the outcome of the Beltane rites. Although, I admit I am slightly disappointed not to have an excuse to draw my blade on the Shade king. Every time he's opened his mouth tonight, I've longed to shut it permanently."

"I hope my jump looked credible," I say.

Isla joins us and links her arm through Mother's, looking extraordinarily pleased by my failure.

Moiron Ravenseeker, the King of Shades, whose hair is the same deep blue color as his son's, steps out of the shadows. "Never mind, my Court of Five friends," he says in a high grating voice. "We may yet decide to attempt another match with Merrin and my heir next Beltane."

Father inclines his head, neither agreeing nor disagreeing, but I know he'll do everything in his power to prevent a repeat of tonight's fraudulent performance.

"Good. We'll return home and consult with our shadow casters. What we desire can always be manifested if our will is steadfast. Princess Merrin of Talamh Cúig, if our court wants you for our queen, in time, we will most certainly have you."

He and his son bow and stride off into the darkness beyond the fires.

Finally, I can breathe freely again.

Isla tugs me to the side, nodding at the spot the Shade king vacated moments ago. "He seems quite keen to make a match between you and his son."

"Maybe I *will* have to marry Kian to escape the Shade prince, then," I murmur.

"Don't be silly. Why not consider the Merit king? He's at your disposal," she says. "It would be a very auspicious alliance, given the geographical closeness of our kingdoms. Same realm. Same landmass. You'd be queen of the Dark Court and princess of the Light, bringing peace to both our lands. Haven't you heard the wise words about loving your enemy, Merri dearest?"

"What?" I stare into the queen's eyes. Does she jest? No, unfortunately, she looks quite serious.

"Just a thought." Queen Isla winks, and then skips off into the forest.

Moments later King Rafael discharges his duties and follows her, his grin wide and his swaggering steps long. The air heats, the warm breeze flavored with longing and joy.

I ponder the queen's words as I slip quietly into the trees, trekking along the quickest path to the castle, alone on this Beltane night of courtship and love.

That Isla would even dare suggest Riven as husband material is deeply shocking and causes me to doubt her sanity.

Well, if our queen is insane, then I must be mad, too, because as I stride through the magical night, a long-asleep part of me wakes, roused by the tempting prospect of Riven and me together.

For one night or forever.

8

Love Your Enemy

Riven

Late on Beltane eve, the door to my prison scrapes open and reveals the air princess standing on the threshold holding a glowing taper in her left hand.

As she strides across the room toward my bed, I force my weight onto an elbow, my heart pounding louder than a kettle drum.

"What a delightful surprise," I say in a bored tone. "Have you brought food? I confess I'm quite ravenous. Please inform your kitchen staff that the portions they serve your detainees are too miserly."

She gives a soft snort. "You think I've had other prisoners before you?"

"I can only assume so. You seem well practiced in the details of detainment. And you're heartless enough. Have you food?"

"No." She kneels beside the bed. "Actually, I have brought something sustaining, but I'm afraid you can't eat it. Now hold still."

Quick fingers delve into the pocket of her barely there gown, the delicate material around her thighs shriveled and burned as though she's been over the bonfires this evening—probably with the insipid Shade prince. Was their leap successful?

"Merri, I must ask you—"

"Shh." She paints a strip of Beltane ash from my forehead to my chin, her touch swift and sure, kindling a fire inside me.

I watch the fast rise and fall of her chest, and my gaze drops to her rosebud lips. My mouth parts, and I shift closer, dragged forward by an uncontrollable force. Why does this halfling have power over me, an Unseelie *king*?

The druid's well never lies—the Princess of Air will be my downfall. I should be repelled by her, not drawn like a dragon to a hoard of gold.

My hand shoots out, and I grip her chin roughly. Since I've been resting in this cell, a little strength has returned to my limbs. I could kill her now, and quickly, too. "You're offering me protection?" I whisper.

In the flickering light of the taper, I cannot see her eyes, but I hear her breath catch. "It's not an offer, Riven. I've already given it to you."

"Why would you do that?"

"You're asking why I want you to survive your injury?"

"Yes."

Wine-dark hair brushes my chest and arms as she leans closer. "You're the Merit king, and over much of my kingdom's history, your court has been our sworn enemy."

A sweet, smoky scent fills my nose and muddles my mind. Silent, I wait for her to continue.

"But contrary to what your narrow mind believes, Riven, I'm not a murderer of the helpless. This is Beltane. It is a fae king's right to receive two blessings on this night."

My chest tightens, then a laugh escapes me. "Oh? And what other blessing have you—"

Without warning, her lips press against mine, silencing my words and dropping me into a raging sea of insanity. I grip her shoulders, planning to shove her away, but her taste, her scent drugs me, and I only move closer. Her air magic slides over my skin, calming, soothing.

What is this? A poisoned kiss?

She whispers my name, and I kiss her with relish, proving myself the worst kind of fool, for I am lost, undone by the sweet sighs of my silver-eyed enemy.

I wrap my hand around her throat as my fingers caress her skin softly. My lips guide hers, deeper and deeper, as terrible thoughts of longing and fulfillment flood my mind.

What do I wish for?

Only total control over the princess of Talamh Cúig.

With a soft moan, she surrenders, and her magic slips away, relinquishing its hold over me. My fingers squeeze her slender neck, capturing her sharply exhaled breath. Heat swirls through my chest, gut, limbs, my body heavy and mind on fire. I could make her mine. Now. And who would stop me?

So this is how it feels to have your obsession at your mercy—equal parts pain and ecstasy, desperate to rush to the finish, while never wanting the blissful feeling to end. At this moment, Merrin Fionbharr *is* mine.

A single tear slides down Merri's cheek, and with the tip of my tongue, I take this, too.

A creature trapped, she cannot move. I nip her lip and draw blood, but she makes no sound, not even a whimper. The room spins as I draw back and stare into her mercurial eyes. They pierce my soul and condemn me, but for what crime, I do not know. What does she want from me?

My dreams provide the answer: *Your kingdom. Your crown. Everything.*

Squeeze, I tell myself. End it now while I have the advantage. If I can leave this land undetected, the Elementals will never know who to blame for Merri's death, retaining peace between our kingdoms.

One strong flex of tendons and bones.

And crunch.

She will be dead.

Gone—unable to plague me with visions of sparkling eyes and a halfling's false promises of joy and laughter. The Princess of Air will not defeat me. Not tonight, and not ever.

But wait...if she's not alive to free me, how will I escape this room? And the castle?

I might rot away in the Seelie lands and leave my people at the mercy of those who long to return to the ways of the Blood Sun ritual and its altar of terror—a dreadful outcome.

"Riven?" Merri gasps, her eyes wide.

She is afraid. And rightly so. Light freckles dust her nose, a glamor of sweetness and innocence. But I am not deceived. This could be my only opportunity to do what I must, the only time she'll come this close.

End it.

End it now.

Fingers dig into my arms as false concern swirls in the silver sea of her irises, her face a mask of innocence. "Riven, you look feverish. Are you all right?"

"Curse your deceitful eyes, Merrin Fionbharr." With a grunt, I shove her away, feeling no pleasure as she slides off the bed and her skull hits the floor with a sickening thud.

"I'm sorry," I say, holding my hand out. "I only meant to throw off the enchantment...your spell of..." I dare not name it. Shouldn't even think it.

"I'm fine. And what are you talking about? I cast no spell."

She lies; I felt the enchantment.

Sitting up, she glares at me through her hair. "You've regained some strength back."

"Perhaps your prison food is not that bad after all." To my disgust, my voice sounds low, an intimate rasp.

Merri flicks her hand and wind whips through the fireplace, a tiny spark eddying inside it that quickly grows into a warm blaze. Gracefully, she stands and stalks forward, eyes feral as her long hair writhes around her shoulders. It seems I've roused the wrath of the Princess of Air.

"So, you wanted to hurt me, Merit? It was a foolish move to reject my blessing."

She thought her kiss was a blessing? Its effect on me was the opposite.

Again, her hand lashes out, this time toward me. My back slams into the mattress. My throat constricts, muscles closing until I cannot draw breath, and my heart pounds a war rhythm against my ribs.

"Stop!" I choke out, pushing against her magic with all the strength I can muster.

A long cry comes from Merri's mouth as she spins in place, arms outstretched and hair streaming as she moves like an air mage—a terrifying wonder.

Wind rips around the room, tearing at my hair and the linen bedclothes, roaring and roaring. Then with a high-pitched whir, it disappears up the fireplace.

Panting and shivering, Merri sags against the wall.

"Your power is strong," I say in awe.

She makes a face to suggest this is not always the case, as if sometimes, she's as weak as I am now.

"It's true, Merrin. You could have killed me with ease."

"Worry not." She walks over and presses a kiss to my forehead. I try not to flinch. "You're safe for now, Riven na Duinn." Tattered gown flowing behind her, she exits the room without another word.

Three bars slide into place on the other side of the door, locking me in.

Sleep evades me as I twist and turn, torturing myself with half-baked plans of escape or getting a message to my sister before she rallies the Merit army and turns the Seelie kingdom to dust.

When I finally drift off, I drop straight into a dream of furious silver eyes and succulent peachy lips beckoning me farther into the dark labyrinth of my chaotic mind.

When I wake, it's still dark, and I'm surprised to feel Merri's unguarded energy thrumming through the walls into my cell. The princess must reside close by.

Very close.

A smile tugs at my lips. If my guess is correct, Merrin holds me in a room next to her chambers, which is convenient for me, because... Well, I'm not exactly certain why yet, but it's a foolish decision on her part. It leaves her vulnerable.

And for some reason, the thought of Merrin Fionbharr close by and vulnerable pleases me, which proves I am sick in the head.

Very sick indeed.

9

Confession

Merri

Despite holding a fae king captive in my antechamber, life at the Emerald Castle continues as it always has. Throughout the days, I pretend to be interested in tedious politics, while stifling yawns until moonlight leads our court into long, extravagant nights of feasting and dancing.

Most mornings, after sword training, I hunt draygonets with Father and Wyn, then in the afternoons, I meet Mother, Isla, and the ladies of the court to practice magic. After we've inflicted injuries, maimed, and healed each other, we eat candy and gossip, laughing until our sides split.

Mostly, I fill my time with trivial tasks interspersed with bouts of training and hunting. I live a life of whimsy and beauty, befitting a princess of Faery, with nary a hardship to bear.

Until the day I brought home the King of Merits and complicated everything.

I suppose I could ignore the Silver King's foreboding energy radiating into my bedchamber night and day and leave Alorus and Magret to care for him. They have the necessary skills to nurse him back to health and don't require my assistance at all. But still, I can't seem to stay away.

It's been a full sennight since I found Riven, and thankfully, he's improving. But I worry constantly that he'll be discovered in my rooms and killed, or perish on the journey back to his court, and all this deceit will have been for naught.

By now, my sporadic visions should have given me a hint, a tiny glimpse into his future—Riven lying in a ditch dead or sitting regally on the Merit throne—but where he's concerned, for some reason, I am blind. And worse, knowing he's near, I'm in a perpetual state of distraction.

Memories of Beltane night and my foolish blessing that turned into a kiss of equal parts hatred and passion taunt me. I felt his longing, then his rage at its existence. He could have killed me. He nearly did. Ever since, I've tried to keep a safe distance between us. But in all this turmoil, only two things are certain: the Merit king is my enemy, and I cannot stay away from him.

Sighing, I dig my fingers into Cara's fur, so soft and warm as she snoozes on my lap.

"Merri," barks a deep voice, jerking me from my reverie. "Am I competing against myself or are you participating in this game, too?"

Oh. I'd forgotten my brother was here.

My gaze skims over my family's secluded garden—the ivy-covered stone walls, tangled weeping cherry branches, and the shimmering pond before finally settling on Wyn's smirking eyes.

"What did you say?" I ask, inspecting his black mane, disheveled and stuck with leaves and twigs as if he's spent the morning rolling in the meadow with a pretty fae. Knowing Wyn, he probably has.

"Nothing important, obviously."

"Sorry, I wasn't paying attention." I pick up a hnefatafl piece and pass it over my fingers. "Fortunately, I could beat you in my sleep."

"That makes sense then. Most of the morning you've been comatose. What preoccupies you, Sister dear? Perhaps fears that the vain Landolin is still plotting to prick his diamond claws into your soft bridal flesh? Or are you dreaming about kissing a beautiful, azure-eyed fae again?"

"Azure! What?" My thoughts dart straight to the king of blue eyes himself...Riven na Duinn. "Why would you say that?"

Wyn laughs. "Well, I've never once seen your attention captured by a golden-gazed fellow. Your blood is heated by the hues of the sea and sky—night-deep indigo, gem-bright cobalt, and sometimes even by a mysterious, starry sapphire. Unlike mine, Merri, your tastes are conspicuous and unchanging."

Guilt stains my cheeks wine-dark. What is obvious to my brother shames me, because after I saw Riven's icy peepers in my dreams many years ago, no others could lure me. Over time, I may have glanced briefly at pale comparisons, but that is all.

If I'd known that the fae who haunted my dreams was my enemy, perhaps I'd have given serious consideration to a union with Landolin and currently be betrothed, preparing for a new life at the Shade Court.

"You wouldn't like it," says Wyn.

I drop my hnefatafl piece. "Wouldn't like what?"

"Life at the Shade Court." Wyn ruffles his hair, creating more disorder. "Landolin is as cruel as the rumors suggest, the court too dark for your liking. There, the pleasures of the night rule, and the practicalities and exertions of the day are barely valued. As a fae of the light, who thrills in the hunt and beauty of the land, you would no doubt wilt away under the shadows of their seven moons."

"Did I speak that thought aloud, Wyn, or did you steal it from me?"

One of Wyn's many talents is the random ability to read minds, and my heart pounds at the idea he may have breached Isla's wards that block my thoughts about Riven. What would Wyn, who is impulsive and unpredictable at the best of times, do if he learned of my secret and believed me to be in danger?

"Ha ha! You should see your face. Have something to hide, do you, sweetest? Fear not, you spoke aloud about the Shade Court, that's all. I didn't pry inside the puzzle of your mind."

I loose a long, slow breath that twirls the cherry leaves behind Wyn's shoulders. Thankfully, he's too busy scowling at the hnefatafl board to notice. Please, *please* don't let him ask any more questions, because he's the one fae who can see through my halfling lies with relative ease.

I long to tell him the Beltane rite was nothing but an elaborate pretense, but the less fae who know about it the better. I hate to think what would happen if the truth made its way back to Moiron Ravenseeker. A war with the Shade Court is the last thing we need at present.

Leaning forward, I skip pieces across the board—*bang, bang, bang*—and take his king. My yawn is wide, my smile triumphant, and his face is as astounded as I've ever seen it. "See? Even half asleep, I still won."

"Son of a draygonet!" He kicks his feet onto the table, knocking the pieces over the board. "Damn. I didn't see that coming. One day, I'll beat you three times in a row."

"Don't hold your breath too long, Wynter. I won't give you any of mine."

He chuckles, gulps from his goblet, then slams it on the wooden table between us. "Listen, I have interesting information to share." His boots hit the dust, and he props an elbow on his thigh, leaning forward. "Apparently, the Merit princess has a gripe with our king."

Heavy as a crystal geode, my heart drops to my stomach. "*What?*"

"Is that the only word you can utter today? You are usually a smidgen more eloquent." A single black eyebrow rises. "Listen, Merri, I overheard Raff and Isla while walking this morning in the Black Forest. They were arguing, and I was sneaking through the undergrowth."

Splinters slide under my nails as I grip the chair's armrests.

Wyn leans close, a chunk of hair curtaining his eye. "What I'm about to tell you is classified. A secret. You cannot tell a soul."

"I know what a secret means, Brother. No need to describe it thrice."

He waits.

I swallow a lump in my throat. "Okay, I won't say a word. Now hurry up and tell me."

"For some reason, Lidwinia believes her brother was on his way to our court and came by foul play and never arrived. His faithful steed returned home alone. The Merit king has disappeared, and neither the princess's consort, the Merit Court's powerful technomancer or their High Mage, Draírdon, can locate him. Riven na Duinn is lost. Can you believe it?"

I nod. I can certainly believe it because I know it to be true. "What a terrible thing," is all I say.

He barks a laugh and slaps his thigh, sending Cara burrowing underneath my hair.

Of course, Wyn is thrilled. He lives for trouble and intrigue.

"Exactly!" he says. "The very idea of it is insane. The Merit Court rudderless and free to do as they please. As you can imagine, Lidwinia swore our king and queen to secrecy. The Merits can't afford to have it bandied about that they're presently without a ruler. Merri, think of it! But where in the realms could Riven be? The possibility that the Unseelie king met a gruesome end while wayfaring is unbelievable, but I find myself obsessed with the notion."

So many questions boil inside me, bubbling up my throat and scalding my tongue and lips. What exactly did the Merit princess tell Isla and Raff? Does she suspect we're holding Riven in our land? And what move will she make next?

"It's shocking indeed. What else did you overhear?"

"Raff sensed a curious being nearby and threw a shield around them, blocking the rest of their conversation. I've told you everything I know. What do you think of the news?"

Tea spills over the embroidered tablecloth as I stand abruptly and brush off my tunic. "I've already given my opinion. What you say scares me. But forgive me, I must go and find Magret. I promised to visit a friend with her, but the morning has passed so quickly, and now I'm late."

Without peeking over my shoulder to see his reaction, I hurry from the garden and head for the castle.

I must find out what the queen knows, and if she believes Lidwinia is a threat to us. Perhaps the Merits are currently preparing to send a war party or a demon monster to battle our mages and destroy our courtiers' homes. Worst case scenario—chaos and mayhem could soon be upon us.

Trekking uphill, I follow the stone wall that encloses the orchard. I round a sharp corner and slam straight into Magret, who is hurrying from the rear of the castle, her eyes downcast.

"Oh, Merri, you're precisely who I was hoping to find," she says, smoothing silky hair around her antlers.

"Hello!" I twist the fabric of my dress. "Can we talk in a little while? I must do something first—"

"I'm afraid this cannot wait." She stares at her boots before reluctantly meeting my gaze.

"What's wrong?"

"I'm worried about your guest. He's not well today."

"But yesterday, he was improving."

"And, today, he was pale and weak when I delivered his breakfast, and even though his wound is healing, and he has no fever, he barely ate a thing." She lowers her voice to a whisper. "The Merit king tells me he must be allowed to go outside."

"That's impossible. He'd be discovered, and Father would take great pleasure in murdering him slowly."

"This is true, but the king says if he doesn't revitalize his life forces in nature, he'll die in your antechamber."

"Did you remove his chains?"

"Immediately."

"Good. That will buy us a little time. Can you bring Alorus to my chambers? I'll find a way to get Riven into the forest today, Magret. I promise."

She flashes a brilliant smile. "I'm so glad. I don't want the king to die."

"I'll see you shortly." I take one step toward the castle's emerald spires, then turn back. "Magret? You like him, don't you? The king I mean."

"Yes. I know he's a Merit, but I can't seem to help myself." She gazes toward the rolling hills wearing a foolish expression. "He smiles so kindly when I tend him. And those eyes, Merri... He doesn't seem like a typical Unseelie—all those horrible stories we've heard. I cannot imagine Riven presiding over such events, let alone partaking in them. And before I enter his chamber in the mornings, I often hear him reciting the poetry of the wild woods, his voice full of sorrow. I refuse to believe he's evil."

"Remember, Magret, succubi are beautiful, yet we don't invite them to our feasts. It isn't wise to become attached to Riven. He wants you to feel safe and secure, so he can gobble you up when you close your eyes and await his kiss."

"Unlike you, I wasn't thinking of his kisses." She laughs, a terribly judgmental sound. "But I promise to heed your warning if I'm certain that you're doing the same."

Before I can muster an outraged reply, she hurries off toward the orchard where Alorus is working.

Shaking my head, I pull Cara from my neck and into my arms. "Come on. Let's go find the queen. Now we have two urgent reasons to visit her—Lidwinia's message and Riven's declining health."

I'd love to include Mom and take her into my confidence, but out of love and worry for me, she'd only tell Father. And *that* would be disastrous.

Shoulders squared, I start up the hillside again.

Now, where might I find the queen at this hour? Perhaps in the High Council chambers with Raff and the advisers? In the falconry with Mother? Or lazing near the river with her ladies? No, when she's troubled, as she likely is with Lidwinia breathing down her neck, she nearly always bakes. I hasten my steps toward the kitchens.

Sure enough, as I approach the stairs leading down to the series of white-washed rooms that form the castle's main kitchen, the aromas of vanilla and chocolate assail my senses. Isla is making brioches again. A loud growl echoes in the stairwell. My stomach clearly approves.

Alone and wiping the massive scarred bench in the center of the room, Isla glances up as I enter. "I was wondering how long it would take you to come find me. Your big-mouth brother has no doubt told you the news?"

"Of course. He thinks he got away with spying on you and Raff in the forest."

She laughs. "You have to love that boy's confidence. Like his father, his belief in his skills is severely overinflated."

"That's true. What does Lidwinia know?"

"Nothing concrete, but it seems she hasn't received my message advising her we're keeping Riven safe. I'll send her another salamander and hope it gets through this time. Thankfully, Lidwinia is a diplomat and, at this point, wouldn't dare accuse us of mistreating a tribe of rabid red caps. But she suspects us. So, as soon as possible, we need to get rid of Riven and send him home. Do you think he's ready for us to find a way?"

"Unfortunately, quite the opposite. Magret says he's taken a turn for the worse, and according to Riven, he needs to connect with the elements to heal, which must be true if he said so. But I'm worried he may be seeking an opportunity to escape. When he leaves, it has to be well planned, so he doesn't perish on the journey and his death start a three-hundred-year war."

Pale eyebrows, dotted with labradorite crystals, rise. "Interesting that his health is connected to the elements. You see, Merri? He's not so dissimilar to us."

I beg to differ.

Isla glides to the largest oven and pulls three large trays out, clanging them on the stove top. With quick movements, she cuts the brioche loaves into thick slices, vanilla custard oozing over the fire opal and sunstone rings decorating her fingers.

"If the outdoors revitalizes him sufficiently, perhaps we should just let him go," she suggests.

My stomach clenches at the idea, but I force my features into a thoughtful expression as I inspect a long, jagged cut in the bench. "Perhaps, but as I said, his departure requires good planning."

A sly smile adorns her face as she eyes me, licking custard from her fingers.

I huff a breath. "Well, Your Majesty, can you assist me to get Riven outside, or do I need to visit the High Mage and seek her help?"

"Draygonets, no! Whatever you do, please don't involve Ether. I can easily cloak Riven. As long as I stay close enough, he'll be invisible to everyone but us. Right now, many of the court, including Raff, Ever, and your mother, are busy fawning over the new falcon chicks. Now is the perfect time to take brioche into the Black Forest and enjoy a picnic. This will be fun! Bring the Silver King and meet me at the stables as soon as you can."

I fly up the fluorite staircases and along the hallways of the royal apartments and meet Magret and Alorus inside my chambers.

Palms on my thighs, I bend and catch my breath. "Okay. Let's do this."

I unlock the door to Riven's room, and the three of us enter swiftly. Wasting no time, I stride straight to his reclining form and commence shaking him awake.

His arms flail in shock. "What are you doing?" The deep timbre of his voice rasps along my spine, heat pooling in my stomach.

"I heard you need some exercise, King of Merits."

Hope flares in his fluorescent-blue eyes.

"Don't get any ideas. I see your schemes brewing, and I must inform you that they'll all fail. Yes, I plan to take you out of doors, but the queen will make you invisible to all eyes but ours. Is that how you want to flee, stumbling across our lands, incorporeal as a wraith and just as powerless? When we allow you to leave, Riven, I promise the circumstances will be in your favor."

A silver brow lifts. "Just Riven, is it? Have you forgotten I'm king of the Unseelie?"

"There's nothing wrong with my memory, *Riven*. While you're at my mercy, I can call you whatever I please."

Rubbing his temple, he sighs. "Fine. Tell me about these *circumstances* under which you'll grant my release."

"For starters, you'll be strong when we let you go, and you will have enough provisions to make it home, so we can't be blamed for your demise should it occur. Now, please, be quiet for a moment while I steal your breath."

"What? Wait, Merrin—" The king chokes as my fingers draw patterns before his startled face, and I take just enough oxygen from his lungs to make him compliant.

I face my co-conspirators who are huddled near the door. "Magret. Alorus, the king is ready for his outing. Now stand up please, Riven na Duinn." It's difficult to watch him rise from the bed, his limbs weak, and the light in his eyes wavering between suspicion and hope.

By way of the castle's hidden corridors, Alorus helps Riven to the stables. Isla meets us in the secret alcove above Jinn's stall and works a fast invisibility spell—a simple enough task for a fae queen.

Cheerfully, she informs the grooms near the front of the stables that we're off on a picnic and taking Jinn with us. The stable hands stare goggle-eyed as we ride away—the queen on her white stallion, Bainne, me astride, Nahla, and trotting gaily beside us, Father's horse, Jinn, who appears riderless.

"We'll take Riven to Emerald Bay behind the ruins, a place of thresholds and open boundaries where every element is heightened," says Isla. "It's the perfect environment to re-energize him."

Hopefully, not too perfect. I'm not ready for him to escape just yet.

10

The Emerald Bay

Merri

Our horses' hooves clip-clop along the city's green-tourmaline pathways, thud over the sun-dappled meadow, then vibrate through the Black Forest, shaking birds from the tangled vines as we travel past.

Riven rides at a slow pace just ahead of Isla and me, the queen greeting tiny creatures with warm laughter and dancing sparks of amber and gold, while I stare at the Merit king's broad shoulders.

I do my best to pretend I'm not admiring the starlight glow of his long-flowing hair, the stunning black metal wreath of intricate patterns that circles his forehead, or the ghostly spikes of jet crystals that are beginning to rise around the circlet. Wait...

What in the realms? Those ethereal spikes weren't there a moment ago.

"Isla, look! His crown is materializing."

She leans over Bainne and speaks in a low voice. "Amazing! The elements are reconstructing his power before our eyes."

"Can you hold him if he regains enough strength to use those powers?"

"Absolutely. He's in our land, Merri, so, I'm naturally stronger, and he's still very unwell. Whoever concocted the poison that struck down an Unseelie king is the being we must fear and find as soon as possible."

"No whispers of unusual sightings amongst the wild fae? No news from the mages?"

"Unfortunately not." She nudges Bainne away from the edge of the ridge we're following. "But we'd better uncover something soon to appease Lidwinia. To say she's a bit upset at the moment, not knowing where her brother is, would be like saying your father only thinks a *little* highly of himself. A ridiculous understatement."

A bank of clouds races across the face of the sun as an icy wind howls through the valley below then wraps itself around our bodies, tearing at our cloaks. I lift my head toward the slate-gray sky, and snowflakes begin to twirl down, their wintry kisses landing on my cheeks and open palm.

"He affects the weather," says Isla. "But why snow, I wonder? When you first met him at the pond in the in-between land, was it snowing then, too?"

"It was." I think of my dreams of blood and snow.

"Merri, go on ahead and ride beside Riven. I want to observe what happens when you interact."

I sigh, my reluctance transforming into a gust of air magic that rustles a family of starlings from their cozy nest. "Must I?"

Isla laughs. "Of course you must. Did you leave your daring nature behind in your bedchamber this morning?" A blonde brow arches. "It seems this king brings out the wimp in you."

"Nonsense." I don't contradict her outright, because I can't—she's correct. I click my tongue and Nahla trots forward.

The king's spine stiffens as I draw up alongside him, but sweet Jinn turns his head to nuzzle my leg in greeting.

I clear my throat. "How do you feel, Riven? Are the elements helping?" To avoid staring at the spectral crown that wavers above his hauntingly pale face, I study the gold-flecked path ahead that winds upward toward the old tournament ground and the ruins of Castle Black.

"The pain is easing."

"Awesome. You'll be as good as new in no time and ready to head home."

He scoffs, his expression puzzled. "Oftentimes, you speak so strangely that I have trouble understanding your meaning."

"Really? For a king, you're a little lacking in the smarts department then."

His lush lips twist. "You see? You speak gibberish."

"Well let me explain why. As you've taken great pains to point out, I'm half human. I'm sure you know that my mother and Queen Isla grew up in the human cities. Becoming fae royalty has changed them, but they haven't lost their love of street slang, as they call it, and other earthly delights, such as pizza nights."

"I see." Frowning ocean eyes clash with mine then flick away to scan the trees. "What are pizza nights?"

"A special night of the month when my family congregates in the kitchen to stuff our faces with pizza. Pizza is...hm...how best to describe it? It's a round base of thin, oven-baked dough loaded with cheese, a rich fragrant sauce, and sweet pineapple. You eat it with your fingers, and most of it ends up all over your face and clothes."

I heave a deep sigh as I think of Max's delicious Hawaiian pizzas. They were always the first thing I asked for as a child when I arrived in the human world with my family on our infrequent trips to visit Great Aunt Clare, who still believes we live in a country called Brazil where my father allegedly runs a charity for homeless children.

Riven grunts. "I have never seen a pine tree that bears apples before. And this *pizza* you speak of sounds troublesome. I prefer to put my food in my mouth, not smear it over my body and clothing."

"Trust me, you'd like it. The way the hot cheese stretches and the oily, juicy—"

"Yes, yes. The fact that it brings you great pleasure is evident, but I have no wish to witness anymore of your ecstasy." Jinn snorts as Riven strokes his neck. "If you insist on riding beside me, please change the subject. You've not told me how your Beltane meeting with the Shade prince went. Are you now blissfully betrothed?"

"Nope. He was as pretty as a peacock and his conversation just as thrilling."

Riven smiles. "Ah, so he was a bore, then?"

"Yes. And worse...I watched him as my mother sang to the court. He stood unmoved throughout, with a sneer slashing his face. I haven't seen Landolin in years. As it turns out, I could have waited longer."

Jinn's bridle chimes musically, making Riven smile. "Never trust a fae who is unmoved by song or music. Their hearts are impoverished wastelands."

Huh. Does that mean Riven approves of music and singing? Or is he describing his own desolate heart?

I breathe in the crisp pine-scented air, then clear my throat. "For my court's sake, I jumped the Beltane fires with the Shade prince, but we didn't manage to clear them. So, he left without a princess on his arm and looked about as relieved as I felt."

Riven's brow creases. "And your family, are they angry at this turn of events?"

"No. Just between us, they didn't like him much either. Now they'll have to find another royal fae to marry me off to. Hopefully, the next one will be a nicer fellow and won't mind a wife who loves hunting and sword fighting and eating left-over pizza in the middle of the night." Giving the king a fleeting smile, I press Nahla into a trot, and we move past him into the dappled tree tunnel.

In silence, our party of three, or seven if I include the horses and Cara who's sleeping under my cloak, makes our way around the old ruins, Riven's gaze like fiery arrows piercing through my shoulder blades and setting my heart aflame.

We turn north and follow a brine-scented passage overhung with billowing branches that broadens and forks out of the thick forest behind the ruins. The trees quickly give way to chest-height, ash-colored shrubs, dragonflies darting through the dog rose that entwines them. These quickly yield to swaying grasses, a wide silver sky, and a dazzling teal-colored ocean.

Our horses pick their way down a pebbly path that leads to the small bay, their hooves crunching stones in a steady, reassuring rhythm.

As we arrive on the beach, the dull sky clears to a bright expanse of blue, marred only by a few wispy clouds brushing the horizon. Seagulls cry. Waves roll lazily onto the rocky shore. And now that Riven seems to have gotten his magical snow-show out of his system, it's once again a beautiful day.

We dismount, letting the horses trot off to forage around the hillside scrub, and Isla carries a picnic basket to a stretch of sand sheltered by a low cliff. She spreads out a large cloth, then places her basket of baked goodies on top of it.

As she arranges the picnic items to her liking, Riven stares at me, his eyes agog. He clears his throat and asks, "Queen Isla, can I offer any assistance?"

Hand raised to shade her eyes from the sun, she gives him a dazzling smile. "Yes. You can best help me, Riven, by sitting down and eating all of the lovely brioche I made this morning. While you're doing that, make sure your body takes all it needs from the Elements and recovers quickly. Then we can be rid of each other."

Clearly confused, he untwists his eyebrows and bows low. "Yes, of course. I shall do my best on all counts."

"Excellent." Isla turns to me. "I have a meeting with Ezili." She points to a nearby slice of land that juts over the frothy waves.

"From those rocks, the invisibility spell will hold, and I'll have a nice view of this cove, so don't get any funny ideas. Either of you."

With a grin, she glides away, sparks trailing from her fingers and embers glowing on the train of her gold dress.

A pair of sea-bright eyes drift toward me. My gaze snaps away and skims over sand, stones, sea, distant rocky cliffs, anything that isn't *him*.

"What now, Princess?" he asks, forcing me to look at his well-built form and chiseled features again. His beauty is a cold, solemn thing and horribly, endlessly alluring.

I'm not lacking in the height department, even so, he's more than a head taller than me, and I strain my neck to keep hold of his magnetic gaze. It glides from my face to my boot tips, then back up again, snagging on my lips. My breath comes out in rapid puffs as my thoughts fly back to Beltane night. The antechamber. Our kiss.

His lips quirk as though he knows what I'm thinking and mocks me for it. "Shall we sit and eat as your queen commanded?"

I nod and sink to my knees, then remove the rest of the food from the basket. As I place flasks of juice on the cloth, then pastries and several peaches, Riven sits opposite, crossing his long legs and looking more like an eager youth than a king of the fae. I pass him a flask and he drinks deeply before wiping his mouth and laughing. "Thank the Blood Sun for pear juice. Replenishing my life force is thirsty work."

I pass him a brioche, which he eats in four quick bites.

"Hungry work, too," I note as I eat my own, transfixed by the movement of his throat muscles and jaw.

Frowning, I say, "Why do you thank the Blood Sun all the time? Isn't that the ceremony where you Merits murdered an innocent from your court every moon turn just for fun? Isla told me you hated it, fought against it, but if that's the truth, I don't see why you'd be proclaiming to be thankful for it all the time."

"Shouldn't you call her *Queen* Isla?"

"No. We're not stuck up in *my* family."

"What?"

"We don't adhere to formalities."

He snorts softly. "Then much has changed since your grandmother's time. Queen Varenus upheld ceremony upon pain of death."

"Yes. She's still the same. You haven't answered my question."

Silver hair tickles my cheek as he leans unnecessarily close to collect more food. "My people are still attached to the concept of the Blood Sun, but I assure you, now that I'm king, we celebrate it quite differently every dark of the moon."

"It's still wrong to refer to it so casually."

"It's a habit. We are Unseelie and don't fear our nightmares as the Bright Court do. What would you recommend I say instead?"

I bite my lip and stare at the smooth arch of his left eyebrow, thinking. "Perhaps you could call it the Living Sun."

"The Living Sun?" He hums and considers it. "That's...actually quite good. I could begin to sprinkle the term into future ceremonies and use it in conversation. For example, like an arrogant king, I could shout it at unsuspecting courtiers. *What in the Living Sun are you looking at?*"

I laugh and, surprisingly, he does, too.

"Today, I could ask you that same question, Princess. Every time I look up, you're staring at me."

Draygonets. I need to get my eyeballs under control. My face heats, and I knock over my flask with a clumsy elbow. "I've been inspecting your eyebrows. Their shape is very...um...kingly?"

He huffs, then polishes off the remaining brioche and four peaches, the whole time chewing and smiling at me. The smile is disconcerting to say the least. Also, I can't help wondering if he took the queen's command to eat *all* of the food quite literally.

"You're not wearing your Merit pendant," I say, employing my famous talent for stating the obvious.

His fingers go to his chest as though searching for it. "No. I despise them and only wear mine for ceremonies and special occasions. But when I do, it's usually deactivated."

"Oh? The King of Merits doesn't collect the points and social statistics so valued by his court." I say, my eyebrows raised.

"Correct. And I hope, eventually, all my courtiers will follow my example."

"You could outlaw the use of them."

"I could. But I won't."

Interesting. This tells me a lot about him. Perhaps Riven na Duinn isn't a tyrant after all.

He wipes crumbs from his black tunic, then stretches his arms and yawns loudly. "I feel amazing. Alive. And so much stronger," he says, springing onto his haunches and jerking forward, pretending to attack me. Shock, horror—the Merit king is being playful.

Scrambling backward, I raise wind magic in my palm and throw it at him. It whips long locks of silver hair around his wild grin and the spikes of that ghostly crown, but doesn't stop him laughing at me.

With impressive speed for one who's been bedridden many days, the king rises and stalks to the shoreline, the wind untangling his hair. Spying something of interest amongst the pebbles, he bends to collect it.

For a few moments, I stay where I am, admiring the set of his shoulders, the tilt of his head as he breathes sea air deeply into his lungs and rolls whatever he's found through his fingers.

Like a bee chasing pollen, I stand and hurry to his side. When he notices me, he releases a long-suffering sigh. I am an annoyance. A nuisance. And above all else—his enemy. I can't forget that.

My gaze fixed on the gleaming horizon, I ask, "What have you found there?"

He glances at the object hidden in his fist. "Nothing. Merrin, do you know where Meerade is?"

Slowly, my eyes meet his. "Your famous owl?"

"Who else would I be referring to? The overly large banded rat peeking through your clothing? The cook in your castle's kitchen?"

"As I've informed you, Cara is a mire squirrel, not a rat. And how should I know where Meerade is?"

"You have air magic like Everend, do you not? She was with me when I was shot. She'd never leave me if she had a choice. I'm certain she's still in your land, waiting for me. Try seeking her on the air currents."

As a halfling, my magic is nowhere near as strong as my father's, not that I'm prepared to admit that to Riven. I'm not sure I can succeed. "She's your creature; does your magic not call to her?"

He scowls at me. "What magic do I possess at present? And for this outing, your queen has cloaked me in a powerful invisibility glamor, which disturbs my energetic frequency. How do you suppose my owl could penetrate a fae queen's magic?"

"I see. Then, of course, I'll try to find her for you. First, I need you to tell me about her."

Riven focuses intently on me, making my heart pound against the cage of my chest, then he closes his eyes. "Meerade is the most beautiful owl you could ever imagine. Half her body is covered in snow-white feathers, and the other side is made of tiny, metallic feathers and—"

"But what does she *feel* like? *Who* is Meerade?"

Earlier, I thought his pleased-to-be-eating-brioche smile was heartbreaking, but the one he wears now, so bright and genuine, would make a Valkyrie cry.

"That's easy. She is the most loyal, wise, intelligent, insightful creature and—"

"Okay. Okay." I laugh. "That will do. Give me a short message for her. I can only send a few words through the air."

"Then just say this…" He swallows, Adam's apple bobbing. "Riven calls you. Come find him now. And, Merrin, when you speak these words, picture me here, my face, clothing, the backdrop, my scent."

My shoulders drop. Must I?

"If you form an accurate image of me in your mind, Meerade will come if she is able."

I close my eyes, spread my fingers and arms wide, and surf the currents just the way Father taught me, seeking the owl called Meerade. Within moments a sharp mind hooks into mine. Meerade—she's close by. "I have her," I say, then send Riven's words to her.

Riven steps forward, his boot tips touching mine. He grasps my forearms tightly and whispers to his owl.

Immediately, powerful wings beat along the airstreams, making me gasp. At the same time, the king and I open our eyes and look to the sky, watching Meerade soar from the forest, over the coastal hillside. Then she lands on her master's arm, screeching loudly.

"She can see you," I say.

Meerade's strange bisected head, soft white and metallic black, burrows into Riven's neck as her squalling turns into affectionate chirps.

Riven's face is a picture of happiness that I long to look away from, but can't.

Cara shivers against my stomach, then pops her snout out of my tunic's side pocket, growling at Meerade. For a timid animal, she often behaves unwisely.

"Stop that," I say as the owl's huge green eyes fix on her. "Do you want to get gobbled up by this formidable creature? If so, I'm sure Meerade is hungry and will be happy to oblige you."

"Rat, rat!" cries Meerade as Riven strokes her feathers and chuckles fondly.

"No, my friend, apparently, it's a mire squirrel. Her name is Cara, and under no circumstances are you permitted to make a meal of her. I'll be most displeased if you do. Have you been trying to find me, Meerade?"

"Yes! Lost king. Lost king! Air princess stole the Merit king."

"Indeed, but only to save my life. And now she is taking good care of me, nursing me back to health, so I can leave with you soon. Can you be patient and wait a little longer?"

Meerade bobs her head, and then rubs her beak along Riven's lips.

"Any news on whoever shot me full of poison?" Riven asks the owl. "I remember seeing Temnen's bird, Olwydd. Then the annlagh, which transformed into a woman and—"

"A woman?" Wild wind whips around us, and Meerade flaps her wings to stay perched on Riven's shoulder. "What did she look like?"

Riven scratches his chin. "I can't recall a thing about her. Only...her voice. I remember that at least, clear and sparkling like a mountain stream. It was very calming. She seemed a benevolent force, but it was a mistake to view her as such. What did you see, Meerade?"

"Smoke. Mirrors." The owl's eyes turn on me, blazing with suspicion. "Wind and rain."

"Nothing but a glamor, then." Riven sighs. "How disappointing. But I would expect nothing less. The creature's power was considerable, its flavor acrid on my tongue."

"Our mages will find whoever was responsible soon, Riven. They have to. Meerade, do you remember anything else about that day? Have you been hiding in the Black Forest, the one that's nestled around the castle ruins?"

"Yes, Meerade hides. When hungry, Meerade eats rats like Cara."

Under my tunic, Cara hisses, this time wisely keeping her snout hidden.

"Meerade, you should stay in the forest while Riven heals. If you need assistance or have a message for us, go to the red willow in the Emerald Forest behind the castle and seek out the green-skinned moss elves. They'll help you. But beware of the golden-eyed air mage who the elves guard. Her powers are bound and suppressed, but I'm warning you in case your paths cross—she's not to be trusted."

A strong grip on my forearm jolts my gaze back to the king. "Could this air mage have shot me?" he asks.

"No. My father would know if her powers were unleashed. As would I—even as a halfling princess, my element is air. I would feel it. It couldn't be Aer who harmed you."

On the rocks, Queen Isla rises from her seated position as Ezili slips back into the water, the sea witch's long hair trailing the waves like tattered seaweed.

"The queen is coming," I say. "Meerade, quickly, you should go. It's best we keep you a secret in case we need a trick up our sleeves or a helper in the forest."

The owl and her master say their goodbyes, and Meerade flies into the trees.

Riven turns to me, smiling broadly. "Princess, I am indebted to you. You were under no obligation to reunite me with Meerade, yet you chose to help." He bows low. Then wearing a serious expression, he places something cool in my palm and closes my fingers around it. "I want you to have this."

My heart booms loud enough to disturb the merfolk kingdom at the bottom of the sea.

Opening my hand, I find a smooth, black stone lying on my palm. "You found a holey stone!" I hold it up and peer through the center hole at the frothy waves. "These are sacred, Riven, and this one is yours. I can't take it from you."

"You can, because I've gifted it to you. May it fulfill its purpose, ward off evil, and keep you safe."

"Thank you." I rub the black stone then slip it into my pocket, picturing the cord I'll use to string it around my neck, so it will lie close to my heart.

Isla saunters over the rocks then the sandy beach toward us, her smile blazing. Her meeting must have gone well.

"Did you eat everything?" she asks Riven.

"Every bite. It was delicious, thank you," he replies.

"Good," says Isla. "You look much better, Riven. Your color's turned from ash to snow, your kingly crown from specter to stone or whatever strange Merit material it's constructed from." She nods at his head. "Will it stay with you now that it's solidified? How does it work?" With a hand on her hip, she winks, and a coronet of flames leaps upon her brow, twisting and turning.

"Impressive," says Riven, his fingers smoothing over a dark crystal spike above his head. "I've often wished for a brighter crown."

"Fiery colors wouldn't suit you at all," says the queen.

"True, they wouldn't. As we near the Emerald Castle, my crown of jet will disappear again. Its nature is druidic and bonded with the elements themselves."

"So it's part of your magic, then." Isla moves closer to Riven, inspecting his crown. "And you couldn't change it even if you wanted to."

Feeling invisible while they chat, I pack the picnic basket, folding the cloth and placing it inside with the flasks and empty wrappings.

"Was that your owl who paid a visit?" I hear Isla ask behind me.

Seven hells. Does she miss nothing?

Riven shifts his weight, his boots scraping over the pebbly sand.

Holding the basket, I spring to my feet and subtly shake my head at the waves. *Don't tell her. Divert her. Speak of her brioche, her flaming locks, her darling amber-eyed baby boy.*

"Yes," says the Merit king in his deep voice. "It was my owl. Your princess found her for me."

"Oh, for Dana's sake!" I cry. "Tell her everything, why don't you?"

Isla laughs, clasping her hands at her jeweled chest. "What? You truly thought I wouldn't notice her, Merri? I'm actually hurt that you believe I'm so blind, so *unobservant*." Her voice drops as flames explode in a ring around the three of us. "So easily deceived. So *un-queenly!*"

Riven steps in front of me, his body forming a shield from the queen's anger. With her fiery nature, often without warning, the queen transforms into an intimidating Elemental being who is, in all honesty, terrifying.

The circle of flames disappears, and Isla smiles. "Oh, don't mind me. I'm just missing Aodhan and grumpy because Ezili was being difficult." She sweeps Riven aside and kisses my cheek. "Merri, you can relax. I don't want to know *all* of the secrets you and Riven have. Only the ones that could put my court in danger. It's a pity Meerade left so swiftly. I would very much have liked a word. She was a great ally when I was detained in your land, Riven. Remember how she convinced you to trust me?"

"I do," he replies. "Meerade is an impeccable judge of character."

"And what does she think of Merrin Fionbharr?" Again, the queen laughs, this time at my face of horror. "Lighten up you two. You're far too easy to tease." She lets out a piercing whistle and Bainne comes trotting through the scrub, followed by Jinn and Nahla. "Come on. Let's ride home. As I said, I'm missing my son, and my king is growing restless for my company."

As I mount Nahla, the queen turns her bright-blue eyes my way. "What's that you're hiding in your pocket and fondling so lovingly, Merri?"

I sigh and steer my horse toward the dunes. "A holey stone."

"Lucky you," she replies. Then, as if I'm a child who knows nothing, she adds, "Take care not to lose it. It'll protect you against evil."

I twist in the saddle and pull a face at her.

"A holey stone found by another and gifted to you is especially potent," Isla says.

What? How does she know that Riven gave it to me?

Riven and Jinn amble past me and Nahla, and a thrush trills from the trees to the left. The Unseelie inclines his head toward the sound, his eyes falling closed as he listens to the flute-like song with a soft smile on his lips.

I recall his earlier words: *Never trust a fae who is unmoved by song or music. Their hearts are impoverished wastelands.* Well, unlike Landolin the Shade prince, it seems the Merit king at least approves of birdsong.

My pulse quickens as I wonder about the state of Riven's heart. By his own reasoning, I can assume it's not a wasteland. Ugh. When will I get over my obnoxious obsession with him? Hopefully, when he departs the Land of Five.

As I rub a sharp pain from my chest, my gaze lands on a few long pieces of scarlet hair hanging from an oak branch to my right. That's odd. We passed no one on this trail on our journey to Emerald Bay.

I slow Nahla's pace and sniff the air. The strands smell fresh, newly placed, the color as vivid as lines of blood welling on sliced skin.

My eyes roll back, pictures flooding in.

Scarlet tresses.

Bloody trees.

Riven lying in the snow.

I shake my head to clear the vision and press Nahla into a trot. I'm losing my mind, and the sooner I get back to my chambers the better. I think I need a very long lie down.

And the king to be gone.

Soon.

Very, very soon.

11

A Spy

Merri

When I enter Riven's room three days later, I find him standing rigidly with his palms pressed against the rosewood cabinet, staring at a section of wall as though he can see the entire kingdom through it.

The frisson of dark energy that rolls off his body gives me pause to question yesterday's decision to remove his leg chain. Perhaps I was too trusting, but I've never been able to bear the sight of a wounded creature trapped.

"Good morning," I say with false gaiety, placing the breakfast tray on the bench opposite the fire. "Are you all right?"

"Perhaps." Every one of the room's seven candles gutter as his deep voice rumbles. "Am I to be served by the Seelie princess this morning? What an honor." He speaks without turning, still focusing on the wall.

He doesn't sound honored, more like furious.

"I wanted to see how you're faring for myself. By the looks of you, it's time for us to plan your journey home. What are you doing staring at the wall, anyway?"

"Losing my mind."

Huh. Me, too.

Turning to fuss with the tray, the thud of Riven's boots is the only warning I get before he grabs my shoulders and presses me against the rough tourmaline-lined walls, the stone scraping my skin through the delicate teal fabric of my gown.

Cool fingers wrap and squeeze my throat, his warm breath gusting over my lips in harsh pants. "Keen to be rid of me, Merri?"

"What? Of course, I..."

Thunder shakes the sky nearby, my shock affecting the weather. For some reason, my power is unusually strong this morning. If I wanted to, I could probably crush his lungs in one inhalation. Tear them from his chest in two. Mince his remains with three.

But I don't move. Barely breathing, I stare at his sorrowful eyes as they trace over my throat, then my mouth.

Giving a low chuckle, his nail trails over the gold falcons swooping down my neckline. "I like this gown, Princess. The feathers are quite entrancing. But I don't like its effect on me." He shakes his head hard, clearing it. "It makes me feel... unsettled."

I draw a ragged breath. "Let me go, Riven. I agree with your earlier claim. You seem to have lost your senses."

"Can you help me find them, sweet Princess of Air?" Then his warm lips press against mine.

I can't move. Don't want to move, not for all the air magic in the seven realms.

"Help me," he whispers, and opens my mouth with his own.

Electricity shoots through my veins.

His kiss deepens, the weight of his body trapping me against the wall. "Are you willing, Merri? Will you save me from this torture."

"Riven...what are you talking about?"

"I don't know...don't care anymore."

Warm hands skim my sides to my waist as he drugs me with slow, mind-melting kisses. Then he wraps his arms around my middle and lifts me off the ground, turning toward the bed.

"Stop! Riven, please." I'm afraid, not of the Merit king, but of myself and of what I might do if I give in to my darkest desires. Once I do, there'll be no turning back. And my heart will break when he leaves. My dreams of him will continue, and he'll haunt my life forever.

Even knowing this, part of me wants to push him down on that bed and take and take and take.

The soles of my boots hit the ground, and he tears away from me and sinks onto the bed, rubbing his face with his palms.

Through a curtain of gleaming hair, he says, "My apologies, Princess Merrin. Life as a prisoner does not suit me. This doesn't excuse my behavior, but I believe my mind has fractured. My thoughts are in tatters, and I no longer know what I'm doing."

Silent, I stare. How do I find the words to reprimand him for starting down a path I secretly long to take myself?

His jaw clenches, a vein in his temple pulsing. "I'm sorry. That wasn't appropriate behavior for a king, for a fae, or indeed any creature. And I don't mean to mislead you with my actions. You're exquisitely lovely, but I'm not in need of a mistress or a plaything. And even if I were, a Seelie princess would be a very poor choice."

Well—a compliment delivered with a brutal insult. Charming. I work hard to keep my expression blank, to appear unaffected by his words. Before, I did want him to stop, but one more kiss, one more plea from his lips, and I would have changed my mind. Even now, part of me wishes I had.

"Can you ever forgive my transgression? I vow I shall never treat you with such disrespect again. I don't know how to make it up to—"

"Of course I can forgive you," I mumble, re-arranging cutlery on the tray. "It is already done. Think no more of it. This chamber has a peculiar energy that we've been unsuccessful in eradicating. I too am affected by its dark persuasions—I was a willing participant in those...um, kisses." Hands on hips, I force a strained laugh, hoping to make light of the situation.

His expression only grows more troubled.

"Seriously, Riven, it's rumored that a long-ago prince used this room for all manner of wild pleasures. I beg you not to think of what just happened ever again." Even though I'll certainly replay those melting kisses over and over, the fragrance of his soft hair as it caressed my cheeks, how perfectly I molded to his body.

Isla and Mother did warn me that pleasure could be magnified with the right male, but they didn't tell me it would be addictive and devastating. Right now, I should regret that I removed Riven's iron shackles yesterday, but I don't regret a single moment of our closeness today, of breathing his essence deep.

I face him with a bright smile. "Eat your breakfast. Isla made brioche for you again. I'll speak to her about getting you out of here, because it's clear the sooner you leave the better. And, I'm sorry, but for both our sakes, that leg shackle should probably go back on."

Closing his eyes, he nods, and my soft heart bleeds in sympathy. He must long for freedom, for home, and his people. Meanwhile, I stand here wishing things were different between us, mooning over him like a lonely leannán sídhe.

After I bid him goodbye, I race through the castle's grand hallways and opulent rooms, seeing only the Merit king's eyes, until I reach the Great Hall where my family is currently breakfasting with a small party of moss elves.

"And she is still secure, you say?" I hear my father ask Tanisha, the leader of the elves.

The tiny matriarch nods her assent, her palm crossing her heart.

Father must be speaking of Aer, the corrupt air mage, who lives in service of the moss elves with her powers bound to the High Mage's.

As he leans back, chewing on a stick of twisted candy, Father's boot thuds on the curved dining table that sits in the center of the hall. The table is laden with treats and surrounded by my family, seven moss elves, and a few favored members of the court.

Only Grandmother Varenus sits upon the dais with her consort, green-skinned Lord Stavros, clinging to pride and formality. With a resigned but withering look at Father's boots, she clicks her fingers and sends a whisper of black moths to tangle in her eldest living son's hair, tut-tutting at him the whole time. He merely laughs and clunks a second boot on the table's edge—a brave and foolhardy fae.

Isla springs from her seat and skips up onto the dais to pass Aodhan into Varenus's arms. The old queen scowls at the babe as though she detests the sight of him, but I see the secret smile flashing across her lips. She adores him as she does each member of her family, even the part-human ones.

According to the tales, once, she longed to drown Mom and Isla in a flood of water magic and cleanse her realm of humans forever. But, thankfully, times have changed.

In fact, here in Faery, change is the only thing we can count on. Kingdoms crumble into ruins while others continue to shine and sprawl ever larger. Old queens and young kings change, too, turning from bad to good and good to bad. I think of Riven and his spine-tingling kisses, wondering which category he fits into.

Ignoring my brother's raised eyebrows and beckoning gestures, I take a bowl of sorrel soup and sit next to the moss elves.

Marelius entertains me with stories of the children's recent antics while I feed baby Velvet tiny pieces of soup-soaked bread. Young Jasper begs me to join him in a dance to the piper's jaunty music, but I decline. I'm still too unsettled by the encounter with the Merit, the hunger in his eyes, mirrored in my soul, and the way it felt to be held by him—perfect, as if I belonged in his arms.

When I finish my soup, I amble over to the banquet table and fill a plate with split figs and cream, then lean against a vine-covered column. Mother notices me and strides over, her green and silver dress floating around her legs.

"There you are, sweetheart." She kisses my cheek. "I've missed you."

"Yes, it's been an age since last night's dinner. Have I changed much since you last laid eyes on me?"

She slaps my shoulder. "Oh, shush. You're so like your father with the constant sarcasm. Even though it nearly explodes Ever's brain to skirt so close to lying all the time, he just can't seem to help himself."

"He'll do anything to make you laugh, Mom. You know that, right?"

"Of course. Sometimes I think it's a shame that it doesn't hurt *you* to lie even half as much as it does him. Perhaps if it did, I'd know more about what you were scheming."

"Me? Whatever could you mean, Mother darling?"

She shakes her head at the guilty blush blooming on my cheeks. "I haven't seen you scampering around the castle much lately, and whenever I do, you seem preoccupied. Off with the fairies as we humans like to say."

Of course she'd notice the slightest detail about me. She's my mother and an astute one at that.

"So, what's been preoccupying you? Has a boy from the court captured your attention?"

Why does it always have to be about romance? I fidget with my bracelet. "Yes, it's something like that." My preoccupation *is* male and he's *in* the court, albeit hidden away from it. And the word *captured* fits the scenario better than Mother could possibly know.

"Be careful, won't you, Merri? I want you to have fun, but believe me heartbreak isn't very amusing."

"That's rich coming from the girl who ran away with a Faery prince after he tried to kill you!"

Laughter crinkles her eyes as she wipes tears of mirth away. I fail to see what's so funny.

"It wasn't like that, Merri," she says. "I was Ever's captive."

"Oh, well that makes it all right then!" My thoughts fly to Riven, imprisoned alone in the ante-chamber, pining for his home, his people, and slowly going mad. Or maybe he was already insane before we met. According to rumors he was—and *is*.

"Just promise me you'll be careful with this boy, whoever he is. As Aunt Clare used to say, handsome is as handsome does. Don't be sucked in by a splendid face. Fae beauty is often a mask hiding unthinkable cruelty. You know this, but please don't forget it."

I look away, remembering the stories about Father before he met Mom, back when he was the Black Blood heir of Talamh Cúig. Whenever I look at my handsome, smiling father, I find those tales difficult to believe. Nonetheless, they've been fodder for many nightmares over the years.

The way Mother talks about the Folk, I think she sometimes forgets I'm half fae and that over her time in Faery, she herself has been remade into an in-between being—not quite human and not entirely Seelie.

"Please, tell me it's not Kian." A deep frown mars her lightly freckled skin.

"I'm not that stupid, Mom. Have a little faith."

"I do. I promise, I do. But you know faeries—their tricks and deceits are legendary. Now don't scowl at me. You wear your every thought on that pretty face. I can't help it if I know when you're up to no good." Her smile disappears. "I'll say it one last time; beware of this boy you're dallying with."

I draw a slow breath. "Of course. And for the record, I believe this fellow is fairly harmless." *For the moment.*

Forest-blade eyes narrow. "Darling, I always know when you're employing your halfling skill of not quite telling the truth. Be careful."

"I will." No lie there, because, much to my eternal annoyance, my mother is nearly always right. If she senses that I'm in danger, then I must be.

Glancing away from Mother, I notice Queen Isla at the other end of the banquet table, piling her plate high as she bounces Aodhan on her hip. I need to speak with her while she's alone.

"Sorry, Mom, I need to finalize arrangements with Isla for this evening. She's teaching me more about manipulating fire with air." Among other things.

"After dinner? Shall Ever and I join you?"

"No. No need. She asked me to come alone. She probably wants to hear my thoughts on a fresh list of prospective husbands and talk about future alliances. I'm sure she's already spoken to you and Dad about it. I wouldn't want to put you through it again."

"Fair enough. It's difficult to hear you spoken of as a pawn in a political game, Merri. But you don't have to agree to anyone until you get to know them first. Don't forget that."

"But Landolin—"

"Your destiny is to marry a prince, maybe a future king, and bring two lands together. Isla has seen this. I don't know how, but she swears this will come to pass. But as your mother, I want you to know this fate needn't be an unhappy one, my love."

Relief and gratitude wash through me. "Thank you. Now it's my turn to offer some advice. You should see to *your* husband. Look at him up there on the dais causing trouble with Grandma Varenus."

She watches Father leaning over the Queen Mother and gesticulating wildly while wearing his most mischievous smirk. "Oh no," says Mom. "What's he up to now? Probably hoping to infuriate her into flooding another banquet. Remember what he made her do last sennight? It took much pleading and many gifts of gold to appease the Dún Mountain dwarfs. They really don't like swimming!"

Laughing, I hug her hard, then stride across the marble floor toward Isla. I think of the queen's prediction, how I'm destined to marry a king, wondering if she's seen *which* particular king.

"How fares your king?" asks Isla in a low voice.

"I wish you'd stop calling him that."

She laughs. "Here, take Aodhan, so I can eat properly. And be honest, do you really want me to stop calling Riven yours, Merri?"

I hug Aodhan closely, burying my nose in his golden curls. "Yes! I really do." My fingers go to the holey stone beneath my spider-web silk gown. I rub the stone's center, the action soothing. "You told me he was dangerous," I whisper. "I should have listened to you."

"Oh? Now the truth comes out." She eats several mouthfuls of fragrant stew. "Mm. This is delicious. What herb has Elowen used?

It's very subtle. Wild aniseed, I think. Now what has Riven done exactly?"

"He hasn't hurt me physically. Quite the opposite."

Isla's fair brow rises. "How interesting. Tell me more."

"I don't want to talk about it. What I do want, however, is to plot his return to the City of Merits. He's in good enough shape to survive the journey. Is it worth considering Ether's help to arrange a portal opening?"

She nods. "It would be simplest. But I'm not yet sure I want to involve her in this mess. Give me time to ponder it." She rubs her hands together. "I feel a baking session coming on. After dinner, I still want you to meet me in the Onyx Courtyard as planned. We can train, and I'll let you know what I've decided."

She hip bumps me and steps backward, arms outstretched toward Aodhan who gurgles as I pass him back to his grinning mother. "See you then, Merri." She smacks a kiss on her child's cheek and spins to face the main table. "Come on you little rascal, let's see what mischief your daddy and Spark are up to."

The king slouches in his gilded chair as he laughs at his mire fox riding about on Balor as she waves Marelius's sword like she's riding into battle. The moss elf gives chase, hooting with laughter.

Isla passes Aodhan into Raff's arms, then sits in the king's lap and straightens his gold and citrine crown.

Wyn and my parents are dancing with courtiers who've recently joined the party, and a throng of winged fae stream in through the enormous doors flung open at the hall's entrance, the bronze, six-pointed star embedded in the ancient wood flashing in the light.

I jostle my way through the assembly, drawn in to dance briefly with groups of revelers as I pass by.

When I reach the doors, Marelius peels away from the crowd, tugging my dress and sending gold feathers wafting into the air. "Princess," he rasps in his deep-forest voice. "Don't leave by this way. The red one awaits. He is not to be trusted."

"The red one? I can handle Kian, but I thank you for the warning, sweet Marelius. I'll be fine."

I skip down the stairs, eager to breathe some revitalizing fresh air before I retreat to my bedroom for peace and quiet and prepare for my meeting with Isla.

As warned, Kian waits along the pathway, leaning against a black wall, his near-permanent sneer morphing into a wide smile when he spies me.

"Princess Merrin, how lovely to see you!" He bows, the tips of his bright hair scraping the ground. "How have your draygonet hunts been of late? Bountiful in the current season, no doubt."

Unless it's the Wild Hunt, he doesn't give two hoots about hunting. He's too busy preening to take part in any useful activity.

Kian snatches my hand and kisses it. To hide my grimace, I spin and walk away, but in the space of two breaths, he's striding beside me.

"Yesterday's hunt was very satisfying," I say, finally answering his pointless question. "I felled five draygonets with my bow, and Mother sent the last three fleeing. You know how they despise her singing."

"They're the only creatures in the kingdom who dislike it," he says.

He emits a hog-like grunt and stops walking, tugging me to a halt as well. "What is that you have there?" he asks, his voice quaking as he points at my chest.

"This?" I hold up the necklace peeking from my dress, my finger covering the hole. "It's just a polished stone on a bit of leather. Nothing of consequence."

Kian's greedy eyes fix on it.

"It is hardly nothing. It's a holey stone. Quite a powerful one." Since Kian's element is earth, he would know, and the hunger emanating from him tells me the stone calls to him strongly.

"I must have it," he says, clawed hand snatching at my necklace.

I jump backward, laughing as I tuck it under my dress. "No, Kian. I found it." Sort of. "It's mine." I take off, striding away as fast as I can without breaking into a run.

Within moments, his heels clack behind me. "What if we bargain for it?"

"You have nothing I want, Kian Leondearg."

"Nothing? I doubt that. What if I were to offer my silence, pay for the stone by keeping your treacherous little secret from your father?"

My heart jolts in my chest as we round a corner. I stumble, and he grips my elbow, steadying me. "What secret?"

"The secret of the Silver King."

I swallow hard, my stomach churning as I face the dirty rotten sneak. "What are you talking about, Kian?"

Wearing a gruesome smirk, he leans close, warm breath gusting against my cheek. "I saw you, Princess. Yesterday at Emerald Bay. I watched you have a picnic lunch with a phantom. At first, I was perplexed. I thought you'd gone mad, waving your hands around at nothing and flirting with the empty air. I sensed there was more to see than my eyes beheld. I squinted. I concentrated, drawing power from earth and stone and, finally, I saw the spectral crown, writhing in a void of nothing, directly above where your gaze was fixed."

Fear ices my veins. I think of the strands of red I saw on our way back through the forest—Kian's hair. "You're the one who has lost your mind, Kian. You saw a figment of your overactive imagination, that is all. A crown waving in the air! What creature could hide in the presence of the Queen of the Land of Five? Ezili was present, too, a sea witch queen, no less."

With one arm looping a jade column outside a house, he spins around it like a giddy child. "No. No. No, Princess Merrin. Your halfling lies don't fool me. I know that crown, those hateful spires of jet. Its terrible, dark shape. That crown is famous throughout the realms, for it belongs to none other than the Silver King. The King of Merits, your father's long-time enemy."

Sheet lightning flashes above. The sky darkens, thunder rumbling in the distance. Kian's low chuckle is vile. He believes he has me at his mercy, exactly where he's always fancied me.

Briefly, I close my eyes and terrible images assault me. The snow. Blood. Riven's silver hair streaked with both, his lips forming a gentle smile as his lifeless eyes stare into mine, blue as a butterfly's wing.

Oh, Riven. No.

"Merri?" Kian shakes me out of my dream. "Merri, what are you doing?"

"Wishing you away."

"Ah, so you admit it's true? You and the queen have the missing king, Riven na Duinn, yes?"

I may be smitten with Riven, but I still don't trust him or necessarily like him. Regardless, I won't ever hand him over to Kian. I won't give him up. Not to this conniving self-serving prig, not to my father, and not even to Raff, our King of Fire.

"We have him, but not for long." I force my lips into a conspiratorial smile. "We're helping him return safely to his home."

Kian's breath comes short and fast, triumph glinting in his eyes. "How did you come by him? Was it you who brought him down? If so, I would love to hear the tale."

I give a breezy laugh. "No. I cannot lay claim to that impressive feat. A being unknown to us felled him. But don't worry. When we find this creature, they'll pay dearly for their crime."

"Give me the necklace, Merrin, and I vow to keep your secret. In addition, you must speak favorably about me to your father, so the next time I press my suit for your hand, neither he nor you will reject it without due consideration. Do these two things and your family will never know that you helped the Merit King."

"What of the queen? She obviously knows, too."

His face reddens at the thought of Isla. Sensibly, he fears her greatly.

"Let's not mention our little bargain to that nosy firebrand."

Charming way to speak of his queen.

"Hmm. Let me think on it. I'll give you an answer tomorrow."

"Certainly, dear Princess. In the meantime, permit me to take the stone as a token."

"Merri, there you are!" booms a voice from behind us. I turn to see Wyn and Ivor trotting down the path, the wolf's black coat ruffling in the breeze.

"Prince Wynter," says Kian as he makes a short bow. He hates my brother almost as much as he hates my father. In both cases, the feeling is mutual.

"Hello, Khan," greets Wyn, grinning as he tucks an unbuttoned black shirt into leather pants.

Kian's nostrils flare. "That's my horse's name."

"Oh, is it? Sorry. I did think it sounded too regal for you." Well in his cups, he staggers over a pebble, then rights himself, raking long black bangs out of unfocused emerald eyes. "Now what could you two possibly be discussing?" he inquires.

Kian thrusts his chin out. "Many fascinating prospects, I assure you."

Laughing, Wyn takes my arm and drags me along the path toward his favorite rear entrance of the castle. Unfortunately, Kian keeps pace alongside us. My brother's wolf bares his teeth and growls at him.

Wyn waves our unwanted companion away. "Begone, Kian," he demands. "Ivor and I will walk my sister to her destination. We don't require the clickety-clack of your mincing steps for sound effect. I already have the beginnings of a throbbing headache."

"That'd be the mulberry wine," I tease.

My brother elbows my ribs, and we quicken our steps, leaving the gaping red-headed beast behind us as fast as we can.

"Until tomorrow, Princess Merrin," Kian calls, his voice edged with the shrill promise of payback.

I clutch my stone, its heat a comfort against the images that invade my mind of white and red and blue.

"Do I want to know what that was all about?" Wyn gives me a tight smile.

"No, Brother. You don't."

Nor would it do him any good to know what I'm thinking—that Kian is all talk and would never dare tell my father that I have the Merit king. Father would love nothing more than a good excuse to crush Kian's lungs, and he'd happily shoot the messenger who delivered such dire news. Kian knows it, too.

So, I won't meet him tomorrow, and because he's not brave enough to risk his life or quite as foolish as he pretends to be, he'll keep my secret.

With a shiver, the truth settles in my stomach—Riven's safety now depends on Kian's cowardice.

It's high time for Isla and me to send the Merit king on his way.

12

The Princess of Merits

Riven

A terrible vision wakes me from my slumber, rattling my bones so hard I lurch into a sitting position. Retching in pain as my eyes search the room, I expect to see only the darkness wrapping my body, but instead find myself immersed in a dream of home. Of Lidwinia in the throne room.

I watch the scene unfold from the Great Hall's marble floor as I stand in the center of the Blood Sun triangle, an insubstantial wraith, a ghost, who no matter how loud I shout, cannot be heard.

The throne room's doors grind open behind me, and the black-armored guards announce the entrance of Elas, Lidwinia's beloved consort and our court technomancer.

"My love," he booms, striding past monolithic columns of black, red, and gold, his dark wings unfurled and trembling above him. "I have news from the Elemental Court. They have our king!"

"*What?*" My sister leaps off the sun throne, her knuckles white around the glowing scepter in her fist. No doubt she wishes to snap the infernal device into a thousand jagged pieces.

The hall's bronze and gold surfaces gleam darkly in the moonlight. I scan the room's shadowy corners and recesses, noting that my sister and Elas are alone, which is the only positive thing about this nightmare I find myself appearing in.

"Those filthy, double crossing sluaghs," she says. "And to think I encouraged Riven to journey to their land. I should have known not to trust them, at least not while Everend Fionbharr still lives."

As Elas arrives below the dais, he unravels a scroll.

Rage seems to have frozen Lidwinia solid as she doesn't speak or even grunt in response. Only trembles. I can imagine what she's thinking—nothing good, that much is certain.

Finally, she speaks. "How I shall revel in bringing about Prince Everend's slow demise, for surely this must be his doing, Elas. No one else would dare hold Riven captive. No one."

"I can't believe fun-loving Queen Isla would do such a thing," says Elas. "And certainly not kind-hearted King Rafael."

"I agree. It's difficult to imagine them doing so. Once, I considered them friends. But they could have changed. Perhaps power has corrupted them and they mean to conquer us just as Father warned. Ruin us."

Elas mounts the steps, and in my trance, I watch his boots stamp the jewel-encrusted steps of alternating colors.

Red. Black. Red. Black. Red. Black. And so on.

Lidwinia sinks onto the granite base of my sun-disk throne, and Elas drops to his knees before her, gingerly holding the scroll out as if it signs his death warrant.

"Hurry up and give it to me," my sister demands.

Frown deepening, he hands it over. "Lidwinia—"

"Shush." The word hisses through the empty hall.

Elas's dark eyes plead for restraint and calm. The scroll's parchment crinkles as Lidwinia holds it to the side, perhaps not quite ready to read it. Unfocused, she stares into the distance.

I tread forward, then up the stairs to stand beside her. I reach for her shoulder, but my hand swipes through the air. "Lidwinia?" I say. "Lidwinia, by the Merits, can you hear me?"

As expected, I receive no reply. Not even an eyelash flickers in response.

For a moment, I watch the mechanical birds swoop through the incense-filled air and take a slow, deep breath.

Home.

I've been longing to see it. But not like this. Not with my sister about to declare war on the Elementals.

She's worked so hard to maintain a level-headed temperament, and like me, has striven to be different than our dead father and brother and always battled against her dark Unseelie nature.

But as she gives Elas a tight-lipped smile, I'd wager my faithful steed, Raghnall, that she's picturing the Emerald Castle razed to the ground, pretty crystals of green and jet sparkling beneath mud and gore and slimy ancient vines. Ever's entrails glistening in the dirt. Maggots feeding on his wife's crushed skull.

These images would sicken me, but not my vengeful sister who killed Temnen and Father and has never shown a scrap of regret over their murders. When it comes to protecting the few fae she truly loves, she's capable of anything.

Elas smiles in return, his fangs stark white against strands of dark hair that frame his face. He squeezes Lidwinia's knee reassuringly, and her shoulders drop a little.

As she opens the scroll and begins to read, her spider, Rothlo, creeps from her hair onto her shoulder, and she pats the creature's spiked, gold legs.

"Well this explains why they haven't replied to my messages," she says. "Who delivered this?"

"Olwydd delivered it to the front gate. The head of guards, as is protocol for anything that bird presents, intercepted and read it, then informed me of its essence. Without reading it myself, I flew straight to you."

"Olwydd, but of course. Wherever there's trouble, my dead brother's hateful bird can be found."

"What does it say?" Elas rises from his knees, kisses her cheek, then sits on the smaller throne beside her.

She thrusts the scroll in his face, and he takes it and reads slowly. With each word he utters, a poisoned thorn pricks my heart.

"*Lidwinia, Royal Princess of Merits,*

In the interests of alleviating your pain, I will deliver my distressing news without delay. The Court of Five have your brother, Riven Èadra na Duinn. Namely, he is being held by Isla Fionbharr, the Queen of Fire and hidden by her accomplice Merrin Fionbharr, the Princess of Air.

At this moment in time, he is alive, but despite my best efforts, I do not have in my possession clear details regarding their plans to either use or dispose of him.

When you take your revenge and retrieve your honorable king, I beg only that as thanks for this information, you dispense mercy upon myself and my intended bride, Merrin Fionbharr, who I solemnly promise to control and punish on your dear brother's behalf.

A place at your court or in the lands nearby is all the reward I seek.

Yours in perpetual friendship,

Kian Leondearg of Talamh Cúig, the Land of Five."

Kian Leondearg. Who is this traitorous Elemental troll turd who thinks himself worthy of Merri? When I find him, I'll smash his skull to pieces.

Blowing out a long breath, Elas unfolds his wings with a metallic tinkle as he waits for my sister's response.

Lidwinia's nails tap against the bronze armrest as she speaks in a sing-song voice that would raise chills over my flesh if I weren't a mere apparition.

"Tinkle, tinkle the faerie's bells ring out. Chink, chink the warrior's armor clatters. A bell. A sword. Both mighty and strong. Laughter and tears exterminate an enemy. Two lovely weapons. But which will I choose, Elas? Which shall I use?"

"Not the sword," I say, my words falling on deaf ears. "Please, not the sword."

"Lidwinia, what will you do?" Elas asks.

"I'll take my warriors and march for the Land of Five. I'll hear them out, but happily kill every last smug and shining Elemental fae if I must."

I kneel at my sister's side and beg her to hear my pleas, but I might as well be an insect on the wall for all the attention she pays me, which is none.

A wing wraps around Lidwinia's shoulders. "My love, consider a moment. You mustn't forget Queen Isla was once your friend, and dare I suggest still is. If she did have our king, for whatever reason, she would tell you. And despite Everend's ill will toward him, I cannot believe Isla would ever permit him to harm Riven."

"But Everend is a—"

"But the missive doesn't mention Ever. And what do we know of this Kian Leondearg? At a long-ago festival, he ran with our rough pack of boys. As I recall, Kian was a good friend of the deceased Elemental heir, Ranier, but he was not well liked by the others. Let me investigate, and I shall—"

"No. The content of this letter, this fae's words must be true. You know it to be so, Elas. Queen Isla has my brother. I must retrieve him and make them pay."

Elas takes her hands and rubs them gently, the contact causing the purple glyphs to dance over her skin. "I'll leave for the Emerald Court tonight," he says in the assured voice of reason. "I'll go in person...a diplomatic mission. I'm certain there is a perfectly reasonable explanation for the queen holding Riven in secret. Isla must have sent word to you, and it's somehow been intercepted, just as your messages to her must have been. Strange forces are at work. Never before have the actions of other courts in our realm been so well veiled to us. But we must be calm."

"*Calm*, is your recommendation, is it? Surely you jest."

"I don't. Think of everything Riven has worked for, Lidwinia. His greatest wish is peace for his kingdom. For you."

"Listen to Elas," I say to no one who can hear me. "You know he's right. *Please, Sister*."

"Tomorrow, we'll march toward the Elemental Court, and Isla can tell us herself why she's holding our king captive," she says to Elas. "And if necessary, justice will be served—with a hearty complement of blood and gore. Hopefully, most of it Everend Fionbharr's."

The edges of the room begin to waver. I look down at my legs, watching them dissolve as I'm sucked back into my body in the cell behind Merrin's bedchamber.

"No," I whisper hoarsely into the darkness. "What I saw cannot have been real."

But deep in my gut, I know the truth—the infrequent visions I have outside of the druid's cavern are rarely ever wrong. This situation doesn't bode well for the Elementals.

I must warn Merri immediately.

13

Return of the King

Merri

"Sister, have you heard the news?" Wyn and his wolf bang their way through two sets of sturdy doors to invade my bedchamber, disturbing my peaceful breakfast.

"Don't tell me someone finally kicked you out of their bed, and you don't know what to do with yourself so early in the morning. I'm afraid you won't find a sympathetic ear here."

Cara leaps from my lap to greet Ivor, who then chases her under my bed, barking loudly.

"Merri, this is shocking..." Wyn begins, his words trailing off as he paces the floor.

My eyes widen as I focus on what he's wearing. "Why are you dressed in armor? You look very fine, but it's a little excessive at this time of the day, even for you."

Fingers raking through his dark locks, he stops before me and bends close. "Merri, Lidwinia and an army of Merits are marching through the Lowlands toward the Dún Mountains as we speak!"

"*What*?" I jolt upright, the tray of toast and tea crashing to the floor.

"They made it through Ithalah Forest and Mount Cúig without triggering any wards or causing any of the Folk to notice and send warnings to the keep. The Merits must be traveling under deep magic. Isla and Raff woke to a message from their princess declaring that she's coming for her brother."

"Her *brother*?"

"Yes, Riven, their king! In a preposterous turn of events, they believe we have him, and if he isn't riding toward them by the time they pass through the Valley of Light, their war drums will begin to pound."

"Oh no. No! This is terrible. Wyn, I..." My head spins, a chill creeping over my flesh. This is *my* fault. My problem. But how do I fix it and keep both Riven and my family safe? "Wyn—"

Muffled banging sounds behind me, a noise that doesn't belong in an Elemental princess's bedchamber.

My brother freezes, listening. "What is that?" he asks, his eyes sharpening to slits.

"What?" I smooth my features into a mask of innocence.

"That noise. Something's in the wall behind your bed."

Hell realms! Isla's wards around my antechamber must be weakening.

"Now, don't freak out…" I draw a sharp breath, fidgeting with my holey stone. "That noise you hear is actually…well, it's the Merit king."

Wyn's skin leeches to white. "What, Merri? No. Please tell me I heard you wrong. Ah, gods, the Merits are going to pull our entrails out through our nostrils today." He drops to the floor, his back against my bed, and buries his face on his drawn-up knees.

"Wyn, pull yourself together. I need your help, now more than I ever have. We need to get Riven out of here."

"We? Who is this we you refer to? It must be some secret partner in crime that you speak of, because you cannot mean me, your devoted brother who you've chosen to keep your nefarious schemes hidden from."

With shaking fingers, I throw a tunic on over my sleep shift. "We don't have time for you to lose it, Wyn."

"Who else knows?"

"Magret and Alorus."

"Anyone else?"

"There might be one other," I say, refusing to meet Wyn's steely gaze.

"Who?" he bites out.

"Isla."

"Who?" He barks a laugh, rising to his feet in a single sinuous movement. "For a ridiculous moment, I thought you said…Wait…you're telling me the queen knows?"

"Yes. Isla knows."

Wyn commences treading the boards. "And the king?"

I sit on my bed and tug on leather boots. "No. Raff has no idea."

Wynter pales further. "I see. The plot thickens. So, what cunning plan have you devised to get us all out of this mess?"

"I'm crafting it as we speak."

"Right. So, making it up as you go, then. Shouldn't you have anticipated and prepared for this outcome?"

"You're right, Wyn. But we didn't predict Kian's meddling. When blackmailing me didn't work, he obviously went straight to the Merits with his snitch-report."

"Whenever that red-headed peacock sticks his nose in, you have to act quickly to shut him down. It was reckless of you to assume he would leave it at that."

"I know. I've been...distracted." I strap leather armor to my chest, then hang my bow and quiver over my shoulder. "I underestimated the damage he was prepared to do in pursuit of power."

"And in pursuit of *you*, Sister. You're what he wants above all else."

That idea turns my stomach. "The damage is done. Forget Kian. Let's concentrate on fixing this."

Wyn stops pacing. "Our family is already riding out to meet the Merits."

"And why did no one think to tell me this?"

"Probably because they feared you'd do something stupid and get yourself killed."

Fair point. I cringe as I imagine their shock and fury when they discovered Isla and I have been harboring the Unseelie king right under their noses.

"Okay, we have to hurry then. I'm assuming Isla will tell Lidwinia what happened to Riven and that she's taken good care of him while waiting for a reply from the Merit Court. That might buy us some time. I need you to help me get the king on a horse. We'll face our family and the Merit princess on the battlefield, then hand Lidwinia her brother while grovelling. A lot. Come quickly. Help me, Wyn. Please."

I unlock the antechamber door and shove it. It doesn't move. I could raise a wind and force it open, but I need to conserve my limited stores of magic in case I need to use it on the Lowlands. "Wyn, help," I say over my shoulder.

Calling on the power of stone, he pushes a shoulder into the oak, and the door clunks open, sending Riven flying across the antechamber.

"Out of your chains and eavesdropping, were you?" I ask.

On the floor, Riven reclines on an elbow, wearing a crooked smile. "When Magret brought breakfast, I recited a druid poem for her amusement. She forgot to refasten them."

Wyn makes a dramatic bow. "Your Majesty, I'm Wynter Ashton Fionbharr, son of Prince Everend and Princess Lara, brother to Merr—"

"Yes, I'm well aware of who you are. Help me up, I stood by that door so long, hoping to hear my suspicions confirmed, my limbs have gone to sleep." Riven's eyes snap from my brother back to me. "Is it true, Merrin? My sister has come for me?"

"Yes," I admit. "Bad timing since we were almost ready to send you home."

"I dreamed of this very outcome three nights ago. That's why I've been constantly asking to see you."

A mixture of dread and guilt pools in my stomach. I've been avoiding him, which was foolish. "What happened in your dream?"

"Oh, nothing of consequence," he says in a tone that suggests the exact opposite. "I only witnessed Lidwinia make plans to destroy the entire Elemental kingdom!"

"Why would she do that?" asks Wyn.

"Because someone by the name of Kian sent her a charming message informing her that your sister and your queen are holding me captive."

"Kian!" I shout. "That backstabbing conniver. He's really done it this time. Wait until Father hears."

Wyn helps Riven to his feet. The king is already dressed in the tunic, leather pants, and breastplate he wore on the day of Isla's picnic.

"How did you know your sister was on the way?" I ask.

"At sunrise, I felt Meerade's presence near the castle. She sent me pictures of Lidwinia dressed in armor and riding Rothlo through your Valley of Light."

"Rothlo?" Wyn's eyes grow round as saucers. "Is that the arachnid monster I've heard many gruesome tales about?"

"Yes, that's Rothlo. Most often she appears the size of a tree spider, as pretty as a gold-dipped jewel, and is relatively harmless. If you're nice to Lidwinia, that is."

"Pretty or not, I'm not too keen to make her acquaintance," admits Wyn. "Let's get you down to the stables. Can you send a message to your sister to let her know you're safe and on your way?"

"Unfortunately not. So we must hurry. Lidwinia has a temper and is capable of wreaking immeasurable damage."

While Wyn checks that the corridor outside my chambers is clear, Riven fixes me with those sorrowful, iridescent eyes. "What's your plan, Princess?"

"A simple one. To ride like the wind and present you to your sister before she starts an all-out war. You should follow Wyn, and be quick about it."

I hurry over to my bed and tuck the covers around Cara, assuring her that I'll return soon and all will be well. Within moments, she's snoring again, and I'm feeling very grateful for my ability to lie. If things go badly, I may never see her again.

The three of us enter the castle's web of internal passageways through a door hidden behind a tapestry in the hall. The main passage follows the external walls of the castle, after a time descending toward the stables. I summon fireflies through cracks in the jet bricks and they form a circle of light to guide us.

We drop through the trapdoor into Jinn's empty stable and find Wyn's dappled silver stallion, Tier, already saddled and stamping the ground with impatience. I quickly saddle Nahla, while Wyn prepares Berry for Riven. Although majestic and tall, she despises battles, hence no rider chose her today. But I know she'll remain calm no matter what happens on the plains, so she'll keep Riven safe.

Vaulting onto Nahla's back, I whisper an entreaty to the wind, calling upon its magic to carry us with speed toward the Dún

Mountains. My hair floats around me like it's made of feathers, and I feel the Merit's hard gaze on me as he climbs into the saddle.

As Wyn mounts Tier, he gives a terrible yell and Ivor appears at the stables' entrance, barking as he joins us. Then we're off, the three of us leaning low over our horses' flying manes.

In no time at all, we're through the city's jade gates and galloping over the golden bridge that leads to the Lowlands, leaving the black-faced cliffs and gushing waterfalls of the town behind us.

After a while, seven tiny arcs appear in the sky circling above the Dún Mountains, Father's órga falcons.

A little farther on and the flat plains reveal two large groups of fae standing opposite each other underneath a dark, leaden sky. At this distance, they look roughly the size of toy soldiers, their armor flashing in the rays of light that break through Father's storm clouds, his fury on display for all to see.

As we ride closer, in the open terrain between the two courts, I pick out Raff and Isla in their glowing armor, flanked by the mages protecting their rulers. Opposite them is Lidwinia, the reptilian-tongued Merit princess in all her glory, sitting atop the gigantic Rothlo.

The stories haven't done Lidwinia justice. She's far more terrifying in the flesh, her battle-ready posture and savage gaze suggesting she can't wait to gnaw upon our freshly stripped bones.

Without warning, a volley of arrows flies through the air, striking Elemental shields on the front line. "Those assholes," I shout, and the Merit king flicks a scowl my way.

"What? I think you can forgive me for swearing in your illustrious presence since your army is trying to kill my family!"

"If that were true, your king and queen would no longer be standing," he replies. "The arrows were a warning."

"This is not the time to argue," Wyn yells as Tier gallops past us.

He's right. We can't afford to waste a single breath. I lean close to Nahla's ear and whisper, "Rás na gaoithe, Nahla, téigh! Go! Go!"

Our horses' hooves barely touching the earth, we race toward King Rafael, who raises his hand high, a sign for our archers to draw their bows.

No. No. Don't fire back, Raff!

I release the reins and stand in the stirrups, my arms reaching for the sky as I prepare to draw down the power of thunder and lightning.

Suddenly, a black and white bird shoots out from the clouds above the battlefield, Meerade, screeching, "The Silver King. The Silver King comes," as she swoops toward us.

Armor crunches as every warrior turns in our direction and Riven's owl lands on his left shoulder. "Halt!" commands the Silver King. "Courts of Light and Dark, lay your weapons down."

Steel clanks as bows and swords are tossed to the ground, the sound calming my speeding heart rate as all fae obey. All except my father.

"Ever, stand down," says Isla, her clear voice ringing out.

Father moves toward our queen, wind whipping his hair around his face. "I don't take orders from the Merit scum who tried to kill my beloved daughter. Even if he were King of All That Is, I wouldn't bow before him."

Mother touches his arm, whispering words in his ear. Releasing a harsh sigh, he flings his sword onto the grass.

With Riven riding between us, Wyn and I guide our steeds past our family, then cautiously into the center of the field.

"Wait here," Riven tells us, continuing on toward Rothlo, who ranges back and forth in front of the Merit army.

Behind us, I hear Raff's voice. "Do you see, Lidwinia? It is just as my queen reported. Your brother is safe, guarded by our honorable Princess of Air."

Cries of "Our king, our king" resound as the Merit warriors bow their heads low at the sight of Riven. Unfortunately, Lidwinia doesn't seem as pleased as the rest of her court.

The long spikes of Riven's ghostly crown have materialized, opaque and solid this time, as if one could be broken off and plunged like a dagger between an enemy's rib bones.

Lidwinia glares at Raff over the tips of Riven's crown. "My *brother* did you say and not *King* Riven? Your form of address makes clear your disrespect for him."

Riven gestures for Raff to remain silent. "Lidwinia, dearest sister, I'm overjoyed to see you, immensely grateful that you've come to my aid, but it wasn't necessary. The tale our old friend Rafael tells is true. Princess Merrin found me injured on the mountain. She saved my life and nursed me back to health in secret to ensure my safety."

While Riven speaks, I dismount Nahla, preparing to address the Merit princess on foot, so I appear peaceful, vulnerable.

"But *who* injured you, Riven?" asks Lidwinia. "That is the question most in need of an answer."

"You're right, Princess Lidwinia," I say, stepping forward. "And our court will not rest until the perpetrator is found and brought to justice. But you must believe me when I vow that your brother was detained in our land only to give him time to heal before he returned home. It was not I who shot him with a poisoned arrow, nor any member of my court, as far as I'm aware."

Lidwinia snorts. "As far as you are aware? How diplomatic of you. And do you think I'm foolish enough to believe the unreliable word of a halfling?" Her gaze moves to Riven. "Tell me, Brother, did the Elemental princess lock you in a cell?"

"No," he replies. "I was held in a room behind Princess Merrin's chambers to keep me safe from...from those who wouldn't look favorably upon my presence."

Eyes the color of golden maple leaves glower. "And were you kept in chains?"

"Yes," says Riven, his fists clenching at his sides. "But not all of the time and—"

"Thank you, Brother. That is all the information I require. Merrin Fionbharr, there is no doubt you held our king prisoner." A thin black tongue lashes between her lips. She flicks her reins, and the giant spider creeps forward, golden legs circling over the bright-green grass around me.

Lidwinia's gaze burns my skin, and I raise my chin in defiance. The spider rears up, its forelegs and pincer-like fangs slicing the air above me. It emits sickening clicking noises that I long to protect my ears from, but I stand tall, refusing to be cowered by this gilded insect. Even though I long to react, I don't step away or resort to a blast of defensive air magic.

As I take a breath to speak, I square my shoulders and force my chin higher. "The chains were only required for my protection and—"

"For *your* protection?" the Merit princess yells as Rothlo lunges close.

Riven pushes me behind him. "Lidwinia, I beg you to wait. Please!"

"*Fine*," she growls out, spinning her creature in a wild circle before stopping in front of me. "If you wish it, Brother, I shall hear the air princess's case and judge its worth, But if it displeases me, then I'll soon be delighting in her cries for mercy."

I take a step closer to the princess, and my father's wind magic rushes forward, circling me, my hair and cloak swirling in the mini tornado.

"If you must take revenge, then take it on me alone. I won't fight back, because I've done nothing wrong, and if you end my life, all will forever know you as a killer of innocents. I'm not to blame for what befell your king, nor do I hold any ill-will or malicious intent toward him."

That's not entirely true since my strongest and most bizarre wish is to keep him in my land, close by. Not to hurt him, just to... I still don't understand what I want with him. But I need to solve the mystery of my dreams about him.

In all truth, I'm as fascinated by the Merit king as I am afraid of him and the strange power he holds over me.

"Sister," says Riven, palms raised as he walks to my side. "I beg you to leave Merrin Fionbharr in peace. She has not sought to hurt me. She saved my life, tried to heal me. In what realm do those acts require punishment? Without her help I would have perished in the forest. *Think.* Her queen is not our enemy; her people are innocent. It saddens me to see you warmongering as our father and brother once did."

"The Elementals innocent? And what of the halfling's father, the Prince of Air? He has been heard calling for your head to decorate their castle's tallest spire of emerald. Is he also blameless?"

"Everend was unaware I was a resident of the Emerald Castle these past days. So, in this instance, he bears no blame. Make Rothlo stand down."

Lidwinia pulls her creature up but doesn't withdraw. "If the Elementals are faultless, then why was I not told you were here under the Fire queen's protection?"

"Lidwinia," says Isla. "On the evening I learned of your king's presence, I sent a salamander messenger to your court and others over the following days."

"Which strangely did not arrive. Do you expect me to believe a Seelie queen's magic could be intercepted?" asks Lidwinia.

"Indeed. You didn't receive my messages, so it must have been tampered with on several occasions," replies our queen, entwining her fingers with Raff's.

"How? And by *whom*?" the Merit princess thunders.

"I might have an idea," I say. "Kian, come here."

Shouts and mutterings fill the air until, finally, Kian is dragged forward, spluttering nonsense as he struggles to break away from the royal guards Orlinda and Marlin. They toss him like a bale of hay, and he lands on his knees in front of Raff.

"Tell them what you did," I say, taking a gamble that Riven's vision reflected real events.

Flames curl from our king's fingertips as thunder rumbles across the sky.

Kian bows his head. "My King, I am innocent."

Raff snorts. "Innocent of what, precisely?"

Long locks of Kian's hair flutter in his ragged, panted breaths, but no words pass his lips.

Flames leap from the king's hands and circle Kian's body, not quite touching his clothes. "I want you to name it, Kian Leondearg," says Raff. "Now!"

"I..." Kian's silver shoulder pauldrons quake. "Your Majesty, I believe I have done no wrong."

Raff sighs, then leans into Kian's face. "I lose patience with you, old *friend*. Did you intercept my queen's messages to Lidwinia na Duinn or interfere in matters pertaining to the Merit king in any way shape or form?"

The sky ceases its rumbling. The wind stills, and even the blades of grass and tiny creatures cowering between them freeze. Not a sound can be heard as we wait for Kian to speak.

"Answer your king!" my father demands as he comes to stand beside Raff and Isla.

Kian sobs quietly.

"By the count of three, speak the words yes or no, or I will crush your lungs and give them to Balor for dinner," says Father. "One... Two..."

"Wait!" Kian raises his tear-stained face. "No. I didn't stop any of the queen's messages, but I sent one of my own, advising the Merits where their king was held."

"Do you know who shot Riven na Duinn?" Father asks.

"I'm not certain. I suspect I saw them briefly in the in-between land, conjuring the fog. I believe the being responsible was well-veiled, hidden."

"Do you recall anything about them?" demands Raff.

"No, nothing."

The king folds his arms across his chest, the air around him rippling with heat as he readies to unleash fireballs and cremate the foolish fae before him. "Fae or beast, give me the name at once."

"I don't know it!"

Father's lips twist in disgust. "Ether, come quickly."

The High Mage materializes between the king and my father, her black eyes wild and fearsome. Cotton-candy hair billows around her shoulders as she smiles, her expression both cunning and benign. "My King, My Prince, how may I help you?"

"Can you make Kian remember?" Raff grins. "Use any method you must."

Ether closes her eyes and reaches for Kian's neck, her palms hovering above his royal blue leather doublet. Words in the ancient tongue spill from her lips, making the world spin fast around us. The Dún Mountains quake, every blade of grass writhes, and the ground roars beneath us.

The moment Ether's eyes open, the storm subsides. "His memory is bound. I cannot break it."

Instead of devastated, she looks strangely pleased by her apparent failure.

Father looms over Kian. "So, you wrote to the Merits without consulting us, putting blame upon my daughter and your queen? Your treachery is complete then, and we are done with you, Kian Leondearg."

"You have always been done with me, Ever. You've never accepted me, never considered me a worthy match for your daughter. Well, now I have brought your enemies down upon you and the kingdom's inferior Queen of Five."

Fury flashes across father's face as lightning strikes the sky. While thunder rumbles, Father says not a word, his silence a warning for Kian to run. And run fast.

In a dangerous move, Kian spits near Father's boots. "This is what I think of the pitiful human brides you and our king inflicted upon our kingdom."

The Prince of Air laughs. "And yet you want a half-human bride for your own. What does that make you, Kian? Me thinks if not a hypocrite, then certainly the lowest kind of fool."

As Father circles him, each thud of his boots creates a clap of thunder. My hands tremble as I feel him call forth the power of the storm. Electricity flashes in silver arcs around his head and hands. The air magic in my blood sizzles, nearly bursting from my skin.

"Brother, be calm," says Raff. "As king, it's my duty to decide Kian's fate, but in this instance, I'll ask Isla to decree a suitable punishment. It was her reign that Kian sought to end with his traitor's note."

Standing silent and regal, the Merit king, his sister, and our court's mages watch intently as our Fire queen steps forward. With a slash of Isla's palm above Kian's head, the flames surrounding him disappear. "Kian, when will you learn that love cannot be bought or sold, forced or fabricated? You can only earn it with kind words, honorable deeds, and a pure and ardent heart—and sometimes by cooking your beloved delicious treats. Wake up. Bury your malice and dark obsessions, for they will never serve you well."

"Yes, My Queen," he whispers, eyes demurely downcast as if he hadn't declared his hatred for her only a moment ago.

A soft smile curves Isla's lips. "Kian Leondearg, I sentence you to be forever banished from the Emerald Castle, the city of Talamh Cúig, and the Land of Five and all its surrounds and people. Anyone who finds you in our kingdom has my permission to put you to death and will suffer no consequences for their actions."

Murmurs rustle through the air—I hear every one of them, outraged and shocked by our queen's leniency. The loudest, most furious mutterings belong to Lidwinia. "Why do you not cleave his head from his shoulders?" she asks, standing tall in Rothlo's stirrups.

"Murder, so final and everlasting, is never our preference," Raff replies. "The queen's penalty is fair and just, and clever in that its torment will last a lifetime. The terror of an execution is but fleeting. It won't be an easy life for Kian out in the wild lands, shunned even by untamed fae who encounter him."

"Although, I'd prefer to finish him off here and now," Father says. "At least I'll have something new and interesting to hunt besides draygonets. I shall look forward to the sport."

Riven emits a shrill whistle and Meerade, still perched on his shoulder, shrieks, "Raghnall! Raghnall! Show yourself."

With a loud whinny, Riven's mare trots up to her master.

I've heard tales of Riven's horse's beauty, and not one was an exaggeration. With her rippling muscles, shining silver coat, and iron-gray mane threaded with moonstone and jet, she's a magnificent beast, who's very pleased to be reunited with the king.

"Raghnall," Riven croons. "It's good to see you." He strokes her nose, then swings into the saddle before turning to his sister. "All is well, Lidwinia. Let's return home and leave the Elementals in peace and with our thanks."

The king's gaze settles on the tip of my left ear. "Princess Merrin, given the situation, I dare not offer you friendship, but you will always have my gratitude. May you be happy and well." He dips his head, flashes me a crooked smile, and then turns his horse about, riding through the line of Merit warriors before I can say goodbye.

Lidwinia's consort swoops from the Merits' front line and drops into the saddle behind his princess. "Hello, Queen Isla. King Rafael," he says, his black wings folding behind him as he inclines his dark head.

"Elas, I'm relieved we won't be killing each other today," says Isla.

"Perhaps next time," interrupts Lidwinia, shocking us all with a broad smile. "You'll be hearing from me after I've had a long talk with Riven. I'm sure I'll be calm and reasonable by then."

"I'm certain you will be," says Isla. "Travel well. I plan to speak with Prince Ever, too. I'd like his agreement to invite you to Samhain again this year. We used to enjoy your court's company in the days before your mother passed to the Eighth Realm and

Temnen came of age. After that, when El Fannon and Temnen attended alone, Merit company lost its shine."

With a cheery salute, the more than slightly deranged Merit Princess rides away, her formidable army turning as one to follow.

"She's really quite lovely when you're on her good side," says Isla, and Raff breaks into loud laughter.

Riven releases his horse's reins, and he and Elas open their arms wide, their fingers reaching for the sky.

A long gash appears in the landscape, displaying a black background dotted with stars and bolts of red energy swirling over it. The Merits ride through the large fissure, vanishing as the magical gateway seals behind them.

Wow. I blink several times, hoping for a final glimpse of Riven's black crown, but it's too late, and all I can see is sky and grass.

Did the king really open a portal, or did a glamor just render the Merits invisible? Either way, Riven is gone, and I doubt I'll ever see him again. Sharp pain twists in my chest, like a knife scraping my ribcage hollow.

Why should it hurt to watch him leave, the fae who likely wants me dead?

I focus on the memory of the in-between place—the frozen pond, the snow, the blade in Riven's hand. I close my eyes, but see only his lips, the corners curved in kissable arcs. The most affecting smile I've ever seen, because it's rare. And honest.

Suddenly, the sky goes black, the lowlands first darkening then completely disappearing, and I'm thrown into a nightmare vision. Aodhan grown, his body tall and muscled but his once fiery eyes dull, translucent, and the veins on his arms and neck mottled gray—riddled with the Black Blood poison.

No.

The image wavers, and I see an enormous oak tree surrounded by twelve cloaked men, druids chanting at night, the black towers of the Merit Castle illuminated behind them in a flash of forked lightning.

One by one the hooded figures speak, a pledge, a promise. "We *vow to protect the key to the riddle of the curse of the Elemental line until such time as the sacred peace-bringers unite—in snow and blood—so mote it be.*"

The tallest figure turns and looks right at me, eyes of vivid purple boring into my soul. Another crash of lightning and the tree explodes, and I'm shot back to the plains, my legs trembling, my heart quaking.

Could this be true? Is it possible that the Merits could be hiding the answer to the end of the Black Blood curse? If so...I can't tell Father or the king—that would mean war. But what if I could find a way to journey there and seek it myself?

"Oh, Merrin darling," calls a voice that, unfortunately, sounds a lot like Mother's and tears me from my tumultuous speculations.

I glance over my shoulder and see her and Dad staring at me with matching knitted brows. I guess I'm in trouble, and it's time to face the music. Smiling innocently, I stride toward them and hope they don't notice my shaking hands.

Mother links her arm through mine and pulls me in the direction of the castle.

"But...what about Nahla? We can't walk all the way home." I point to my horse eating grass nearby.

"Don't worry," Mom replies. "Wyn will see her back home safely."

My brother ties my horse's halter rope to Tier's saddle pack, his green eyes and a smirk flashing amid unruly strands of black hair. I blow him a kiss, which he catches as he laughs.

"We have a lot to talk about, Merri," says Father.

"Oh, joy," I mutter, his armor scraping my flesh as I take his arm.

"So," he says in a disturbingly calm voice. "How shall we punish you for deceiving us and keeping a Merit who once tried to kill you hidden in your rooms?"

"Punish me?" Ugh. I wish I'd bolted for Nahla and ridden away. "But there's no need. I had the queen's full support. We couldn't tell you, Father, because of your illogical unreasonableness when it comes to Riven na Duinn. Surely, you understand that."

Thunder rumbles overhead. "Illogical! I am not—"

"Ever, leave her be." Mom stops and whistles for her horse, a dappled gray stallion she named after her human boss, Max. Jinn appears first, trotting through the army of Elemental warriors, Max's white mane flying close behind.

My parents mount their horses, then Father extends his hand and pulls me up in front of him. "Merri is correct to point out the queen's role in this matter," he says to Mom. "It's Isla who must be dealt with."

"Good luck with that," I say. "No doubt she'll turn you into a tall piece of charcoal." I laugh partly in relief as we take off at great speed, because continuing this conversation while riding will be impossible.

When we arrive on the silver pathway before the Great Hall, we pass our horses' reins to the guards. My mother kisses my cheeks, advising me to return to my chambers to rest, and I smile and nod as if I plan to do just that. But I have other ideas.

I clutch the holey stone around my neck, and something unfurls in my chest, a warm feeling of certainty, a crazy scheme unfolding.

My wild dreams have meaning—the snow, the blood—I'm sure of it now. I have a role to play in the Silver King's fate—to save him from untimely death, just as I did in the forest. This is my destiny, to do it again. And again and again if necessary.

Other things I must spend time considering are his fleeting smiles and the way he watches me. And kisses me.

Whatever this strange allure is…I'm resolved to explore it.

I can't leave things like this.

I won't.

Then there's the vision of Aodhan and the key to the Black Blood curse that's possibly hidden somewhere in the Merit City. The idea that I could save them both—a current king and a future one.

Heat floods my veins—a mixture of fear, excitement, and…something I dare not name.

The dark clouds part, clearing the sky.

"Riven," I whisper. "You think you've seen the last of me, but I promise that you haven't. Not by a long shot."

14

A Wolf and a Boy

Merri

For the next three days, the Elemental Court is in an uproar, courtiers reeling from our close call with the Merits, my parents in constant talks with the king, queen, and the High Mage as they work to discover the identity of the creature responsible for the felling of Riven na Duinn.

Outwardly, I continue on as usual while I bide my time until the fourth night after the Lowlands skirmish when everyone is attending a lavish feast in the Great Hall. Everyone except my brother.

Bearing offerings, I carry a tray laden with wine, steaming bowls of pasta, and freshly baked bread to Wyn's chambers. Creamy Alfredo, a human dish Isla introduced us to, is his favorite meal, which he regularly bribes the cooks to make for him. Tonight, I'm doing the bribing.

With the tray balanced on one hip, I knock on his door and wait, the fragrant steam making my belly rumble.

"What?" he barks out.

"It's Merri. Open the door. I come bearing gifts."

"Open it yourself."

I blow a lemniscate pattern on the heavy bolt and it begrudgingly shudders open. With my mind, I turn the handle, kicking the door wide as I enter. "You should lock your door properly when there aren't any guards stationed outside it."

"Why should I?" Wyn asks, sprawled in an armchair by the fire, his wolf lying at his feet. He smirks over his shoulder. "I have no enemies in this castle and little to be afraid of."

Laughing, I set the food on the table in the middle of his messy sitting room. "Yet the most powerful of all the Merits spent weeks living right under your nose and you had no idea. Is he not your enemy?"

"I'm not sure. And, regardless, I lived to tell the tale. Speaking of noses, what is that divine smell?"

"Pasta Alfredo. Come eat with me….unless, of course, you aren't hungry."

I make a show of arranging candles and cutlery while my brother tells Ivor to stay put, and then crashes over furniture in his haste to get to the table.

"I wasn't at all hungry until that smell hit my nose, but now I'm positively famished." He plants a kiss on my cheek and scrapes a chair out, head bowing over the bowl and his fork digging in before he's even seated properly. "This is bliss." He sighs and then side eyes me. "So, what do you want from me in exchange for this feast, little pest?"

"Who me?" I ask, rounding my eyes to shining orbs of innocence.

"Yes, *you*. How will I be paying for you to badger the cooks on my behalf? They despise making mortal food."

"First, you can tell me why you aren't attending the court banquet."

"Simple. Because I'm too bored to bother, and no faery girl entrances me. I'm obsessed with thoughts of visiting the Shade Court. It's rumored they have some very fetching human slaves right now. I have dreams of freeing one."

"Wyn, the Shade Court is not a place for you to loiter. You're not nearly as heartless as those fae are."

He grunts. "Well, perhaps I'll have to try harder to fit in, then."

After I eat a few mouthfuls in silence, I lean back in the chair and watch Wyn stuff his face like a pig at a trough, thinking how best to phrase my request. As always when it comes to my earthy brother, the blunt approach is best.

"I made the pasta myself, Wyn, to pay for your silence."

"What?" His hand freezes in the action of running bread through the creamy sauce.

"You heard me. I need your silence."

"Damn." He pushes his bowl away. "I wish you'd said so first, and I wouldn't have started eating."

"Yes, you would have. You can't resist this dish, hence why I chose it."

"Tell me and be quick about it." He lifts his palm. "Wait. On second thought, allow me to drink my fill of wine first to lessen the shock, for I'm certain it will be a bad one."

I refill his goblet, and he closes those glittering eyes and drinks deeply. He lets loose a great sigh, cracking a lid open. "Well? I'm waiting."

"All right, here it is. I'm going to follow Riven to the Court of Merits and—"

"*What*? Merri, are you insane?" Wine spills from his cup, drenching the fur and garnet trim of his dark-brown robe. "How could I possibly assist with such a terrible scheme?"

"I need the High Mage's help to enchant the court so nobody will look for me or wonder where I've gotten to. At least until I arrive safely and make my place in the Merit Court. You can help by making sure Mother and Father are distracted while I speak to Ether."

"You *are* mad! Ether will not help you, and Lidwinia will have your head after what you did to her brother."

"What, saved his life so she would have the pleasure of looking at his handsome face for countless moons to come?"

"Handsome, is he?" Wyn bellows. "Now I see what you're about. You're smitten by the bluest bloody eyes in all the realms. And then there's the fact that Father despises him. Of course, you would find Riven irresistible."

"Oh, do grow up, Wynter! I'm not a fool. Even if his eyes were as blue as the Emerald Bay, it would take a lot more than that to bewitch me. I'm not a child anymore."

"The Merit king's eyes *are* bluer, and you're following a fool's dream."

"What I'm following is my destiny! Riven's life is in danger. I've dreamed of his death all my life, and I know I can prevent it. I stopped it in the forest, and I'll be called upon to do it again. I know it, Wyn. Why else have these dreams been given to me?"

"But why should you care if he gets eaten by a selkie or drops off a cliff never to be seen again? You've saved him once already, so consider your destiny fulfilled, and save *me* from the wrath of our parents. They'll murder me if they ever find out I'd aided you in this reckless venture. Are you trying to ruin my life?"

"Wyn," I say, rising from the table and kneeling at his feet. I grip his hands tightly. "Please, Wyn. I wouldn't ask this of you if it wasn't necessary and urgent."

He stares at the crackling fire, refusing to meet my gaze. I conjure a gust of wind, and the flames disappear. He turns his scowl on me. "Merri, bring the flames back."

I send another gust to reignite the fire. "Consider this for a moment: if you had a chance to return to the human world in secret and slake your obsession with mortals. Would you do it?"

"In the blink of an eye."

Of course he would. He hasn't been to the mortal realm since he was a boy of twelve and still begs our parents to take him. When they refuse, he spends a sennight searching Ithalah Forest for a portal that doesn't exist.

Mother has sworn me to secrecy about the one in the Moonstone Cave and the mages who can open it, because she knows that if Wyn discovered these secrets, he'd be lost to her forever. Such is his fascination with the human realm and its people.

"Well, if you help me now, I vow to do the same for you—assist you in any way possible—when your opportunity to fulfill your dreams arises." I thrust my hand forward. "Deal?"

Eyes sparkling, he shakes my hand. "Ah, Merri, you're merciless. Of course you have yourself a deal."

Squeezing his cheeks, I smack a kiss on his lips. "You're the best brother in all the realms. Will you take care of Cara for me while I'm gone?"

"As though she were mine." He laughs. "Do you realize the Merits may not be happy to see you?

"I do. And I might not make it out of there alive."

He blows a hard breath. "Tell me what I must do."

"It's simple. Stick close to Mother and Father tonight, distract them each time they wonder where I am. It won't take long for me to ascertain whether Ether is willing to help."

"Why *would* she want to help you?" he asks.

"She once told me if I ever needed assistance, she'd be there for me. I'm going to test that offer."

"Fine, then." He stands and brushes breadcrumbs from his robe. "I suppose I'd better dress for the Night Court. Go to Ether and take the órga falcons with you. If you find you must leave for the Merit City in a hurry, send Taibsear to fly over the Great Hall's roof window closest to the dais, then I'll know you've embarked on your foolhardy journey and begin praying to the Elements for your safety."

"Thank you, Wyn. You're as annoying as a prickle in my boot, but I love you endlessly. You know that, right?"

"I do." He enfolds me in an earth-scented hug, and then shoves me toward the door. "And I love you, big sister. I wish you luck in saving your king."

15

The High Mage

Merri

After covert trips to the kitchen and the library, I return to my chambers and pack a satchel with two simple gowns, some traveling food, and the smallest map of the Merit City I can find. Then I dress in leathers, a warm tunic, and a cloak. I push knives into the outside pockets of my boots, hang a smaller blade around my neck from a leather pouch, and last of all, strap on a small sword.

I hope I'm ready for anything.

Staring at the looking glass beside my robe, I tie my long waves back and practice a smile for the High Mage. With excitement sparkling in my eyes, I look wild, unhinged. But, fortunately, Ether views a dash of madness as a positive personality trait. Mages. They're very strange beings.

I conjure a glamor of servants' clothing, then skulk through the shadows to the High Mage's abode tucked against the northwest corner of the city walls, the órga falcons flying high above.

Thankfully, along the way, I only encounter two drunken sprites who can barely hold their wings off the ground and would have no hope of seeing through my hastily constructed glamor.

In the past, my parents have warned me not to disturb the High Mage in her home, and until this evening, I've had no reason to disobey them.

The outside of the house is small, unremarkable, and most definitely glamored. The unassuming facade helps to calm my nerves as the falcons alight on the wrought-iron porch, wailing at me because I tell them to wait.

I knock twice on the white door, and it glides open, revealing an enormous antechamber streaked with colorful beams of light that shine through the stained-glass ceiling, the candlelight acting like daylight in a stunning trick of light magic.

Five dark alcoves line the edges of the hexagon-shaped room, and standing in the archway of the one opposite me is Ether, her body shining as bright as a full moon, and her dark, opaque eyes as impenetrable as the fortified tourmaline that covers our city walls.

"High Mage, I'm so sorry to disturb you."

"Nonsense, you aren't the least bit sorry." She smiles. "What you *are*, Princess Merrin, is hopeful, eager, and perhaps a little frightened of what's in store for you. I've been expecting you. Come, we can speak in my sitting room."

She leads me into another room that takes my breath away. The white walls are decorated in silver and gold Elemental symbols, and the ceiling is wide open to the stars. A light jasmine-scented breeze wafts from above, much warmer than the air outside.

Candlelight illuminates masses of vines twisting down the walls, framing enormous floor-to-ceiling mirrors that even in the dim light, somehow portray our images. In her reflection, Ether wears a crown of seven golden halos, and I can't help but gape at its magnificence.

"Look behind you and see your own crown. It is quite a spectacle."

"What?" I spin around and regard myself in the mirror, my loud gasp echoing into the night sky. I reach above my head to touch the silver spikes in the tall crown above it, but my hand only swishes through air. I step closer to the mirror. "How? What is this?"

"It is a crown, Princess," she says dryly.

"Yes, but if this is a glimpse into the future, it doesn't make sense. Aodhan is the Land of Five heir. I'll never be an Elemental queen."

"Perhaps not. Nevertheless, this is the crown you will one day wear, fashioned from veins of meteoric silver that were long ago embedded beneath an ancient castle, forged by mountain goblins, and revered and protected by your husband-to-be."

I think of Riven—his crown of jet spikes—and how my own is its match in silver.

Ether points at an ornate narrow chair. "Please, Princess Merrin, take a seat, for what is a conversation if it's not held in comfort?"

"An argument? I'm not sure. I don't have time for riddles…"

"Yes, true. You are running short on time," she says. "Therefore, move quickly, and please *sit down*."

With a resigned puff of breath, I sink into the chair.

In one graceful movement, Ether settles opposite. She nods at a plate of chocolate chip cookies sprinkled with spikes of lavender in the center of the table. "Please, have one," Ether says. "These are your favorite, a recipe our queen remembers fondly from the human world."

"Yes, I love these. But I've eaten more than my fill of dinner."

She laughs. "Nonetheless, before you leave this evening, Princess Merrin, I believe you shall sample this batch. And, as you know, I'm never wrong. Now, how may I help you?"

I take a deep breath. "I need to follow the Silver King to the Merit City, and I beg you to help me get there as quickly as possible."

Black eyes stare at me, harvesting my hidden thoughts and desires. "Why?" she asks.

"Because I've dreamed of saving his life for as long as I can remember."

"But doing it once was not enough for you. Interesting." She leans over the glass table, her gaze penetrating deeper. "And why do you care if Riven Èadra na Duinn lives or dies? Is he not your father's enemy?"

"Yes, is the answer to the last question…and the first I'm not so sure about yet. But one thing I do know—all fae heed the messages in their dreams. Riven's life is connected to mine. I don't understand how or why, only that he's going to need me to save him a second time. Will you help me, Ether?"

Cold fingers dig into the flesh of my wrists as she tugs me to the edge of my chair. "More words, royal halfling. I need you to tell me *more*."

Dropping my head back, I gaze at the stars, wondering how I can make Ether understand. "I feel drawn to the Merit king and... Maybe I'm a tiny bit obsessed with him. Somehow and in some way, Riven na Duinn's destiny is entwined with mine. Also, I had a vision that the key to ending the Black Blood curse is hidden somewhere in Riven's land. Ether, if what I saw is correct, I could save Aodhan, too."

"Yes, and I believe you will." A smile glows on Ether's face, warming her usual impassive mask. "Your words ring with truth, dear one. Take care to always wield your halfling ability to deceive with caution. Here in Faery, it's a powerful weapon. I'm pleased with what you've shared. Therefore, I will help you."

Relief flows through me. I dip my head in a bow. "Thank you, High Mage. I'm very grateful."

"You must go to the Merit City and find the hidden verse of the curse. There you shall see your true destiny revealed. The question is, when the crucial moment arrives, will you recognize it or deny it?"

After a moment's thought, I give the only answer I can. "I will do my best to follow my true path."

Ether nods. "Ensure it's the path of your heart, for that is the only one worth turning your life upside down and back to front for."

That sounds fair.

"Of course," I agree. "Now, how can I travel to the City of Merits? Is there a portal you can open?"

She laughs. "The Moonstone Cave portal will take you anywhere I direct it. But please don't tell Rafael or Wynter this, or they'll bother me no end. And we cannot have the Seelie king and prince making mischief across the Seven Realms, can we?"

"Certainly not. What a terrible thought. Can you take me through tonight?"

She smiles at the cookies. "Take one, eat it, and then you'll be ready for your adventure, Princess."

My hand hovers above the plate. "Wait. What about my family? Only Wynter knows of my plan to leave. My father's storms will wreak havoc when he finds me gone."

"Leave Ever to me. I'll place an enchantment over the whole court, barring your brother, of course, and everyone will keep forgetting you exist until they see you again upon your return—a harmless misplacement spell."

Forget me? What a horrid thought. I picture Mom's loving smile, her lame jokes, and comforting hugs. Sighing, I pick up the cookie with the most chocolate chips.

As I bring it toward my mouth, Ether's hand tightens around my wrist again, tugging it so the cookie lies between us.

"Vow that you will follow your heart's path and no other," she hisses.

"I, Merrin Airgetlám Fionbharr, do solemnly vow upon the Elements Five and on the blood of mine and all who carry it within their veins to choose the path of my heart as it is revealed to me, in all instances. This I promise you, Ether, High Mage of Talamh Cúig."

"Good." With a quick yank, she brings my cookie close to her chest, dips her head, and spits on it. "Eat this, and then we shall depart."

The human half of my stomach roils in disgust, but the rest of me, as wild and strange as Ether is, understands the profound power of body secretions. "This will protect me?" I ask.

"It will connect our life forces. I'll know if you need me."

Ignoring the way it glistens, I shove the cookie in my mouth, chew quickly, and swallow it down. I make the mortal all-is-well symbol that Isla and Mom taught me, giving Ether the double thumbs up.

"And so it is done," says the mage, looking unusually happy. "Time to go." She stands and opens her arms wide, her body glowing like the midday sun. "Come into my arms. You'll be safe. This is the quickest passage to the cave and will ensure we won't be seen."

"Can you send Taibsear to fly over the Great Hall's window closest to the dais? Then Wyn will know I've left."

"Consider it done."

Okay, then. I step into her blinding light and allow her to enfold me.

"Close your eyes and tamp down your power, Merri. Air rules the mind and your thoughts race endlessly. Let them be quiet. Relinquish control to me."

I begin a silent chant.

I am at peace with all.

Like a cloud, I drift and flow.

Let go. Let go. Let go.

"Very good," says Ether.

Then my world turns black.

When I open my eyes, I'm sitting on the floor of a cave, surrounded by rainbow moonstone stalactites. A large curtain of water cascades into the pool in front of me, the burbling sound both calming and energizing.

"Well, that was something," I tell Ether who bids me to rise with her palms.

"You must stay silent and walk through the water while I focus on the place you wish to land—their Great Hall, perhaps? You might find a civil audience there if the Merit princess has softened since her brother's return. After all, it was not you who injured him."

"Yes, but who did, High Mage?"

Ignoring my question, she asks one of her own. "So, to the Merit Hall, then?"

"No. If you can manage it, I'd like to arrive wherever Riven may be. He's my likeliest ally."

"That remains to be seen. Now into the pond with you. Quickly, if you will."

The waist-deep water is as warm as the Lake of Spirits. "It doesn't wet my clothes at all."

"You're half fae. A mortal would be saturated. Walk through the portal's curtain, Merrin. Do it now."

Ether begins to hum. The noise of swarming bees fills the cave, the loud drone reverberating off the crystal walls. Then her chant rises higher, sounding like a thousand voices of the spirits of our people, the Tuatha De Danann, have joined her. Perhaps they have.

"Goodbye, Ether. And thank you," I say as I duck under the waterfall, its warmth spilling like silk over my shoulders. "Take care of my family."

I don't hear her reply because, for the second time tonight, everything goes black.

As dark as Jinn's shiny coat.

As hard as the Dún Mountain diamonds.

Colder than Ether's fathomless eyes.

And then a light appears to guide me through the void—as blue as Riven na Duinn's sorrowful gaze.

16

Kill Her

Riven

The night is dark in Blackthorn Forest, the moon hidden behind a veil of rippling clouds. And other than Meerade's distant hooting and Lidwinia's steps disappearing into the thicket of metallic, glowing trees, all is quiet.

A sennight ago, while I was in the Land of Five, a tribe of aggressive eyendric elves, who live beneath the forest, began hunting beyond their territory. Since my return, the druid's well has shown me many images of them planning an attack on the city. A foolish endeavor on their part.

Tonight, Lidwinia and I, the most skilled hunters in the kingdom, are searching for the elves' underground lair. We plan to frighten the moonlight out of them before offering to resolve any grievances they hold against us.

As I trek up a thickly wooded hillside, a dull thud sounds behind me. I freeze, searching the surrounding area with my superior night vision. I listen for Meerade's warning, but hear only the rush of my pulse in my ears.

A loud crack echoes through the night forest. Something moves in the undergrowth.

Silence. More silence. Then another snap of woodland debris.

I close my eyes and use my druidic senses to sift through the deeper shadows, expecting to feel my sister's energy close by. But, no, it's not Lidwinia's form I collide with, it's something foreign, unknown. Clenching my fists, I hone my focus until I find the thing I seek.

Yes, there it is.

Wrapped in a purple forcefield of unfamiliar swirling magic crouches a cloaked figure only several steps down the hillside, poised and waiting to spring.

Seven hells. My knuckles crack as I attempt to infiltrate the supernatural barrier. The spell at work is strong, impenetrable, and I cannot perceive through it or recognize the being it protects.

Slowly, careful not to make a sound, I withdraw my sword.

I take three long steps, fast as the wind, and then leap, my aim not to kill, but to reveal this creature's nature.

A scream rips through the air—its tone feminine. Perhaps I'm dealing with a rogue banshee.

The creature is quick and on its feet before I land, slashing a small sword at me. It is weaker than me, of course, but strong enough to put up a decent fight. I step back and forward in time with its panted breaths and harsh grunts.

It repeats my name in a guttural voice. "Riven. Riven. Riven."

Is this a plea or a curse?

I parry, spin, then slash at the being's cloak, planning to draw only a little blood. It swears and turns to flee. I grab it by the back of the neck and tug it close as I sheathe my sword and go for my dagger, pressing it against warm, supple flesh.

An Elemental-style sword thuds to the ground.

"Riven." The dark hood slips back, the cloaking magic slipping away to reveal pale skin and bright green eyes.

"What the Blood Sun? Merrin!"

"Yes, it's me. I'd appreciate it if you'd kindly remove your knife from my throat."

Still in shock, I scrape the blade against her jugular vein. "Did your father send you to try and finish me off?"

"What? If you really believe that, I give up on you, Riven. You might as well go ahead and kill me now." Her cool breath kisses my face, the impact of her wildflower scent catapulting my thoughts into chaos.

The tip of my knife presses into her tender, white throat. With one tiny movement, the life of Merrin Fionbharr would cease, thereby ending years of torment from her impudent smile and dancing eyes.

"Can you do it?" she taunts. "Are you brave enough? Kingly enough? Or *foolish* enough? Kill me and my family will be at war with yours for all eternity. Is that what you want?"

No. I don't want war, but I do need to end this infernal anguish.

Since I left Talamh Cúig, I've barely thought of anything *but* the untrustworthy princess of the Elemental Court. Is she here as her father's spy or to end my life? Whichever it is, most likely both, she's up to no good. That much is clear. But whatever it takes, I must protect my kingdom from the fate of the Black Blood curse so that Merrin Fionbharr will never control me or my kingdom.

Ever.

Killing her now would be reckless, and as I stare into her emerald eyes, I cannot bear the thought of slicing her throat and watching the life bleed out of them. Am I too soft-hearted? Not quite. A slave to her whiplash smile? No doubt.

Sighing, I release her, take a step back, and bow low. "Apologies, Princess Merrin, I thought you were an eydendric elf. Their warren is nearby."

She folds her arms across her chest. "Yet when you learned it was me, the tooth of your dagger hovered ready to bite. You knew who I was and still contemplated my end. I saw it in your eyes, Riven na Duinn."

Since I cannot deny it, I remain silent, inspecting her clothes, noting the weapons she likely believes are hidden against her body. She paces a circle around me, and I spin slowly to keep her in sight.

"You're looking well since I last saw you," she says in a light voice. "Filled out quite a lot. You're almost brawny, really."

"And why should my good health surprise you? In your land, I was depleted. Ill. Barely a man, with not even a quarter of the strength of a king of the fae."

A delicately shaped eyebrow rises. "But that was mere days ago. How quickly you've rejuvenated. Is this what you normally look like? Or has Merit technology improved upon your form somehow?"

I unclench my jaw. "You see before you a king, supported by the power and magic of his land and people. As a halfling, perhaps you cannot fully appreciate this phenomenon. Now it is time for you to explain how and why you've come here."

"With the Elemental High Mage's assistance, I came through a portal."

"Your *High Mage* helped you?"

"That's what I said, didn't I?"

"It's extremely unlikely she would meddle in my land. I sense a halfling's lie has fallen from your lips."

"Then you must believe I'm a very formidable being if I have the ability to materialize in your kingdom on the strength of my own powers."

She has a point. Only the strongest of mages can open and control portals, and she certainly doesn't look as if she's been traveling for days. Therefore, Ether must have helped her. But why?

"And for what reason are you here?"

Her rosebud lips part as she glances to the side.

"If you refuse to tell me, then you must leave immediately and by any means," I say, advancing until her back hits the trunk of a tree.

"Are you going to press your dagger against my throat again?"

Without intending it, I do exactly that, this time beading a drop of blood beneath her chin.

"Riven! *Stop that.* Now!" comes an all too familiar voice from the bushes to my right.

With a sigh, I step away from the Elemental brat, sheathing my knife as I face my sister. "Lidwinia, good. As usual, your timing is impeccable. You can assist me in the task of taking this reckless interloper prisoner. I believe she'll fare better under your care. My fuse is short tonight."

"An *interloper*? Come now, Brother, Merrin saved your life. Slicing a girl's throat is not the traditional way to welcome an honored guest to our land."

"Honored guest? *Her*? Did you forget that the being who shot me on Mount Cúig has not yet been apprehended? Until then, no Seelie can be trusted." I stride toward the Elemental and tug her off balance, twist her arm behind her back, and then push her in front of me as I whistle for Raghnall.

"*Riven*," says Lidwinia. "Your mare isn't here. Did you forget we transferred into the forest?"

Yes. Unfortunately, I had forgotten. "Of course. Of course," I say, not exactly admitting to my blunder.

Lidwinia pries the Elemental princess from my grip, drawing her close with an arm around her shoulders. "Hello, Merrin. I, for one, am very happy to see you, although I admit this is quite the surprise. Riven has helped me realize that, if not for you, he would have perished in your land, therefore I am in your debt and owe you a rather large apology. You'll find me a good friend to those who care for my loved ones. I promise you'll be safe in our kingdom. Tell me, what does your family think about your travels?"

Merrin crosses her arms and lifts her chin. "They don't know I've left. The court has been enchanted with a misplace-me spell, which will last until I return."

"What? Why would you do such a—"

"Hush, Riven." My sister turns back to the Elemental. "Let's return to the castle and get you settled. Over a large slice of sweet pie, you can entertain me with the tale of why you're here. Have you ever transferred before?"

"I haven't," says Merrin, shuffling away from my sister as if Lidwinia might bite, which she sometimes does.

Lidwinia laughs. "You'll be fine. It's easy. And don't worry about Riven. Since his return from your kingdom, he's been unusually grumpy—even for him. Transferring is quite safe. Only powerful fae can travel this way, which is to say, mostly only the royal family. I'll take you in my arms, and all you need to do is relax and—"

Without thinking, I dash forward and drag Merrin toward me, her back now aligned against my chest. "I'll take the intruder. When you transfer with others, Lidwinia, you've been known to reassemble their particles in, how shall I put it? An unusual manner."

"That's only happened once or twice. Remember the pixie who arrived at court with an arm growing from her knee? Mentally, she was never quite the same either." Lidwinia's eyes narrow. "And why do you care what shape Merrin arrives in, Riven? A moment ago, your blade was ready to slice her into pieces."

Before I can answer, a gust of wind blows hair in my eyes, then Meerade alights on my shoulder. "Silver Queen. Silver Queen," she croaks, hopping from one foot to the other.

"Where have you been?" I scowl. "You're making a habit of turning up after all the excitement is over. What's this silver queen nonsense?"

Meerade's green gaze fixes on Merrin, and Lidwinia laughs at my stunned expression.

"Her? You're severely mistaken, Meerade. 'Tis only the Elemental princess, found lurking in our forest like a hungry sluagh intent on poaching its next meal."

My owl flaps her wings, covering my face with hair once again. Meerade can be a spiteful creature.

"Where shall we materialize?" asks Lidwinia.

"The dungeons?" I suggest. "Or perhaps the Black Tower?"

"That's where King Rafael was imprisoned," says Merrin. "So, you're taking revenge on me and locking me up?"

My sister rolls her eyes. "Try again, Brother. Personally, I think the White Tower would do nicely. Queen Isla enjoyed her time there. It's both comfortable and luxurious."

My shoulders slump. "No. I have a better idea. Stay still if you don't want to arrive addled," I tell Merrin as I scowl at my sister. "I've decided I'd like her closer, so we can keep an eye on her. Mother's old room will do nicely."

"*Mother's room?*" cries Lidwinia, her orange eyes nearly dropping out of her skull.

Before I can justify my decision to my irritating sibling, I draw the Elemental close, our bodies dissolving in the transfer.

I only hope that by the time we materialize, I can explain my bizarre choice to myself.

17

Court of Merits

Merri

For two days, I've done nothing but languish in the dead queen's chambers—which sounds creepy and morbid but is, in fact, the furthest thing from it.

Queen Ciara's four interlinking rooms are enormous, bedecked in opulent gold and royal blue, and contain an overabundance of lush furniture from which to enjoy the view of the Obsidian Sea through the balcony windows. Resting here, waited on by Merit servants as though I'm on vacation, as the humans call a respite from their work, hasn't been a hardship at all.

Since Riven refuses to see me, and Lidwinia insists I delay my tour of the city until she can accompany me after tonight's banquet celebrating her engagement to the court's technomancer, I've had little to do but bide my time.

The Merit princess claims her brother is a danger to me at present. It will pass, she says, yet refuses to explain why. I have no choice but to trust her—she's fae and cannot lie, so she must believe it's not safe for me to be alone with the king for now.

By the time Riven left my land, I believed we'd developed a fragile, burgeoning friendship. But two nights ago in the forest, when he realized who I was, his chilly reception couldn't have made me feel less welcome. So, it seems he despises me—which only makes me determined to find out why.

I rock back on my heels, returning my focus to the dressmaker's tower where I stand on a vermilion, ivy-wrapped platform, frowning and huffing as I'm fitted into an outfit of Merit finery for tonight's banquet.

"Stop moving," chides Lidwinia. "You'll ruin the fit."

"Really, Lidwinia, I'm truly grateful for the effort, but this is unnecessary. I brought a gown with me. It'll do fine."

The princess sighs. "Take a break, Sartornalia," she tells the light-weaver elf who's been working hard with both magic and thread. "I need privacy to admonish Princess Merrin for spoiling all our fun today."

Collecting scraps of cloth as she goes, the elf retreats through an archway and down a winding staircase.

Lidwinia ruffles the layers of my gown, an unusual combination of variegated-green strips of gossamer material and stiff metallic panels woven in bright strands of silver that match my eyes.

"This dress couldn't be more perfect for you, Merri. You look like an empress." Rothlo scuttles from Lidwinia's shoulder to her hand, the spider's numerous emerald eyes inspecting my gown. I hope she approves.

It's difficult to believe this is the same enormous creature Lidwinia rode to the Lowlands, but she assures me this golden-legged critter is one and the same.

"If I resemble an empress, then it's a barely dressed one," I say, swishing the dreamy fabric around my legs. "It doesn't leave much to the imagination. One glance and the viewer sees all."

"Come now, don't be so prudish." The princess laughs. "Seelie fashion is hardly neck-to-toe sacking."

"I'm more comfortable wearing something simple," I grumble.

"Such as hunting leathers? That's what Riven said about you, too."

Riven? Why would he deign to voice an opinion on my preferred style of clothing?

The dressmaker's room occupies the entire top section of a Merit tower. Round with six arched floor-to-ceiling windows that allow afternoon sunshine and a refreshing breeze to dance through the space, it has spectacular views.

The window I face displays the black and white towers that pierce the sky from the middle of the ocean, linked to the land by a spiked-metal footbridge bisecting between them. From my chambers, I can see these fascinating towers, and I've spent hours contemplating their transitory nature.

"Why do the towers disappear and reappear like that?" I ask. "Are they real or mere illusions?"

Lidwinia snaps her tiger eyes from my gown to my face. "They're quite real and will show themselves when necessary."

"But who controls them?"

"The towers? They're my mother's creations. She controls them."

"But she's...deceased," I say, immediately regretting my words as sorrow shrouds Lidwinia's features.

"Sadly, yes. Mostly."

"Mostly? What do you mean?"

"At my father's request, our High Mage, Draírdon, used the darkest of magic to bind her spirit to the towers, hoping to suspend her in eternal torture. Unlike the old king and my brother, Temnen, Mother was a sweet soul, and she resonates with the bright energy of the White Tower. It is mainly there that her consciousness resides."

"How cruel your father was."

Green spikes of hair writhe like baby serpents as she tilts her head. "Yes, but his plan to cause her endless pain failed. Riven and I often visit, and we know she receives great comfort in this. Also, she can sense the true essence of any being who enters the tower and accommodates them accordingly. The atmosphere, lighting, and warmth all adjust to the guest's intrinsic nature, ensuring they're treated exactly as they deserve."

I hop down from the platform and walk to a window. As I lean on the stone sill and scrutinize the towers in the sea, they flicker like a dream. "Is that why you suggested I should be housed there when I arrived? So you could test me."

"Yes," she admits. "But instead my brother decided to place you in my mother's old room. Interesting choice, no? He refuses to answer questions about why he's done this, but I suspect he didn't want you to be judged or found lacking in any way."

"Your brother is strange indeed. If he's a danger to me, as you say, then why would he care?"

She laughs through her nose. "I think this dress might change his position in regards to you."

My pulse beats slow and hard, my thoughts spinning and crashing in a terrible muddle. I turn to face Lidwinia. "Isla was kept in the White Tower."

"Correct. And for this reason, Elas and I knew we could trust her and should help her and Rafael escape."

"Because your mother liked her," I say.

Lidwinia nods, and I recall Isla's tales of the floating lambent lights, the hearth that lit its own fire, and the sweetly scented bath water that was filled and heated by unseen hands.

A thin black tongue flickers between Lidwinia's teeth as she smiles at me. "Your current queen's heart was deemed pure, and my mother liked her very well. Of course, when I heard Isla had captured Riven, I thought perhaps ruling a kingdom had corrupted her. But the unknown being who felled our king and the banished Kian were the real problems, not you. You, I trust, Merri."

"Why?"

"Because Riven does, even though he acts as if he doesn't. Deep down, he trusts you."

"Surely not! He should just put me in the White Tower, let your mother be the judge. Maybe then he'll grant me an audience. Even the night I arrived, in the forest, he could barely look at me."

She smooths her purple-patterned finger down my dress's plunging neckline to where it ends at my last rib. "Do not worry. This dress should rectify that. I predict his gaze will fall upon you many times tonight, and if you wish to save him from a life of misery, the first step is to not reject his attention."

"But as I explained yesterday, my dreams foretell that I'll save his *life*. His state of happiness is of no interest to me." That's not entirely true, and I steel my features against a small grimace of pain that never comes. Interesting. My body thinks I *care* about the Merit king.

"That remains to be seen. Either way, you look lovely, Merri," she says, guiding me toward one of the long, mirrored panels that line the walls between the window arches. "See?"

The mirrors reflect my image a thousand times over as I circle the room, studying my outfit. Do I wish to capture Riven's attention and have him find *me*—a halfling who entertains notions of being a king's savior—perhaps lacking in some way? Excitement and fear shiver down my spine.

"This will do nicely. Thank you, Lidwinia. I must admit it's an improvement on my hunting outfits."

Laughing, she strides over to an ornate crystal cabinet that rests against the opposite wall on a stepped dais wrapped in jade and ivy. "I know something that would perfectly match your coloring and gown." She takes a key from the pocket of her metal-studded corset and opens the cabinet door, retrieving a tall crown of dark, glittering spikes.

"Wow. What material is it made from?"

"Meteoric silver."

I fail to contain a loud gasp as she places the crown on my head. I stare at myself in the glass as my hand shakes, touching a spike with great care. This is the crown I saw in the vision in Ether's sitting room on the night she opened the portal.

"Who does this belong to?" I ask.

"It was our queen's."

My jaw drops further, my blood roaring in my ears. "But—"

"Of course you cannot wear it this evening. I was merely curious to see how it looked on you, and the answer is very, *very* well. Almost as if it were fashioned for you alone, Merri."

A resounding knock startles me.

Lidwinia turns toward the door. "Ah, that will be your maid come to return you to your chambers. She's eager to apply Merit designs to that lovely long hair of yours. And after a couple more adjustments are made, the dress will be brought to you this afternoon. Now run along. You should rest before your official introduction to our court. Every member will be interested in making your acquaintance. And since it's my betrothal banquet, Riven has no choice but to play nice tonight."

I arch a disbelieving eyebrow, and she barks out a laugh, making Rothlo run for cover under her corset's pointed collar.

With deft movements, I redress in my soft tunic and pants, and then return to my rooms with my maid, Alina, wild butterflies dancing in my stomach.

Tonight, I'll see Riven again.

And I hope he doesn't kill me.

18

To Dance with a King

Merri

Many hours later, I sit at the far end of the Merit high table, swallowing my last mouthful of dessert and trying to stop my gaze from flicking toward the king. My eyes, the foolish appendages, do not obey.

Tonight, there is no sign of the weakened fae I helped nurse back to life in my antechamber. Riven's dark, richly embroidered clothes, towering crown, and strong, sinuous movements are those of an austere and powerful Unseelie king—albeit one who won't speak to me.

Before dinner, Elas insisted I dine with the royal family on the dais, sparking hope inside me. But when I mounted the steps,

Lidwinia brought me to stand before Riven, and he promptly extinguished any burgeoning warm feelings.

Seated on the sun throne, his bored gaze slid from my head to my toes. Then, as he stared somewhere over my left shoulder, he nodded once and resumed his conversation with the High Mage, Draírdon.

At least Meerade greeted me politely from her master's shoulder, although she did call me queen again, her mistake amusing Elas greatly.

Sipping wine, I survey the Merit Hall, and the surrounding conversations dissolve. Rowdy courtiers gather on either side of the old Blood Sun ritual fountain, a channel of water that runs from a point on the dais around the floor of the room in the shape of a massive triangle, the base forming a moat near the entrance to the hall.

Like the beams of Riven's sun throne, every burnished surface in the hall flashes with metallic brightness, the effect dark, dramatic, and sometimes blinding. A series of alternating black, red, and gold columns soar upward to meet the grand ceiling, where moonlight shines down in circular rays through domed windows.

Mechanical birds flit through the warm, heavily scented air and swaying palms and copper braziers add to the tropical atmosphere, reminding me of tales of the night markets in the Hidden Realm's Meedyean Kingdom, where the sun turns the fae's skin every shade of gold.

Despite the warmth of the Merit climate, the fae are as varied in color as those of my own land—their skin glimmering in hues of silver, brown, black, ivory, green, and some even variegated, like dazzling rainbows.

The wicked king El Fannon and his repulsive son Temnen have been dead many years, and still the air resonates with darkness. Cruelty once reigned supreme in this court, and tormented spirits still haunt the hall, evidence of the lives lost to the Blood Sun ceremony that Isla and Raff had the misfortune to witness in extremely gory detail.

Thankfully, when Riven ascended the Merit throne, he transformed the ritual into a celebration of life, not an end to it for some unlucky fae every moon turn.

Needing a respite from being the center of attention, I rise without a word and sneak down the left side of the dais steps and merge with the crowd.

Courtiers dance in elaborate patterns over the black marble floor while I stand at the back of the assembly and gaze up at the high table, pretending I'm not searching for any fae in particular.

Lidwinia looks resplendent in a gown spiked with gold, a glowing scepter in her hand, and Elas seated beside her with his wings flared dramatically. Behind them, a magnificent backdrop of stars sparkles through a window as wide and tall as the castle itself, a breathtaking sight. I scan the fae seated at the table again, unable to find the person I seek.

The Unseelie king has disappeared.

After scowling his way through the betrothal ceremony and dinner, Riven has vanished in the short time it took me to descend the stairs and walk to the rear of the hall. He must have transferred directly to his bedchamber, so he can grumble privately to Meerade until he falls asleep—no doubt the highlight of his day.

If only for the sake of appearances, why couldn't he speak civilly to me tonight? Would it have been so difficult a task? His coldness wounds like a knife, hemorrhaging loneliness and homesickness from my heart.

How I wish I could send a message to my family and hear news from them in return. But it's impossible. A letter from me would break Ether's enchantment, not only confirm I'm missing but also reveal my location. Then my father would unleash an almighty storm on the Merit City and raze it to the ground.

Not an ideal outcome if I'm determined to save their king, which I am.

My disturbing train of thought and the clove and frankincense-scented smoke curling through the hall make me dizzy. I urgently need a large dose of fresh air.

Positioned opposite each other in the middle of the hall are two giant alcoves opening onto long balconies and the star-studded sky. A perfect place to recharge.

As I weave through the crowd, I choose the balcony to my right, the one with the best view of the cliffs and the dark Obsidian Sea.

A warm breeze rustles the sleeves of my gown as I walk to the stone balustrade and lean my elbows against it. I stare across the ocean toward the ebony and white towers that rise from the middle of the water like two needles embroidering a pattern of stars on the fabric of the sky.

Out here, the noise of the fiddles, bodhrán drums, and dancers' caws and hoots is muted, and I feel calm and sure of myself once more.

Stepping onto the bottom rail, I lean over the balustrade, rough stone grazing my belly as I spread my arms wide.

I call the wind to whip around my body. "Come Zephyr, softest, sweetest queen," I whisper. "Come bless your wandering child with your comforting caress."

The wind obeys and twines my limbs, tugging my hair from the complicated style Alina created earlier, and billowing most of it out toward the ocean. I laugh and laugh with joy.

I wish I were a bird, a falcon. Indeed, if I were my father's son instead of his daughter, I could shift into a griffin, dive from this balcony, soar into the night sky, and then return home.

Home.

What am I doing here in this dark place of metal and magic?

Self-doubt claws again at my insides, but I sweep it away with a harsh sigh, refusing to submit to it. My purpose is sound, my intentions pure. I'm here for two reasons—to save Aodhan from the curse and Riven from himself. My dreams and visions prove the Silver King needs me, that we're somehow connected—he just doesn't know it yet.

"Take care or you'll fall to your death," comes a deep voice from the shadows—the Merit king himself. "Unless, like your royal male line, halfling Seelie princesses can shift into giant flying creatures. If so, then by all means, Merrin, leap."

The king leans against the same balcony as me, the distance between us vast. He grips the balustrade tight enough to crumble it to dust, so his bones, not mine, will more likely end up smashed upon the rocks.

"Thanks for mentioning I'm a halfling, Riven," I grumble. "It's exactly what I need reminding of while alone in a foreign kingdom, treated like an outcast."

"Pardon?" he says. "I cannot make meaning from your soft, hurried mutterings."

"Then come closer."

Wind rips the circlet of silver feathers from my head. I whip my hand out to catch it, laughing as I miss, and it tumbles down, down, down.

A silver shadow blurs beside me, and then Riven hands back the circlet, his brow twisted in a frown. "You don't like the diadem our smiths made for you, Princess?"

"No. I mean, yes, of course. But they shouldn't have gone to any trouble. I rarely wear such finery back home. And if I do, I like to weave circlets from fallen vines and leaves."

His frown deepens. I've angered him. I didn't mean to sound ungrateful.

Placing the circlet on my head, I arrange my hair around it. "It's beautiful, Riven. I'm truly honored by this gift. I shall treasure it."

He makes a huffing-grunt, sounding like an angry bear. "If you really cared for it, when it tumbled, you would've commanded the wind to return it."

"I could have, yes, but Lady Zephyr appreciates pretty gifts, too. I thought she might enjoy playing with it."

Silent, he turns his gaze toward the towers in the sea, his knuckles standing out white against the balustrade in the moonlight.

"I love the circlet, Riven."

"How can anyone be sure whether you're speaking the truth or telling easy lies to flatter and win favor? This halfling skill must make it difficult for your people to trust you."

"I can't tell *easy* lies. And, if possible, I prefer to avoid them at all costs. Lies twist everything into inextricable knots."

"Some fae prefer their communications complicated," he replies.

This conversation skirts close to an argument, and a change of subject is in order. With a puff of air, I blow hair from my face. "You don't seem all that happy to be celebrating your sister's betrothal. Do you not approve of Elas?"

"Of course I do. I gave Lidwinia permission to wed a fae who's not of royal lineage gladly and wholeheartedly. And, even if I didn't like Elas, I still would have done the same. All fae should have the ability to choose their partners."

Oh. I wasn't aware he had a heart, let alone a whole one.

"Well, then, what could be causing your ill-tempered mood?"

He sighs. "I have a lot on my mind."

"A problem shared is a problem halved."

Blue eyes bore through me. "Which fool ever said that?"

"It's a human saying. One that is quite true, I believe."

He snorts. "For princesses perhaps. Not for kings."

I take deliberate slow breaths, tamping down my anger. "Why haven't you answered my requests to meet with you?"

"Merrin, I must ask *you* something," he begins, completely disregarding my query. "My sister..." He trails off, inspecting the oak tree's dara knot on his ring—a symbol of power, destiny, leadership, and wisdom engraved on soul-mirroring silver. "Lidwinia insists I ask you to dance," he states, those startling eyes immobilizing me.

"And you certainly don't look happy about it," I reply, hoping he'll disagree.

Silent, the Silver King stares.

"Fine. Shall we get it over with, then?" I suggest.

"Of course." With a barely concealed grimace, Riven offers his arm.

I take it and gift him with my brightest fake smile. "Cheer up," I say as I close my eyes, conjuring a great gust of wind. It blasts Riven's hair out behind him, then tangles silver strands around his crown and the sharp points of his ears. With a flick of my wrist, I smooth out the mess, restoring his elegant glory.

"A nifty and annoying trick," he says, looking down his nose at me. "You're brave to toy with an Unseelie king."

I laugh. "Other than transferring, I've yet to see you perform even a simple conjuring. Perhaps because you can't."

"I'm not a trained monkey. Since we no longer participate in the Blood Sun ceremony each dark moon, what do you imagine powers our magic and technologies?"

I shrug. "I'm sure you can't wait to tell me."

"My druid's magic harnessed from my own bloodletting. Without me, this land and all its creatures would crumble into the very sea you look upon. How's that for a parlor trick?"

"Your own *bloodletting*? Sounds positively gruesome." I force a fake shiver and stifle a laugh, pleased to see him grit his teeth at the edges of my vision.

I glance down, finally noticing our arms are still linked and how close we're standing. He notices, too, his eyes wide as he steps back and tugs me into motion.

We stroll into the Great Hall and join the crowd on the dance floor, my mind and senses already spinning. Moon and flame light the room and enfold me in a sensual ambiance as Merit pendants flash in the darkness, making me squint against their glare.

The king's pendant lies dark in its gilt frame against his leather and velvet tunic, proof he wears it purely for ceremonial purposes, as he once claimed during our picnic at Emerald Bay.

We pivot and face each other, our reluctance to begin a vibrating wall of dense energy between us. The music is loud, the crush of bodies uncomfortably hot, and I grow warmer as Riven steps closer.

The king takes a breath, his lips parting to speak, but before he utters a word, Meerade swoops from a lofty rafter and lands on his shoulder.

"Where is your rodent, Queen?" she screeches like a petulant toddler. "Where rodent? Where? Where?"

"Cara is at home, and she's a mire squirrel, not a rat. And, also, I'm not a queen but a princess of the Seelie Court. Don't you remember visiting us when your master was wounded in the Land of Five?"

The owl ruffles her feathers, the white fluffing up prettily and the black metal ones standing on end like tiny plates of armor.

"Silver. Silver. Silver," she repeats while directing her mechanical eye at me in a strangely accusing fashion.

"Meerade, mind your manners," says the king. "Princess Merrin is our guest."

Interesting choice of words. He should take his own advice and be more pleasant, too.

"It's fine," I say, adjusting the circlet on my brow. "Direct communication is always better than secrecy and avoidance. Say what you think, Meerade." I smirk at Riven, hoping he'll take the hint.

Meerade pecks at my circlet. "Wrong crown!"

Pain and something undefinable flashes over the king's face. "Be gone now, Meerade. Merrin and I must dance for my sister's pleasure."

He tosses the owl into the air, and she flaps away, screeching what sounds like *foolish Riven*. She flies toward the dais and lands on the back of Elas's wing.

Riven holds his hands out toward me. "Shall we?"

I step into his embrace, and his arm snakes around my waist, tugging me close.

I'm about to give the nod to commence our dance, when a blur of movement catches my eye—a girl spinning like a top, surrounded by a group of horned fae cackling and pushing her around each time her speed slows.

"Is that—?"

"A human? Yes." Riven looks over his shoulder.

Standing frozen in the king's arms, I watch the girl's hair fly like tangled black garlands, her arms floppy, reminding me of the dolls

Mother used to make from cloth and the protection spells that she sung into them as she watched me play with Balor when I was a child.

"Her name is Summer. Draírdon found her at the Shade Court, near senseless and raving mad. He bargained for her, brought her home, and now she is a favorite of our court."

Nausea stirs my still-digesting dinner. "I thought your court had given up the despicable hunt for change bringers. Riven, you have to send her home."

"Of course. I wish to do so, but she won't leave and insists she's the bride of Winter, whoever that may be, and that she must wait for him to find her."

Winter. Could it be...? I think of my raven-haired rogue of a brother, the male version of this beautiful waif, and shake my head at the floor.

"Do not worry, Princess. Lidwinia and I keep watch over her. These days, we don't promote torture in our court. Now hold on tight." He spins us into the dance at breakneck speed, and every dream I've ever had of him coalesces and moves along with us in my periphery.

Riven by the pond. Riven with snow falling on his shoulders. Silver hair in the snow, trailing through blood. Vacant blue eyes staring at the sky, seeing nothing.

Dead.

With his full lips pressed into a grim line, he whips us around faster, and I grin at his scowl and summon a tiny tornado. I throw my leg out and force us to change direction, dancing widdershins.

I expect him to laugh at my trick or at the very least smile, but he doesn't. The skin on his palm heats, burning my own, but I don't allow him to take back control of our dance.

Tonight, I'm in charge.

Harnessing the wind's power, I slow our movements and speak firmly. "Tell me about the hidden verse of the Black Blood curse, Riven."

With the flick of his chin, he banishes my air magic and brings us to an abrupt halt. A wild dance continues around us, the human girl, Summer, still spinning and spinning.

Behind us, the Celestial Skyway pulls into the station, visible through the windows at the rear of the throne. Latecomers disembark from the elevated rail car—a group of spindly pixies, their gray skin corrugated like tree bark and black wings spiked with glowing thorns—falling over each other, drunk with laughter and Dana knows what other enchantments.

Riven's chest labors like bellows, his eyes glowing so intensely they're a trial to look at. Not once during our dance did he appear breathless. My request has shaken him.

"What do you know about it, *Merrin*?" he asks in a rumbling growl.

I lift my chin. "Nothing. Only that one exists, and it's the key to ending the curse. I need to find it and help Aodhan. I don't want him to suffer as the past Elemental heirs have. I believe it may be concealed somewhere in your city."

"And I believe the time has come for you to return to yours." He thrusts me from his arms as if I'm covered in poison ivy, paying no mind to the nearby Merits who gasp in shock. "*Now*."

Full of power, the word echoes in my skull like an incantation. But I can't be swayed, *won't* be swayed from my purpose.

Teeth gritted and palm outstretched, he takes a determined step forward as though he's about to cast me into another dimension.

Could he do that?

I press my heeled leather shoes into the marble. I won't retreat.

His other arm shoots out, and then, thankfully, Lidwinia slips into the space between us, pressing him backward with her palm on his chest.

"Riven darling," she purrs, sliding her arm around his waist and smiling up at him.

Of course he would have to be the tallest fae in the room, probably in the kingdom. Right now, I find it a very unlikable attribute—which is entirely nonsensical.

"You're terribly dour on such a happy night and have come quite close to ruining my mood. Is that what good brothers do, ruin their sisters' special occasions?"

"Lidwinia, you don't understand…She—"

"*She* is a guest at our court, and you need to make up for your bad behavior tonight by granting me a special wish."

"What? Another? I've already danced with her at your bidding," he says as though I'm not standing beside him with fully functioning ears. "What more would you have me suffer to purchase your contentment this night?" He lifts his crown and rakes fingers through his hair, his expression terrible to behold. The crown goes back on, and he sighs. "But of course. Name your price, Sister, and I shall pay it, though not gladly."

Ouch. My palm goes to my chest, pressing against the holey stone.

Lidwinia tsks. "Stop that. Do you know who you sound like at the moment? Our terrible brother. I was going to ask you to glamor Merri from Draírdon's notice, since only your power surpasses our mage's, and he's been leering at her all night. But after hearing those ungracious words leave your lips, I think I'll beseech you to perform a different task."

Silent, Riven squares his shoulders, his iolite gaze hardening.

"Tomorrow, you will take Merri riding and show her one of our favorite picnic places."

"But I have duties to attend to," Riven says through gritted teeth.

Probably only a whole lot of scowling and grouching at his courtiers.

"And now you have one more." Lidwinia twists her fist into the fabric at Riven's neck, tugging him close. "At breakfast, I'll give you instructions. Tell me now if you'd prefer to break your sister's heart on such a memorable night, because if you do, I'll need a little notice before I see you next, so I can summon the will to speak to you."

"Fine." Sweeping his hand before him, Riven bows low, then rises to kiss Lidwinia's cheek. "It will be as you wish. I shall be your humble servant on the morrow and perform every duty that you set out for me to my best ability."

Lidwinia smooths a lock of his glossy hair from his cheekbone. "And you'll perform them with a smile, I hope."

"Oh, now you ask for the impossible." He cuts a quick bow in my direction, stares at my fancy boots, and mutters, "Goodnight,

Merrin." Then he turns and departs through the main entrance, brushing off eager courtiers like swarming bees from a branch as he goes.

Halfway to the golden doors, his body wavers and a glamor settles over his regal form, and instead of the Silver King, a blond-haired youth exits the Great Hall in his place.

"Impressive," I say to Lidwinia. "I had no idea he could change his entire appearance like that."

"Indeed," says Elas, sidling up to his betrothed. "Our king has many hidden talents." He flares his black metallic wings, enfolding Lidwinia's shoulders. "Shall we dance again?" he asks, sharp fangs poking over his smile.

"As long as you promise not to drink from me if it's a slow dance, then yes. You know it drives the court mad with blood lust."

"Of course, my beloved. Anything you wish."

Lidwinia smiles. "Don't worry about Riven. He often leaves banquets early because he's much too serious to have any fun. Perhaps when he marries, he'll allow himself to be happy again, as he was when our mother was alive."

Riven married? What fae could ever meet his exacting standards?

Elas slips Lidwinia's arm through his, and they glide toward the middle of the dance floor. Sliding off the happy couple, my gaze lands on the spinning top in the corner, the mortal girl, Summer, still dancing at breakneck speed and circled by unfriendly looking fae.

With a glare fixed on the court's High Mage, who's conducting her movements with high-pitched screeches and twirling fingers, I carve a short path through the crowd toward them.

"What are you doing?" I ask as I come up beside the mage.

"Enjoying ourselves," Draírdon replies, his focus on the girl. Then his murky brown eyes cut my way, nostrils flaring as if he smells something bad. "Oh, it's you, the halfling princess."

Standing this close to the spinning girl, I see the sheen of sweat on her pale skin, her gray dress so damp it's transparent, and how uncannily similar she is to my brother.

Dancing before me with her shaggy dark hair, black slashes for eyebrows, generous mouth, and luminous green eyes with a feline tilt, is the female twin of Wynter Ashton Fionbharr. Vulnerable and in danger.

"This is cruel," I say, and the group of pixies surrounding the girl laugh. "I thought torture was history in this court."

Draírdon scowls. "The past, the present—it is all the same." He dips his head close to me and growls, "But she's fine. She loves to entertain, listen." He waves his gnarled hand, and she comes to a giddy stop, her body heaving as she pants, exhausted. "Are you having fun, Summer, my dear?" the mage asks.

"Oh, yes." Her eyes are glazed, unfocused. "This is a great party. So much fun."

"She's enchanted." I cross my arms, tapping my toe against hard marble. "At present, she's incapable of knowing pain from pleasure, Draírdon. But no girl, fae or otherwise, would enjoy such mistreatment."

"She will come to no lasting harm under my control, I promise you that much."

I note the words *no lasting harm.*

"Let me dance with her."

"You? What for?" he spits out.

"She is pretty and reminds me of my brother. I'm a little homesick this evening."

He leans in and whispers, "Well, no one is preventing you from leaving our court, Princess Merrin. Run along back to the Land of Five whenever it suits you. The sooner the better."

"When our king, Rafael, was a *guest* of your court. He didn't have the luxury to run along home when he felt like it."

Draírdon caresses the mottled skin of his throat. "Yes. I remember his visit fondly. In fact, the last time I saw your king, he was barely dressed, iron-cuffed around the neck, and snarling while the blood from his slashed chest streamed into our Blood Sun altar." Closing his eyes, a gruesome smirk smears his face. "A truly wonderful memory. One of my most precious."

The reedy lament of pipes and heady swoon of fiddles winds sinuously around my limbs, making me sway. I grin lazily at Draírdon, hoping I appear thoroughly enchanted by the music. With the snap of his fingers, the human girl stops spinning.

"Dance with her, then," croons the High Mage. "It will amuse me to watch you relate to your human kinfolk."

Rolling my eyes as I sweep past him, I clasp the girl's shoulders and say, "Dance with me. I'll keep you safe." I take her arm and guide her through the crowd, away from Draírdon and his sycophants. Drawing her close, I begin to dance, slowly and rhythmically.

Her body is limp against mine, humid puffs of breath from her moist lips warm my shoulder. "Are you all right?" I ask. "Do you need food? Water? Anything you require. Please let me know, and I'll make sure you get it."

I wait for a reply, but none comes.

"Summer, listen to me. I can help you. Why were you in the Shade Court when Draírdon found you? Did you fall through a portal from the human realm?"

This time she answers with small kitten-like mews.

Curse that mushroom-faced mage and his cruelty. Why has Riven done nothing to stop this? Most likely because he's too high and mighty to care about the plight of an insignificant human.

Rocking her gently, I whisper soothing words. "Don't worry. I'll find a way to help you return home."

The music stops, and she draws back, her vacant eyes wide. "Why would I want to go home? I'm waiting for someone. Can't leave until he finds me or he never ever will. We're from different worlds, you see."

The enchantment is deep if she believes she'll meet her beloved in the Merit Court. My heart bleeds for this girl, her dire situation, glamored, alone in a vicious fae court. So unfair. So tragic. It's true that faeries have always lured and prized human visitors, but in the Bright Court, even Grandmother never treated them so cruelly.

"Who is this fae you expect to make the acquaintance of?" I ask.

"The winter prince. We are fated."

The winter prince? She couldn't mean my brother, Wyn. Surely not.

Over Summer's shoulder, I see Draírdon creeping toward us, a sneer twisting his mouth. "Time to give her back," he says. "We have need of entertainment. Your plain dancing style amused me, but the human performs better solo."

"I'll come find you," I whisper, my words soft as a feather's stroke as I kiss her cheek. Summer doesn't look at me, simply follows the mage like an obedient automaton.

I close my eyes, power trickling into my fingertips. "Vengeful tempest come," I bid. "Greet the putrid-colored mage in the manner he deserves."

Wind whooshes from my right hand. It lashes toward Draírdon, then slams into his back, tumbling him face first into a towering plate of candied puddings on a nearby dessert table. He goes down hard, then jackknifes upright again, thick, sticky sauce covering his face.

As he curses and splutters, his blackened gaze finds me surrounded by a circle of fae who stifle their laughter behind claws and folded wings.

The human stands frozen between the fae and the mage, her eyes fixed on the floor glittering in the light of the brazier's flames.

"Don't move," I say, willing her not to flinch a muscle, so she'll avoid Draírdon's notice.

Energy vibrates around the mage's body. It buckles and an invisible wall of power detonates, blasting toward me. I send up a shield of air magic, no match for Draírdon's strength, but I refuse to be an easy target. A moment before the magic hits me, he grins and yanks the force back into himself, playing a cruel game.

Inclining his head in a pretend bow, he points at me like a scolding tutor, then pivots and scurries away to clean himself up. I may have made an enemy of Draírdon this evening, but at least I'm keeping him away from the human for the time being.

With quick steps, I close the distance between me and the girl and link her arm with mine. "Come with me, Summer. We'll say goodnight to Lidwinia and get you tucked up somewhere safe."

"But the dancing—"

"Can wait until tomorrow. You're in Faery. It's really not that hard to find a party to attend."

I take her hand and tug her limp-limbed body up the stairs to the dais, coming to a halt in front of Lidwinia and Elas who have given up dancing in favor of gazing into each other's eyes while they share wine from a single goblet. A sickeningly sweet spectacle.

"I see you've befriended our human visitor," says Lidwinia, smiling as though there's nothing wrong with the girl slouched beside me.

"It's hard to make friends with a thrall," I say.

With a thud, Elas drops his goblet on the table before him. "No permission was given to enthrall the girl."

"Then your High Mage assumes he doesn't need it. I'm going to bed. Can I leave Summer safely in your care?"

"Of course," replies Lidwinia. "We'll make sure her room is guarded and that no one can enter this evening."

Emphasis on this evening. I suppose that'll have to do for tonight. I'm too tired to argue, but I won't be tomorrow.

"Thank you." I smile. "And congratulations on your betrothal. I wish you eternal happiness. The banquet was delicious." Except for the soup garnished with the crunchy black spiders' legs.

"Did you have fun?" asks the princess. "Our courtiers enjoyed meeting you."

I think she means *ogling* me, because although not many Merits dared to speak to me, I certainly felt their eyes on me, their magic reaching out, grazing my skin with invisible tendrils. It wouldn't surprise me if Riven had warned them against talking to me, which would be petty of him. And typical.

I curve my lips in a smile and say, "Yes, thank you. It was an entertaining evening." But not in a wholly good way.

I squeeze Summer's hand—more for my comfort than hers, because, in her current state, the human is beyond both fear or care. "Goodnight, Lidwinia, Elas. I'll see you tomorrow."

"Yes. You'll need a good night's sleep to bear your outing with Riven. He's been in a tiresome mood of late."

Truer words have never been spoken.

Departing via the stairs next to the dais that sweep toward the west wing of the castle, I wonder how I'll survive more than a single hour in the company of the Silver King without pushing him off his horse with a swift gust of wind.

No matter what happens tomorrow, I need him to reveal what he knows about the Black Blood curse. Or at least give me clues to where the final verse might be stored.

I enter my chambers and flop backward on the bed, my thoughts whirling.

When I first arrived in the Merit Kingdom, I was optimistic and believed I could face the challenge of Riven's prickliness with ease. Now, I'm not so sure.

And my problems are three—the curse, the king, and the bewitched human girl.

19

Ride with Destiny

Riven

The rocky cliffs behind the castle descend through a steep forest of larch and pine, the crisp scent of the trees distracting me from the irritating presence riding beside me.

For the thousandth time since we set off today, I wonder how a fae who bears the weighty title of the Silver King could allow his sister to direct him to take an Elemental halfling on a quaint little outing. A picnic, of all things. "Damn ridiculous," I grumble under my breath.

"What did you say, Riven?" the aforementioned halfling asks.

By the Merits, she has better hearing than Meerade. My fingernails dig into the thick leather of Raghnall's reins, and I roll my eyes toward the treetops.

"Nothing important, I assure you." I turn my head and fix a foreboding frown on her. "In case you've forgotten, it's *King* Riven."

Merri leans over her sorrel mare's neck, and I notice that its mane is nearly the same shade as her hair, copper red under the green light of the tree canopy.

Laughter peals from her smiling mouth. "I'm afraid calling you that might be problematic. You see, if I use your title, then it's only fair that you should use mine, but I don't like being called a princess of anything. So I'm afraid I'll have to decline. Call me Merri, because to me, you are Riven, and Riven you shall remain."

Anger detonates in my skull, my thoughts tumbling and colliding as heat rushes from my chest to my gut in a disturbing mixture of fury and pleasure. Her disobedience wakes something deep inside me, a wild creature who enjoys the sound of its name spilling from her lips. Uttered in her sweet, husky voice, the word is foreign to me.

Riven, she says.

Who is this person she speaks of so breezily? Surely not a king, the most powerful fae in the Unseelie kingdom. *Her* Riven sounds like a friend. A lover even.

A spark of need ignites inside me, blazing into a fireball of longing. I quickly douse it, and it settles in my stomach like a lump of coal. Cold and heavy, it grates against my organs, whispering its name over and over.

Loneliness. Loneliness. Loneliness.

"I heard that," Merri says, and my blood gallops through my veins.

Her horse falls behind mine as the path through the trees narrows and forces us to ride in single file. Unfortunately, this new configuration doesn't stop her speaking.

"I know you're lonely," she says. "Even when Isla was at your court, she knew it, too. She believes—as do I—that you've created this problem yourself, and you simply need to choose happiness, reach out and take it. But that would involve opening up to others and the risk of getting hurt. Given your childhood, the way your father rejected you, I understand why you're reluctant to do this."

Thank the Blood Sun she cannot see the gray light of power seeping through my clenched fists, unleashed by the roiling twin emotions of embarrassment and fury.

I press my palm against a dull ache in my chest. "Perhaps it's just my journey through life, my fate to be unloved, reviled, and feared."

Behind me, the princess draws a deep inhalation, no doubt preparing to impart a sage-like answer to further infuriate me.

In the distance, Meerade emits high-pitched calls as she scouts the shallow valley below. "Be quiet," I tell the princess, listening with my head cocked. I wait three heartbeats. Four. Five. But only silence resounds. "All is well. You may commence your lecture."

She snorts. "Never mind. My wise words would only fly above the spikes of your great crown of consequence."

Crown of consequence? What does she mean?

Unbidden, my hand swipes the air above my skull. This morning, I chose a silver coronet of black diamonds and darkest carnelians, simple and well-suited to the day's purpose. But it's worrisome indeed if Merri can see the ethereal crown, made by the mountain goblins and bound to me in ancient druidic magic. The goblins made Mother's crown, too. But not Father's. I always found that fact fascinating. It made me wonder what the goblins knew about him that the rest of the court did not.

I consider the circumstances that cause the spectral crown to appear when I'm not wearing the physical one. When I sense danger, draw powerful magic from it. Or if I'm aroused by extreme emotions, such as anger or...other potent sensations. Today, only the third reason applies.

"Oh, this is lovely," Merri says as the trees give way to a captivating view. "I pictured all of your land to be dark and miserable, but this valley reminds me of home."

Will she still think it's delightful when the ferocious, fanged butterflies swoop, or the aggressive mechanical-hearted rabbits give chase, both tragic failed experiments of Draírdon's?

Only the strongest rays of midday sun push their way through the trees, but in the valley below, sunshine floods the land, casting a golden-green glow over everything. My chest expands on a deep breath, the fresh air infusing me with a warm peace and a flash of empathy for my Elemental companion.

"You haven't seen much of the city, then?" I ask, shifting my weight back so Raghnall halts.

Merri pulls up beside me. "It seems no one has had time to show me around, and I've been warned it would be dangerous for an Elemental princess to wander about alone. But I'm bored, Riven, and seriously considering stealing a disguise and taking myself on a tour. I've heard the Merit taverns are very entertaining."

I choke on my next breath. "Please. I beg you not to visit them. They're full of cutthroats and grifters. In fact, you shouldn't go anywhere without an escort. Tell me when you plan to have this adventure, and if I cannot take you myself, I'll send a guard to accompany you. Then you can traipse about the city in full disguise and stand a chance of returning alive."

Her brows arch, mercurial eyes widening. Then she smiles, the expression disarming, brighter than the sun, and for some reason, more pleasing than the sight of my beloved land spread before me.

What in the Merits could cause such sappy feelings to flow inside me?

Our horses ambling side by side, we start down the hillside in the direction of Citrene Creek, a favorite destination of mine since I was a child and a place of serene beauty.

"Where are we going?" the princess asks as she scans the lightly treed terrain.

"You'll soon see."

I feel Merri studying me, so I turn my glare on her, disappointed to find it isn't me who has captured her attention but my horse. Her gaze treks over my silver mare's coat and dark mane braided with rough diamonds and highly polished garnets that look as juicy as ripe berries.

"Your horse is beautiful," she says. "What's her name?"

"Raghnall."

"Hm... Raghnall. Interesting." She rolls the name slowly over her tongue. "Isn't that a male's name, though?" She smiles sweetly, diminishing the sting of her insult. "Raghnall means strong, so I find it strange that you, of all people, chose it for your gentle-natured mare."

Me of all people? What is that supposed to mean? Also, she hasn't seen my horse on a battlefield—Raghnall is far from *gentle*.

"With those words, Princess, you prove yourself narrow-minded. My horse has suffered much at the hands of Temnen and his band of sycophantic fools, and still she retains her strong, faithful heart. No creature is more deserving of such a powerful name as my Raghnall."

Bored of flying above us, Meerade swoops down and lands on my shoulder pauldron, sliding along the angled metal until she's leaning against my face. "Meerade stronger," she squawks indignantly. "No companion is as faithful as an owl."

"Indeed, my jealous friend." I caress her, the metal feathers clinking musically. "My owl is upset," I tell Merri. "You see, Meerade means pearl, and she believes that since she is steadfast in nature and untiring in her commitment to me, she deserves a name of greater significance."

Merri laughs, and I hide my smile by feigning great interest in the view to my left.

"Oh, I see," she says, "Perhaps something like Cathal, which means great warrior, would be more fitting."

A laugh rumbles from my chest, and this time, I brashly show my smile to the halfling princess. Meerade's wings flap above my head, and she screeches, the sound nearly destroying my hearing.

"No? You don't care for it, Meerade?" Merri asks, meeting my owl's gaze, the glass and metal eye spinning in displeasure, a warning sign that sensible members of my court would immediately retreat from.

Merri strokes Meerade's wing, and I flinch away. For an insane moment, I thought she was reaching for me. How stupid I am.

"Perhaps you've forgotten what pearls are known for, Meerade." says Merri. "These mysterious jewels of the sea signify great wisdom and serenity, alongside unparalleled integrity and loyalty. A pearl's power is in its ability to reveal right from wrong, good from bad. Valuable attributes indeed, and if I were you, I wouldn't complain of bearing such an auspicious name."

Meerade emits a high-pitched whistle followed by a succession of bright chirps, then flaps from my shoulder onto Merri's, burrowing her face under the girl's thick hair and nuzzling her neck.

I watch them with a strange hunger, then nudge Raghnall forward. "Come. I grow hungry. Let's waste no more time."

At the lowest point of the valley, we follow a stream as it weaves through the thick copse of trees along Citrene Creek. A comfortable silence enfolds us and, for the first time today, I fully relax in her presence, the weight on my shoulders easing, and my thoughts meandering through the environment, connecting with it.

The peace doesn't last long, however, because without warning, she starts to hum, her voice leaping around from a low range to alarmingly high notes, like a willow warbler calling for its mate.

The corners of my mouth fold into a grimace. "What is that?"

"The song? You don't like it?"

"Ah. Well, not exactly. I suppose I don't mind it. It's very different than a usual faery tune."

"That's because it's a human song. My mother, Lara, taught it to me. It's called I Will Always Love You."

My chest squeezes tight. "An unusual name," I grumble. "I prefer titles such as Seachrán Sí."

Her laugh tinkles out like chimes dancing on winter branches. "Set Astray by the Fairies? I'm sure you do prefer it, Riven, King of the Unseelie."

"Ah, finally, you address me in the appropriate manner."

She smirks, then smiles properly. "The song I was humming is actually quite catchy. You should listen to the words."

"Must I?"

"Indeed. You must."

The warbling increases to an astonishing degree, this time accompanied by dubious lyrics I've never before heard the likes of. Bewilderment compresses my brow so severely I'm certain I've caused permanent damage to my muscles. "Please stop. I cannot bear the maudlin sentiment." Or the repulsive words of love befitting only the ears of children or intoxicated milksops.

She laughs, and then, thank the old gods, goes silent. When I sigh with relief, she mutters the song's vexing words under her breath, taunting me with her grin.

"Stop it," I warn.

"Of course," she says, looking pleased with herself.

I watch as she scans the tree canopy and then fight a groan as she sighs with deep contentment.

Why is she relentlessly carefree and happy? Shouldn't she be worried that I might choose to keep her in my kingdom forever? Or worse, that she might lose her life and never see her home again?

This girl is a mystery to me, likely because she's a halfling. I've never enjoyed the company of humans, and what is Merri but half one? No wonder her presence unsettles me.

"Your woods are brimming with wisdom, Riven. The tree spirits here are strong. They reach out to me, welcoming me with reassuring whispers. I like *this* part of your land very much."

I doubt the dryads are *welcoming* her. The Elemental princess is a dreamer who believes the best about her surroundings—the woods, trees, the damned sky, but also about my sister, and worst of all, *me*. I wonder if she'll live long enough to one day regret her childish optimism.

"Can you hear them speaking too, Riven?"

"What? The trees?" I ask, pretending I've forgotten her last words when I remember every one I've heard her utter. "Of course. This is the ancient druidic forest of Blackthorn. The unseen beings and creatures that dwell in its rocks and waterways help fuel my kingdom's power."

Rust-colored eyebrows rise. "Blackthorn, huh? My mother came from the human city of Blackbrook. It's similar in name, is it not?"

Another scowl wrings my brow. "Barely. And it is of no significance."

"If you say so, Your Majesty." She dips her head in a bow, mocking me as only she would dare. "And is Blackthorn Forest's magic dark, like your Blood Sun ritual was? To me, it doesn't feel that way."

I roll my eyes toward a golden birch, releasing a sigh. She speaks as if she's an authority on all the wild beings of Faery, when in reality, she is a mere babe compared to the archaic entities that dwell here waiting to swallow her whole with glee.

I clear my throat, my mind abuzz with conflicting emotions—misery and a horrid longing for something I dare not name. "The Lady is strong in the Elemental woodlands, Merrin, but here in the Merit Kingdom, the Horned Lord, Cernunnos, rules. It is by his benevolence that we continue to flourish."

"Are you a druid yourself, then?"

"I respect and am guided by their ways. Theirs is the oldest of sacred paths—and I strive to walk along it with an unsullied heart, just as *they* did when they prevailed here long ago."

"Unsullied? What do you mean by that?"

Raghnall's step falters on a rock, but she soon regains her balance. I, however, do not.

The lump in my throat swells like slow-death candy, and shivers roll down my spine in alternating waves of fire and ice—a frigid cold to match the discomfort I feel around this subject and wicked heat because...well...because of the very ideas it inspires.

Fire.

Ice.

More fire burning hotter, the flames licking low in my gut as images of Merri in my arms burn me to a cinder.

"Riven?" Her mouth gapes open. "You look feverish. Are you all right? Before, did you mean... Were you telling me that you keep your *body* pure? As in..."

As her voice trails away, I keep my face averted, afraid she'll see my depraved desires written clearly upon it, the terrible, unwanted heat sparking in my eyes.

I nod and confirm her suspicions, cringing at her sharp intake of breath.

Now she knows that I, Riven Èadra na Duinn, king of all the Merits and Unseelie creatures, have never once lain with a fae. Yes, I've been tempted, and on more than one occasion I came close to losing control.

Very close indeed.

When I was younger and hadn't committed to the old path, courtiers, the wild fae, river nymphs, dryads, even the leanan sidhe tried to tempt me with their caresses. But I was strong and resisted, mostly because whatever my wicked brother did, I did the opposite.

Many times, I've pondered the idea that if Temnen had been kinder, not so cruel, perhaps I would have indulged in an Unseelie prince's darker tendencies. Perhaps his and my father's ways forged the king I am today. A pure one. A lonely one.

Meeting the Seelie princess after years of dreaming of her enigmatic eyes, guileless smiles, and wild, carefree laughter, has challenged my resolve to focus my energy, my strength on my kingdom alone.

But I *will* remain steadfast and committed to my purpose. For me, there is no other choice.

And yet...I burn to ask how many lovers she has taken in her life. She's young, but fae of both the Light and Dark Courts relish in uniting their bodies with others. For all fae, it is as natural as breathing air, well, except for *me*.

Still, I yearn for knowledge of those who have touched her—their names, where they live and—

"*Riven*," she shouts, dragging me from my spiraling thoughts. "Will you answer my question?"

Heat sears my cheeks, and I dip my head so my hair wings my face, hiding it from her. "And why is it your business to ask a king such intimate questions?"

She puffs out a long breath, and russet and gold leaves fall from the trees, dancing around her shoulders, then landing on her cloak like nature's embroidery, a gift for the Princess of Air. "Well," she says. "If you won't speak of past dalliances, what about love, then? Have your feelings been engaged before?"

"Love!" I scoff. "What is love but a series of curses cast upon a soul? You should be well acquainted with this concept since the Black Blood curse has infected your family's heirs for many generations."

"You're wrong. They may have been cursed, but it was always love that saved them."

"And you talk too much, paying little mind to your surroundings and giving far too much attention to the inner-workings of the minds of those in your company. Look, we've arrived at our destination." I sweep my arm around, indicating the small clearing beside the creek surrounded by a half-circle of sacred oak trees. The Druid's Circle.

I ask Raghnall to stop, and she does.

Swinging off my horse, I say, "Dismount, and we shall eat. Are you very hungry?" I hope she is, because if her mouth is occupied, she won't bother me with endless chatter. And questions. Always the difficult questions.

"Actually, I'm ravenous. What delicious treats have you brought along for us?" she asks, smacking her lips together.

I stare at the velvet rosebud of her mouth, its shape so enticing, so fascinating. I wonder what *she* tastes like?

Those lips part, and she speaks. "Riven?"

"Hm?"

"Where's the food?"

Food?

Blood Sun, the picnic food!

I picture the hamper Lidwinia presented me with at breakfast this morning, the fresh bread rolls, fruit, and pastries spilling from under a silver-and-gold-checkered cloth, exactly where I left it on the high table. My ribs contract around my disappointment, the shame of my carelessness a sharp pain beneath them.

I inhale raggedly. "What is forgotten is forgotten. It matters not," I say in the haughtiest voice I can summon, releasing Raghnall's reins so she can forage around the undergrowth.

Uncertainty flickers in Merri's eyes. "Right...so perhaps you forgot your favorite goblet or knife, but you didn't forget to bring any food. Did you?"

How can I admit that my state of agitation when I departed caused me to leave the hamper behind? She will think me an utter fool.

I straighten my spine and glare at her. "I plan for us to feast off the many delights of my land."

"Oh?" Her dazzling smile is back. She seems impressed. "So, you'll be hunting and cooking for me then?"

"Well...not precisely." I'll use magic to prepare food for her. I'm a king of Faery, not a kitchen maid. "Wait and see. I predict you'll be pleased with the results."

I offer my hand to help her dismount, but she ignores it, alighting with speed and elegance.

I spread a dark saddle blanket embroidered with constellations near the water's edge and beckon her over. "Please sit down, Princess Merrin. I'll gather our feast."

Astonishingly, she obeys without complaint.

Meerade follows me into the trees to search for wild greens, berries, tubers, and herbs, her rasping barks sounding suspiciously like laughter.

"Be quiet," I tell her as I shove mushrooms into the pouch I carry. "You've seen me hunt and gather food enough times in the past. There's nothing funny to see here."

She hoots louder as she takes off through the leafy branches, returning to the creek and the pretty halfling princess.

When my pouch is full, I wend my way back along the riverbank, stopping to grab a fat trout from the rocky stream. I smile at my catch. *This should satisfy the halfling's fastidious demands.*

Although, where Merrin Fionbharr is concerned, I can be certain of nothing.

20

The Nicor

Riven

When I return to the clearing, Merri glances up expectantly. "Oh, you've caught a fish. I thought I heard you say you weren't going to hunt."

"What I've done is called *fishing*. Have you not heard the term before?" Turning toward the trees, so she doesn't see me wince at my impulsive words, I search the undergrowth for wood.

While the girl watches my every move, I pile up kindling and heavier branches, and then start a fire with magic. I quickly gut then wrap the fish in foraged herbs and leaves, tie it to a branch resting between two logs, and then roast it over the fire.

When my mouth is watering from the fish's smoky scent, I kick down the fire and lay scrubbed tubers in the coals, leaving them to cook.

I fetch the water pouches and hand her one, then watch her throat ripple as she drinks deeply. After I break the fish into portions and lay the feast out, I rest back on my haunches and contemplate my work.

Yes. Our meal looks most pleasing, and I used barely any magic to create it. Perhaps I am a cook after all and should offer my services to Estel in the kitchens whenever I grow bored with my kingly duties, which is a far too frequent occurrence. Presiding over court schemes and politics is a chore I'll likely never come to relish. Yes, I was born to rule but certainly wasn't raised to it. That was Temnen's role. May Dana save his putrid soul.

"Eat," I say, directing my open palm toward the food.

Folding her legs underneath her green and gold tunic, she takes a handful of berries, popping them in her mouth. Bright red drops of juice bead her bottom lip, seizing my attention.

She swallows, then inhales a fast breath. "Riven, I need to speak to you about the human girl at your court. About Summer."

I arch an eyebrow, but offer no comment as I begin to eat.

"Your High Mage is abusing her."

Chewing slowly, I sift through memories of the human at court, reliving each time I've seen her, the images shuffling through my mind's eye. "Impossible. I've given orders that she's not to be harmed, nor is any fae or *being* for that matter, including Draírdon, allowed to lie with her by means of trick or enchantment."

"Okay," she says. "Regardless, I've witnessed her being treated poorly, made to dance, and sing, and abase herself for the entertainment of others. She's underfed, dehydrated, and at a breaking point. Your mage is stretching the meaning of your orders to a ridiculous and dangerous degree. How can you allow this?"

Could I perhaps be oblivious to acts of cruelty performed right under my nose? It *is* possible. I've been distracted of late.

"Allow it? I've never seen evidence of it."

"Then you are blind. Anyway, I'm telling you it's happening. Send her home," Princess Merrin demands.

"I cannot. She doesn't wish to leave my court."

"If she were in her right mind, I assure you, she'd run screaming from your throne room. So you'll do nothing and permit her to be danced to death. Is that what you're saying?"

"No. I'll forbid Draírdon and his associates from being alone with her." I scan the nearby branches for my owl. "Meerade, shortly you must leave us and pass this message to our High Mage. Tell him that when I return, I'll have new orders for the court regarding our human visitor. In the meantime, he's not to go near her."

A wide smile blazes across Merri's face, and Meerade screeches, "Mushroom mage! Trouble!"

"Mushroom mage?" I mutter. "Wherever could she have heard such a strange term?"

Merri's cheeks stain crimson. "I have no idea," she says, wincing as though caught in a lie.

"Be at ease. I'll place Lidwinia in charge of Summer. You may see her whenever you wish, and if you find a way to convince her to leave my city, then with my blessing, she may go."

"Thank you, Riven. I hardly slept last night thinking of the girl's suffering. With great power, comes great responsibility. The strong must strive to care for those who can't look after themselves."

"Yes. Unlike my father, I agree with this sentiment."

The brilliance of her smile dispels the shadows on the dappled bank. Why must she look at me this way? As if she sees beyond the crown, deep into my being, and is *fond* of me, *likes* me. And even more staggering—is happy to be in my company.

Of course, if she knew my innermost thoughts, she would flee and never look back.

With fleeting glances, I observe the Elemental halfling, watch how she folds the fish around berries before placing it in her mouth. Every movement is slow and deliberate, her face expressive, showing unabashed enjoyment, as if she lives each moment to its fullest.

Merri appears grateful for each experience, more druid-like in her bearing than I am at present, my mind a mess of conflicting desires.

To harm, to hold. To crush, to caress. To protect, to kill.

Choices. Choices.

A soft laugh wakes me from my musings.

Merri.

"What?" I ask, blinking away visions of scarlet hair floating on a bed of snow.

"Look at Meerade." Merri points to the trees. "She's trying to befriend a tiny bird. The wren is rightly terrified."

"Yes, the bird is smart." The smoky flavor of the fish explodes in my mouth as I chew quickly. "Meerade is like a wolfhound who thinks they're a tiny lapdog. One affectionate kiss from that hooked beak and her friend the wren would be no more."

"My dad's dog, Balor, is like that, always knocking moss elves over in play. He has no idea why they run when he bounds toward them with his tongue flapping in joyous greeting."

I cringe at the thought of Everend Fionbharr and his devil hound. Out of all the fae in the seven realms, why must Merri be *his* daughter?

"Riven? When you and Lidwinia left the Lowlands, how did you and your entire army disappear as one through an opening in the air?"

"Simple. If our Merit powers are strong enough, as mine and Elas's are when combined, it's possible to transfer large groups at the same time."

"Impressive."

I take more fish and crispy tubers and continue to watch her as I eat. For a spoiled Elemental royal, she's uncommonly interested in her environment. Compared to the ice princess of my dreams, she is not at all how I imagined she would be.

"Oh," she says, a perky expression chasing away her thoughtful one. "I've been meaning to thank you for the beautiful chambers you have me situated in. It's very generous of you to put me up in such luxury when I would've been content with a room above the stables."

A hot knife digs between my ribs. Damned embarrassment again. I grunt and say, "It's nothing. You should see *my* chambers."

Both our eyes widen at my words, then with a shudder, she says, "Oh. Well…" her gaze skimming the nearby bushes.

I clear my throat and capture her attention. "Last evening, why did you say that all your kingdom's heirs have suffered from the curse of the fated mates, but just before, you stated that love saved them. It cannot be both. Do King Rafael and Prince Ever still suffer now they are married to their chosen ones? And…" Before I change my mind, I take a quick breath and ask the question that brims behind my lips. "By all accounts, their marriages are love matches. Has love not made them…happy?"

She smirks. "I thought you weren't interested in *love* and its effects. But because I'm nice, I shall answer you anyway. Yes, they have suffered much. And, yes, love has made them happy. With a force as powerful as love, it's possible and sometimes preferable to exist in a state of constant flux. A deliciously painful condition, I've heard Mother describe it."

Delicious? I doubt that very much. It sounds extremely unappealing to be at the mercy of another fae or, worse, *human's* words and actions, vulnerable and weak if they shun you. This *love* business does not appeal to me. No thank you.

With my gaze tracing the contours of her face, it's my turn to give an exaggerated shudder. "How unpleasant," I say, focusing my attention back on the food.

She laughs at me again, then kneels to grab a handful of tubers, shoving them into her mouth. "Delicious," she says, repeating the word that's echoing through my skull.

Now only one tuber is left, and I quite fancy it for myself. In a blur of movement, I snatch it up, grasp her wrist, and place it on her upturned palm, closing her fingers around it. Her breath hitches, molten silver swirling in her wide eyes.

Let her go, I tell myself as my grip tightens on her bones.

Let her go.

Let her go.

But I don't.

I can't.

Like a tree coaxed by the sun's light, I lean closer, enthralled. The tug between our bodies is an insidious vine of magic, as old as the sorcery that runs beneath the earth, lives in every breath of air, drop of water, and burning flame.

One half of my mind wishes to strangle her here and now, eradicate the risk to my kingdom, for she can only bring its downfall. Why else would I have dreamed all these years of her blood on my sword? The other half of me, regrettably, burns to close the distance and taste the berries on her lips.

Crouching, I rock forward on my heels, then back again, unable to decide which direction I want to move—toward the girl or away—all the while, tormented by a vision of white and red. Snow and blood. Blood and snow. And Merri. Always Merri.

I can't stand it.

I cannot bear it.

Closing my eyes, I clear the horror of the vision with a hard shake of my head.

Now where was I?

Ah, yes. Staring at the mesmerizing ruby of the halfling's parted lips, the moisture glistening within.

Her eyes stare back as I inch forward, my own mouth parting. She should run, but she doesn't flinch or move a muscle.

No.

No.

Another head shake brings clarity.

Don't forget who you are, I tell myself. My mother's child. Not my father's. Never his. *Do not forget it.*

I begin a rousing internal lecture meant to banish thoughts of Merri for once and for all. I recall that the magic of the high druids was most potent when they were chaste and focused on their purpose. In my case, my focus is my steadfast mission to heal my land from the scars of El Fannon's rule, not to leap in and out of beds whenever someone takes my fancy, diluting my power.

That would be folly. The madness of youth. The deficiency of a selfish and untrained ruler.

Then I remember the chaos of the kisses I stole when I was imprisoned in her hidden chamber. Who kissed who first? On Beltane eve, it was her. I resisted, and then I didn't. And the other time... My blood quickened. My magic, too. And what happened? I nearly killed her then and there.

A kiss. A kill. A killer-kiss. Is this all I'm capable of when base feelings are roused? Harshness, violence? But never anything...*softer.*

My thumb strokes the silky skin of her wrist as she shifts forward, her short breaths loud and ragged in the silence. Unable to break her gaze, I dive forward, eager to drown in a pool of silver.

Closer.

Then closer still.

A loud screech echoes from the trees, and I reel back and swear, saved by Meerade's hunting noises as she heads back to the castle to deliver my message to Draírdon. Thank the Blood Sun because I cannot and *will not* allow myself to bend to the will of the Black Blood curse.

Ever.

Abruptly, I rise, knocking the last tuber from her hand. "I must check on Raghnall," I say, which is a ridiculous notion. My horse needs neither a nursemaid for a master nor any such hovering attentions.

A few strides into the brush, and I find Raghnall tearing bark from the trees. I rest my face against her warm coat, breathing deep her calming scent. I stroke her mane and murmur, "I don't understand what's happening, my friend. I'm not myself, and it terrifies—" A blast of dark energy strikes my gut, the force so strong a bolt of nausea makes me retch.

A creature has arrived in the vicinity, its nature vile indeed.

My heart vaults, blood forking through my veins like lightning. The halfling is alone! Leaving her unprotected, even for a moment, was a bad mistake. Perhaps a fatal one.

With my magical shield up and sword in hand, I dart back to the riverbank, skidding to a stop at the edge of the trees when I see Merri conversing with a creature in the water.

"No..." I whisper, fear quaking my bones. This creature will snatch the halfling away forever if I make the slightest sound or sudden move. Although this callous, shape-shifting nix usually hunts farther north, near Port Neo, he is, unfortunately, well known to me.

Frustration curdles in my gut. In the blink of an eye, I could blow the beast to pieces, but I won't dare, because in the same amount of time, he could reach out and take Merri to her death.

I can't risk it.

Sheathing my sword and drawing my magic inward, so it vibrates close to my skin, I move carefully forward, whistling a jaunty tune. I want him to know I'm aware of his presence but believe he's not a threat. Casual interest is what I hope to exhibit.

"Good day, Nicor," I say, infusing my voice with warmth and activating the subtlest glamor to appear smaller, weaker, *friendlier*. "How has the fishing been of late?"

Nicor's dark head snaps up, a snarl splitting his black lips. "Good day to you, too, Silver King. The fish are as vapid and boring as ever. They make a bland and uneventful meal. But I am very pleased you've kindly brought me a tasty treat. I shall relish it greatly."

Merri looks over her shoulder at me, revealing a bright smile.

To my eyes, the nix is an unpleasant sight, his mottled gray skin peeling off in rotten layers, black hair tangled and stinking like putrid weeds, fanged teeth dripping drool as it speaks. But the princess will see a different sight—a beautiful youth, his gaze wide and innocent and pleading for her help. Even his grating voice will sound melodious and smooth to Merri's ears.

With a wet sucking sound, Nicor drags his wiry body farther out of the water and up the bank. Closer to Merri.

This creature is no ordinary nix. He's one of Draírdon's half-mechanical experiments, a heartless puppet of evil. One side of his body is covered in black and silver metal scales, the bones inside fused with nickel and gold and horrendously strong.

Grinding my teeth to stop from rushing forward or releasing a blast of magic, I will my pulse to slow, clear my head, and focus my thoughts. I can't afford to make one wrong move or the halfling princess will pay for it with her life.

Merri turns back to the nix. "I'm afraid we only have a handful of berries left over from our lunch. But you're very welcome to them."

A barbed tongue lolls over its chin. "Tell your king that this paltry offering isn't the delicious meal I was hoping for." He licks his lips, drool stringing from his chin to his chest, but Merri only smiles at him, no doubt wondering why the handsome stranger is suddenly sounding a trifle insolent and rude.

"Well, he's not really *my* king." She throws the rejected food toward the trees, a treat for the birds and wood elves. "Would you like to accompany us back to the palace for dinner tonight? You're sure to find something more to your liking there."

"That is kind of you," says the nix, his voice now as savage as his gaze. "But I've already found something to feast upon, and the old king, El Fannon, granted me leave to eat whatever or *whoever* took my fancy should they pass along my banks."

This is correct. My father did indeed grant this terrible boon. A boon I cannot rescind and am bound to abide by.

The nix grins, his fangs chattering, spiked tail swishing with impatience. "Do I speak true, King of Merits?" Nicor asks.

"Indeed, you do." I take three large but slow strides forward then drop to my haunches beside Merri, subtle magic expelling calm authority from my every pore. "But in regards to this contract you made with my deceased father, I propose we make an adjustment to it in this instance. For amusement's sake."

A hiss wheezes from the creature's lungs as it reels backward. "What? Why would I agree to this?"

"Because she is *mine*." I say, bracing my muscles against the piercing pain of a part lie. None comes. She is in my court, under my care. Therefore I speak the truth.

Mine. Merri is mine.

I dare not hint at who she really is—a princess of the Seelie Court. If Nicor knew this, he would snatch her without delay, drag her under, kill her slowly. Painfully. Horribly.

"If you say so, King, then I must believe you. And, since you are our sovereign, I shouldn't try to take what is yours. But, by the rules agreed to long ago, I *can* should I still choose to. Which I believe I do, choose to take her from you, that is."

"As is your right, Nicor of the Dark Weeds. Unless... Unless you wish to barter with me and strike a new bargain. Purely for entertainment's sake, of course. Your reputation for craftiness precedes you. I doubt I could best you." Pain explodes inside my skull, and it takes all my power to keep my face a passive mask of friendly interest.

Merri's silver gaze is wide, bouncing between me and the nix, only now sensing that the appealing boy might be a danger to her. She wriggles backward a little.

"Also," I say. "These banks you've presented yourself on aren't your usual grounds. One could suggest that you're beyond your territory."

A snarl grates the air. "My territory was not clearly defined by your father."

The princess startles, and I put a calming hand on her knee to keep her still. Were she to run, the nix would drag her under with a splash, and her diminished air magic would be useless against this ancient creature, made one hundred times more diabolical by Draírdon's meddling.

"A mistake that I myself would not have made," I say with a light chuckle to arouse his anger.

Nicor's scales rattle and stand on end. "You fool. You will regret your insolence. You may be king for now, but I am as old as these waters I dwell in, and I recall when you were born. Such a shining, handsome child of silver. I remember the depths of your father's disappointment because you carried no true royal Unseelie characteristics, like your brother's antennae or your sister's tongue. How El Fannon wailed with grief when you showed yourself to be your mother's son and followed the path of the druids. Walked in the light, like one of *them*. Weak, your father said. My son is weak."

A one shouldered shrug and a smile. "You tell me nothing new. I've lived all my life in the shackles of his disappointment. The chafing wounds have healed."

The nix's lips compress. He wishes to rile me. To make me lose control. He slithers closer to Merri, bends his head, and takes a long inhalation, drawing her scent deep, taunting me with his hungry, quivering mouth. A slight tremor vibrates over Merri's skin, but she stays silent, just as I will her to be.

Nicor clacks his teeth together. "Are you aware of the rumors that make their way through the shadows of our land, King? The ones that whisper you shall not live to reign over us for very long?"

These words unsettle me. These words remind me that I sit beside and protect the girl who I've long dreamed will be the cause of my dethroning. Of my death.

Why do I not end this now and let the nix have her?

I unclench my jaw. "I am aware, yet I pay them no heed. Tell me, is this how you wish to delay your meal, Nicor, trading insults back and forth as children do?"

With a roar, he lunges for me, drawing back at the last breath, just before his fangs strike the flesh of my neck. Breathing slowly, rhythmically, I smile and click my tongue four times, as if chastising an errant hound. "Now, now, noxious nix. Try to show a little patience."

"Then hurry, King, and let us bargain for your halfling, and when I win, I'll take not only her, but your eternal agreement that I may expand my territory to encompass the entire Land of Merits."

I incline my head, a respectful gesture that hides my fury. "Indeed you ask for much, therefore I shall propose the terms of our bargain. If she agrees willingly and without coercion to go with you, you shall have her and all the territory to hunt in that you desire."

A rabid growl rumbles in his chest, a protest on his black lips.

"Wait," I command. "I will allow you to use magic for one more thing, because you're already wearing a glamor. And if I were you, I'd use it to wipe her mind of this conversation, then all she'll see is

276

your charming visage. I'll even stand by yonder tree, so she'll forget I ever spoke to you."

"Riven," says Merri. "I don't think this is a good—"

"Shh, all will be as it should," I tell her, then face the nix. "Well? What say you? Are you game or not?"

Hunger twists his features, revealing his desperation, his great need to consume the tasty girl before him. Recklessly, he says, "Yes. The bargain as you have worded it is struck."

His gnarled fingers snap between Merri's eyes, and her gaze turns vacant, her muscles soft and pliant against me.

"Good. We have made our agreement, and so the result shall be unchallenged," I say, standing abruptly and shoving hair from my face. As my arm swings downward, I flick two fingers at the nix's heart, destroying his glamor of innocent beauty.

Merri's eyes widen subtly.

Stifling a laugh, I walk to the oak tree, then cross my arms, and lean a shoulder against it. I didn't say I would refrain from using magic. Foolish Nicor. Greed and arrogance made him a careless bargainer.

He slides backward and sinks soundlessly beneath the water to chest level.

"Are you all right?" Merri asks with a frown. Having forgotten the recent conversation, she's likely wondering why the elegant young man has turned into a gruesome monster.

Nicor smiles, revealing a row of gray, pointed teeth. "No, girl. I require your help. I may have injured my leg badly and may soon have trouble staying afloat. I do not wish to die today. Will you come into the water and save me?"

"Save you? How would I do that?"

A mechanical arm shoots toward her, muscles rippling over metal bones, the palm outstretched in appeal. "Take my hand. Come in the water beside me, and I'll put my arm around your shoulders. It will be easy for me to use your strength. I promise."

Merri leans forward, and for a moment, my chest clenches, every tendon taut as a drawn bowstring.

"No," she says. "I don't want to help you. You're a creature of the fae. You'll heal in time."

Nicor splutters, those ugly teeth gnashing. "But you're beautiful. We will make a perfect pair down in the deep-dark beneath the currents, me, and what is left of you."

"I thank you, but I prefer the light. Be gone now. I have much to speak of with the king. Go hunt your fish, old nix."

With an enraged screech and a massive spray of water, Nicor springs from the river, both hands outstretched, aimed at the princess's throat.

I grit my teeth, drawing magic through the earth, and throw a spear of power at the nix's heart. Before it reaches its mark, an arc of silver flashes, Merri's lightning-fast response as she withdraws a knife from her boot and lunges to meet the nix in the air, plunging it deep into his corded neck. She tumbles to the ground with a thud, and my magic detonates in the water. Useless.

"Merri," I yell, running to her side then gathering her in my arms.

Squealing and cursing, Nicor clamps his fingers on the gushing neck wound and sinks underneath the water, leaving a swirl of blood and gore on top, the only remaining sign of its malevolent presence.

"Merri, are you hurt?" I ask, using my mind and hands to gently prod for damage. Thankfully, she feels perfect. Wonderful and...unbroken.

With her palms braced against my chest, she pushes out of my tight embrace and shoves onto her feet. "I'm fine, Riven. No need to fuss."

Cracking her neck side to side, she surprises me by summoning a whirlwind that combs through her hair, rearranging it before the tempest funnels back into the sky. "At least I can say I've finally had an adventure in the Merit Court."

"I'd wager that was not the kind of entertainment Lidwinia had in mind for you today."

Swiping mud from her tunic, she looks up wearing another of her charming smiles. "Nonetheless, it *has* been diverting."

Beyond my control, my eyes narrow into a glower. What type of Seelie princess would call a near-fatal attack a diverting experience? Not a typical spoiled one, that's for certain. And how did she move faster than my bolt of magic and then raise a strong wind immediately after? It appears her magic is not as diminished as she would have me believe.

After collecting the remains of our picnic, I return to our horses who are eating grass under an oak tree, serene and unaffected by the drama with the nix.

With my back to Merri, I pack Raghnall's saddlebags. "We should leave now," I say in a tone that brooks no argument.

"Yes, master." Merri's reply is soft but not *too* soft that I can't hear it.

An intoxicating fragrance of wild dog roses invades my nose, befuddling my mind as Merri plants a kiss on her horse's forehead, the halfling's body too close to mine for comfort and any clear thinking on my part.

An arm slung around her steed's neck and her expression curious, she says, "I'm surprised you didn't transform into your creature before. You saw through the nix's glamor from the start, didn't you?"

"Yes, his trickery can't fool me. But, alas, I cannot shift. I rescinded the ability when I began lessons with the druids."

"It was fortunate I was here to save you then," she says in a mocking tone, as if she means the opposite—sarcasm, as the humans call it.

And this is the problem with a halfling, one can never fully trust them. I grit my teeth and vault into Raghnall's saddle.

As Merri mounts her horse, a necklace swings from the folds of her tunic, the black holey stone I gave her, hanging on a finely braided cord of leather. My hand goes to my chest, fumbling for the arrowhead necklace lying against my skin. Merri's arrow.

We take off through the circle of oaks, the sun warm on our backs. As we ride up the valley into the depths of Blackthorn Forest, ascending the mountain toward the city, she is silent, leaving me to my thoughts, which are unbearable, tumbling and clashing like churning waves. Maddening and ungovernable.

Today, I tried to construct a wall around myself that would stand against her sunny smiles and bright, curious nature. Render me impervious and keep her out. This wall made of prejudice and suspicion collapsed the moment I saw her with the nix, vulnerable and in danger.

I know I should have let Nicor take her and remove her from my life forever.

But I didn't.

I *couldn't*.

And now, my failure to let another monster deal with her while my own knife remains bloodless will haunt me forever, because my visions clearly tell the tale—if Merri lives, my kingdom falls. It must be her blood that runs in rivulets through the snow, not mine.

For the sake of the Merits and the land I hold dear, the blood must not be mine.

Never mine.

"Riven?" Her voice whispers through the pine needles, sliding along the skin of my throat and face, like a caress.

Without taking my eyes from the path ahead, I grunt in reply.

"Just a warning, I plan to explore your city tomorrow, no matter what you have to say about it."

And here it is—another opportunity to get rid of her. What I do with it remains to be seen.

I breathe a sigh through my nose. "I'll have suitable clothing brought to your rooms in the morning."

Her head whips around. "Thank you! That will save me from searching for the laundry and stealing them."

I stifle a rare laugh, but not a wry grin. "'Tis no bother. Just don't say I never give you anything."

21

My Killer, My Love

Merri

The morning after my picnic with the Silver King, I wake with a heavy heart, longing for home and my family, questioning my sanity and reasons for staying here.

A sour taste in my mouth, I shake off the bedclothes and my nightmare of cruel hands wrapping my throat and squeezing.

In the dream, a dark voice demanded to know why I was here in the Land of Merits and what I wanted. I couldn't reply. The answer is far too complicated.

I lie in bed wondering what I *do* want. Without a doubt, to save Aodhan from the curse. But should I follow my heart and pursue the Merit king, make him kiss me again as he nearly did yesterday on the banks of the creek? Or is it best to ignore this pull between us, find the Black Blood curse, learn all I can about the Merits and their magic, and then leave, taking this information home to my father and Raff and help keep my kingdom safe?

And even if I wanted to draw Riven closer, do I possess the power to do so?

Yesterday, he made it clear he's attracted to me but also despises the fact. There is one thing I'm certain of, though—giving my heart to the King of Merits would be the worst decision of my life. And this leads me to the ultimate question. Even knowing this, can I stop myself from throwing my bleeding heart at him, anyway?

Sunshine blinds me as I sit up in bed, swathed in silk and furs and rubbing sleep from my eyes. My maid must have entered while I slept and opened the heavy drapes, revealing a beautiful cloudless day through windows set high above the Obsidian Sea.

Gold vines, leaves, and flowers glint prettily in the light, my gaze skimming over them and landing on the pile of clothes folded at the foot of the bed.

I scramble through the cut-velvet curtains that hang from bedposts as tall as fir trees, leaping onto the floor to inspect the molded leather armor, roughly woven pants, tunic, and cloak that together form my disguise for today's tour of the city.

The king followed his words with actions, which surprises me. A warm but foolish glow fills my chest.

After a visit to the bathing room and a bite to eat, I waste no time pulling on the new clothes. I strike poses in front of the gilt-framed mirror in the main chamber, grinning as I admire the snug fit. Oh, how I prefer the simplicity of brown and gray garments to delicate rainbow-hued gowns.

As I braid my hair into a thick rope I can easily conceal inside my hooded cape, several hard knocks wrap against the entrance to my rooms.

"Come in," I call, expecting to see Lidwinia or my maid, Alina, waiting on the threshold.

The double doors swing wide and reveal Riven standing in a wide stance, his leather-bound arms folded over his sculpted ornate breastplate, dressed for court business or a tithe audience by the look of him.

"Good morning, Merrin." He steps inside, mouth downturned and his haunted gaze skittering over the furniture and walls, no doubt assaulted by old memories. Sympathy pangs in my chest.

"Morning," I answer, giving him a warm smile that I hope will help chase away his ghosts. "Thank you for these clothes. They're absolutely perfect."

"I'm glad they fit. I chose them myself."

"Sounds unlikely." Hands on my hips, I twist from side to side, the cloak twirling around my calves. "But if you say so, Riven, it must be true. I had no idea you possessed the eye of a tailor."

He gives me a heart-stopping smile, making me stumble and flay my arms about to regain balance. His smile broadens as he appraises the fit, sending a bolt of heat to my stomach. "Well, I didn't say I made them. But I do take good note of details, such as the particulars of your form."

My mouth dries, and I force a grin. "Indeed, your talents are surprising. Are you my tour guide today?"

"No. Thorne shall accompany you."

"Thorne? Your friend the hedgehog, I presume?"

"I'm not *that* cute, Princess," says a tall fae as he steps out from behind Riven. "And I'm considerably more skilled with a sword than those prickly creatures."

With my mouth agape, I take in the newcomer. He's right. He's not cute. Frightening is a better description. Dressed in similar clothes to mine, he's the same height as his king, has a mop of short dark hair, a slightly crooked nose, and typical glowing faery eyes of gold. He's brutish, even handsome, and then he smiles. With a gruesome metallic grind, two formidable rows of jagged black teeth snap together. No, Thorne isn't cute. Not at all.

"If you've finished fussing with your appearance, we should leave right away." Thorne bows his head as we duck past the king and through the door.

Marching along the corridor in front of me, Thorne speaks over his shoulder. "If you'd like to see some interesting sights, Princess, you should pick up the pace. The market is only open for a couple more hours, and it's an opportunity to view the fae who don't often attend the court."

"Because Riven won't let them?" I ask, seeking confirmation he is a terrible king, a horrible fae.

"No. It's because they're wild and don't care for formality and extravagance. Riven invites all fae to court, even the ones who disgust him."

I grunt in reply, digesting the idea of Riven as a benevolent ruler.

We pass along wide, windowless hallways of black and gold, descend a series of shining onyx staircases, march through a large reception room, then follow a maze of narrow corridors for some time before we come to a carved stone door.

"Are you taking me to the dungeons?" I ask as Thorne pushes on the white stone.

"I wish, but, alas, no." He tugs two Merit pendants from beneath his cloak and passes me one. Like Riven's, both screens are inactive. "This is one of the more discreet exits from the castle that will lead us directly out into the city."

"If I have to wear this, shouldn't it be blipping and flashing like everyone else's will be?"

"No. Since Riven has been king, many no longer use the pendants as point collectors and data analyzers. Besides, we'll draw less attention to ourselves without the damn things squeaking and beeping."

That makes sense. The ornately framed screen hangs heavily around my neck as we descend a final set of steps. At the bottom, Thorne places his palm on a copper pad beside another white door. The door beeps, sliding open to reveal a cobblestoned street nestled between the narrow walls that line the top section of the town.

Bolts of blue sky are visible between roofs and the edges of buildings, not a cloud marring them. My magic sizzles along my skin, stimulated by the warm, spicy air. The smell of baking bread affects my stomach in particular, which growls as loudly as Balor on the hunt.

"Forgot to break your fast, did you?" asks Thorne, shortening his steps to match mine as we stride along the street.

"Not at all." Excitement curdled my gut this morning, so I only ate three slices of a spiky fruit that tasted pretty good even though it smelled like my brother's boots. It wasn't nearly enough fuel for an adventure. "I can't wait to see the city."

Thorne side-eyes me. "It's more akin to a fortress. Come, let's head to the market where you can purchase fripperies to your heart's content."

"Only if they're edible."

He squints, laughs, then directs me to hurry along with a violent hand gesture.

If the Merit City is a fortress, it's quite a spectacular one—flames, roving bands of musicians, and a myriad of rich colors enliven the deep slick shadows, creating a festive atmosphere under the industrial towers and spires of the castle. Market days are lively in any town, I suppose, even in the Unseelie kingdom.

As we trek, keeping to the edges of the growing crowd, I inspect the impressive Merit buildings.

Wrapped in black stone, they're patterned with straps of tarnished silver and copper, a mesmerizing mix of dark, burnished hues against the bright, soaring glass panels that jut from the structures at steep angles.

On the whole, the town reminds me of the human realm's modern factory districts, but one designed by an architect with a love of wildness and whimsy. Ivy, vining roses, and purple wisteria creep like pretty nightmares along arches and walls, growing vigorously in jets of steam and nearly obstructing the city's cogs and machinery.

While I'm busy gaping at the sights, Thorne elbows me out of the pathway of a fast-moving faun whose curling horns nearly take my head off. "If you close your mouth and open your eyes, Princess, I believe you'll have a better chance of navigating without causing or receiving injury," Thorne advises.

I draw my hood lower to hide my grimace. "Thank you for the tip. I can see why Riven sent you in his stead today. He wanted me to spend time with someone as equally infuriating as he is."

Thorne laughs and gnashes those frightening teeth at me before quickening his stride.

I jog to pull alongside him again. "Who are we posing as today? Cutthroats? Thieves? A dancing duo?"

"No. Traders from Port Neo."

"Ah, hence the fetching wicker basket decorated with small anchors you're carrying." I raise an eyebrow at the enormous odd-shaped woven bag he wears hitched over his shoulder. "It's very convincing and definitely declares we're not basket weavers."

"Beg your pardon? I crafted this myself."

A snort escapes me. "That explains a lot."

"You may laugh all you like, Princess. Every wonky weave and uneven stitch is mine. This bag happens to be my pride and joy."

"My sympathies then, Thorne. You need a different hobby."

Like a maze, the streets climb in a haphazard pattern up and down the town's jagged mountain until, finally, they open onto a large flat section of the town bordered by trading stores and stalls.

We stop and rest against a low wall with a view over the busy market, late morning sun warming our backs. A flock of seabirds cries in the distance, the sound drifting down to mingle with the cheerful noises of the market.

For the capital of the Unseelie kingdom, the atmosphere in the Merit City is surprisingly uplifting. It doesn't feel like a foreboding or dangerous place. What was Riven worried about? I could have ventured out alone without a problem.

In the city square, tree-lined walking paths spread out in geometrical designs, and at the center sits an enormous glass building called the Meritorium. The structure's dramatic slopes and planes bring back memories of the museums I visited with my parents in the human world many years ago, and I'm eager to see what treasures lie inside it.

"That's where Elas works, isn't it? In your technological advancement center?"

Thorne nods. "Yes. And you'll find our princess there most hours of the day and night, too." He tugs my cloak. "Come. Let's find something to calm that growling stomach of yours. It has quite the vocabulary."

We cut through a narrow street, arriving at the entrance to the market plaza without incident, but the moment we begin following our noses toward the food stalls, everything changes.

A dark vibration thrums through the air, but for no visible reason. None of the fae snarl or yell, or attempt to bite me. It's subtler than a physical threat. It's a feeling, an unpleasant sensation of being watched by an unknown entity.

I keep my head low, my eyes peeled, and don't mention my concerns to my companion. If I did, he'd only rush me back to my chambers as though I'm a child in need of cosseting, which I'm not. Far from it. Growing up with a brother like Wyn, I was quite young when I learned how to put up a decent fight.

Besides, I wouldn't mind an opportunity to show off my knife skills, then Thorne might stop believing I'm a spoiled Seelie princess. He might even tell Riven I can look after myself and am no average, helpless halfling.

The smell of garlic and spices teases my nostrils. "Look over there—dumplings." I point at a stall opposite. "Praise the Elements! They're just what I feel like eating."

Drooling, and guided by blind hunger, I bolt toward the stall's tantalizing aromas, my eyes fixed on the fragrant steam curling from an array of pots and pans.

One step, two. Then three, four, five, and an unseen force hits me, flinging me into the air, then backward into a table of wares. Leather-bound books and paperweights tumble to the ground around me. Wincing in pain, I whip my head up, and a cart full of Titherian elves careens past.

If not for Thorne's quick action of shoving me out of the way, they would have made a pancake out of me. And, sadly, I would have died hungry.

Looking suspiciously close to laughter, Thorne offers his hand, but I push it away. "If you'd thrown me any harder, right now, you would be scooping pieces of me into that fine basket of yours, and it would be quite the gory trip back to the castle for you."

I leap up from the gravel and pile books back on the table, smiling at the stall owner. "Sorry, Sir. I don't think anything was broken."

The troll has so much hair covering his face, I can't tell if his grunt is an acceptance of my apology or if he's preparing to wallop me with his ax handle.

A gold coin flings out of Thorne's bag, spinning like a top onto the stall's wooden table. The troll grunts again, this time in a slightly less murderous register.

"Take a silver leaf from our librarian's book, Princess, and try to be a little more grateful," Thorne says, watching me pick tiny stones from the points of my ears. "I just saved your life."

"That *troll* is your librarian?"

Thorne doesn't answer, just tugs me toward the dumpling stall. "I've never been assigned to play nursemaid before. You must be important somehow for him to care about what happens to a Seelie royal."

"By *him*, do you mean your king?"

"I mean my best friend, Riven, who, yes, happens to bear the title of the King of Merits." He sneers down his long nose at me. "One he doesn't wear lightly, I might add."

"Why do I get the feeling you don't like me much, Thorne?"

"Probably because I don't like you very much." His expression softens as mine collapses in sorrow. No creature enjoys being loathed.

When we arrive at the stall, Thorne elbows his way to the front of the rowdy line of fae, dragging me along with him. "We'll take forty of those. A mix of all fillings," he tells the rotund brownie behind the counter.

I tug his sleeve. "I'm not *that* hungry."

"Who says they're for you?"

Utensils fly, metal clangs and bangs, and Thorne turns to me with a rough sigh. "Look, I apologize for not wanting to be your new best friend, but you're the daughter of the one fae in all the realms who wants Riven's head on a stake and his guts torn out and burned, preferably while he lies there watching. I have good reason to be suspicious of you."

"That's rather graphic. And, really, my father's not that bad."

"Says his pampered daughter! In practice, you're Riven's enemy, which makes you mine, too. What I can't figure out is why he didn't send you off on a tour alone today and let the cretins and lowlifes sniff you out, deal with you in their own special way."

The brownie's eyes widen in recognition as he makes an exchange with Thorne—a large steaming parcel for a handful of coins. The cook bows. "Commander Thorne, I am honored."

"No, you're not." Thorne waves a thick hand in the brownie's face and it goes slack, then twists back into the original scowl he was wearing when we arrived.

"You wiped his memory. Neat trick," I say as my hand tears into the packet and retrieves a hot dumpling.

We walk toward a copse of trees beside the square and take a seat on a low wall, a quiet spot to eat our meal and watch the passersby.

Thorne swallows a dumpling whole. "I don't understand why you're so impressed by simple magic," he says, chewing with his mouth open. "Can't Seelie halflings perform any tricks?"

Instead of a dumpling, hot anger scalds my tongue. "And I don't understand why you have to be so forthcoming with every one of your vile thoughts."

"Because I'm interested in hearing yours." He taps my temple. "I'd like to learn how your mind works. And because I'm Unseelie, we rather enjoy shocking others."

"Right. So, you're seeking to understand your foe then."

"Yes." His eyes bug out. "*Duck!*"

"What? Where?"

Thorne pushes me to my knees and throws a rock at the tree behind me. A bronze raven-like bird with eyes of black stone swoops into the sky in a clatter of metal feathers, squawking off toward the sea. Olwydd, Temnen's familiar.

"Good riddance, you scum-sucking, skinny-bellied sky rodent," yells Thorne through cupped hands. He turns to me with a rueful expression. "That's the deceased prince's bird, brings trouble with it that one. He was going for your eyeball."

"Ouch. I thought it was Olwydd. I've heard all about his past crimes. Why in the realms hasn't he been banished yet?"

"Oh, he has. But that doesn't stop him from appearing like a harbinger of gloom at least once a sennight."

"Tell you what, if you lend me your bow, next time he shows up, I'll shoot him right between his pebbly eyes for you." Blood warming with excitement, I hastily swallow my third dumpling, wipe grease onto my cloak, and hold my hand out for Thorne's weapon.

He laughs and shoves his seven-hundred-and-fifth dumpling into his gob, chewing open-mouthed as he shakes his head. "I'll hold on to my bow, thank you very much. Come on. Do you want to take a proper look around or not?"

He strides off, leaving me to gawk at a tall figure whose black hood suddenly peeks from behind a tree trunk, then disappears in the blink of an eye.

I walk backward in Thorne's direction, half close my eyes, and open my senses, searching the air currents for any clues to the spy's identity. I get nothing, only a distinct sense of malice sullying the air. Whoever this person or creature is, they're employing a protection spell, their essence hidden behind it.

My heart thumps hard, but I'm not scared, because I already know who it is. Riven, the Merit king himself. It has to be. Who else knew about today's plans and could conceal their scent, their flavor, from the Princess of Air? I touch the pommel of my sword, pat the knives strapped to my body, then spin on my heels and chase after Thorne.

We munch, or I should say Thorne munches, on the last of our lunch as we pass through the maze and enter the Meritorium via a door hidden in a hedge.

Our visit is quick. I chat to Lidwinia about the market, admire Elas's latest invention and the beautiful interior, meet a few workers, and then we leave.

Lidwinia advised Thorne he'd do best to treat me like a visiting military dignitary. So, to my surprise, he takes me on a tour of the courtiers' apartment complexes, the business district, the weaponry, forge, and the guardhouse, and all the while, the unknown presence slips through the shadows behind us. Hand on my weapon, I keep my lips sealed tight.

When we arrive on the outskirts of Blackthorn Forest, the edge of a dark cloak flies between tree trunks on the hill to my left. I smile. At last, our pursuer comes closer.

From the direction of the trees comes a grunt, followed by the sound of stones sliding. A flash of blue eyes, and then a thud. Someone has fallen over.

Thorne jolts forward.

"Wait," I cry out, gripping his arm.

"For what, Princess? I was only going to suggest we return to the castle quickly. Someone with ill intentions has been following us. I'll return alone and hunt them down."

"No! Let's do it now. Together. I'm quite good with a sword, much better with a bow. But, nonetheless, two is better than one in any fight, wouldn't you agree?"

"Are you deaf? I said I will hunt them *alone*."

"But they're right over there in the trees. Possibly injured and—"

"I don't care how expertly you wield a weapon. Riven would have my guts for breakfast if I returned you with even the slightest scratch. My job is to keep you out of harm's way, not thrust you into the middle of it."

"And who do you imagine would want to follow two simple traders from Port Neo?"

"Whoever they are, they know very well we're not traders."

"So someone from court, then?"

"Not necessarily." He starts up the hill that leads to the castle, tugging me along by my tunic sleeve like I'm an unwilling donkey dressed as a trader.

"But, Thorne, it has to be someone from court," I say. "What outsider could manage to breach your wards, your famous sea guards, and fierce forest defenders? I've heard it's nearly impossible to break into your city."

"Not necessarily."

"Stop saying that."

"Listen, don't tell your Fatuous Father of Storms, but if somebody used very strong magic, dark magic, Unseelie magic, it could be done."

"So, therefore, it has to be one of your own!"

"Perhaps, Princess. Perhaps."

Could it be Draírdon? No. Absolutely not. No cloaking spell could possibly contain his diabolical scent of week-old mushroom and cabbage soup.

Therefore, it *has* to have been Riven.

22

On the Merit Throne

Merri

When we reach the castle, Thorne shoves me through the side entrance without thought or ceremony. "Don't worry, Princess. I'll find the spy and deal with them promptly," he says, slamming the white door in my face.

The sound of his boots clacking against cobblestones grows distant as he runs off, and I lean back against the door, listening. I don't know why he's bothering, because I'm certain he won't find anyone. By Thorne's own admission, the only creature able to breach the Merit wards is most likely one of their own.

Prime suspect: *Riven na Duinn.*

I recall the energy of the dark presence tracing my steps today, then think of Riven's smile this morning—smug and pleased with the fit of the clothes he chose, a touch of possessive fondness flashing in his eyes.

Am I foolish for believing we have a connection, no matter how fragile the thread is?

Yes. Of course, I'm a fool. Because why else would he follow me around the city if not to fantasize about my demise? But that fleeting smile he tries not to show me, those steamy kisses. He cycles through more temperature changes than a human washing machine.

Out of all the fae I've ever met, the Merit king is by far the most annoying and confusing.

There's one way I can eliminate Riven from my suspicions that he was spying on us today, and it can't be achieved if I return to my chambers in a foul temper.

Pivoting on my heels, I climb the stairs that lead to the throne room, then slip into the hall through a side door. My breath snags in my throat as the sight before my eyes stops me cold.

Riven himself languishes on the sun throne while a writhing mass of courtiers fornicates at his feet. He stares past them, his fingers tapping on the edge of the sun disk, legs spread wide in a slouch, and his demeanor exuding leashed power and open boredom.

Jarring music saws through the air, the fiddlers on the dais inciting anger inside me with their frenzied rhythms. Cries and moans compete with the sickening grate of music as thoughts of the human girl flood my mind. My heart lurches. Is Summer among the group performing for the king? Peering around a column, I check. No, thank the Elements, I don't believe she is. The pain in my temples eases slightly.

Outside, afternoon light still glows over the city, but in the throne room, a false night has descended. Flames dance in the braziers, and stars glitter between the coppery rays of the sun throne. A spell of darkness has been cast, a perfect backdrop for decadence.

Riven's midnight. Riven's pleasure. What an Unseelie king wants, he gets—even everlasting shadows.

I picture those cold blue eyes stalking me today, then the Emerald Castle and the small cell hidden behind my bedchamber's wall. I recall Riven drawing me into his arms, his touch urgent, unpracticed, and my body responds as if his warm lips touch mine now.

Oh, *Riven*. What might we become if you could only set aside your prejudices?

I brace myself for when he rises and joins his moaning courtiers. When he does this, I know all my hopes will shatter, and still, for one stupid heartbeat, I consider remaining while he removes his dark clothing, the spiked crown, and all of my regard for him. I could stay and watch. For scientific purposes, of course. And to slake my curiosity.

No, I tell myself. *Don't be a fool.* The Silver King's passion laid bare is a sight I don't need to see, could never *unsee*. It's time to flee, but quietly. Willing my wild pulse to settle, I slither backward. One step. Then two.

"Merrin," calls a deep voice, the tone hard and merciless. "Come here. Why do you lurk in the shadows?"

Draygonets! This fae's hearing is exceptional—almost as good as mine.

"I wasn't lurking exactly," I say, chin raised and shoulders squared as I stride to the bottom of the stairs below the dais. "Merely hiding."

With the click of his fingers, the music changes to a soft and lilting tune. "Come closer."

Must I?

With sluggish movements, I ascend the stairs until I'm standing on the edge of the dais, as far away from him as possible.

"Closer."

When I stand tall in front of the writhing mass of bodies, I fix my gaze on a spike in Riven's crown.

He asks, "How was your day? Did you have the adventure you wished for?"

I cup my ear and lean forward theatrically. "Pardon? The festivities below are rather distracting." My eyes narrow, flicking downward.

Riven's bright-blue beams drift over the fleshy mound of limbs, then rise and settle on my face. "Oh, them," he says, as if he'd somehow forgotten there was an orgy taking place on the tips of his boots. "Leave," he commands, and like terrified roaches, seven courtiers leap up and scurry into dark passages.

A corner of his mouth tilts upward, as though he's attempting a smile. "So?"

"So what?"

"No need to play the fool, Merrin."

Okay. Perhaps he thinks I'm a natural one.

He waves his hand at the black and silver throne to his right. "Sit and tell me about your day."

Sit on a Merit throne? That doesn't seem appropriate.

Collecting my thoughts, I continue to stare, and his icy-blue eyes glare back. He raises an eyebrow, then nods at the empty seat beside him, not the one Lidwinia usually perches on. It's the dead queen's throne. I can tell because it's almost the same size as Riven's and perfectly matches Ciara's crown of meteoric silver spikes.

"I'm really not dressed for it. I'm covered in—"

"Sit."

Wrapping my dirty cloak tightly around my body, I obey and sink into the throne's plush black cushions beside the king. Other than a few guards, the cavernous hall below is empty.

I scan the channels on the floor that form the triangular-shaped Blood Sun altar, green flames from the braziers reflecting in the water. I recall the story Isla told me about the sacrifice she witnessed. The bloodbath. How our Fire king's essence once streamed in fresh bursts into the bowl on the dais.

My stomach churns, nausea washing through me. Then I remember—if not for this king beside me, blood would still flow through the altar, freely and frequently.

Time passes in silence counted in slow, hard beats of my heart.

A mechanical bird swoops from the metal rafters, an orange flash turning translucent as it passes through each beam of moonlight. I feel the king's gaze on me, tingling over my skin before he speaks.

"You have no points collected on your pendant." His intense gaze drops to my chest.

"Because I didn't activate it."

This must please him because he smiles broadly. "I heard you toured all the places any self-respecting warrior would wish to visit."

My stomach clenches. "How do you know that?"

"I know everything that happens in my kingdom." He leans closer. "And I have a very nosy sister who enjoys gossip."

With a soft sigh, I flop back against the throne. "In your kingdom, are only males allowed to show interest in important things and places?"

"Are you suggesting that art, dancing, and healing are trifling matters?"

"Of course I'm not!"

"Neither am I. Look at the throne you sit upon. It was built for a strong queen, a warrior. The clothes you wear now are quite fit for purpose."

"What a shocking thing to say. I'm not sure who you mock more, me or every Merit queen that has ever existed."

He blinks rapidly. "I... I didn't mean—"

On the inside, I wince. I don't want to anger and alienate the Merit king. I should be pleased he's invited me to sit beside him and not lash out just because his motives confuse me.

"I'm sorry, Riven. I'm tired and irritable. Please ignore me."

"An impossible task," he murmurs.

I'm not certain if I've been complimented or insulted, so I say nothing in response.

His hands make fists on the throne's armrests. "I suppose you didn't see our library, then?"

"Elas said all your tablets are in the Meritorium. I went there."

"I'm referring to the old library. The buried one. With the *actual* books."

"Where? I didn't know one existed."

"It barely does. It's only a ghost of a library. With the advent of technology, my father outlawed leather-bound parchment and scrolls, let the whole lot sink beneath the earth, a cavern as tall as the throne room, lined and piled with books and books and still even more books."

Squirming on the edge of my seat, I ask, "Will you show it to me?"

"Yes. Yes, I think I will."

"Now?"

"I'm afraid not." He laughs, fingers reaching for the lock of hair curtaining my eye before his hand drops, clenching on his thigh. "I have a High Council meeting to attend shortly, but I'll take you to see it one day soon. I promise."

Or I could go by myself. "Where is it exactly?"

"Situated in a very dangerous place. You shouldn't go alone."

We'll see about that. It sounds like a perfect place to hide an ancient curse. "Right. I'd better leave you to your meeting, then."

A strong hand grips my knee. "Before you go, will you do something for me?"

A lump constricts my throat. I swallow twice to dislodge it. "If I can."

Something akin to excitement glows in his gaze. "I want you to perform air magic from the throne. Or...the dais will do."

Wait... *What?*

Hiding my surprise with a shaky smile, I say, "I must remind you that the limited magic I have as a halfling is even more diminished in your land. But I'll give it a try. What type of trick do you wish me to attempt?"

"Anything. Surprise me."

I think I can handle a trifle of greenery compulsion, make the leaves in the room dance a little without too much effort.

Standing at the front of the dais, I raise my open palms, thrilled when a flash of energy licks down my spine.

All right. I can do this. I close my eyes. Slow my breathing. Then focus on the air prickling against my skin, the particles raising every hair on my body, the tiny bumps spreading over my flesh.

Lightning flashes. Thunder cracks.

Yes. I can definitely do this.

My stomach tightens. My toes curl as power vibrates along my spine, through my chest, out the tips of my fingers. Then I whisper, "Lady Zephyr, I call thee, Air. *Come.* Do my bidding. Source of life, obey me now. Wing and feather. Storm and sky. All in soil that's green and living, bring them, bring them *now.*"

Thunder crashes again. Once. Twice.

The wind funnels from my fingers, moving outward, and then every branch, leaf, and curling vine in the room unravels, reaching for me. I smile as I feel them writhe and dance in the breeze. Then as one, the plants release a terrible groan, and my body jolts forward, white light exploding inside my head.

The king disappears, the room, too. The wind lifts me, and I float in a cold black place, an unknown place, buffeted but held safe, while every living thing in the Merit Hall creeps and winds around my limbs.

This feeling is what humans describe as heavenly. Blissful. Here and now, me and the air Element, together and in control—this is everything. This is home.

"Merrin!" a voice shouts, instantly breaking the spell.

When I open my eyes, Riven stands in front of me breathing like a warrior mid-battle. His hands hover over my arms, preparing to grab me. Perhaps to shake me out of my trance. A silver aura surrounds his body, his crown. Worry and awe line his face.

I glance down at my body. Vines wrap my legs, torso, arms. Dirt and tiny bugs crawl through my hair, over my skin. I laugh, delighted by my achievement.

"Move aside," I tell him, and he obeys.

As I draw the remnants of power back inside me, the greenery moves in reverse, unwrapping, wriggling backward along the floor, winding up columns and around ceramic pots and palm trees.

I wipe my hands on my cloak. "So, how was that?" I ask. "Entertaining enough, Your Majesty?"

"It was..." He shakes his head. "Incredible."

It certainly was. The vines should have unraveled a little and danced for me, yes. At least, I hoped they would. But I shouldn't have had the power to do *that*. Something strange just happened. A power circuit formed, connecting mine to the king's and feeding off it in a feat of shocking, primal magic.

Riven looks as stunned as I feel, so I'm guessing he sensed our connection, too. He must have.

My heart pounds, limbs trembling. I'm thirsty, hungry, and completely exhausted. After my stellar performance, I need a long lie down. Or a large goblet of wine—or three.

I dip my head in a bow. "Goodbye, Riven."

He does the same, which is an odd thing for a king to do to a princess. "Goodbye, Merrin."

When I reach the last stair, I pivot on my weak legs, facing him again. On the throne, the king is a glittering silver statue, waiting for me to speak.

"Oh, and, Riven, I meant to ask earlier...where have you been all day?"

His brow furrows. "Here. Where else would I be on the day of my courtiers' petitions?"

"Sorry. Could you please say where you were again?"

His voice deepens. "I just told you, Merrin. I've been here all day—in the throne room."

Well, that confirms it. He cannot lie, and he spoke the words. Therefore, he can't have been the spy. If not his king, then I wonder who Thorne has trapped or killed.

I'm so tired I can barely walk straight. I need to curl up on my bed and think about today's stalker. Then, tomorrow if possible, I must discover where the king spends his time when his legs aren't grafted to his throne, find the curse, get the hell out of here, and forget about my naive dreams of saving him.

As I climb the seemingly endless stairs to the queen's chamber, a flash of red catches my eye. At the edge of my cloak sleeve hangs a long strand of straight hair. That's strange. In this kingdom, I've seen hair in all shades of earth and sky, but none this exact shade of rich scarlet.

I hold it up to the light of a stained-glass window. Is it mine? The color is a little too bright, and my hair is wavy, but Wyn often jokes I shed more fur than Ivor. It must belong to me.

I round the corner to my hallway and find Thorne standing in front of my door, arms crossed over his rumpled tunic. "Princess!" he calls as he glances up. "Come quickly. I must speak to you."

I take off at a jog and am beside him in a flash. "Who did you capture?"

"That's the problem. No one." He rubs his stubbly chin. "I stalked and hunted, but somehow this creature kept ahead of me, always hidden behind a veil of magic. I tracked them through the forest to the sea, and there they disappeared. No trace. No scent. Nothing. They're strong, Princess. Very strong."

"Or if not them, whoever's protecting them is powerful."

"Don't worry." Thorne bows. "I'll speak to Riven and search again tomorrow. Whoever this creature is, we'll find them." He spins on his heels, preparing to march away.

"Wait a moment, Thorne." I narrow my eyes, concentrating hard on the lie I'm about to utter. "The king has asked me to meet him after dinner to talk about my family. It's just...well, I seem to have forgotten the place he mentioned." I squint at the ceiling. "Let me think...it was something like—"

"The druid's well," says Thorne helpfully.

"Ah, yes! That was it. Thank you."

He shoves his hands in the pockets of his loose pants. "It was an easy guess. If our king isn't on the throne, in the forest, or engaged in weapons training, you're almost certain to find him in the cavern."

Excellent. I need to find the right person to ask for directions and make sure I pick a time to visit the druid's well when Riven is extremely busy elsewhere.

If what I seek can't be found in the cavern, then the only other place I know that might be worth a search is the buried library.

Of course, if I can't find the curse in either of those two places, my task becomes impossible—and I may have to ask Riven himself for help.

I shudder at the thought.

23

Poisoned Kiss

Merri

O ver the next seven days, Thorne's extensive hunts throughout the city and surrounds uncover nothing and nobody. All traces of the being who followed us a sennight ago have been wiped clean from the land, and even the Unseelie king has been unable to uncover a single clue.

Meanwhile, I've spent my days traipsing about the castle dressed in finery, joining every activity I chanced upon in the hope that someone would disclose the location of the druid's well.

I've spent hours in the Meritorium, feigning interest in Lidwinia and Elas's work and asking leading questions.

I attended tea parties, dances, magical discussion groups, herb gathering excursions, and even cloth dying sessions held by the light weaver elves in the dressmaker's tower.

As a result, I collected tips on Merit dance styles, herbal lore, dark spell casting, and cloth weaving with metallic fibers but not one scrap of information about the location of the druid's well or when the king usually visits it.

The last two nights, I invoked a weak veiling spell, donned my trader's disguise, grabbed a stolen quiver and bow, and searched the city high and low for the curse. Not once did I sense a location where it might be kept, which leads me to believe that it's definitely somewhere in the druid's well—wherever that may be.

Why didn't I ask Isla where this mysterious well is located? She's been there, seen the scrying fountain with her own eyes, and I'm a fool for not thinking of this before I rushed from the Land of Five without a proper plan.

Currently, it's day three of my search of the Merit City, and I've almost given up hope of ever finding the curse. The last thing I want is to have to ask Riven where it's hidden, but as each day passes, it's looking like I'll have no other choice.

With my shoulders slumped, I head to the walled garden that's recently become a refuge, my boots scraping along the path. I breathe a sigh as I push open the wrought-iron gate, slump on the dark crystal bench, and let the hood of my traveler's cloak fall to my shoulders.

This garden is a peaceful place. Blood-red roses ramble over obsidian-lined walls and creep up trees, winding around branches.

Today, seven ravens croak from the wall's ledge, preening each other's feathers.

Sometimes, the deceased king's clockwork cat, Meyet, visits at the same time as me, and I watch him leap through the garden with the wild faery cats. But, so far, I'm yet to see another fae here.

At the moment, there aren't any noisy felines present, and I'm free to lie on the bench, close my eyes, and recall the interesting seating plans of recent court dinners—Summer beside Lidwinia and Elas and me on the king's right.

Lately, Riven has been polite, civil, and sometimes even smiles at my bad jokes. But if he knew what I've been up to, gallivanting around his town in search of Merit secrets, he'd probably lock me in my chambers and throw away the key—even the score between us.

Only once in my late-night expeditions did I feel the presence of the spy outside the Meritorium. Excitement vibrating inside me, I drew my sword and called the creature forth, but the cowardly being stayed hidden. And I remained safe.

In truth, I'd have preferred to fight, exposing the infiltrator's identity and myself as much more than a helpless, spoiled Seelie princess.

"I don't care what the surly Silver King thinks of me," I say to the puffy clouds gathering in the sky.

I blow dandelion seeds into the air, and they swirl and form the shape of a tall, jagged crown, beautiful to behold. Damn Riven again.

A loud screech from above makes me jolt upright, and a rough voice says, "Meerade cares about king."

Squinting into the oak tree, I see Riven's owl swaying on a low branch. "Hello, Meerade," I say. "How long have you been hovering up there?"

"Long time." Her head bobs twice as she stretches her wings. "Queen, come. Time to find the message you seek. Come now. Come."

I cock my head. "You want me to follow you?"

She bounces on the branch. "Come. Come!"

"Where to exactly?"

"Secrets hide in Riven's well. Old secrets time to tell. Meerade show the Silver Queen."

"Queen Ciara has been dead a long time, Meerade. It's best you accept that and stop calling everyone who crosses your path a queen."

"Only one is queen. Come. Come!" The owl screeches and flies over the wall, and I hurry through the garden gate and follow her.

Before long, we're trekking down narrow passageways at the rear of the castle. After a time, we come to a small landing with a door hidden in the wall. Meerade settles on my shoulder and presses a triangular recess in the bricks. The door opens, and we pass through it, then follow the stairs downward.

In the claustrophobic passages, the air is damp and musky, but, finally, the ceiling grows taller, and I can breathe a little easier. We turn a sharp corner, and a large stack of boulders at least three times my height blocks the path forward.

I peek through a tight gap in the rock wall into an enormous cavern of sparkling limestone, the space lit by torches burning on four sconces. The infamous druid's well is a cave beneath the castle!

"Meerade," I say. "Is Riven likely to come here soon? If he finds me in this place, I'm as good as dead. Or at the very least, banished forever."

Metallic feathers clink as her wings flap beside my head, and she drops to the ground. "Go inside," she tells me, hopping through the gap in the rocks.

As soon as I follow Meerade through the tight space, she flies to the quartz column that grows from an island of rough stone into a chest-height well and lands on its edges. "Come quickly!"

Wasting no time, I pad through ankle-deep water that floods the bottom of the cave, glad that I'm wearing boots. All is silent except for the eerie echo of water dripping from the ceiling.

With my heart pounding, I lean over the well and peer into the glowing surface of silver liquid, praying for something to happen. I wait.

And wait.

And wait.

Meerade hops onto my shoulder and bores her gaze into the side of my head. But, still, the magical well does nothing.

I look around the cavern, spending an agreeable few moments picturing the Silver King prowling about his lair before I lose patience.

"All right, Meerade. So, I'm here, but how am I meant to find the hidden curse?"

"Look down. Look," she demands, pecking lightly at my ear.

I squint harder, my breath agitating the mercurial water and forming loose swirls across it. "There's nothing to see."

"Ask. Ask!" says the owl on my shoulder.

"Ask?"

I'd imagined the curse would be carved on a tablet and buried underneath earth and stone, not as words floating on the surface of a well. But if there's the slightest chance that asking might reveal it, then for my family's sake, I'm prepared to beg.

I grip the edges of the well and close my eyes, summoning what little power I have. "Ancient waters and enlightened druids, I beg you to show me the location of the Seelie curse, wrought by Aer that poisons the blood of the Elemental line. Where shall I seek it? Show me now and show me true."

Wind whips through the cavern, tearing at my hair and buffeting my body. Meerade releases a deafening screech. "Look, look!" she says.

I open my eyes. Familiar words drift along the surface of the well, the Black Blood curse in dark curling letters. I quickly read the verse about our princes, how they must marry the chosen ones selected by the curse maker, Aer, or succumb to a slow and painful death.

Then the section that my family believes to be the final verse appears:

"*If by another's hand the chosen dies, then before their blood fully weeps and dries, black will fade to gray, gray to white, and white to never. Never was the darkest taint and never will it ever be.*"

A green film clouds the water, the words dissolving.

"Is that it? I know this part already, Meerade. It's the secret verse I need to find."

"Patience," croaks the owl.

I swallow a groan and wait.

Condensation falls from the stalactites above.

Drip. Drip. Drip.

My heart thuds against my ribs.

Bang. Bang. Bang.

Then it happens—the water clears and more words appear.

I read them aloud in a low, shaky voice.

"A halfling defies the..." Words catch in my throat, and I gape at Meerade, hardly able to believe what I'm reading.

"Go on," she says.

I take a breath, and then try again.

"A *halfling defies the Silver King.*

From dark to light, her good heart brings.

Enemies unite. Two courts now one,

Should merry win, the curse is done.

Not Faery born,

But human sworn,

One celestial day,

She'll wear his ring."

The room spins around me, blood rushing through my veins. "Incredible! It could almost be about Riven and me. But that...that can't be possible...me and Riven—how could we cure the curse? I must've read it wrong."

Silently, Meerade grooms my hair with her beak, lightly nipping the point of my ear.

I swipe her face away. "But right there as plain as the dirt beneath my nails, the words state, should Merry win—all right, all right, so my name is spelled wrong, but which other halfling could it be referring to? And if it is me, what exactly am I meant to win in order to end the curse? A battle with whichever fae or creature I've dreamed will one day kill Riven?"

"No. No," Meerade says. "King's heart. King's heart."

"The king's heart? Are you suggesting that me and Riven... Do you mean..." My words trail off as the ground trembles.

Stalactites break from the ceiling and spear the ground, forming a cage of glittering spikes around me. Hair curtains my face as I bow over the well and grip the edges tighter, not daring to turn around because I already know what I'll see.

"King comes. Meerade go now. Not want trouble, Queen. Meerade not want trouble." She rotates her head and stares over her shoulder in that alarming way owls do.

"You really must stop calling me queen," I scold. "I've told you many times; I'm a princess of the Land of Five. A *princess*, understand?"

"Princess for now." With those disturbing words, Meerade wriggles between the limestone bars and swoops out via the tunnel we entered through.

On the other side of the cave, Riven materializes, first as a shadowy ghost who quickly solidifies into the formidable Silver King, a terrible storm brewing in his eyes.

"Amazing," I say, forcing calm into my voice. "Transferring is very cool, wish I had that ability."

"Cool? The temperature has nothing to do with it."

Oh. Of course, my Earth slang would make no sense to him. "Where my mother comes from, that's a compliment." Instead of appeasing him, this insight appears to make him angrier, and a silver-black aura glows around his body.

"What in the Blood Sun are *you* doing here, Merrin? I made Lidwinia vow never to tell you about this place and—"

"Please don't involve your sister. It wasn't her who led me here."

"Then *who* was it?"

Biting my lip, I remain silent. I don't want to betray the darling, title-confused owl.

Riven's eyes close, his head dropping back toward his shoulders. "*Meerade*," he growls.

I hold his gaze as he stomps toward me, the water underneath his boots reacting like hard stone. His hand swipes the air between us, and my stalactite prison disappears.

A muscle in Riven's jaw ticks as he stands with his arms folded, brooding silently.

Taking a calculated risk, I decide to pretend everything's normal. "Well, you're in a charming mood today."

"I've just found you snooping in my private space, a sanctuary that's sacred to both me and my people. What did you expect, applause or me to offer you a goblet of my finest stag's tear wine?"

"A drink would certainly be nice. I wouldn't say no."

"Why did Meerade bring you here?"

My fingers burrow into the folds of my tunic, squeezing and twisting the fabric. I could make up an excuse. I could lie. But I won't. "I'm looking for the answer to the Black Blood curse. And I found it in your scrying well."

A subtle vibration passes over Riven's body, his eyes wild. "You *found* it?"

"Yes." I take a big breath, then chance another risk. "It says that together, you and I can end the curse and bring peace to our lands. Isn't that what you've always wanted? Peace?"

His lips compress, and he vibrates harder, fists clenched against his sides.

I'm tired of pretending this man means nothing to me, exhausted by constantly suppressing my feelings.

Riven na Duinn is the fae I long for in my dreams and tempts me like no other. And now, the curse has confirmed our combined destiny—who and what we are to each other.

A soft breeze tickles my palms as I lift them, raise a small squall and throw it at Riven. It flaps his black tunic against his legs, the silver threads on the thick material glowing brighter and brighter. It tears his hair, rippling it out like moonlit ocean waves.

"Come closer," I whisper, compelling him. Demanding it.

"What are you doing?" he bites out.

"Showing you I'm not the weak halfling you've decided I am. Even here in your kingdom, I have power. Power over you."

With one long step, his body is flush with mine, his palms bracketing my cheeks. "I've never thought you weak, Merrin. Not once."

My heart dances as his lips lower to mine, not touching, not quite. He sighs against my mouth, and then he's kissing me. I part my lips, not participating yet because I want him to know that he chose this. That *he* started it. Not me.

Then he presses closer, his fingers burrowing into my hair, taking hold and twisting it. With a gasp, I kiss him back, losing control of my magic as the wind whirls faster around us, the sound of a hurricane in my ears.

"Merrin," he says between kisses. "Your gale will knock us over."

I break away with a smothered laugh. "Sorry." I click my fingers, and the wind falls away. "The curse… Riven, do you think it's about us? You and me, together like this, perhaps we can…"

He sighs, his palms holding my face and calloused thumb stroking my lower lip. "The druid's well has been wrong before. When Rafael and Isla were imprisoned here, it showed me images of the old Queen of Five dying, and I knew I had to help your king escape before your land was left without a ruler. But Varenus still lives. Besides, what you speak of is impossible. If I could control you, things might be different."

My jaw drops with an audible click. "What did you say? *Control* me?"

"I have racked my brain and tortured myself but come to the resolution that there will never be enough magic in all of the seven realms with which to govern you. What am I to do with you, Merri?"

Ice-cold anger melts the warmth in my belly. I grip his wrists and shove his hands away. "I'm disappointed, Riven. I never imagined your mind was so small that you'd ever wish to control a girl. You're not a king. You're a fraud. Why bother kissing me if that's what you think?"

"You don't understand. Your very presence compels me to kiss you. But mark my words, if we walk this path, one of us will be the ruination of the other. This outcome is inevitable. I've seen it happen in the scrying well over and over, and that's why I wish to control you, Merrin. If I could have you and find a way to contain your power to keep you from fulfilling the foretold destiny, then I would kiss you again and again. Otherwise, I cannot trust you with my kingdom. Your parents are my father's sworn enemy. Your queen caused the death of my brother."

"You hated your father, and that worm Temnen deserved to fry! And it wasn't our queen who plunged the sword into his heart. Surely you know who it was." The name of his sister presses against my lips.

"I don't want to lessen your power for *my* pleasure. I only want to prevent you from betraying me as the visions predict. If I risk involvement with you, in time, I would no longer see you clearly and, therefore, place my kingdom in peril. Indeed, I would lose sight of myself."

"So, you're saying you like me, but you don't trust me."

He nods.

Lightning courses through me, anger exploding out of my palm as I strike Riven's face.

Breathing roughly, he touches his cheek but says nothing.

"That's right, I slapped you. Do you know how insulting your words are? In the depths of your heart, do you truly believe I'm capable of causing harm to anyone in your kingdom?"

"Not intentionally, of course, but..." Jaw clenching, he rubs the side of his face, his hair rippling like liquid silver.

"There's something else, isn't there?" I ask. "Something you're not telling me."

The cavern floor becomes a thing of great fascination to him.

"Look at me, Riven, and say it," I snap.

Ocean eyes lift, seven realms of pain swimming in their depths. "No matter how strongly I'm drawn to you, these facts remain—you're half human and could never be the Queen of Merits. Why should I waste time, perhaps grow attached to you, when nothing good could ever come of it?"

Pain twists deep in my chest. "You can't be serious. Your brother, Temnen, tried to wed Isla, a full-blooded human! She could have become a Merit princess and maybe even a queen if your father's schemes for him to replace you as the Merit heir had been successful."

One side of his lips twists into a cruel smile. "Never. Temnen was toying with Isla only to torture Rafael. I assure you he had no intention of *marrying* her himself."

I stab a finger near his face. "Then you're small minded. Prejudiced. And I couldn't be more disappointed in you."

"I'm simply a realist. Your blood is tainted. Your humanity makes you weak and unstable."

"And, therefore, unworthy of you."

His eyes darken. "I did not say that. Nonetheless, all fae believe humans are the weaker race. How can you not understand this?"

Seeking calm, I draw a slow breath. "It's *you* who doesn't comprehend me or the world in which you live. My humanity drives me to prove myself, to be my best self. And being half-human gives me a greater reason to be steadfast and true. My otherness makes me *more* worthy, not less, and if you can't see this, then I say good riddance to you, Riven na Duinn."

All my life in Faery, I've felt like a royal fraud. But as I speak these words of self-belief, I know that deep down they're true. I wholeheartedly believe them. So, I'm at least thankful to Riven for helping me make this discovery.

For a fleeting moment, I consider showing him my gratitude with a punch to his perfect nose. But, no, he's not worth the sore knuckles.

I walk backward toward the tunnel, away from him and his horrible, sorrow-filled eyes. "Perhaps one day you'll be brave and choose happiness, take what you want. Maybe you won't. But this much is clear, our dreams unite our fates. Until the day of reckoning, I ask you to stay away from me."

"Merri, please understand I don't say these things to hurt you. If I ignore the truth and follow my desires, one day I'll be the death of you."

"What do you mean?" I ask.

"My visions. In the druid's well and at night when I sleep…it's always your blood I see on the snow. On my knife, it is *your* blood. You'll bring the downfall of my city unless I stop you, and my dreams tell me that I *do* stop you—by killing you. Go home, Merrin Fionbharr. Go home and be safe from harm."

So the rumors must be true—the Merit king *is* insane.

Without another word, like a rejected hound, I retreat to my chambers to lick my wounds.

24

High Council

Riven

H*alflings lie.*
Halflings deceive.
Halflings sulk and make kings grieve.

For the last three evenings, Lidwinia has seated the Elemental princess on my right side during dinner, effectively destroying my appetite.

Last night was particularly unpleasant. Over five seemingly endless courses, we ate in strained silence while Meerade gave a running commentary from her perch on my shoulder. "Black," she said, as her beak dipped into my mushroom and sorrel soup. "Hairy," as I took a mouthful of the boar-snout stew. And, "mine," at first sight of the steaming baked trout.

Merri, wearing a gossamer-thin gown of shaded silver and black, obligingly fed my owl from her own plate, cooing and whispering the whole time. It was beyond tedious.

Unable to bear the tension, I broke my vow to ignore her and, for want of something better to say, haughtily declared, "Someone made a mistake and dressed you in my colors."

Eyes fixed on Meerade, Merri fed her more fish, this time extracting the piece from *my* bowl. "Nope. They're mine actually. You can't have exclusive rights to a color scheme just because you're king."

Without comment, I turned to watch a blood pixie throttle her partner in an argument over a goblet of garnet wine as I mouthed the word *nope* three times, wondering why in the Blood Sun Merrin would choose to speak like a Port Neo dock worker instead of a princess. Most likely because of her unusual parentage.

She delivered a blunt lecture on my lack of manners, then answered my further polite questions in as few brusque words as possible. So in revenge, I broke my habit of rarely dancing and chose the second-most beautiful fae in the room to spin around the dance floor, self-righteousness swelling in my breast. Only to have it dashed by disappointment when I noticed Merri leaving early.

Not long after, I retired to my chambers and spent a sleepless night reliving the sweet smiles she granted Meerade versus the scorn in her eyes when she looked at me. A torture more thorough than even Temnen ever devised.

As a result, my mood is foul as I grind my teeth and pace outside the Meritorium, debating whether or not to enter. I can't even recall why I'm here, but since I am, perhaps I can seek Lidwinia's advice about the Elemental princess. No! That's a foolish idea. My sister will only laugh at me.

Why am I worried, anyway? I should be happy Merri is ignoring me. It's what I want, isn't it?

No. No, it's not.

Yes, I want her to return home where she'll be safe, where her bright smile and mesmerizing gaze can't torment me to death, but I don't want her to *despise* me. That's an unbearable outcome.

With a groan, I swing open one of the smaller glass doors to the Meritorium. Meerade flies from the shoulder of a tall figure in my periphery and sweeps inside with me, attacking the seven shadow ravens that have been bothering me all morning.

Damn phantom birds.

I spy Lidwinia and Elas with their heads bowed over the polished granite benchtop that dominates the center of the main workroom. Batting at the incorporeal ravens, I make my way toward my sister.

Meerade skids to an ungraceful landing on the work table, tumbling scrolls, writing implements, and plans to the floor.

Without looking up from her work, Lidwinia asks, "What's troubling you, Riven?"

"What? Why would you ask that?" Stupid question. I already know the answer.

"Well, your mood is so black the grief ravens are following you. Their constant flapping is ruining my concentration. Make them leave."

"Téigh vah!" I tell them as I take a seat, watching the bad omens dissolve mid-air with seven plaintive croaks.

Elas flashes his fangs in a friendly smile and nudges my leg with the edge of a wing. "Have you come to offer your opinion on the latest upgrade to the Merit pendants?"

"Nope," I answer, trying out the halfling's strange word and deciding I quite like it. "I wish to be distracted from my gloom. Can either of you help me?"

"Only if you're prepared to describe what you wish to be relieved from," Lidwinia says, fitting delicate crystals into a pendant with what appears to be the longest pair of tweezers in the seven realms. "Also, there's a council meeting shortly. We don't have time to entertain you."

"A council meeting? Blood Sun save me," I mumble, my mood plummeting further.

"Well, Brother, what's going on?"

I place my crown on the table and grimace. "The Elemental princess needs to leave and—"

"No. She doesn't." The purple scale glyphs on Lidwinia's arms flare bright. "What do you think of her?"

Silent, I stare at my crown and stroke the sharpest jet spike, blood beading on the tip of my finger.

Lidwinia elbows me in the ribs. "She's very nice for the daughter of a sworn enemy. Don't you agree?"

My head jerks up. "No. I don't agree. She's argumentative, foolishly inquisitive, her incessant questions bordering on the outrageous. Anyone who saw the way she treats me would think I'm the local swineherd flirting with her on market day."

"Flirting? So, you like her, then?"

"*Like* her? Are you deaf, Sister?"

"Not at all, *Brother*." A despicable smile curves her lips. "I hear you very well. And see things far clearer than you."

"And what are these *things* you see?" I scoff.

My sister raises her brow, her mouth forming the smug smile again.

"Speaking of seeing things, when will you next see Merrin?" asks Elas.

I glare at him. "How do I know? As Lidwinia pointed out, she's my natural-born enemy, not my besotted bride to be."

Lidwinia laughs. "I never said the word bride. What about you, Elas? Did you mention marriage or a union of any kind between Riven and Merri?"

"No." Elas rubs his mouth, hiding a smirk. "By my best recollection, the only one of us talking about weddings and brides is our king."

"Oh, forget it. I wish I hadn't said a word." I shoot to my feet, stretch and crack the bones of my neck, rolling the tension from my shoulders. "You're both unbearable, and I can't stand another moment of your company. I'm leaving now."

"You'll have to put up with us shortly at the council meeting. In the meantime, I wish you luck with your...problem." She cuts an insolent half bow.

Elas does the same, then says, "Do say hello to Merri for us."

With their snickers raising hackles along my back, I push through the door and use magic to slam it behind me.

Elas's words taunt me. *Say hello to Merri.* No, thank you. I'd rather crush her body to mine and kiss all traces of Seelie princess from her being.

Change her.

Make her *Unseelie*.

A queen.

Queen of Merits.

And forever *mine*.

The terrifying turn of my thoughts freezes the blood in my veins. I inhale a deep breath of brine-scented air, spinning slowly with my face turned toward the sun, letting it melt the ice in my chest. Finally, my pulse slows.

I inspect the clear blue sky, relieved that the grief ravens are nowhere in sight, and only gold-winged butterflies flutter over the gardens. Distant conversations drift on the breeze, the murmurs audible over the noise of turning cogs and pumping steam.

All is as it should be. My people fare well. My kingdom, too. At present, my mind and heart are the only things in danger of disintegrating. But there's a remedy for that—I must get rid of the Seelie princess.

Without purpose, I head toward a line of trees, ambling along, my thoughts a war zone. Meerade flies above, regularly diving low to seize a tasty spider or insect to supplement her breakfast.

An idea haunts me—that a life shared with Merri, devoid of loneliness and sorrow, might only be a single choice away. I have two options. Remain alone, forever embittered. Or turn against everything my kingdom once stood for—domination, supremacy—and follow my selfish desires, taking my enemy's daughter for a wife.

And if the prophecy is true and Merri and I are the keys to ending the Black Blood curse, then our union would unite our lands and bring about long-lasting peace. But then there are the visions to consider. The snow. The blood.

In truth, both outcomes are equally terrifying.

As I cut across a narrow path in the direction of Blackthorn Forest, a gravelly voice calls my name from close behind, halting my steps.

I turn quickly. Damn—it's Thorne. How did his presence escape my notice? I pivot and keep walking.

The staccato thud of boots draws closer, and then Thorne is beside me harrumphing like an old goat. "You're in a hurry," he points out unnecessarily. "Did you forget that you'd left me waiting for you outside the Meritorium?"

What? My thoughts scramble, rewinding. Right. So, the tall figure resting against the building was Thorne. Seven hells. I must be losing my mind. "And what if I did forget?"

"Since you are the king, I suppose you're entitled to leave your friends and brain behind once in a while." Thorne catches my arm. "Going somewhere interesting, Riven?"

"No." I shake him off with a shrug and a brutal side-eye. "Just planning to check the wards along Citrene Creek." I continue walking, hoping he won't follow, but within seconds, he's at my side again, whistling like a river maid who's caught herself a nice juicy farm boy for lunch.

"Why?" Thorne asks.

I sigh. "I want to ensure Nicor hasn't been slithering around the new boundaries attempting to breach them again."

"I see." Thorne is silent a moment, giving me hope that this conversation is over. He harrumphs again, and I brace for his next words. "And no doubt you want to reminisce about the time you spent by the creek with the Seelie princess."

"Minus the nix's attack, no doubt I do," I snap, furious that my motives are so transparent.

Thorne is my closest friend, and if he already understands my feelings to this extent, then I don't see why he should be spared the entire embarrassing truth.

Feeling slightly deranged, I smile and say, "Actually, there is a lot to consider when I think about Merrin, for example, recently she slapped my face—"

Thorne chokes on a gasp, then yelps, "Ballocks, no!" tripping over his boots before righting himself.

Grinning, I thump his back, causing him to stumble again.

And then, as the forest closes its twisted branches around us, I continue my declaration of madness. "She did. I swear it's true. It is amazing that an Elemental fae would dare to abuse an Unseelie king in such a way, as though I were a mere servant. But I confess, Thorne, when she did it, I experienced the darkest of thrills. She slapped me hard, too, a crime punishable by death, and it was the most enjoyable event of my life. Can you believe it?"

"Good gods, no," says Thorne. "What I do believe is this—you, my friend, have gone mad, and your Seelie guest is a downright fiend."

"Indeed. I wish you'd seen Merrin a few days ago. She transformed before me on the dais, and like a queen, she commanded the air element and brought every living plant in the throne room under her spell. I suspect that, at the time, if the castle walls had fallen on my shoulders, I still couldn't have looked away from her."

"As pleased as I am to behold you so witlessly enchanted," says Thorne, his puzzled expression indicating otherwise, "I regret I must ruin your plans to meditate on the princess. Your presence was required in the High Council chambers some time ago."

I stop dead. "Damn it. I'd completely forgotten. We'll have to transfer there straight away."

Thorne gnashes his metal teeth. As a lowborn, he cannot transfer alone, and like most fae who can't, he despises the often painful sensation of being dragged along for the ride.

"Hurry. Grip my arm," I say as he takes a step backward into a pine tree. "Come now, Thorne. Who's the fierce fae guard? Is it me or you?"

"You're far grumpier than I am. Does that count? Riven. Wait..." He stills, sniffing the air. "Did you feel that? An interference in the energy web, possibly an intruder. We should investigate and—"

I laugh. "Good try, Thorne." Then I pull him close with one hand, lightly boxing his thick head with the other. "Your games can't distract me."

In a flash of heat and light, the magic dissolves our bodies into whirling particles as Thorne screams like a colicky changeling.

We materialize in the castle's armory and march up the stairs that lead to the council room, otherwise known as the war room.

"You arrived swiftly," I tell my sister as I push through the oak doors into the fire-lit room. It's daylight outside but forever-night in here, a place where secrets are born and nurtured.

Lidwinia's thin tongue flickers over her grin. She enjoys taunting me about my lack of Unseelie attributes—the curled tails, leathery bat wings, and alarmingly spiked breeding organs of past princes and kings. It used to bother me, this difference, my family believing I'm inferior, but after I met Merri in the in-between place and saw longing in her eyes, I stopped caring.

"And you took your sweet time getting here, Your *Majesty*." Lidwinia lifts Rothlo from her shoulder, placing her pet on her palm.

Besides Thorne and me, five others are seated around the oval table in the center of the windowless room. My sister and Elas, Tyzagarne, the fearsome half-giant and former right-hand conspirator of my father's, Chancellor Mareous, the sea witch who is worth the city's weight in gold for her enduring loyalty and wise, measured council. And, of course, Draírdon, the repellent, overbearing High Mage.

I take a seat, nod solemnly at Draírdon, and offer a tight smile to the others. Thanks to Merri, I can no longer look at the High Mage without picturing a wrinkled, moldy mushroom.

After giving me a grudging bow, Draírdon rasps, "Your Highness. A king's worth is only as valuable as his respect for his people, and arriving late to an official engagement, be it a ceremony or a meeting with one's councilors, is a violation of your vow to serve them."

Blood Suns save me from this fool. I spear him with a silent glare and hold it until he looks away.

Elas clears his throat. "Before we start, I have news on the eydendric elves. Their lair has been disbanded and the leaders recently seen in Port Neo. We'll need to keep an eye on the situation, but I don't believe they're an immediate threat."

"Good," I say, my gaze still on the High Mage.

"So, what's the order of the day?" asks Elas, tapping a quill on a sheet of parchment.

"As you well know, Elas," says Draírdon, "We must solidify our plans to move against the Elementals. There is no better time to act than when we have the Prince of Air's child in our hands. We would be fools to waste such an unexpected opportunity."

"What plans?" I ask. "I've given no orders to hatch any such schemes."

"Yes, My King," Draírdon wheedles. "Indeed, you are correct. However, Tyzagarne and I, wishing only to save you from the tedious task, took it upon ourselves to commence work on them. I believe you'll be extremely pleased when we outline our strategy."

"Your beliefs are incorrect!" My fist thumps the table, and Lidwinia jumps as the floor and walls shudder.

Draírdon doesn't blink. "Majesty, if you will only consider the situation we find ourselves in. We have their princess. Why not take their kingdom, too?"

"Because, Draírdon, I do not want it. My dream has always been peace. Why must you always seek to conquer others? You have a high mage's considerable power and court position. As king, I tolerate your disrespect as repayment for the dedication you've always shown my family. I turn a blind eye to your games of minor cruelties, even though I disagree with them. Is all this not enough for you?"

I turn my glare to Tyzagarne, whose yellow eyes drop to his fur-covered palms. "I will never move against the Seelie kingdom unless they move against us first. Do you understand?"

"I agree with our king," says Elas.

Lidwinia drops Rothlo on the surface of the table, and the spider rears up, her front legs slicing the air in front of the High Mage. "My brother has my full support in this matter. We should work toward making the Elementals our allies."

Mareous rises, pearl-threaded hair of moonlight and seaweed writhing around her lithe body. "I stand with the Silver King and will strive to make his wishes a reality and to unite the Unseelie and Seelie lands before tragedy befalls us all. Look, and I shall show you the future that you long for, Draírdon. Look, and witness the horror."

She throws her head back with a loud cry, and water pours over the table enclosed in an elongated bubble.

Inside the sea witch's undulating globe, ghastly scenes of violence and war play, showing not only warriors and battlefields affected but every creature of fae, every blade of grass and tree, all burning or screaming in terror and pain. The land around is ravaged and dying, castles crumbling to rock and tumbling into the sea. Devastation. Horror.

Only a madman would desire this outcome. "Enough," I whisper. "I've seen enough."

Instantly, the scene dissolves, the water frothing and churning back to Mareous, disappearing down her throat while she moans and shakes with power. Then it's finally over.

She returns to her seat, her ocean eyes on the mage, asking a question that he'll never be able to answer correctly.

I touch her arm gently. "*Don't worry*," I tell her in my mind. "*He cannot move without us. A coward at heart, he'll never dare. He's terrified of you.*"

Mareous is young but her inherited magic is incredibly old and strong, and when united with my sister, Elas, and myself, we're unconquerable.

"You've seen the outcome of a war with the Elementals. Do you still have nothing to say?" I ask Draírdon.

Tyzagarne speaks. "The vision did not appeal to me. So, for now, I will do my best to please you, Silver King. I will work no more on these plans against the Land of Five and its rulers."

Draírdon stares at his bearlike accomplice, outrage blazing in his eyes.

"And you?" I ask the mage.

"My sentiment matches Tyzagarne's. I will not move for now."

"Then we are agreed, and the meeting is at an end." I get to my feet and signal for Thorne to do the same. "After witnessing the decimation of my home, I find I have no patience left for trivial matters. Let's continue in three days."

Thorne and I leave the High Council room as quickly as possible, then stroll back through the castle toward my chambers. If I'm to survive another night of the halfling's company, I need sleep before tonight's feast.

When we arrive at my door, Thorne says, "The presence near the forest; let's hunt it tonight."

"I look forward to it. After dinner, meet me in the armory."

Thorne bows and strides off, disappearing down the staircase at the end of the hallway.

Feeling better than I have all day, I grip the sides of the door frame, lean forward, and stretch my shoulders. A nighttime hunt will keep my mind off Merri.

And then tomorrow, I must decide what to do with her.

25

Death Becomes Her

Merri

T he night is moonless, the dark so deep that when I wake up suddenly in the middle of it, I need to use magic to seek the menacing current that shook me from my dreams of blood and snow.

"Merri," says a voice, its timbre low and thick with longing.

Is it Riven?

"Give me your seer's necklace made of stone and power. Give me your heart so I may own that, too. Do it now. Avoid all woes. May it be right. May it be so."

I do know that voice. It's not Riven's but *Kian's*! What in the freaking realms is happening?

As I lurch into a sitting position, I throw up a barrier of air magic. The blast of energy flings the intruder through the air, thudding them against a wall. My eyes adjust to the darkness, showing me the bronze bird, Olwydd, flapping near the door, the cord of my holey stone hanging from its claw.

"You devil creature. Give that back to me, dammit!" I send a gust of wind to extract the necklace, but it merely buffets the bird around while it squawks loudly.

Then it screeches, the sound morphing into words as Kian's voice comes trumpeting from its beak. "Thank you, Merri, for such a lovely gift. I shall treasure it dearly. As I will cherish you when you're mine."

I leap out of bed and stalk toward Olwydd, my hands fisting the silky material of my nightgown. "Kian? Can you hear me in there, you cowardly, shriveled piece of dried-up pig's prick? Give me my necklace right now and scram before I summon the guards. When our court learns of this latest prank, you and whoever your accomplice is will be in so much trouble. There won't be a single cave or rock crevice for you to hide in all the seven realms."

"Ah, but I shall have *you*, Merrin darling, and that is all that matters. If you want the necklace that your precious Silver King gave you, you'll have to come and get it. Follow me if you dare."

As I lunge for the necklace, the door to the hallway opens by itself, and Olwydd flies straight through it.

Panting with fury, I shrug into a cloak and slip my feet into soft boots that I leave unlaced. Then I shoot out after the bird, immediately spying it hanging upside down from a gilt-framed painting of Riven's mother.

First, I throw magic at Olwydd, then one of the knives that I always wear strapped to my calves. Both bounce off the metal casing of its body. With the force of the wind behind it, the knife should have pierced his evil little heart with ease. But it didn't.

Unfortunately, it seems I need the Merit king by my side for my powers to have much effect in this infernal city. Any rational person would have left four days ago after they slapped an Unseelie king for insulting them. But I've never claimed to be sensible, and I'm not about to start behaving that way any time soon.

As I follow Olwydd out to the stables, I have the welcome realization that even thinking about Riven makes my power surge and flicker over my skin. This gives me hope. If I can keep him in mind and draw on his magic, then I should be able to defeat Kian and Olwydd and reclaim my holey stone. I refuse to leave the Merit City without it.

Shafts of moonlight illuminate the stables as I walk through the open doors and toward Olwydd, my gaze fixed on the necklace dangling from his beak.

He's perched on a high beam of oak, too high for my hands to reach, but the white-lightning sizzling from my fingertips will have a good chance of hitting its mark.

Picturing Riven's hand holding mine, I focus the energy and push it out of my palms. With a resounding crack, it hits the bird and ricochets off.

Kian's laughter fills the air.

Impossible! He took a direct hit. That bird should be baked. I raise another bolt of power, my focus faltering when the light in front of Olwydd shatters like a pane of glass and Draírdon appears. In a smooth acrobatic move, he tumbles from the crossbeams and lands in front of me.

I scream like a banshee and fire a sizzling sheet of lightning at him.

With a single wave of his palm, it disintegrates, and blinding purple energy envelopes me. I fall to my knees as the worst pain I've ever felt saws through my skull.

Now two laughs reverberate in the darkness—Kian's and the High Mage's.

They stand before me, blood gleaming from their smiles, proof of the dark magic they've been harnessing to shapeshift and control the mechanical bird.

"You're dead," I spit out as fury like I've never known spills over my cheeks in the form of scalding-hot tears.

Kian laughs again, slipping my necklace over his head, then picking up the stone and peering at me through the hole. "You're in no position to make futile threats, Merri darling. Hmmm. Oh, yes. This necklace suits me very well. I promise to take care of it for you. Now say the words to make it mine, and we may decide to let you return to your bed. Isn't that true, Draírdon?"

Draírdon says, "Nothing promised, nothing gained. Nothing ventured, plenty of pain."

The buzzing in my head increases. The High Mage is torturing me! I swallow a moan of agony and lean toward him. "When Riven learns of your treachery, mushroom face, you'll be a goner, too."

"A *goner*?" Draírdon sneers. "Your princess speaks strangely, Kian. A defect of her parentage, no doubt. After I've wiped your memory clean, halfling, that weakling Riven will never find out. You'll forget I was ever here. So, quickly now. Transfer ownership of the stone to Kian and ease your suffering."

"Being a good king doesn't make Riven weak. And you can go suck on a dead donkey's tail, because I'll never give the power of my holey stone to that psychotic strutting peacock."

Draírdon leans close, his iron-tinged breath nauseating. "Are you sure about that, my pretty little halfling? Its power is of no use to you here. At present, you can barely ruffle a whisker on my chin. For a Princess of Air, you're useless, pathetic."

If I can manage to draw more power from Riven to bolster mine, then Draírdon is wrong. I just need to buy a little more time to get the necklace back. I'm not giving that up. Riven gave it to me. It's mine. "I'll never speak the words, so do what you will to me."

"So be it," says the mage.

I conjure a vision of Riven along with a ball of lightning that crackles and whirs in my palm. Before I can toss it, the mage draws a knife and slices his forearm. Dark blood spills on the sawdust floor, and my head drops back, my magic fizzling out.

"No!" My arms shake and I can barely focus on Draírdon's triumphant sneer.

With a click of his fingers, he produces iron handcuffs from a slit in the air and slips them over my wrists, fastening them tightly.

Stars spin inside my head as cold iron takes effect, slurring my thoughts and words. "How did you carry these and not weaken your magic? It's...impossible."

Draírdon runs a claw along my cheek. "Oh, Princess, when you live in the shadows, almost anything is possible. Now sleep."

I focus on an image of Riven's eyes and let my body flop in a heap, pretending to faint.

The mage turns to Kian. "Put her on the horse. She shouldn't wake until I come to you tomorrow night."

"Why not do it now?" whines Kian. "It's the perfect time. All fae in the castle are unconscious under your spell. Let me take her from this land before they rise."

"You fool! Without another death, I cannot hold the spell much longer." Draírdon's eyes narrow. "Unless you would like to offer your life, Seelie lord? I'm certain I can find a use for a bonded princess of your court, halfling or not. Show me your throat."

Kian whimpers out a protest, and the mage spreads his arms toward the ceiling and begins a chant. Although the words of his spell are indistinct, they grate my insides, shredding my skin raw.

Barely conscious, I'm flung over a saddle and Kian mounts behind.

"You remember the directions?" echoes the mage's voice. I turn my head toward the sound and watch through heavy eyelids.

"Yes," replies Kian, the horse dancing beneath us.

"Good." Draírdon tosses a polished labradorite, the stone of transformation, into Kian's palm. "The blood of seven fae has ensured no power great or small will stand against you as long as you have this stone. Do not lose it."

Kian takes it and kicks the horse into motion. Then we're off, racing beneath the dispassionate night sky, wind tearing at my clothes, my body buffeted about.

After a while, the clopping of hooves over pavement changes to rhythmic padding on soft earth. Somewhere nearby, waves crash into rocks, the sound growing closer with every breath. Before long, the breeze brings the strong scent of brine and the sound of gulls cawing in the distance. Then the horse's hooves are thudding along sand, tiny grains flicking up and biting my face.

We're at the beach. No. This is bad. Bile rises up my throat, and I retch against sweaty horseflesh.

My mind reels as I picture Kian carting me on to a ship that will carry us away to some far-off land where I'd never see my family again. Or Riven.

We stop, the horse's sides heaving with each steaming breath.

Riven where are you? I need help. I search the air currents, seeking any sign of him, finding nothing and no one. It's just me, the horse, and my revolting kidnapper.

"Here we are, Merrin. If the journey woke you, do not fear, you won't be conscious for much longer."

Kian dismounts and hauls me off. He throws me over his shoulder and walks up a shadowy hill, then downward for a time, his boots crunching over unstable rocks. He stops on the precipice of a cliff and slides me down his body, my back pressed to his chest.

My feet hit the ground, and every part of me trembles, including my eyeballs. I peer into a black void and feel the ghosts of old reaching from the foul pit below.

Without another word, Kian shoves me, and I somersault down.

Down.

Down.

And still farther down I fall to a likely painful death of shattered bones and splattered flesh.

Suddenly, my breath whooshes out of me as I collide with something soft, not pillow-soft, but it's certainly not as hard as rock or the ground. I slide down a great hill or pile of something or other, cartwheeling and tumbling until I hit a solid barrier. I open my eyes, and in a great shaft of moonlight, I see books. Books. And more books!

Weak from iron sickness, I push onto my haunches and look up at the almost-full moon that fills the gaping hole above and dusts my skin with silver light. Heart thundering in my ears, I scan the space and find I'm surrounded by various-sized mountains of books and rubble, some intact shelves still lining the sides of the narrow cavern that is so deep I wonder how I'll ever get out of here.

This place has to be the ruins of the sunken library Riven mentioned. To think I was so desperate to visit—but not like this, weak, overpowered, and a prisoner of the pathetic Kian Leondearg.

Across the room, the end of a rope ladder hangs a little way off the ground, and Kian scurries down it in a rodent-like fashion. "I'm pleased you're still alive, Merrin. If you give me your trust and make the holey stone mine, I'll ensure you will remain unharmed."

It will be a bright day in the Shade Court before I'll give him anything other than a punch in his ballocks.

I rub my temples as he jumps from the last rung of the ladder and minces his way over piles of debris. "The stables…" I say, my memory of the night's events foggy, faulty.

He leans down, inspecting me closely. "Yes, I captured you in the stables. Do you recall anyone else being there, you sweet docile thing?"

"No." I'm certain that there was someone, but for the life of me I can't recall who. I think for a moment and give up, shaking my head. "Just you and that horrible beady-eyed bird. What are we doing here?"

"Wouldn't you love to know. Since your hateful father caused my exile, I've been watching you, planning to make you mine."

My insides roil at the thought of being Kian's *anything*. "So that was you the day of the market, following me, and many nights since. How...how have you gone undetected in the city? And how did you get through the king's wards?"

"The *king*, the *king*," he wails. "I'm entirely sick of that particular fae. Anyone would think the seven realms revolve around him."

"He's the Unseelie king, Kian. At least one of the kingdoms revolves around him. Don't be a fool. How did you avoid his notice? And his royal guard has been hunting you for days. How did you evade capture?"

"Questions. Questions." Kian drops to his haunches, lifts my limp, heavy arms by the shackle between my wrists, then leans his bony cheek into my palm, forcing me to caress his skin. "I have friends in high places. That's all you need to know."

He drops my hands and brings his parted lips close.

Gagging at the thought of his mouth touching mine, I struggle hard against his cruel grip. He laughs and twists the sensitive tip of my ear. I kick him and spit on his boot, growling like Balor does when he's in hot pursuit of a draygonet.

I can barely remember how I came to be in this sunken library, how *he* managed to chain and drag me here. But suddenly I remember something very, very important—an image of the Court of Five High Mage, Ether, spitting on my cookie the night I left home. She said it would connect us, that she'd know if I needed her. Well, I can't think of an occasion I would need her more than now.

I draw my focus inside and call her in my mind. *Ether...*

Ether...

"Look at me, Merrin," shouts Kian as he shakes me by the shoulders. "Look. At. Me!"

"*Stop.* That hurts." I risk speaking the mage's name out loud. "Ether? *Ether*?"

"Be quiet!" He shoves me hard. "How dare you invoke that old crone's name."

I fall back and stare through a veil of tears at the bright moon smiling down at me. She offers reassurance. Comfort. I take neither.

"Ether can't help you now. Nor can righteous Riven or your foul-tempered father. You're mine, Merrin. And when we leave this place for our new home, I vow that you will earn your keep in blood and tears. Mark me, this is the last time you will ever dare think yourself above me."

"You never change, Kian. And you'll always be wrong and out of touch with reality, too full of yourself to bother achieving anything by way of honor and hard work. Instead, like a foul odor, you blow in and out, an insignificant annoyance incapable of any lasting effect. That's what you are, Kian—a stinky, treacherous, cheating cloud of nothing."

"I've had enough of your mutinous words for tonight, Merrin Fionbharr. You shouldn't treat one who holds your fate in the palm of their hand with such open disdain. Close your eyes and sleep now."

He takes something from his breast pocket—black powder—and flings it at me. Metal shards explode in my head, the pain excruciating.

"You killed me," I say as my skull squeezes tighter.

"No, Merrin. I would never go so far." Kian straddles me, then licks my face from chin to eyeball. I retch, nearly choking on vomit. "I need you alive, Princess mine. For always and forever more."

My eyes roll to the side, locking on a blurry image of an enormous brass clock that ticks high up on a wall. "Clock's broken," I slur.

Tick-tock. Tick-tock.

"Just let me go," I beg.

"Never."

Tick-tock. Tick-tock.

"Please. The pain..."

Ether, where are you?

Kian, let me die.

The pain increases. Then the moonlight dims, the darkness transforming into a translucent obsidian mirror. I gaze through it into an empty, endless night.

I am nothing but white-hot pain.

Then thick, oozing anguish.

Then just...

Tick.

Tock.

Nothing.

26

Library of Souls

Riven

"**M**ove!" Thorne growls. "Or your boots will be splattered." For the fifth time this evening, his body bends violently as he empties what's left of his guts over the pavement.

With my usual impeccable timing, I step behind him and pat his hunched-over back. "I'm sorry, Thorne, I can see I must arrange more transferring practice for you."

Glaring at me, he wipes his mouth. "I'd rather have my teeth pulled, ground up, and fed to me in my porridge."

I laugh. "That, too, can be arranged."

We've spent the last hour transferring all over the city, our deadliest swords strapped to our bodies and magic primed with druidic rituals, searching for a trace of the mystery interloper. So far, our efforts have been in vain.

When we hit the outskirts of Blackthorn Forest, my worldly sight dims, and my inner perception blazes with a vision that shocks me to the core. Bathed in moonlight, in my mind's eye, I see the enormous broken clock in the sunken library, its pendulum swinging to and fro.

Tick-tock. Tick-tock.

The fact that the clock is awake disturbs me greatly. Its magic can only ignite when a life form of consequence enters its domain—fae or human. Instantly, my thoughts leap to Merri. Was she foolish enough to journey to the library on her own?

I focus my concentration internally and search through the ruins. It doesn't take long to find her, lying unconscious surrounded by books and broken gilded rafters.

There's no time to give Thorne any warning. I grip his shoulder and dematerialize faster than I've ever done in my life, picturing the old library, my thoughts focused on a book about the goddess Arianrhod that I saw cushioning Merri's head in my vision.

When I open my eyes, my jaw drops in shock. We're standing on the edge of the library crater, not at the bottom of it where I'd planned to arrive. How did this happen? I've never miscalculated a transfer before.

I clench my teeth and attempt to transfer again. It doesn't work. Nothing happens, and only a slight buzz of particle disturbance runs along my skin. A barrier of foreign magic encircles the crater and is somehow preventing me from moving through it.

"By the Infernal Sun, Thorne, Merri is down there, and I cannot transfer to her. Whoever she's with has the ability to obstruct an Unseelie king's power. This is disastrous." I take a step closer to the mouth of the crater. "Stay there. Don't follow me."

As I throw myself into the cavern's dark maw, Thorne lunges for me, his claws scraping my bracer. "Riven, wait!"

Roaring, I run and tumble down the wreckage of the ancient Library of Souls, my body rolling at the bottom before I leap onto my feet, sword drawn.

In the charged silence, the moonlight reveals Merri curled over a small pile of books, her wrists shackled. I see no creature hovering nearby, but their malevolent energy coats her form like tar.

The magic I desperately will into my limbs doesn't spark, not even a little. Only a cocktail of panic and terror shoots through my veins. My power is blocked—inert and useless. Without it, how can I destroy Merri's captor and remove her to safety?

A thud sounds as Thorne lands beside me, drawing his sword and slashing at the air.

"Damn you, Thorne," I hiss. "I told you to stay put."

He chuckles. "Since when do I listen to you?"

"Never." I take advantage of the cover his sword provides and scuttle crab-like toward Merri. Taking great care, I inspect her.

I'm relieved to find no obvious injuries, but her pulse is weak from the poisoned chains. I try to blast them off and am unsurprised when my magic fails once again.

"Now's the time to fight, Princess," I say, my voice hoarse. "Don't give in to the iron. Fight it with your every breath. *Please.*"

She groans in answer, but I don't hold much hope—like Thorne, she never listens to me either. Croaking sounds come from the mouth of the cave, the seven grief ravens cawing together around the edge.

Death is coming.

Thorne shuffles backward, moving closer to us. "Riven, get up! Something is—"

Before he can finish, an explosion of light blinds me momentarily. I throw myself over Merri, protecting her as rocks, plaster, and gold dirt rain down. What the hell just happened? I shove onto my feet, my gaze searching the cavern and sword swinging wildly.

Thorne is gone. Where in the Blood Sun is he?

"Thorne?" I bellow, my pulse roaring in my ears. "For Dana's sake, answer me. Are you all right?"

A moment's silence. Then an insidious chuckle comes from a small branch of the cave directly in front of me, followed by a voice slithering out of the darkness. "Poor impotent Silver King. Do not fear. Your friend may well survive after a long period of sleep. Or perhaps he won't. After some time has passed, Merri will most definitely wake, but by then, it will be too late for you, and she'll already be mine."

"Show yourself!" The muffled echo of my words answers me. I wait, counting heart beats.

One, two. One, two. One, two.

My patience snaps. "My power is blocked, yet yours remains. You're a gutless coward if you refuse to face me. Forever unworthy of a princess of the Bright Court." My knuckles crack on the sword hilt, blood and rage priming my muscles for a fight to the death.

Stones shift and crunch as a pair of boots treads over the ruins. A red-headed fae emerges from the shadows.

"You!" I snarl. I cannot believe the pompous peafowl from the Land of Five stands before me, the one who was exiled for implicating Merri and the Fire queen in my capture.

In what realm is it possible for *him* to best Thorne and me?

I must stay calm and *think*. I fold my fury over and over until it's the size of a lump of coal and lodges in the middle of my chest. I nod toward Merri. "Can't you obtain a girl without knocking one unconscious and stealing her?"

He laughs again and draws his sword. "For Merrin to be stolen, she would need to belong to someone first."

"She *belongs* to her land," I roar. "To her family and loved ones, and most of all to *herself*."

"And now, as you can see, forsaking all others, she belongs to me."

Kian Leondearg inhales a long, smug draft of air through his quivering nostrils. He had better make the most of it, because his breaths in this realm are numbered. He just doesn't realize it yet.

I circle him slowly, my muscles drawn taut, ready to pounce.

"So this is all about, Merri?" I ask.

"Of course. As it has always been."

"Why the obsession?" I slash my blade through the air in a lemniscate pattern. "Did she make you cry once, and like a pathetic milksop, you vowed to have your revenge and one day conquer her?"

Madness glints in his eyes. "Merrin and I are made for each other. I knew it the very moment I saw her."

"When she was an infant? An appalling concept, proving your words are those of a deluded psychopath."

Kian palms something on the left side of his chest, then thrusts his hand toward me. A bolt of purple shoots out, and I sidestep it with ease. My power might be suspended, but I'm fast, and Kian is flustered and slow.

He clutches his chest, spewing childish insults that make me feel pity rather than fear. Then I remember Thorne lying in the dirt. And Merri.

Rage shudders through me.

I have curses I wish to hurl at him, too, but I plan to deliver every one of them with the edge of my sword.

Before he has time to activate the damned thing in his breast pocket that enables his magic, I run at him with an ear-splitting war cry. He blocks my blade with his own, and we slash back and forth, sliding up and down the hills and valleys of decayed books and scrolls.

The clash of metal and our labored grunts punctuate each violent move, keeping time. Lunge, slash, parry. Slash, parry, slash. Forward. Back. Circle. Slash. Slash. Slash.

Mold and the sour smell of fear saturates the air, telling me that Kian's corpse will soon be contributing to the rot in the cavern, not mine. He's afraid, and the heady scent of his terror calls to my Unseelie nature, honing my movements, making them sharper. Faster and deadlier.

I lead the brutal dance and spin him in a swift pattern as we range from wall to wall. On top of the highest mountain of books, I lunge, drawing my dagger from its belt, and aim a killing blow at the Elemental's neck. Before my dagger bites his flesh, a blast of magic rips it from my hand. The blade flies down one side of the hill, and the blast sends me somersaulting to the bottom of the other.

Kian sheathes his sword and leaps down the hill of debris after my blade, which has landed beside Merri, within reach of her limp hand.

"No!" I yell, scrabbling across slippery paper and earth toward them.

Kian snatches my knife from the ground and slashes wildly at Merri, her sharp cry of pain searing my soul.

I make the sound of a wounded bear—half roar, half cry. "You said you wouldn't hurt her! If you have, runt, you'll pay with eternal suffering. I vow it."

Kian hunches over her like a sniveling bag of blood and bones. "She'll survive. 'Tis only a tiny wound. I needed a little more blood, more power in order to kill you, Merit. You shall be the one to suffer, not I."

He tosses my knife to the far reaches of the cave. As he does this, without warning, Merri lurches up and stabs Kian in the armpit with one of the tiny bone daggers she wears. Then, while he's reeling in shock, she throws herself on him. He topples backward as her bound hands claw at his chest, tearing fabric. A triumphant yelp, and she flings a tiny stone across the cavern.

Kian howls, scrambling after it.

"Stop him, Riven," yells Merri. "The stone powers his magic. Quickly!"

I hurtle across the cave and leap onto his back. We crash on the ground next to a sludgy quagmire of filth. We both roll onto our feet at the same time. Kian draws his blade, and as he raises it, his eyes narrow on the labradorite stone shimmering on the edge of the pool of quicksand-like mud. The gem must be powerful indeed because he spends a moment too long contemplating making a dive for it instead of fighting me with his sword.

I regain his attention with the edge of my blade as it clangs on his vivid-blue armor. Puffing and glowering, he attacks, but without the stone, his efforts are weak.

One slash. Two. Three. Four more, then our swords lock, and I wish I still had the dagger he threw away so I could gut him with it. Kian presses his weight against my sword, his arms shuddering. I push back with all my might, silently thanking Thorne for the endless, punishing hours of daily training he makes me endure.

Heat boils inside me. If I were human, I'd be sweating rivers by now. But I'm not. I am fae, the king of the Unseelie.

With a grunt, I step back, and Kian stumbles. Then I feint, and he retreats again, slamming against the wall and going for his pocket.

"Bad luck. Your little toy is gone." Lightning fast, I slash his sword from his grip, and it clatters to his feet.

Blood drips from his arm, white bone glistening from an ugly gash, and I bare my teeth in a merciless grin as I kick his sword away then close in.

Gusts of his sour breath fan my face, and I wrap one hand around his reed-thin throat, not squeezing yet. Simply waiting.

"I shall enjoy making Merrin cry," he wheezes. "After I kill you, she will live to regret every humiliation she inflicted upon me."

"And how do you plan to defeat me? Currently, you're powerless. But that's your usual state, isn't it, Leondearg? You've always been *less* than any creature around you. Even slugs, maggots, rotting corpses."

He spits in my face and then bursts into tears, snot hanging from his pointy chin.

The holey stone I gave Merri dangles from his neck. With a hard tug, I break the cord and pocket it.

Eager to finish him off, I shove him to the ground. As his power ebbs, mine flows through my veins, strength returning to my body.

I could pop this fae's head like a grape or rip his coward's heart from his puny chest in the blink of an eye. But, no, given what he's tried to take from me—Merri and my best friend—his death must be slow. And satisfying.

Kian writhes on his back. Flipping his body, I push him face-first into the pool of thick mud, muffling his blood-curdling screams.

Trembling with rage, I hold him in place. Not pressing hard enough to snap his neck or suffocate him, but making sure my nails pierce his skin and that he'll stay conscious for as long as possible. And die slowly.

The grief ravens cry shrilly above. My vision tunnels to black as the library disappears, my entire being focused on the Seelie's muffled death cries. His body flails, and I keep the pressure steady, allowing a small pocket of air to form. Extending the horror.

"Riven, enough. End it. Please."

Merri's voice releases me from the trance, and I contract my fingers fast, breaking the vermin's neck. I stand and step backward, scanning the cavern. The Seelie is dead. But where is his talisman, the source of his foul power?

I search the shadows until I find the stone, then pick it up, its dark magic burning the pads of my fingers. With a snarl, I toss it at the ground, the heel of my boot chasing it fast and smashing it into fine powder.

A putrid green light and a noxious smell explode in the cavern. Thankfully, both dissipate quickly. I crack my neck, moving it side to side, as the remainder of my power returns, vibrating first in my chest, my gut, then snaking through my limbs like molten lava. The spectral crown of jet appears, buzzing and flickering on top of my head, a sign I am fully restored. An Unseelie king once more.

"Riven, my chains." Merri collapses against a ruined velvet sofa, her skin deathly pale. "Hurry."

I stumble over to her, and with a single thought, crack the iron from her wrists, then carefully help her onto her feet.

"You found me." Merri smiles and lifts her hands toward the sky as snow falls from the cavern's opening and eddies around us, just like it does in my visions.

I step back, fear jumbling my thoughts as she collects a flake from the air and places it on her tongue. "See? This snow can't harm us, Riven. It's a manifestation of my joy, my relief that, tonight, we survived the terrors of our visions. We did it. *Together.*"

Our visions?

I think of my dreams and the pictures in the scrying well that began the day she was born, back when I had no clue what she would come to mean to me.

There is no pond of silver in this library. No tree of gold. But, still, I can't deny that most of the events I foresaw in the druid's well have come to pass.

I first met her at the pond. It snowed then, too. The ancient library clock is gold, its rusty tick-tocking akin to the cracking of branches. The knife. Her blood. It has all happened. Yet neither of us are dead.

Yet.

"Wait here," Merri says as she strolls to a corner of the cavern, searching for something. She returns with my knife and softly opens my palm, laying the blade on it. "Look at your knife, Riven, covered in blood—my blood—and both of us are safe."

Mesmerized, I stare at the dark red color, and then without wiping the knife, I sheathe it. "You'll be safer when I get you out of this library. I wish I'd ordered the infernal thing to be filled in years ago. Come."

"But Thorne—where is he?"

Thorne. Of course. How could I have forgotten him, even momentarily?

We find him lying under a fallen beam, its weight supported by the frame of a huge window. I remove stained-glass fragments from his body and then feel for his pulse, relieved to find he still has one. Merri and I crouch next to him, and we take his body in our arms.

"Close your eyes," I tell her. "It will help prevent nausea when we dematerialize."

We transfer out of the library, intentionally landing close to the cavern's entrance to give Thorne a chance to recover. He wakes, rolling onto his side, then vomits on the grass. "What happened?"

"Quite a bit," I tell him. "Rest a while before we return to the castle, and I'll fill you in over breakfast."

"Breakfast? No thank you." His eyelids flutter, and he collapses against the ground.

I push onto my feet and go to Merri who stands nearby, watching the russet sunrise on the horizon. "Are you all right?" I ask.

She walks into my arms and wraps her hands behind my neck. "Riven. Yes, finally. All is well."

Her voice is soft, her fingers warm against my skin. I should push her away. But I don't. I can't.

"Consider how the night's events played out. Instead of killing me as your visions foretold, you saved me." She laughs softly. "Then, of course, I saved the three of us by getting rid of that stone. But, Riven, don't you see? You're not the monster you believe yourself to be."

"Maybe I'm not a monster, but I can never give you what you desire. Go home, Merri. Go back to where you belong, where people love you and will keep you safe. Take the human girl with you. Get as far away as you can from the influence of my court. Your mage can release Summer from the thrall she suffers under and return her to the mortal world."

Instantly, her gaze turns wintry as she drops her arms to her sides. Mine remain wrapped loosely around her waist.

"If that's what you wish," she says, "then so be it. I'll not stand here begging you to see sense."

"I am glad," I say, the words slicing through my skull like a lie. "I'll help you contact your mages and—"

"I don't need your assistance. Now that I'm no longer iron-sick, I'm certain the Elements will hear me. I'll be gone before you know it." She moves to leave my embrace.

"Wait." I tighten my arms around her, and for a moment, hope sparks in her eyes. I draw a painful breath. "Where did Kian get the stone? Do you remember the presence of another being? He can't possibly have achieved what he did alone."

Confusion clouds her expression. "There *was* someone." She rubs her forehead. "I...I just can't remember."

"Fae or beast? Male or female?" I press.

"I don't know. A female, perhaps. Their image is blocked to me. I can only feel their energy and extreme hatred for me. I'm sorry."

Then this being is strong, and my troubles are far from over.

Merri's lips touch mine, soft as butterfly wings that land for only a moment, drawing power. She walks toward the trees and calls out the name Ether. Wispy clouds form the letters of the being's name and float upward before the wind whisks them away.

A Land of Five mage appears, her billowing mane of hair so white it's translucent. She's wrapped in flowing silks of silver and has eyes as dark as the eternal void. Her face is tranquil, her smile warm and reassuring, then she speaks, and something deep within me quakes.

"Merri, child. How lovely to see you. I should have known you wouldn't call me when your life was in danger, but instead when your heart is. You've always valued sentiment above sense. Do not take my meaning wrong; for this reason, I respect you greatly."

The mage gives me a pointed glance. "Many a fool could take your lead, Merrin, and rule by their hearts, thereby improving their realm's happiness and prosperity immeasurably."

Ether criticizes the way I rule my kingdom, but I can find no words of defense.

"I did call for you, High Mage, but my pleas were blocked by magic." Merri curtsies deeply. "Thank you for coming."

"Silver King," says Ether. "I hadn't taken you for a fool, and we all make mistakes from time to time. I ask you this—will you learn from yours before it's too late?"

I've no idea what she's referring to. It could be any number of things. Still, I incline my head respectfully. This Elemental mage is older than time itself and most likely precedes the druids. She could turn me to dust with the snap of her fingers. I'm not about to argue with her.

"No? Are you still oblivious?" She tsk tsks like a disapproving nursemaid. "You disappoint me."

Wonderful. I'll add her to the ever-growing list of those who find me lacking.

Something in her expression tugs a memory I cannot place. A thread of dread that connects to nothing solid. I've never met the High Mage of Talamh Cúig before, so there's no reason for me to be wary of her. And yet...an irrational fear settles deep inside me.

Merri frowns, giving her full attention to the High Mage and excluding me by turning away. "Ether, there's a human girl in the city. Her name is Summer, and she must return with us. Can you wait while I find her?"

Stepping forward, I clasp Merri's arm. "No need. I can send for her and—"

"No," the mage's voice thunders. "In the time you wasted speaking, I have called her forth. Silver King, I suggest you take your hands off what isn't yours to touch."

I do as Ether bids but not without considerable effort. My mind wants Merri gone. It seems my body does not.

Leaves tremble in the branches above, and a limp-limbed girl drops onto the ground. The human, dressed warmly as though ready to depart on a journey.

"Summer," says Merri. "We're returning to my home, the Elemental Court where light lives in the hearts of nearly all the creatures in its bounds. There, I promise you will be well-treated. Safe. Do you wish to come with us in free will?"

Summer shudders. "Does the Winter prince live there?" Her voice is low, a breeze rustling through reeds.

My boots shuffle around the uneven ground. I want to see the smile I'm sure Merri will be giving to the girl.

"Yes, indeed. Prince Wynter resides at my court."

She speaks no lie. I know that's her brother's name.

"Then, yes! Of course, I want to go with you." Like a child, the bewitched human spins three times. "Let's go. Please, hurry!"

Wearing a mysterious smile, Ether opens her arms. Merri takes the human's hand, and they step toward the mage.

The princess gives me no backward glance nor any parting words. Not one. Not even goodbye.

"Merrin...wait," I say. "You forgot something."

She turns, her expression blank and spine set in a rigid line. I put the holey stone in her palm, and she stares at it like it's a poisonous snake but pockets it anyway. Still, she says nothing.

Why won't she speak?

"You can't even say goodbye to me?" I ask. "Nor grant me a wish for a long and happy life?"

"I suppose I can try." A stiff smile freezes on her face. "Goodbye, Riven. I'm very grateful you came when I needed help—these words I can say with ease. But the things I wish for you are my own secrets to keep well-guarded. One day, if you can raise the courage, you're welcome to come and find me and ask me to unlock them."

And with those words, the apricot-colored sky folds over itself like a freshly laundered sheet, and Merri, the mage, and the human all disappear within it.

The Elemental princess is gone.

From the Court of Merits.

From my life.

But not from my dreams.

As I crouch down to tend to Thorne, the library clock taunts me from the inky depths below.

Tick-tock. Tick-tock. Tick-tock, it says.

Time is running out.

27

The King Must Choose

Riven

After the halfling princess returned home, I assumed I would swiftly forget her. After all, the scene in my visions—the snow, a violent death, my blood-painted knife—it had all come to pass, and we'd both survived with our kingdoms still standing. But I haven't forgotten Merri. Far from it.

A full moon's turn has passed, but the dreams persist in an even more disturbing form. Instead of daggers and rust-colored blood, scarlet hair twines my fingers, smooth skin pebbles under my touch, and a wild silver gaze melts from the heat of our kisses.

These images torture me more than the visions of death ever did.

What do they mean? The answer is simple: if I allow desire to bring me to my knees, my obsession with the Elemental princess will tear me from my path and cause me to neglect my city.

But I won't let it.

My kingdom must come first. Always. The druids taught me to focus my power for the good of my land, not to deplete my life force in lusty pursuits.

All I learned from my father was that I never wanted to be like him. After he rejected me, I only had the druids' wisdom to nourish me, and I refuse to dishonor their legacy by failing them and my people now.

This morning, Meerade still sleeps on the metal beams at the foot of my bed, and I lie wretched and despondent under the furs. I cover my eyes with my arm and beg the gods to release me from my tortured thoughts and grant me a little more sleep. But, alas, peace must wait.

A loud knock sounds, and my attendant, Tiernan, enters bearing breakfast. He places a tray beside the bed and opens the curtains. Late morning sunshine streams over the black and gilt walls.

I squint against the glare then at the silver eyes staring at me from within complex patterns on the wallpaper. Why must I see Merri everywhere I look? I shake my head to clear the illusion.

Scowling, I watch Meerade hoot awake and fly onto Tiernan's shoulder.

"Good morning, Your Majesty. And Meerade." Tiernan's leathery wings unfold as he bows, his draped sleeves skimming the floor. "Can I get you anything else?"

I force a less threatening expression. "No. That is all."

Tiernan glides toward the exit, my owl whistling sweet nothings in his ear. She wants his help to gain entry to the kitchens, where she'll eat copious food items not intended for her. As always, the fae is her happy and obedient accomplice.

"Wait…tell the bards I don't want them to perform tonight. I'd prefer the court to eat in silence."

Tiernan's black brow rises. We've been friends since he tended me as a child, and for a Merit, he's a kindly soul. "But, My King, you've told me many times that a meal cannot be enjoyed without music. What will the courtiers think of this change?"

"I don't care to guess. See it done."

"Yes, Majesty. Of course."

"Thank you. And, Meerade, I'll call for you after training. Please don't eat too much. Remember how sick you made yourself yesterday?"

She answers with a shriek, then says, "Queen," her favorite word of late.

As Tiernan departs, leaving a trail of glittering bronze dust behind, I recall what I said to Merri on the way to Emerald Bay. Three lifetimes must have passed since that day when I smirked and told her to never trust a fae who doesn't enjoy music—that their hearts were impoverished wastelands.

With those words, I never imagined I'd be describing my future self.

Ignoring the breakfast tray, I walk out onto the balcony and survey the city, my gaze trailing over the sea to the single tower piercing the sky. Today, the black one is hidden and only the white is visible. *Mother*. I should visit her soon. Share my sorrows. Repent my sins. Request absolution.

The softest breeze caresses my bare chest, sending my thoughts reeling toward the Princess of Air.

Again.

The city has been awake for hours, and I've spent my time lying in my chamber feeling sorry for myself, achieving nothing. This can't go on much longer.

A horn blows in the distance, Thorne telling me to hurry up and get to sword practice. Good. I look forward to the distraction.

I frown down at the linen pants barely clinging to my hips and glamor up suitable fighting armor. Every blow Thorne strikes upon my unprotected body will be a welcome punishment for my over-indulgent brooding.

After strapping on my favorite sword, the one I nearly killed that bogtroll Kian with, I jog to the training yard, quite enjoying the bemused greetings from the courtiers as I pass.

I round the wall and see Thorne's teeth flashing at me and wish I'd stayed in bed. He looks far too pleased to see me stumbling through the gate, a mess.

"Riven, you look pained, and you're not even wearing a circlet like a proper king would be at this time of day. I suppose this means you're still moping, then." He slashes his sword through the air between us.

"Correct. But I trust you'll help me see the error of my ways."

"Gladly. With each and every bite of my blade." With those words he lunges, landing a brutal blow on my shoulder before I even have a chance to draw my sword.

"Is that all you've got for me?" Wincing in pain, I stalk toward Thorne and mutter, "*Go harder. Faster.*"

He stops in his tracks, brow hiked high. "Is that *glamored* armor you're wearing? It's sort of wavering in and out."

"What do you think?" I snarl.

"That you're an idiot. And I refuse to take it easy on you just because you've—"

"I know it. Stop talking."

He charges, and I lurch backward.

My mind is a mess, my limbs uncoordinated. This fight is a joke.

Swords clashing, our feet work fast. I clang my blade against Thorne's chest plate, then stumble as he feints and slices his steel across my bicep. Pain bites hard, its toxic drug sluicing through my veins. Grunting, I spin on my heels, my face raised to the sun.

I turn to Thorne and close my eyes, taking a long breath. Then I open my eyes and lift my sword as he lowers his own. "Come on," I say through gritted teeth.

"Riven, wait. Stop." He circles me, frowning. "Raise a barrier and protect your bare flesh."

"No." I growl and attack him with renewed energy. The combat grows fierce, our harsh breaths and soft grunts a comfort to me. Every strike of his blade is a blessing.

We scrape back and forth until I have him pinned against the wall, my sword at his throat. "You let me win."

"And you're bleeding," he says.

I peer through my glamor at the dark rivulets trailing my skin, the red blood pooling on my bare feet and the ground. "Yes."

I laugh, and he hits my shoulder with his palm, spinning my body and slamming me into the wall. I slide down it to the ground and fold my arms over my knees, then brace for what's coming: conversation—the worst part of our battle. The question is will I let him defeat me?

He sits beside me and spears me with his amber gaze. "I never took you for a coward, let alone a fool. Just go to her, Riven. Be hers, and she can be yours. Can you not see that Merrin is perfect for you?"

"Perfect." I scoff. "Perfectly capable of destroying me."

"So then you *are* a coward."

"Think of the city! My kingdom," I boom.

"What of them?

"She's a halfling. A *Seelie* halfling."

"And the Elementals take full-blooded humans for brides all the time. If anything, it's only made them stronger. Faery blood has always required a little fortifying by the human race. How have you forgotten this?"

"Because, for the longest time, we Merits have considered ourselves above the corrupted frailty of humans."

"Get over yourself. Take her for a lover, and I wager all your problems will disappear. I promise you, my friend. All you need is a good—"

"What about my druidic path?" I'm not sure I want to hear his answer, because I think I already know it.

"As you learned, Riven, but chose to repress, druidism reveres pleasure as a creative force, especially if you integrate and channel it responsibly. This is what the druids taught you. I know because you relayed many of your lessons to me when we were younger. Some of the most powerful druids had lovers, equal spiritual partners. Why have you decided to delude yourself about this?"

"Because I..." Sighing loudly, I grab a handful of glittery dirt and let it run through my fingers. "When did you become so smart?"

"I've always been brilliant. I suggest you speak with your sister. Take her council in the matter. Much joy awaits you, my friend. And my greatest wish is that you will be brave enough to reach out and take it."

Joy. For me? It seems unlikely.

Merri's parting words about her own secret wishes for me echo in my mind. *One day, if you can raise the courage, you're welcome to come and find me and ask me to unlock them,* she told me, her face solemn.

She thinks me a coward, too.

All this time, I've considered my self-sacrifice as courageous, even heroic. But perhaps Merri and Thorne are right. My vision came true, and we're both still alive.

Then there's that damned curse, those final words that allude to Merri and me being the missing part of the puzzle—that together, reigning as one, we'll create the peace I've long wished for. If all this is possible, then why do I resist?

Thorne slaps my back, jolting me from my thoughts. "I shall leave you to your self-torture. Should you need me, you know where I'll be."

"In the alehouse as usual?"

Laughing, he stands and brushes gravel from his leather pants. "Listen, if you decide to visit Lidwinia, I suggest you deal with those wounds first. In a heartbeat, she'll see right through that shoddy glamor you're wearing and have my head on a pike within two."

"Of course," I agree. "I will." Soon.

After he leaves, I sit on the ground for hours, wrestling with what-ifs and letting my blood congeal in the dirt. When I can no longer bear it, I call down magic and seal my gashes. Then I leave the practice yard with haste, eager to test my resolution on my sister—hear myself say the words. Make it real.

I get distracted and transfer to Citrene Creek, sit on the bank, lost in memories of the picnic and the horrors of the nix nearly taking Merri from me.

By the time I leave, the gloaming wraps a purple sunset around my shoulders as I stalk toward the city in search of Lidwinia and Elas. I find them in the first place I look, alone in the Meritorium, heads bowed over a complicated contraption, bolts and metal shavings piled everywhere.

"I'm off," I announce casually as I stride through the glass doors.

"Oh? And where are you going?" my sister asks, not bothering to raise her head from her work.

"I'll get Merrin. Bring her back here."

Lidwinia's lips tilt in a not-so-secret smirk. "Why would you do that?"

"She belongs here." I brace my feet wide, lift my chin.

"Tell me more," she urges, finally lifting her head to bore her orange gaze through my skull. A stool squeaks as she pulls it out from the table, indicating with her head that I should sit.

I prefer to stand. What I have to say won't take long, and I haven't time to linger. "With me, I mean. She belongs here with me."

"At last! What took you so long to realize this?" asks Elas. "We knew as soon as Merrin turned up here telling Lidwinia her role was to save you from some terrible fate that something big was about to happen."

He rushes over and gives me a brutal one-armed hug as though I've announced we're the victors in a seven-year war or something equally momentous.

"And then you were so desperate for her to leave before you caused her some mysterious harm. We knew, didn't we, Lidwinia? You and the Seelie princess are a match made in Tír na nÓg, if ever there was one. We've laughed so hard at your blindness our stomachs ached."

"Let him be, Elas," Lidwinia chides. "You know Riven has always taken his time to make significant decisions." She leaves her work and joins me on the polished concrete floor, pressing a kiss to my cheek.

"I must depart tonight before I change my mind. I won't stay long at Talamh Cúig, but if Everend kills me, the scroll that makes you and Elas rulers in my stead is signed and sealed in the Great Vault. When I arrive safely, I'll send Meerade back with a message."

I hug her and transfer straight to the White Tower. When I enter the enormous circular room, five floating glass balls of various sizes greet me with their golden light.

Mother.

Parting soft jewel-hued veils, I move slowly toward the sun bed and sit on its edge, my fingers burrowing into the thick, white covers. I lie back, warmed by the blazing fire, and stare into the void of the tower's open ceiling, imagining a future with Merri.

With my mind, I show the dead queen my plans, my wild hopes, and ridiculous dreams and wait for her reaction. In return, she gifts me with images from my childhood, happy days bathed in the warmth of her love.

Then the pictures shift, and I see Merri wearing the crown of meteoric silver, her smile as luminous as the glittering spikes, and me standing beside her, my grin even brighter. I look different. Changed. I hardly recognize myself.

Golden light streams over me as Mother blesses my plan to leave my kingdom and pursue the daughter of the Land of Five. She communicates in images and a smattering of words that sound in my mind.

I thank her aloud, promising that when I return, I'll bring Merri to the White Tower at the time of the Blood Sun when Mother's energy is the most vital, and she can materialize and converse.

Closing my eyes, I transfer to the council chamber in search of the High Mage. It's empty.

Next, I follow a hunch and materialize in the Starless Dungeons. There I find Draírdon and Tyzagarne skulking around the dank cells beneath the castle, engaged in what they loosely describe as a kind of maintenance inspection.

I stare blankly at them to indicate my doubt.

Tyzagarne's shoulders hunch. Draírdon's sneer grows. It's clear the only objects these two schemers are interested in maintaining are their personal coffers.

They bow, the giant's effort respectful, the mage's bordering on offensive.

"I'm glad I've found you together. I wanted to inform you that I'm leaving for Talamh Cúig. Draírdon, I'll require your assistance to open a portal and—"

"I beg your pardon?" says Draírdon. "I must have misheard you. I thought you said you were—"

"I did. And I am." I face Tyzagarne. "Speak to Princess Lidwinia. She has my instructions and will wear the crown in my absence." The giant shifts from foot to foot, huge jaw hanging loose.

"Go. Do it now. You know where she'll be hiding."

Another bow and his footsteps shake the foundations toward the exit. When he's gone, I narrow my eyes at Draírdon. "If you have something to say, spit it out."

"Your Majesty, I must express the greatest objection to your plan. Think of your father's legacy. Consider—"

"Your disapproval is noted. We can argue about it when I return. I'm in a hurry."

I must leave before I lose my courage.

Crossing my arms, I say, "The cave at Nemiah Bay where the human often wandered will be the perfect place to depart from. Unbeknown to them, humans in Faery often possess an innate sense for finding gateways where natural energy concentrates. Don't you agree?"

The scent of Draírdon's fury fills the air. His lips form a thin smile with malice lurking at its edges.

Lately, he's seemed more hostile than usual. Perhaps he's sulking because I sent his human pet away with Merri, but I suspect there's more to it than that.

Draírdon was always Temnen's creature, not mine, and he was grief-stricken when my brother died. Even though it was my birthright, I don't think Draírdon ever believed he would have to see me take the throne.

Well, for better or worse, I'm the King of Merits, and whatever ridiculous scheme Draírdon plots now, it will have to wait until I return.

Grime-colored eyes lift and narrow. "Do not go to the Elemental land, My King. Furthermore, do not take their princess, your father's enemy, as your consort. I beg you not to dishonor his memory with an irreversible violation of your Unseelie nature."

Me? Dishonor my father's memory? Every Blood Sun ceremony, King El Fannon dishonored it himself. And in addition, he was the worst father in the history of Faery.

Stepping closer, I loom over the mage. "My father's honor is not your concern." Despite my effort to control my temper, my voice comes out in a low snarl. "But, regardless, I require your assistance to open a portal. Together, our magic will be strong enough."

He doesn't back down. "I cannot in all good conscience help you bring about the downfall of our kingdom. I will not be complicit in the polluting and dilution of the royal Merit bloodline."

A good conscience is the last thing I could accuse him of having. "At this point, Draírdon, I only wish to visit Merrin Fionbharr, not pledge my life to hers."

I sense his power fighting against his restraint, longing to lash out and consume me. Spine cracking, his stooped goblin body unfurls to its full height, which isn't very impressive. "I refuse to participate!"

"So be it." I dematerialize before he can get another word in, making a mental note to send a message to Lidwinia. She'll need to watch him closely until I return—which will be soon, I hope. Then I'll deal with him myself.

Moonlight illuminates the entrance to the Selkie Cave as I materialize on the hill above it. I walk through the scrub onto the beach and call Chancellor Mareous to join me.

Within moments, I hear her siren's song. She glides over the waves, then pads up the beach barefooted, her hair glowing a lustrous kelp-green and pearly silver.

"So, you think I can help you open a portal, Silver King?" Tiny fish slide and leap along her mesh gown. With a dark smile, she cuts her hand through the air and they fly like a sheet of liquid lightning toward the sea.

"Of course you can. Your power is immense, Mareous. Together we can do anything."

"Prejudice and the trauma of your past have made you blind to the truth. The Elemental princess is the one you can do anything with, not I."

She circles me, her critical gaze no doubt seeing through the glamored leather armor I haven't had time to replace with real clothes. "This is how you've chosen to present yourself to your prospective bride? In your sleeping attire?"

"I was in a hurry, and also...there *is* the glamor."

"That trickery will not deceive the eyes of the Seelie royals. What in the realms were you thinking?"

I grin at my bare chest and feet. "Nothing intelligent. Obviously."

A long blue nail taps her cheek. "Then I shall gift you with a more suitable outfit. Be sure to wear it with pride."

She throws her head back and releases a plaintive wail, and hundreds answer her call. Mer-creatures appear and surround me, their arms hung with fine cloth woven from plants of the deep, embedded with the finest iridescent shells and black pearls.

In a storm of magic, they wind these items around my body, sew panels together, and step back as one to admire their efforts.

"Much better," declares the sea witch as she places a circlet of driftwood and sea glass on my brow.

Humbled, I bow and thank Mareous and her glittering subjects for their generosity.

Mareous's cold palm smooths along my cheek, her head angled and eyes narrowed as though she'd like to bite my face off. "Silver King, surely you must know that portal energy is not ours to manipulate."

"I suspected as much," I admit.

She waves a hand at the horde of merfolk behind her. "But we can boost your power and help you transfer directly to the Seelie Court."

My brow rises. It's impossible to transfer such a great distance. When I traveled to the false meeting with the Seelie king, Raghnall and I materialized in Ithalah Forest, and then rode to the northern side of Mount Cúig.

I take the sea witch's hands. "Let's try."

The merfolk form a circle around us and begin chanting a mournful song. Mareous and I direct our gazes to the stars as power rushes through us, forming a ring of silver light around our bodies. The waves gnash, wind roars, and images shuffle through my mind. Merri. Lidwinia. Meerade. Merri again.

Meerade! Damn, I almost forgot her. "Hold," I tell the people of the sea, and the energy stabilizes. I shout Meerade's name, and it echoes across the land.

Within moments, her wings beat the air nearby. She penetrates the circle of magic with ease and lands on my shoulder, giving my ear a savage bite.

The silver ring of light reappears, and then the transfer is upon us—a powerful one.

As the earth trembles below my feet and my body shudders, I say to Meerade. "Do not fret. I would never forget you."

She emits a volley of high-pitched noises, and as my muscles begin to dissolve, a final thought occurs to me. If Merri greets me half as joyfully as Meerade just did, I shall be happy.

Then...

We are gone.

28

A King Defied

Merri

"That male dancing near your parents has lovely horns and a very pleasing rear aspect," says Grandmother Varenus from beside me on the dais.

For the thousandth time this evening, I roll my eyes toward the vaulted glass ceiling. The stars twinkle down, laughing back at me. "Yes, but the front view is not so agreeable."

"You are too fussy, Granddaughter. Choose a courtier to dance with this evening. Just one. It will be over quickly. I've watched you cry enough glamored tears into your goblet of wine, souring your stomach."

Grandmother is one to talk. In her time as Queen of the Curmudgeons, she spoiled countless lovers' fun, including my parents'. Thankfully, she's mellowed somewhat with age. But granted, there is truth in her words. I've moped far too long, so tonight, I think I'll humor her.

"Fine. For your entertainment, I'll dance with the beautifully horned one whose bottom so entrances you. After that, do you promise to stop bothering me?"

"Delightful news!" She claps her hands, and a cloud of snow-white moths the exact shade of her hair explodes around her. Some fly toward the dancers, and others die on the obsidian spikes of her crown. "I vow to give you peace for the rest of the night, Merri. That is my best offer." Her smile turns dark. "But take the horned one to your bed and eradicate the foul memory of the arrogant silver beast, and perhaps then I shall offer you more."

I cut her a bow, then traipse down the stairs and join the revelers on the dance floor. Wearing a tight smile, I tap the muscular fae Grandmother selected on the shoulder. With a wide grin, he takes me in his arms, and we spin around the room together.

I think of Grandmother's second request and study the fae's handsome angular face, his dark hair and neat beard.

No. He's not for me. I prefer fair males who look like stars that have fallen into the realm of Faery.

As we dance, my partner, Ollen, entertains me with his life story, then tales about his large family. I try to pay attention, but it's difficult. Nothing holds my interest of late.

In the distance, a guard interrupts my parents and speaks with urgent gestures, then they leave together through the Great Hall's doors.

Strange. What could possibly be so important that would drag them from their fun?

Two dances later, the music slows, and Ollen's gaze turns lusty. I search my body for an answering warmth but find nothing, not even a spark. This is wrong and only prevents Ollen from finding a companion for the evening. I should end this farce now.

I'm about to excuse myself when someone clears their throat behind me. I spin around and see my parents before me holding hands, their expressions of shock terrible to behold.

"What's wrong?" I ask in a trembling voice. "Is Wyn all right?"

Mother says, "He's fine, Merri. Nothing bad has happened. You have a visitor, that's all."

"What? A visitor? *Who?*"

Father inclines his head toward the hall's entrance. I follow his gaze and find the Silver King standing there like a glittering statue with Meerade perched on his shoulder.

Nausea washes over me, then joy. I need to sit down. No—a lie down would be better. Hopefully, with the Merit king.

With a measured pace and his gaze fixed on me, Riven walks forward, his owl giving the evil eye to the stunned courtiers frozen mid-dance.

I stare open-mouthed at Mother, then grab my father's arm. "Don't hurt him, please."

He laughs. "I wouldn't dream of rearranging a hair on the head of your greatest protector, the fae who liberated you from the horrors of the cretin formerly known as Kian Leondearg."

"Wait. Did you just call the Merit king my greatest protector? Exactly how much wine have you drunk?"

"As always, the perfect amount." Smirking, he sweeps his arm toward the golden doors. "Go, my love. Greet your beau."

My beau? By the Elements, who has stolen my father's body?

My heart pounding in time to my heels clicking over the floor, I meet Riven near the far end of the hall. We stop within a hand's width of each other, our chests laboring.

Fists clenched at his sides, the Merit king's gaze is fierce. "Merri."

Words fail me. I lift my palms in a helpless gesture of confusion.

He smiles, takes my hand, and tugs me through the doors and down the external stairs. Then we're alone, stars whirling above us, around us—inside of us.

On the dance floor with Ollen, I couldn't summon a flicker of desire, but now... Now my entire being is incandescent, burning.

"I've missed you," Riven murmurs, pulling me into his arms.

"Missed you! Missed you!" Meerade repeats, nearly destroying my ears.

I stroke the snowy-white side of her feathers. "I'm so happy to see you, Meerade." My gaze cuts to Riven's. "But you, I'm not so sure about yet."

"Never mind. You'll find me very patient."

"But I can't believe you're here! How? Why? And did you even consider I might not have missed you in return?"

"No. Not once," Riven says, stepping back and taking my hand. "Quickly, Princess, show me to your chambers, and I promise when we're there, I'll answer each one of your four-hundred-and-seventy-five questions in earnest."

"Your arrogance is shocking," I say with a smile, then tug him through a side entrance to the castle and up to my chambers.

On the threshold of my rooms, Riven says, "Meerade, this is one doorway through which you cannot accompany me." Then he asks, "Merri, is your Cara inside?"

"Yes, sleeping."

"Wake her, then."

I open the door and give a piercing whistle. My mire squirrel squeaks, peeking from under the bed covers then scampers along the floor, up my gown, and into my arms.

Dropping a kiss on her nose, I say. "Show Meerade the kitchens. You have my permission to eat anything you like."

More squeaking ensues, then she leaps to the floor and races off. Meerade flies above her along the passageway, and as they disappear around a corner, the owl says, "Follow rat. But do not eat."

We laugh at our creatures and stumble into the room, wrapped in each other's arms. In the distance, the waterfalls of Talamh Cúig roar. The fire next to the bed spits and crackles, and I'm certain my wild heartbeat is louder than both. I pray he cannot hear it.

Riven tips his head toward the door in the far corner of the bedroom. "Are you going to lock me back in the cell where you tortured me ruthlessly?"

"I never once harmed you!"

"True. Not intentionally. But you unwittingly inflicted great suffering with your mocking eyes and teasing smile."

"Now you're making fun of me," I say, placing my fingers around his throat and squeezing gently.

He chuckles darkly. "Who were you dancing with before?"

"Why? Jealous?"

"Of course. Give me his name."

"It doesn't matter. He wasn't important. It's time to tell me why you're here."

"Isn't it obvious?" he says, pulling me closer.

I bite my lip and shake my head.

"No? You have no idea?" His face inches closer, his lips parted. "For this," he whispers, closing the distance between us.

Our lips meet, and the room spins. Ice. Fire. Then red-hot longing burns through my veins. I press into Riven's warmth, and his hands slide to my shoulders, my wrists, and then he wraps me in his embrace.

Not breaking our kiss, I push against his chest, creating enough space for me to unfasten his cloak. With a rustle, the heavy material falls to the floor, and my fingers work on the pearl buttons on his midnight tunic.

"Wait, Merri." He folds his body around mine, presses his face against my neck, and takes a long, shaky breath.

"What's wrong?"

Deep sapphire eyes meet mine, tiny bursts of gold glittering in their depths. "I've never done this before. And I want to. So badly, but..."

I stroke his cheek. "But what, Riven? Tell me."

"As king, my strength is immense...were I to lose control... I'm afraid I might hurt you."

My heart bleeds. "That's impossible. When we're together, we create a circle of power that feeds and bolsters the other's. We make each other stronger. Together, we're equal, Riven."

I entwine my arms around his neck, and as our lips meet, a wild wind howls outside and rattles the windows, causing leaves to skitter against the glass. Lightning flashes, followed a moment later by a crack of thunder.

Riven chuckles against my lips. "You're wrong. You're more than my equal, a Queen of Storms, you destroy me, and I never want you to stop."

His lips seize mine, and he kisses me over and over, soft as a love spell, then hard and punishing, and oh-so-perfect. I groan and press closer, feverish and melting under his touch.

The sound of the distant waterfalls disappears, replaced by Riven's sighs and ragged breaths as we work to tug his arm bracers and tunic off. Then we remove my gown and keep going, our hands shaking, our movements fast and clumsy, until we're down to our linen undergarments.

His hungry gaze roams over me. I inspect every impressive inch of his body.

Silver hair flows over his shoulders, the tips curling around the glowing Dara knot tattoo on his chest, a larger rendering of the druid's symbol for strength and wisdom that's engraved on the ring he wears on his finger.

"Interesting fact," I say, pointing at his tattoo. "Oak trees are resistant to lightning,"

His smile is quick and brilliant. "Yes. Whenever you defy me with your storms, I'll simply stand strong, waiting for you to come back into my arms."

"Riven, it sounds as if you're hoping this will be more than one night. Is that true?"

He nods. "I want all you're prepared to give me. Everything. Forever."

"So, a partner or a consort, then?" I ask.

"No. A queen who will unite two kingdoms, help me end a curse, and share a love that was long ago foretold."

"You believe the words of the Black Blood curse?"

"Yes. Listen," he whispers before repeating the final verse.

"A *halfling defies the Silver King.*
From dark to light, her good heart brings.
Enemies unite. Two courts now one,
Should merry win, the curse is done.
Not Faery born,
But human sworn,
One celestial day,
She'll wear his ring."

"Merri, even if I were foolish enough to still deny my feelings for you, those words are irrefutable, for they describe you and only you. A halfling who is not Faery-born, your name, Merri. Also, your mother was fully human when you were both conceived and delivered. It was only after she married Everend that she became something other, no longer human and yet not quite fae. I'm the Silver King. You are my queen. For me, there can be no other, nor do I want anyone else. We're meant to be."

"Yes." My heart dances as he says things I never dared dream. I step closer and stroke his cheek. "And if you need further proof, think of the curse your High Mage put on you to prevent you aging past the year of one-and-twenty until you met your mate."

"It was a blessing, not a curse, and the powerful sea witch Mareous cast it not Draírdon, who has never once performed a single kind act toward me."

"That makes sense. The first time I met you, at the pond, you looked so young, but the second time, when I rescued you in the forest, you'd changed and grown into a man."

"Because of you." His lips brush mine. "Merri, I've been a fool. Blind. Obstinate. Fighting my fate for no good reason. Can you ever forgive me?"

"Yes. In a breath. It is done."

"Can you love me?"

"With all my heart," I reply.

His answering smile lights up the room and every shadow that dwells inside me.

"Then I pledge my life and love to you, Merrin Airgetlám Fionbharr. You are mine, and I am yours, if you will have me."

"I will." My palm presses over the center of his tattoo. Even in the middle of his chest, I can feel his heart pounding.

"I love you," he whispers.

"And I love you, Riven Èadra na Duinn." I press a slow, teasing kiss to his mouth. "But I believe we've done quite enough talking. Now it's time for you to *show* me your love."

With one arm, he pulls me against his body. "You're still wearing the stone I gave you." His finger strokes from my chin, slowly down my throat, to the holey stone between my breasts.

Raising an eyebrow at the leather strap around his neck, I lift the arrow strung on it and rub the tip between my fingers. "And this thing you wear is mine."

"It is. You see? Even though I fought my feelings for you, deep down I've always known who you are to me. My partner. My mate. My beloved. Dearest Merri, you have defied me over and over, and, finally, you've prevailed and won. As it was written long ago, so it shall be. Forever and ever."

We seal our future with a kiss that promises eternity and leaves us panting, desperate to become one. I take his hand and draw him over to the bed where we remove the last of our clothing. Then we're divested of all glamor, trickery, and costumes, our souls bared to each other.

He stands proud, a fine tremor running over his body. I slide under the bed furs and beckon him to follow. Before I can blink, he's beside me, over me, kissing and caressing my skin as his body shakes.

"Are you afraid?" I ask.

"No. It's only...this feels too good. It's the strongest magic I've ever experienced, and I'm not sure how to control it."

"Stop trying. I'm not a fragile flower. Let go and follow your instincts."

"Merri," he whispers, fingers cradling my jaw. He kisses me, taking and taking until I moan beneath the weight of his body. Needing more.

"Please, Riven. Don't wait."

Body quaking, he fights harder, drawing out my torture. Then with a gut-wrenching groan, he gives in to his need, his voice hoarse as he surges forward. "I'm done fighting a war with myself, battling my desires and my longing for you. Done with it...forever."

"Praise the Elements," I say with a giggle.

He whispers a curse, then his body moves in a delicious rhythm. We hold each other as if the seven realms are breaking apart, as though these are our last moments alive, and he is precious to me and I to him. And it's true.

Nothing is more important than Riven. I've known it all my life. Every dream has told the tale. And now, nothing stands between us. Not even a breath of air.

The sounds we make are the purest song, every movement, a sacred dance. Heat coils inside me. Wind rages around us, tangling our hair together. White and red. Blood and snow. Dreams and visions. The past and future.

My teeth scrape his lips, and he moans my name—again and again.

Our pace is wild, frantic, perfect. Then everything explodes.

Snow and blood.

Blood and snow.

As was foretold.

The howling wind subsides as we slowly recover, our limbs entwined. I rest my head on his chest, my fingers caressing what is finally mine. Riven. The Silver King.

"I can't believe I waited so long," he says. "Why didn't you tell me it was like this?"

I laugh. "I did try."

"Think how well we could have occupied ourselves during your time at my court."

"Yes, so many wasted opportunities."

He wrestles with my limbs until I'm seated above him. "And now, we must make the most of every moment."

I answer his grin with my own. "You are wise indeed, My King."

"My King, you say?" His smile turns devious. "Finally, you decide to address me correctly."

"Ah, but then who am I to you?"

"My goddess. My Queen. My only and everything."

"An acceptable answer. Now, let's not waste a moment more of this magical night."

He rises to rest against the bed head, pulling me onto his lap. Then our bodies speak for us, telling stories of love and devotion.

Only many hours later, when dawn creeps across the floor, do my eyelids grow heavy. "Riven, I still can't comprehend why you've never done this before. You must've wanted to so many times," I say with a contented sigh.

"Yes, quite badly after that fateful day at the pond." He kisses my tender lips, his fingers gently stroking over the steady beat of my heart. "But I've been waiting."

My limbs ache, my insides are raw, and I've never felt better in my life. "What for, my love?"

"For you, Merri." He flops onto his back. "Always for you. Now, let's sleep a little. We'll need to be alert tomorrow, because we must marry as soon as we wake and put an end to that infernal curse."

"Yes. But tomorrow is already here."

Which means, by the Elements, I'm getting married today!

29

Should Merri Win

Riven

Flanked by three Elemental mages, Merri glides toward me as I wait on an altar twined with flowers and vines, erected in the grassy oval of the ancient tournament site below Castle Black's ruins.

Last night, Merri broke me, and, today, resplendent in silver and gold, each step she takes toward me brings her closer to becoming my queen and making me whole again.

I only wish my sister were here as witness, but we dared not wait a moment longer than necessary in case our marriage somehow puts an instant end to the Black Blood curse.

And, besides, when we return to my land, we'll have a coronation ceremony to look forward to.

The three mages, Terra dressed in black and purple, Undine, a vision in iridescent blue, and Salamander with her flaming hair, hand Merri to the High Mage. Ether guides her up the opal staircase, bringing her to stand beside me.

Smiling serenely, Ether takes our hands and joins them together. The crowd cheers, and Merri's family claps. Even her father.

Merri and I laugh like spell-addled fools, and my heart overflows.

Merri's silver crown of diamonds and rainbow moonstones sprays colors over the black and green tunic the people of the sea made for me and the large assembly of creatures—elegant fae, gnarled gnomes, goblins, trolls, and fauns, to name a few.

There are no moss elves present, because today of all days, they must work extra hard to keep the air mage, the originator of the curse, tethered to her forest prison.

"Finally," says Ether. "After moons and moons of planning, I have the pleasure of presenting you to each other. Merri, the Silver Hand, I now give to Riven, the Silver King who she shall rule. Your blessed union will bring peace to our lands and put an end to the oldest blight on the Seelie kingdom, the curse of the Black Blood princes."

Ether smiles at me, and with dawning alarm, images flash across my mind of a willowy fae dressed in silver, drawing a golden bow and aiming it at my chest.

"You!" I say. "Back in the forest on Mount Cúig, it was you who shot me with the poisoned arrow. You who tried to kill me."

The courtiers growl and snarl, and the palace guards raise their swords, the tips pointing at me.

Ether's laugh chimes, echoing through the glade like birdsong. "Well, yes, that is correct, Silver King. I did shoot you, but only to bring you under our princess's care. To deliver you to each other. The path was, unfortunately, longer than I foresaw, but today you both stand where destiny commands you must."

Merri says, "So, the first time I met Riven, that was you, too. The purple mist in the Lowlands was yours, and you created a portal space that allowed our kingdoms to meet."

"Yes." A field of silver glows around Ether, and she grows taller. "It has always been I, intercepting messages and working to bring you together."

Merri squeezes my hand, and we grin at each other as dozens of swords in the crowd are sheathed. "Well, thank you," she says to the mage. "I'm grateful for your help."

"But instead of shooting me and risking an all-out war, I don't suppose you could have simply told us about our destiny?" I ask.

"I could have, yes. And you would have fought the outcome by all possible means. Some fae cannot be told and insist on learning by experience. Do you deny this is so, Merit King?"

"No." I laugh and cut a low bow to the mage. "You're correct. I wouldn't have listened. And even though that arrow hurt like blazes, you have my eternal thanks. To you, I forever owe my happiness."

"Ether, we should hurry," says Merri. "Let's see if we can break that damned curse."

The mage inclines her head, and then speaks the binding words. We repeat the vows, swearing to the Elements Five, to our lands, and to one another.

"By the Blessed Five that binds all matter together and the eternal powers of the oak, Merrin Airgetlám Fionbharr and Riven Èadra na Duinn, I declare the Light and Dark Courts of Faery united and you to be husband and wife, Lady and Lord, Queen and King. May your sacred union bring everlasting bliss." Ether spreads her arms toward the Court. "Seal your vows with a kiss, then turn and face your loved ones, born anew."

Our lips meet, and the altar quakes beneath our feet. Baby Aodhan, the current Land of Five heir, releases a bloodcurdling scream. A series of violent shivers wrack his body, and his mother, Queen Isla, holds him tighter, worry darkening her eyes from bright blue to indigo.

Aodhan's skin turns green, then a dark cloud rises from his body and dissolves in the air. With another wail, he loses consciousness, waking a moment later to give his parents a cheerful smile.

King Rafael's palms hover above his son's forehead, sensing deep into the child's being. "The curse is lifted," he cries jubilantly, and the crowd answers with wild hoots and cheers.

Merri wraps her arms around me, and we laugh and sway with joy. "We did it, Riven. It worked!"

As I inhale a sharp breath to answer, a disturbance parts the crowd behind us. I turn in its direction.

A tribe of moss elves runs toward us along the aisle of meadow flowers, their high-pitched voices piercing through the din. When they're a little closer, I make out their words. "Run," they yell. "Run."

A vicious wind rises, howling and groaning like a fear gorta on the hunt for food to fill its skinless corpse. The sky turns black, then all falls silent, every courtier, including the moss elves, going still.

"Riven?" Merri's voice shakes as she reaches for me.

I attempt to lift my hand to clasp hers, but nothing happens. Paralyzed, I can't move a muscle. But, for better or worse, I can hear and see *everything*—Merri's mouth, frozen in a silent shout, her eyes wide with terror, the seven órga falcons and diaphanous-bodied sylphs immobilized as they fly in a lemniscate pattern through the clouds.

Meerade is on top of the altar, wings spread as if about to take flight, Cara perched beside her. Strangely, Merri's brother stands close to the ever-twirling human, Summer, his hand lightly resting on her forearm, his expression pained.

Thunder cracks. Lightning slashes across the sky. Rain teems down, and Aer, the Sorceress of the Seven Winds, appears at the foot of the altar.

Once upon a time, the air mage's beauty was celebrated throughout the kingdoms, but Lara's powerful voice took it from her when she tried to murder Prince Ever here at the ruins of Castle Black. Water streams around Aer's dull-brown eyes and down her wrinkled skin, drenching her straw-colored hair.

Internally, I call upon the oak and the old gods of the forest but receive no answer. No matter how hard I will it, I cannot move.

The royal family are statues, every creature and courtier, and my Merri, too. We're suspended in a terrible spell, all except for Ether who strolls calmly down the steps to meet Aer.

"Sister," she says. "It has been a long time between disagreements."

"Disagreements? Ha! Today's squabble is much more than that." Aer weaves her way through the courtiers, tearing wings and horns with cruel fingers as she passes. She comes to a halt in front of Ever, strokes his hair, then gives his snarling mouth a lingering kiss.

Aer returns to stand before the High Mage. "Just because I've always wanted a prince of Talamh Cúig for my own, you've thought me worthy of contempt. Well, I have finally beaten you, Sister."

"Not yet," answers Ether.

Aer cackles, and my skin chills in response. "Thanks to you, *Sister*, I have suffered endless, wordless years in the dark under your binding spell. But I've kept a lovely surprise for you that helped me wait patiently, knowing that if one day my curse was broken, the provision I wove into its creation would convey me to the center of the event that ends it—*with my powers intact.* So I can *destroy* you all."

Ether smiles and flings her arms toward the sky. But nothing happens. She gives a cry of frustration as her sister laughs.

"No, Ether, you cannot shift into your creature because my spell prevents it."

"Nor can *you*, or you would already have taken your dragon form." Ether throws a bolt of white energy that sends the air mage tumbling through the crowd. "Fortunately, you aren't strong enough to fully bind *my* power. Hurry and dust yourself off. Let us see if you can defeat me."

The mages drop into combative stances and magic, dark and light, blazes between them. The smell of burnt flesh assaults me, overpowering the tangy scent of the ocean.

With a guttural roar, Aer runs and pounces on Ether. Lightning flashes, the rain pelting down harder. The sisters somersault back and forth in a ball of wildly churning limbs. They smash into the trunks of the sacred hazels, roll precariously close to the high cliffs that drop down to the gnashing jaws of the sea, waiting to consume them whole.

Then the mages are up on their feet, bolts of magic slashing both ways, bloody gashes lacerating their bodies.

Thunder rumbles the sky. Cracks splinter the earth, great chasms opening up, one swallowing a whole line of fae into its depths.

The mages disappear from my frozen line of vision, past the sacred hazels and up onto the rocky hillside the ruins sit upon. I can't see what's happening, but I hear it. Snarls, thuds and crashes, and horrible screams of pain.

Then Ether is shot back into the oval, rolling and rolling until she's stopped by the statue-like bodies of a group of courtiers.

On the ground, Ether leans on an elbow, panting hard as her sister strides closer and closer. "You're a fool, Aer. When you made the curse, you bound part of my powers to its end, decreasing them, but you had to do the same to *your* power to make it work, didn't you? You've made yourself *weak*."

Again, Aer's cackle sends shivers down my spine. "We are equally diminished. But *you* are soft and kindhearted, and I am not. I *will* defeat you. Now get up, so I can finish this!"

Ether pushes onto her haunches and points her fingers at Merri and me. With a loud roar, white light connects us, forming a triangle of magic between the three of us.

"Join hands," yells Ether.

With a grunt, I move my arm, then grab Merri's hand in an iron grip. Power rushes through me, my body shuddering with the force.

The sky goes black then flashes silver, the storm overhead growling and roiling like a wild beast in a cage. Aer harnesses the lightning's energy, sending bolt after bolt at Ether.

Stumbling and rocking backward with each attack, Ether somehow gets to her feet. She cries out to Dana and the Powers of Five and harnesses the quicksilver energy arcing between us, shooting it toward Aer, who leaps sideways a little too late, taking a hit to her side. She drops like a wall of bricks, cursing and writhing in agony.

Aer is down, but Ether doesn't move in to finish her off. With her arms raised to the sky and her eyes squeezed closed, she mutters a low chant in an unfathomable language.

"Riven!" Merri tugs my arm, not letting go of my hand to retain the circuit of power. "I can move my upper body, but not my feet. I'm stuck, and we need to get over there and pummel that shrew before she gets up."

My mouth goes dry, my heart raging against my ribs. "I can't move either. Nor can I manipulate this magic your mage has created."

"Dammit, *Ether*," screams Merri. "Come out of your trance. This isn't over. We need you. Now!"

The mad air sorceress lifts her head and levers her body's weight onto an elbow, and, still, Ether continues to chant.

I try to direct the magic into my legs, leaning forward, imagining running or transferring. Nothing happens. It's as if my feet have grown unbreakable roots into the earth. "High Mage, I beg you, help us!"

Aer pushes onto all fours, her hollow gaze full of bitter hatred. "Spawn of Everend Fionbharr, the curse is done, but you have *not* won," she screeches, blood trickling from the corners of her mouth. "Winds will whip, sparks will fly, waves will churn, earth will rumble. And the coldest heart in the land will melt for one he can never possess."

She points at Merri's brother, Wynter, whose emerald eyes burn back at the mage. "Prince of the barren earth, buried within it you must be for at least seven days and seven nights, and until you—"

"*Now*, Merri. Now!" commands Ether. "You're the key to the riddle, the vessel of our power. Release it *now*."

Our bodies jerk as the three of us concentrate our power into a stream of the brightest, purest light I've ever seen. It blasts from Merri's outstretched palms directly into the air mage's heart, instantly exploding her into tinkling shards of mirrored glass and black feathers.

"By the Five, all wake," cries Ether, and the rest of the court begins to move, lingering enchantment making their limbs slow and awkward.

Ether disappears, reappearing a moment later beside Wynter. She presses her palm against his heart and speaks quickly. "Prince of the barren earth, buried within it you must be for at least seven days and seven nights, and until your heart's love unearths you. Then free and forever blessed you shall be."

Wynter's eyes roll back as Ether's tempered curse takes hold, and he blacks out, swaying. Before he drops to the ground, he wakes with a grimace and buries his face in his hands.

Ether gently uncurls his fingers and clasps his hands tight. "You can bear this curse with ease, Wynter Ashton Fionbharr, Prince of Earth. I promise you this. You *can* and you *will*."

Merri's mother rushes to Wynter, gathering him in her arms as the human girl dances a slow circle around them. The rest of the royal family, including the formidable Varenus, surround Merri and me, clapping our backs and peppering us with kisses.

The mages, Terra, Salamander, and Undine sweep all remnants of their sister, Aer, into a fast-woven basket of young hazel branches. Ezeli, the sea witch queen, takes it from them, swearing to bury the remains in the deepest part of the ocean as she dives off the cliffs into the Emerald Sea.

Soft skin meets my lips as I kiss my new wife's hand. "You did it, Merri. You've won. The curse has ended. From this moment on, all our dreams will be dreamed together."

"And I'm so thankful. But, Riven, now that Wyn—"

"Wyn will find a way," says Ether. "He always does."

Prince Ever addresses the High Mage. "What will happen to our land and to the Lake of Spirits now that our air mage is gone? The Elements are out of balance. Our magic systems and entire kingdom will collapse."

"No," says Ether. "All is well. Before I dealt Aer the blow that felled her, I cast a spell that bound Merri's and your power to the source. You, Ever, must forever remain in this land to stabilize it. Merri's union with the Silver King has made her very powerful.

You witnessed the incredible force that she and I wielded when we linked our magic. She is free to move between the Land of Five and the Merit Kingdom at will. Talamh Cúig will endure."

The mage kisses Merri's cheek, then mine. "Together, you are the solution to the problems of the past, but Merri is the key to the future, the silver hand that controls the Unseelie king's power. Follow her council with diligence, Riven na Duinn, and you cannot fail."

Merri grins. "Did you hear that, Riven? Apparently, I am *wise*."

I pull her close. "I have no doubt and hereby promise to heed your every word and treasure you forever and always."

"Are you happy?" she asks.

"As never before. Now let us go and celebrate our wedding."

"Are you suggesting we skip the feast?" she asks, her face a mask of false shock.

I pretend to consider this, but my mind is already resolved. "Well...surely as the guests of honor, we're allowed to be a little late."

She kisses me, and snow begins to fall. Soft and pure and as welcome as winter light, it dances around us.

"Yes," she whispers. "I imagine we'll be very late."

Epilogue

Wynter Ashton Fionbharr

I n the Land of Five, there are no more Black Blood princes, and only one of the Elemental sons is cursed—me, the Prince of Earth.

Aer's words, tempered by Ether, roll night and day through my mind. A torture, a torment. A promise of things to come. Things that will never be.

Prince of the barren earth, buried within it you must be for at least seven days and seven nights, and until your heart's love unearths you. Then free and forever blessed you shall be.

Until my heart's love unearths me. What foolishness! There will be no fated mate for me, for I could never value such a terrible gift.

No poison creeps through my cursed blood, and yet my heart is stone cold, any golden vein of warmth buried in deepest soil long ago, back when the Elements first formed me.

Buried already, dark earth surrounds me, lays heavy as a grave upon my ribs and my limbs. But I smile and laugh and pretend it's not true. Not the way of things.

But it is.

Yes, *it is.*

And so, I drink and drink and watch the enchanted human as she twirls and twirls, for soon she will be gone from the Bright Court. Summer to my winter. Fire to my blood. Earth to my ashes. Ashes to my earth.

Because of her—I see no other.

The girl my sister will send home.

The Shade Court wants the girl back, Merri says. *We'll send her home to protect her from them.*

But the girl they long for, I am destined to retrieve.

And though I'll never want her insipid-human love, there are other things she can give me.

She won't be safe unless I follow and protect her.

So she'll never be Landolin or Moiron Ravenseeker's toy again.

The summer girl is mine.

Forever mine.

Not to love.

But to own.

As it should be—a faery prince and his human pet.

Forever.

Thank you for reading King of Merits! Keep turning to read an excerpt of the full-length prequel, Prince of Then, which tells the tale of the first Black Blood prince, Gadriel and his human fated mate, Holly.

Excerpt Prince of Then

Prologue

Once upon a time, the Faery city of Talamh Cúig was a place of peace, where the Elements co-existed in perfect harmony and gifted the people with their ancient nature magic.

Sisters—the Elements were five in number.

Ether, the soul who bound them together.

Terra, who loved to play in the dirt.

Undine, bathed in blue.

Salamander with her hair on fire.

And Aer, who longed to rule over all, but none more so than Gadriel, the raven-haired prince with eyes of brightest sapphire blue.

But what will a shunned air mage do when she learns that love cannot be forced?

Seal the prince's fate.

Poison his blood.
And curse his line forever.

The Cursed Prince – Chapter 1 – Gade

"Gadriel, I see you at the water's edge. Surely you don't wish to hide from me," calls a voice, soft as the summer breeze and just as sweetly cloying.
Nothing.

I know exactly who that voice belongs to, and I definitely want to hide from her.

Scooping my sword from the ground, I duck behind a tree trunk and quickly tie my belt around my hips. When I glance up, she's in front of me—Aer, standing in the forest, her impossible golden beauty shining as bright as the midday sun.

"Hello, Gade," she says, smiling and blushing like the maid I'm well aware she isn't. Far from it, for she is as old as the earth beneath my feet, more lovely than the sky, as tempting as a cool lake, and more terrifying than the wildest of flames.

"Kiss me," she breathes, pressing her palm against my still-wet chest.

To balance my powers, I've bathed in the Lake of Spirits—the source of our kingdom's magic—and now, the six-pointed star glyph on the back of my hand glows brightly, fully charged, Aer's hungry gaze fixing on it.

"I knew you'd come soon," she says, the thin straps of her creamy gown slipping halfway down her arms. "I knew you couldn't stay away."

A wry smile twists my lips. "Of course I couldn't. It's been a month since I last visited the lake, and my powers were ebbing."

She steps closer, crushing pine needles underfoot, the smell invigorating. "How old are you now, Gade?"

Why she asks when she already knows the answer is beyond me. "Eighteen."

Her fair brow rises. "A man now, and so tall and strong. I predict that today will be the day you'll finally kiss me."

"You're an Elemental mage, not a faery. Me dallying with you would be like a forest stag trying to win the heart of a princess in the highest tower. Or the dark sea longing to hold the moon in its slippery embrace. Ridiculous and impossible."

The pine trees groan. Limbs and twigs snap as her gold eyes darken, the first signs of her anger. She steps back, her long fingers curling into fists. "I've been patient, young princeling. I have courted, and I have waited, and my desire for the great king you will one day become has been my only sustenance these long years past. And you repay my dedication and steadfast love with insults?"

A sour taste fills my mouth as I recall her past attentions, the lavish presents she gifted me each celebration of my birth, the precious jewels, the poems. The many times her regard made me feel akin to an insect drowning in a pot of the sweetest honey.

For many moons, I've thought nothing of her lingering touches, her heated stares. Why would I? She is a mage. I am a prince. Never in the history of Faery has one been interested in the other.

"Oh, Gadriel, how I tire of this game."

"What game? If you play one, I do not know it."

Her brittle smile twists into a snarl. "Are you really so naive, handsome Prince of Five?"

I'm not. It is only with Aer that I pretend to be.

Her knuckles bleach white around a thin branch as she snaps it from the ash tree behind me, leaning too close. "I am ready to be yours and can wait no longer for this to be done. But I can't force you. You must choose me, and the time has come to do so."

My frown grows. "Choose you for what?"

"To be your bride, of course." A sly smile spreads over her face. "In all the seven realms, there is no one who will love you as I do. I shall be your forever queen."

With those words, the first tendrils of fear snake through my stomach.

She is deadly serious, and a *deadly* Aer is a grave problem.

I draw a quick breath, then force a smile. "You're an Elemental mage. It cannot be. What about your sisters? Think of Ether, Terra, Undine, and Salamander."

"What of them?"

"It would put the Elements, no, it would put *everything* out of balance—the whole kingdom would be at risk. You, the air mage, cannot rule over your sisters. It is impossible."

Translucent yellow eyes turn opaque, and she strikes, pulling me close as her sickly sweet lips coax mine to open.

The air mage kisses me.

Fingers digging into her shoulders, I shove her away. "I do not want you, Aer. What you wish for will never be."

Thunder shakes the sky as her fury surges through the air, an acrid scent. I have made a grievous mistake. A terrible error of judgment. I should have taken more care with my words and let her down gently.

"I insist that you *do* desire me." Her gown wavers then melts away, and she stands before me naked, her body luminous, glorious, and a bizarre contrast to the ugly contortion of her features. Eyes squinting. Brow lined. Teeth bared and elongating.

It's such a strange sight that laughter explodes from me.

Aer's gold eyes turn black as she covers her chest with her arm, and then the gown appears, enfolding her curves again. "You dare to laugh at me? You ignorant, ungrateful fool. Do you not realize I hold your fate in my hands?"

My blood rushes through my veins, and I shake my head, stepping backward. "Aer... You misunderstand..."

She opens her mouth, and a screech like the sound of a thousand wailing harpies shreds the air as I fall to my knees, clutching my chest.

Then there is only pain.

And more pain.

Agony is my blood, my soul, my very name.

I am agony.

"Aer..." The word croaks out of me, the taste on my tongue like bitter poison, thick as it slides down my throat. "What have you done?"

Silver fire licks over her arms, the wind whipping her hair around her shoulders like serpents seeking prey to strike. Purple clouds race above, then explode with a thunderous boom. Lightning flashes. The forest floor shakes.

"I curse you, Gadriel Raven Fionbharr and all the future heirs of the Throne of Five. In your blood, the blackest poison will bloom, gifting you the cruelest death. You will burn, and you will moan, and pray to all the gods that love will find you fast. Your pure heart will turn to coal heartbeat by heartbeat, breath by breath. You will hate and, finally, you will love, but find your true mate you must—or die a slow and painful death."

My every muscle taut and trembling, I struggle to my feet and face her, my hand crushing my sword pommel. "You must truly loathe me."

"No, fair prince, it is the opposite. I will love you beyond the veil to the depths of the underworld and back. This is the price you'll pay for not surrendering your heart to me as you should."

But the punishment isn't equal to my supposed crime. Aer's revenge is savage. Never-ending.

"Punish me if you will, but not the innocent souls in my line who come after me. In what way will my children's children have wronged you? Your curse is unjust."

"All is fair in matters of love and rejection. But I am not without mercy. You are the most fortunate of your line, for you will keep your Powers of Five. Future princes of your land will rule one element only, yet I'll allow you to retain them all. See? Am I not a merciful mage, Gadriel?"

There is only one answer to that question, and she would not like to hear it.

"And you still *live*, Gadriel. I could slay you this moment with one breath, but I do not. And I've given you part of the key to easing your misery—to remain alive, you must find a mate before the poison has run its course. It won't be an easy task because the mate I select may not be fae and may view you as a monster, just as you view me now."

"Not fae? What else could she be?"

"Perhaps a troll. Or a human."

"No, wait, Aer. Please do not—"

Closing her eyes, the mage begins to chant, softly at first, then growing louder and louder until blood trickles from my ears.

Through the pain, I can only make out a little of what she says: "*Black will fade to gray, gray to white, and white to never. Never was the darkest taint and never will it ever be.*" Then she mutters in a low, guttural voice, the words an incoherent song that splinters my bones and grinds them to dust.

Clutching my head, I drop to my knees again. "Please, Aer. Stop!"

The sky clears as she turns away, her billowing robes dissolving into the forest until only her voice remains. Floating on the breeze come whispered words of ruin—*a halfling, a king, dark and light, and Faery born.* They all mean naught to me.

"Farewell, Black Blood Prince, first of your cursed line. Your pain will one day cease, but your kingdom's suffering will be endless. My gift to you is the Black Blood poison. This gift is your curse, and when your bones are ash, your son's curse to bear, and so on and so on. Until the end of time."

Like a volley of poisoned arrows have pierced my chest, agony shoots through my veins and settles in my skull. And then there is no Lake. No forest. No warmhearted Prince of Five.

Only blackness remains.

And then nothing.

Nothing.

Keep turning for information about other books in the series!

Also By Juno Heart

Prince of Then: Gadriel and Holly's story, the prequel.

Prince of Never: Ever and Lara's story.

King of Always: Raff & Isla's story.
King of Merits: Riven and Merri's tale.

Ebook & paperback covers

Hardcovers

I also write about damaged heroes and the girls who heal them under a steamy romance pen name. Stay tuned for steamy fae books coming soon and Wyn & Aodhan's stories!

Join my newsletter list and be the first to hear of new releases, read-first opportunities, and other sweet deals.
You can sign up at my website: junoheartfaeromance.com

About the Author

Juno Heart writes enemies-to-lovers romances about cursed fae princes and the feisty mortal girls they fall hard for.
When she's not busy writing, she's chatting with her magical talking cat, spilling coffee on her keyboard, or searching local alleyways for a portal into Faery.
She also publishes books about damaged heroes under her spicy contemporary romance pen name.

For release news and sales alerts, join Juno's newsletter!

Website: Junoheartfaeromance.com

Email: juno@junoheartfaeromance.com

Come say hi on Tik Tok!

Acknowledgments

Thank you for reading Riven and Merri's story! I hope you enjoyed it.

I love hearing from readers, and I'm so grateful for every kind email and thoughtful review I've received. You guys rock! Massive thanks and virtual hugs for taking the time to reach out and, also, for sharing my stories with your friends!

Huge thank yous to Amelie, Anna, Ken, and Jennifer from Bookends Editing for your awesome feedback and support. Thank you for helping me make Riven and Merri's story a whole lot better!

Massive thanks to the awesome designers for the beautiful covers, saintjupit3rgr4phic for the eBooks and paperbacks and Covers by Juan for the hardbacks!

Until next time,

Juno X

Printed in Great Britain
by Amazon

41936346R00239